I0699005

THE FORBIDDEN TEARS SERIES

# Paradise Breached

AWARD-WINNING AUTHORS

## Sam Withrow
## & Amelia Pinkis

This is a work of fiction. Names, characters, places, and incidents are products of the author's imagination or are used fictitiously and are not to be construed as real. Any resemblance to actual events, locations, organizations, or persons, living or dead, is entirely coincidental.

## FRESH INK PRESS
### Cape Coral, Florida



Cover Art: David Leahey
Editor: Natalie West

# CONTENTS

# ACKNOWLEDGMENTS

First and foremost, to my incredible fans — you are the reason this book exists and the reason I keep going, even when my caffeine levels are dangerously low. Your enthusiasm, passion, and sometimes completely unhinged theories about my characters bring me so much joy. Thank you for embracing my world and making it your own.

To my husband, Jim — thank you for your patience and unwavering support and for tolerating the many late nights when I insisted, "Just one more chapter!" (We both know that was a lie.) You are my rock, my reality check, and the one who makes sure I occasionally see the sun.

To my daughter, Loryn — you inspire me daily with your creativity, kindness, and ability to make me laugh at the most unexpected moments. You remind me why stories matter. I can only hope my words bring others the same magic you bring into my life.

Finally, to my sister, Mary Ellen — your time, dedication, and willingness to help with promotions, events, and book signings mean more than I can express. Your honesty, insight, and the occasional eye roll have helped shape this series into what it is today, and I wouldn't have it any other way.

Writing a book is a journey, but having all of you by my side makes it an adventure. Thank you for being part of this crazy, wonderful, word-filled ride. Now, let's do it all over again, shall we?

*Sam Withrow*

This has been one of the most creatively challenging and rewarding years of my life. I'm overjoyed to share this story with the world and, very soon, to bring another little soul here to share in the love.

To our fans, thank you a thousand times and again for all your encouragement and support. I hope you love following Brie on this journey as much as Sam and I love bringing it to life.

To my friends and family, your love and support throughout this process has been incredible. May a lifetime of love, gratitude, and unsolicited deadpan witticisms help to repay this unpayable debt that I owe you. Sharona, your beautiful brain and radiant soul are compelling reasons for continued belief that there is good in this timeline. I love you forever. Maysa, the day the threads of our lives started to braid together was a blessed one. I hope I can shine as much light into your life as you've shone into mine. Natalie, the world owes you a great debt for keeping me on the side of the angels. I love you forever, you absolute nova of talent and will. A special thanks to Arianne, whose keen eye and beautiful mind have helped guide this project in more ways than one. I love you, my heart. Daniel, Taylor, and Patrick, Louis and Jaclyn, Dylan, Hayden, Mom and Dave, and Dad — you've made me who I am, and I love you forever.

Alex, you made me believe in soulmates and destiny, and I wouldn't trade the life we've created for anything. I love you. Auden, Anakin, Aria, Adeline, and To Be Announced… I love you, forever. Happy reading, my favorite people.

*Amelia Rose*

# Paradise Breached

# PROLOGUE

"Wrath is cruel and anger a torrent,<br>
but who can stand before envy?"<br>
Proverbs 27:4

It was a horror. There was no better word for it.

The old king of Elysium looked down at the table, staring past the shattered remains of a sculpture to the broken figure of a man that lay within. If one could still call him a man. He wasn't sure how anything in such a state could be living.

*Absol. My dearest friend.*

He was emaciated, hardly breathing, his heartbeat visible through paper-thin skin stretched taut over a mangled ribcage. Scars, bruises, and signs of abuse, the likes of which the ancient king had never seen, colored every inch of his battered body.

Tears stood in King Enoch's eyes. It hurt to look at him.

Raphael stood on the opposite side of the table, ministering to his patient, muttering a steady stream of ancient incantations as he raised vial after vial of golden liquid to the fallen Elysian's lips. Bundles of dried herbs from the celestial gardens burned in ceramic bowls, and pungent, medicinal-smelling smoke wafted through the infirmary and out to the arena next door, drifting over the wall engraved with names of Elysium's missing and dead.

Most of the Elysian Guard had deployed into the Time Seas, hunting for the shards of Baal that threatened the borders of their realm.

The remaining few had worked tirelessly to determine the nature of the strange sculpture the human girl had used to behead Mammon. When they'd finally managed to crack open the dark sphere encased in those looping stone antlers only to find the broken form of Absol's Elysian body inside, the chamber had fallen silent with a stricken hush.

Absol was one of their brightest. No one could get past the shock.

Enoch took a step closer, pressing his fingertips to the table. "Who did this to him?"

Raphael shook his head, never breaking his incantations.

The king asked again. "Is it within your skill to heal him?"

At this, the archangel fell abruptly silent, staring at the ruined body before locking eyes with his king. "Call Sabriel."

With that, he went back to his chanting.

Enoch's jaw clenched. Sabriel was the Angel of Miracles. One did not send for her unless hope was all but lost. He turned slightly and gave a curt nod to his attendant, who saluted and quickly left the room.

Once he was out of earshot, Raphael cleared his throat. "Sire, the implications…"

Together, they turned to the memorial wall, to the hundreds of names carved in white stone, stretching far into the distance.

There were times when it almost blended in with the scenery.

Other times, it was the only thing they could see.

"Tend to him with all the skill you possess," Enoch answered quietly. "We must find out what could have done this to him, and how. Beyond that, Absol is one of our own, and I will do everything within my power to see him restored."

Raphael nodded silently, his hands moving once more, administering the medicine.

The king cast a final look at his friend before turning to leave. At a different time, he might have stood vigil. But the enemy was upon them, and this was not the only tragedy that had washed up in his halls. It wasn't until he reached the door that he turned again to speak.

"And Raphael? Once the troops have returned from their patrol of the seas, come to the Great Hall. You are summoned to a council of war."

Absol stirred feebly on the table, and they both fell silent.

"Bring Sabriel quickly. We could certainly use a miracle." With that, Enoch swept out of the room.

# CHAPTER ONE

## One Small Step

It's rare, those nights when you expect to see something you've never seen before, rarer still when you unexpectedly see two.

*"Did I hear somebody ask for a miracle?!"*

There was a roar of laughter as the patrons of the Mad River Cafe turned their eyes to the person speaking — a barrel-chested man who had parked himself beneath the TV. Clive Emerson was the unofficial mayor of the town, though he was, in reality, a television repairman. At sixty-two, he'd taken to giving these types of performances, thick thumbs stuck into his belt loops, straining his suspenders to the brink, but it wasn't often he was treated with such an audience. It felt like the entire town had crammed themselves into the diner, and it was still early evening. He rose to the occasion, puffing himself up like a southern preacher who'd set out that morning for the chapel, and found himself at a diner instead.

*"Because I think we're all in for one in T-minus just about an hour!"*

The diner let out a cheer and went back to their excited chattering.

"Order up!" rang a voice from the kitchen.

A team of waitresses had been refilling drinks and providing a steady supply of diner fare for hours, getting half the orders wrong, as they couldn't stop stealing glances at the fuzzy-pictured television mounted in the corner of the little restaurant. If you could call it a restaurant. It was more of a hole-in-the-wall — a diner attached to the only gas station in the little California town, where teenagers came to make eyes at each other over bottles of soda, and adults brought their broods of children for special occasions or on muggy summer nights when it was too hot to cook indoors. It was a popular haunt in a town of admittedly limited options.

But they'd never had a crowd like this before. A solid third of the town's residents were crammed into the booths, socializing around the bar and spilling into the patio area in the back. The establishment had set up extra picnic tables to accommodate everyone, and the manager had brought his own television from home to mount on a bench outside. Every once in a while, someone had to jiggle the metal rabbit ears to fix the picture, but it was only a matter of time before someone knocked it loose again. A band on the radio sang to their lady love, calling her "Sugar, Sugar" and "Candy Girl."

The entire town had come alive — neighbors, friends, and families, all thrumming with eager anticipation, all expecting to see something no one had ever seen before. Not that you'd know it to hear them. Everyone had suddenly become an expert on things like program alarms, contact lights, and entry vectors. The fact that no one present had even heard these terms until a few days ago did nothing to stop them from discussing these subjects like their opinion held the weight of a Greek philosopher in the ancient Senate.

The pressure had been steadily building, and the walls had started to vibrate with the churn of the crowd. Once in a while, the gravity of the moment would overwhelm someone, and they would drift outside to sip their soda or beer and stare up at the evening sky.

"Order up!"

There was no end to it. A waitress, whose name tag identified her as Daphne, wiped some sweat from her forehead and paused by the register, watching as one of the others went racing back to the kitchen.

They'd known it was going to be a busy day. The kitchen manager had been prepping for weeks, ordering extra supplies from the grocers and stocking the bar with enough peanuts and tiny napkins to sink a small ship. Daphne had gotten there early and expected to stay late. But this had exceeded all expectations.

The door opened again, and two more families came rushing inside. *"We're here!"*

*"Did we miss anything?"*

Daphne let out a sigh, blowing damp hair off her face. The television antenna, wrapped in a layer of aluminum foil and held together with duct tape and hope, had knocked loose again, but one of the busboys was already running over to fix it. From the sudden uproar in the corner, it looked like Clive was getting up to give another speech.

"Mama, can we go home yet?" asked a small voice.

The waitress startled to attention and looked down at the girl swinging her feet against the counter. It was little Susie Perkins. Her family had gotten there early, too. She'd been there so long her mother had ceased to notice her, and the child had decided to sulk.

"In a little while, pumpkin," answered Mrs. Perkins, distracted.

"But why do we have to *be* here?" the girl whined. "What's the point if there aren't going to be any aliens?" She jutted out her lower lip. Her science teacher and parents had finally sat her down to temper expectations after her drawings in art class had repeatedly featured little green men. She had listened to them stoically and had yet to get over her disappointment.

Her mother sighed. "Why don't you go play tag with the other kids? Look honey, they're having so much fun!"

Susie scowled. She'd had her fill of socializing. The precocious ten-year-old hadn't wanted to come in the first place, and by her estimation, she'd suffered enough indignities for one night. Her mother had dressed her in the pink-checkered gingham sundress she hated, styled her hair in pigtails, and, worst of all, told her to play with the other children.

"I'm an apex predator, mama," she answered with an adorable scowl.

Daphne turned her head quickly to hide a smile.

"What?" Mrs. Perkins glanced down in alarm. "What was that, sweetheart?"

"I am an apex predator," the girl repeated. "I haven't fought my way to the top of the food chain to be forced to play childish games." She poked a french fry into her puddle of ketchup and refused to make eye contact.

Mrs. Perkins' lips pursed together. She was a good mother and tried to be patient, but there was a limit to these things, and the child was well past it. "Susie," she said in a carefully measured tone, "you haven't fought your way to the top of anything, and it isn't nice to take credit for the totality of human achievement to get out of playing tag. Now go outside and get some fresh air. Let Mommy and Daddy talk with our friends for a little bit." Her tone was even and pleasant, but a maternal warning flashed in her eyes.

Susie knew better than to press her luck. She hopped down from her chair and headed outside, pausing when Daphne winked and slipped her one of the special "mooncakes" the chef had prepared — glorified doughnuts filled with colored custards.

It was a balmy midsummer night, cooler outside than in but still uncomfortably warm, the kind of night that lured people outdoors and then attacked them with mosquitos. Susie made her way toward the woods, fidgeting in the itchy gingham and wishing she was at home. She turned in a last-ditch effort and saw her parents through the glass doors, talking and laughing with the neighbors, before sighing and trudging slowly across the field. The long grass scratched against her legs, and a breeze drifted down from the trees, scented with sycamore and pine. As she got closer, her eyes lifted past the shadowed canopy to the stars, wondering when the extraordinary event would happen so they could all go home.

"I really don't see the point if there aren't going to be aliens," she muttered aloud.

The wind stirred again, and she stopped, lifting her eyes to the heavens.

She had to admit it was beautiful. So deep in the country, without light or noise, there seemed nothing between her and that wide open sky. With a soft sigh, she squinted her eyes and reached up a hand, using her thumb to hide the moon and then reveal it again.

*There, and gone. There, and gone.*

Could there be other things out there? Other people, even? Was it really possible that one day they might discover that in a vast and brimming universe, they weren't alone?

She was still staring when she heard it.

A slight rustling, a snapped twig. Susie's skin prickled, and her eyes snapped back to the woods. At first, she thought it was a dog. The gas station attendant's Labrador had gone missing a few days back. She and some of the kids from school had gone out looking for it.

"Cooper?" she called softly, edging a step back. "Is that you? Come here, boy!"

Another rustle. Too big for Cooper.

She let out a silent gasp and jumped back as the branches of the silver-lit trees rattled and the bushes beneath them shook. Whatever was out there, it was coming closer. Other sounds drifted from the shadows — footfalls and a muffled curse. She was about to call out again when a voice suddenly broke through. "Brie, are you sure you even *saw* a light?"

"No more sure than usual," another voice answered, "but Azrael's glass can't always be wrong. It's navigating us somewhere. Eventually."

"What if it isn't?" A third voice rang out, feminine and angry. "It's been showing the same thing this whole time. What if we're trapped in this forest until the end of our days?"

"Sherry, don't be so dramatic—"

"I'm not being dramatic — the situation *is* dramatic. We have *no idea* where we landed. Plus, I got bit. No, not bit — *swallowed*. By a *mountain*.

A mountain tried to *eat* me. I'm tired, I'm hot, I don't see how humans manage to eat these rations and call them food, and I've never gone this long without seeing signs of civilization, or more importantly, *a macchiato*, in my *life*. I'm being the appropriate amount of dramatic."

Susie stared at the treeline, openmouthed.

"Look, we have to catch a break at some point," a man's voice answered, moving steadily closer. "I mean, the law of large numbers says we've got to. Right?"

There was a brief pause, then several voices answered at once.

"Shut *up*, Cameron."

The bushes parted, and she saw them.

There were six covered head to toe in mud, lurching with ungainly synchronicity out of the trees. One was brandishing a magnifying glass, and another held a glowing rectangle above its head.

That one seemed angry.

"I can't get a signal. And the GPS still isn't working. You'd think by now at least one satellite would have—"

They stopped cold at the sight of Susie in her pigtails and little pink dress, still clutching her custard-filled donut.

There was a moment when nothing happened. Then the tallest one growled.

"By the Staff of Moses — what fresh hell is this?"

Susie dropped her mooncake. "I knew it," she whispered, eyes wide as dinner plates.

The creature who had spoken stepped forward. He looked human enough, except for his sheer scale. He was hulking, nearly seven feet tall, with black braids that swung to his waist. He wore what looked like gold wrist cuffs and ancient Roman battle gear. The ground trembled as he moved, and Susie shrank backward.

He smiled, baring all of his teeth. "Excuse me, youngling. My name is Ephriam, and these are my comrades. We didn't mean to frighten you. Might we trouble you for a glass of water?"

The child stared at them solemnly, nodded once, then turned and raced back across the field to the diner as fast as her little legs could carry her.

"Mama!" she called, feeling the eyes of the strangers behind her. "Mama!" She burst through the glass doors, ran up to her mother, and tugged on her skirt, unable to claim her attention. The table was crammed, and everyone was chatting and laughing. She drew a deep breath and tried again, much louder this time. "MOM!"

A sudden hush fell over the diner as every person swiveled around and every eye turned their way.

Mrs. Perkins flushed, speaking through clenched teeth.

"There's no need to shout like a hooligan. What is it?"

Susie looked back evenly, matching her gaze.

"There are some aliens outside, and they'd like a glass of water, please."

At first, it was quiet. Then, a titter of laughter rippled through the diner.

At that point, her father pushed to his feet, red-faced and fuming, a half-drunk milkshake still gripped in his hand. "Susie, for the last time, there is no such thing as aliens. Now, this is a special night, and I won't have you ruining it with any of your fantastical…" He trailed off, staring through the glass doors.

A collective gasp rang through the diner.

Six people stood in a line outside the window. Two of them were nearly seven feet tall and dressed like gladiators. Two were wearing fishing waders made entirely out of rhinestones. All were waving awkwardly. All of them were covered in mud.

One of the gladiators tapped on the window, speaking politely through the glass.

"If it isn't too much of a cliche, please take me to your leader."

♦    ♦    ♦

The six strangers were ushered into the diner in a flurry of sound and movement. They stammered out a steady stream of thanks, but it was nearly impossible to hear them over the clamor of voices that had risen in their wake — a hundred people, each shouting over the other.

"How did you get *that* lost?"

"Would you like a mooncake?"

"Is that a real sword?"

"It doesn't have to be. Jesus, Bill — just look at him."

Questions echoed from one corner of the room to the next, rising in pitch and frequency as more people clambered out of their booths, crowded away from the forgotten spectacle behind them, and focused on the new one that had just walked through their door.

"Did they fall into the river?"

"I heard there was a mudslide up the ridge in Malheur."

"And they made it all the way to Mad River on foot?"

"Someone tell me honestly, is that purse a rhinestone trout?"

One of the strangers, an enchanting man with ocean-blue eyes, started to laugh. It began quietly but quickly rose beyond his control. His shoulders shook, and pine needles rained from his chestnut hair as he lifted a hand to cover his mouth.

"Unbelievable," he murmured.

The shortest of the women spun around with a scathing glare.

"What could possibly be so funny?" she demanded, hands on her hips.

"Nothing, Sher," he answered quickly, trying hard to contain himself. "But, the Malheur forest? Mad River?" He waited a beat, then cracked up again.

She scowled. "I don't see what—"

"*Malheur* means misfortune," he interrupted, his voice tinged with a trace of rising hysteria. "We started in misfortune and ended up by the Mad River." He shook again with laughter, unable to restrain himself. "It's the least subtle metaphor the Universe has ever thrown. It's like being hit upside the head with a stick labeled METAPHOR in big, block letters."

There was a moment of uncomfortable silence before Ephriam spoke. "Cameron, can you name one instance when your well-timed and hilarious jokes have made anyone laugh other than yourself?" His voice was like ice, his arms folded across his chest. The cuffs on his wrists glinted menacingly as he waited for a reply. "No? Then, I cordially invite you to *get a grip*."

Cameron bit his lip obligingly, but the chuckles continued.

After consuming several pitchers of water, the shock of their sudden appearance was fading, and a few details had emerged. The mysterious figures from the woods were, of course, not aliens, to Susie's unending disappointment, but lost hikers: three men and three women, all definitely the worse for wear but pleasant and courteous enough and certainly in such pitiable states that you couldn't help but feel sorry for them. The two normal-sized women who'd introduced themselves as Sherry and Brie said they were nurses; Cameron, the handsome one, was lost to his fit of giggles, and the red-haired man was apparently a policeman. There was no accounting for the two unnaturally tall ones dressed for an ancient battle, but even so, the townsfolk figured they must be decent and worthy of some charity despite their uncanny heights and bizarre choices in clothing. The group had gotten lost in the woods and had been hiking toward civilization for the past ten days with nothing but the supplies on their backs.

A table had been cleared for them. They clustered around it, sipping water and trying to compose themselves.

It was unclear whether they'd made much progress.

Brie, one of the nurses, deliberately ignored the hysterics of her blue-eyed boyfriend, shaking a few more pieces of the forest from her long brunette curls before pouring the unnaturally tall woman another glass of water. "Try to drink, Tavi. Maybe it'll help."

The warrior nodded grimly and sipped with a martyred expression. Though all six companions had undoubtedly been through the wringer, there was no doubt that Tavi was in the worst shape. She gritted her teeth and sipped slowly, gripping fiercely at the cup.

"Can I get you anything else?" asked a waitress, appearing from nowhere. For the last twenty minutes, the entire town had been clamoring for a better view. Visitors were few and far between, and usually someone's extended family. She couldn't remember the last time they'd seen somebody new.

"Some more water, if it's alright," Brie answered, smiling sweetly. She'd yet to look at a menu. She'd yet to progress past the feeling of hard linoleum under her shoes.

"Could we get something to eat?" added Tavi, eyeing a pile of french fries at a neighboring table hungrily. During their time in the woods, dinner had consisted of dehydrated rations and whatever they could forage.

"Of course, dear, anything you like," the waitress soothed, shying away from her leather battle gear and alarming collection of knives. "All of you — anything you like." She whipped out her order pad. "What's your pleasure?"

"Cheeseburgers," rumbled Ephriam, looking comically out of place against the Americana backdrop. It would have felt more likely to suppose he'd escaped from some movie set, the kind where people communicated in monosyllabic grunts and talked mostly with their swords. "With bacon." He looked at the quailing waitress and gave her his best attempt at a smile, hoping this might speed the process along. When this clearly unsettled her further, he added, "Please."

"And any fresh fruits or vegetables you have," added Mike, giving Sherry's hand a squeeze below the table. "This one's been dying for a banana." Throughout their ordeal, the man had grown increasingly protective, offering his share of their drinking water and using his jacket to pillow Sherry's head as she slept. Even now, sitting in the relative safety of a diner, she was always somewhere within his reach.

"We have banana splits, so I'm sure I can find something," said the waitress.

"I'd love a banana split," Brie chimed in, mouth watering at the thought of ice cream. Trudging through the wilderness, it had been nothing except Mike's rations and a handful of roots Cameron claimed had medicinal powers but had only succeeded in making everyone sick.

"Why do you prefer the fruit to be sliced?" Ephriam asked. "Is this superior?"

It took Brie a second to catch up. "No, it's a dessert," she explained, glancing nervously at the curious patrons. Her friends stood out on the best of occasions, but things were always more challenging in close quarters. Already, a few children had begun to point with delight at their assorted weapons, whispering behind cupped hands and fencing each other with plastic spoons. "Banana splits for everyone, if that's alright. Do you take Visa?" she added, suddenly remembering nobody had any cash.

The waitress frowned. "Like a diner's club card? We're not as fancy as all that. But don't you worry, hon, this is on the house." She cast another glance around the table, lingering a moment on both Ephriam and Tavi before heading off to the kitchen.

Brie stared after her, puzzled, before leaning slowly back in her chair. It felt strange to be sitting still, let alone sitting somewhere indoors. She felt as though she hadn't stopped moving since fleeing the shores of Virginia. She looked around the diner for the first time, taking stock of her surroundings. While the layout was predictable and familiar, it was suddenly easy to see all the details she'd missed in the flurry of their arrival: the beehives, the pink dress uniforms, the kitschy Americana trinkets decorating the walls — not to mention the music.

*My candy girl? Really?*

"Must be some sort of themed restaurant," she muttered.

"What was that?" asked Sherry.

"Just noticing the vintage vibes," Brie answered with a tired smile, leaning against her arm. "Don't you wish people still dressed this way?"

The chef must have caught up on his orders because as food poured from the kitchen and hit the tables, the general mayhem of the diner dulled from a roar to a gentle buzz. Music crooned softly in the background as Brie and Sherry looked around. Circumstances aside, the scene was rather quaint, right down to the group of over-sugared children dancing in front of the jukebox. It was a charming combination of grass stains and floppy ribbons. Several of the girls were sporting Mary Jane shoes.

Sherry wrinkled her nose. "What's the point of wearing vintage if it's just going to end up smelling like grilling lard?" Her stomach let out a loud growl. "Though I have to admit, I'm desperate for anything that hasn't been freeze-dried and rehydrated with river water."

Just then, Clive Emerson sidled up beside them, beer belly jiggling, eyes twinkling, bearing a platter of mooncakes. He placed the desserts in the middle of the table and pulled up a chair, which groaned under his weight as he settled down.

"Brought you a little sugar," he declared, smiling at each of them, "get some color back in your cheeks. Standing outside like a bunch of strays, banging on that window, it looked like you'd battled your way here from the gates of Hell itself."

The friends stared back in silence before their eyes dropped to the cakes. They weren't wild about the strays comparison, but the man might have a point. Brie shivered in spite of herself while Mike let out a pitiable sneeze.

"Go on, eat," the man urged, pushing the plate toward them. "And while you wait for your meal, you can tell us how the devil you ended up in our humble town," he continued casually, meeting their blank stares with a winning smile. He spread his arms wide, gesturing to the television. "And on *today*, of all days."

Brie looked at him curiously.

*What's so special about today?*

A swift glance around the table and the question was quickly replaced by another: What the hell were they supposed to say?

They'd done a fine job so far, shrugging off the ceaseless volley of questions with the same vague replies: we were hiking, we got lost, and *please*, is there any coffee? They were in such a disheveled state that those generalities had been more than enough to suffice. But the longer things had time to settle, the easier it was to see the gaping holes in their story. The man had asked directly, but what were they supposed to tell him? What story could they possibly give that wouldn't land them in the nearest psychiatric facility?

In the silence that followed, Ephriam snatched up some pastries for himself and Tavi before leaning back in his chair with a pointed expression. After so many days traveling alongside each other, Brie could guess his thoughts as if he'd said them out loud:

*"We followed your magical magnifying glass here. Your pendant is responsible for this entire debacle. You tell him what happened."*

Her pulse quickened as she glanced anxiously around the table, but unfortunately, it seemed to be a shared opinion. Mike and Tavi were focused on their plates, Cameron was deliberately avoiding eye contact, and even her faithful Sherry was looking the other way.

*Traitors.*

She took a slow sip of water, debating what to say.

*I could always go with the truth.*

*I stood trial in the celestial realm of Elysium because my family heirloom necklace, which has helped us take down one ancient demon and escape another, might be too powerful to entrust to a mortal like me. Luckily, the Archangel of Death intervened on my behalf by delivering one helluva prophecy that's thrown us all into some ridiculous quest. My boyfriend Cameron is the Elysian prince. He has a secret brother I just found out about, and these two oversized barrels of laughs wearing battle gear are elite Elysian guards sent to help and protect us. My best friend Sherry and her boyfriend Mike got kidnapped into joining this misadventure very much against their will, though they've rolled with it admirably. Oh, and the mortal sin of Gluttony, which is actually a hurricane-sized swarm of nightmare creatures named Baal, attacked us after a lovely afternoon at a Virginian jubilee. To save the town, we had to trap the demon on the moon, which is the very place we were coming from when we teleported into the middle of nowhere, wandered through the woods, and met all of you.*

She paused a moment longer, considering this.

*…Or we could lie.*

"We had a rough week," she finally answered, twisting her fingers together nervously. The others glanced over with matching, caustic expressions, and she carefully avoided their eyes. Fine, that was a *bit* of an understatement. "We decided to get away from it all for a while, do some hiking, and camp a few nights under the stars. Everything was going fine, but I guess we wandered farther than we thought. We ran into some weather, got lost, tried to find our way back, and wound up here."

*Eating mooncakes.*

Clive frowned in disappointment. It was one of the most exciting things to ever happen to their sleepy town, and she'd managed to make it sound almost mundane. A hiking trip gone wrong? They were dressed like strung-out circus performers! Where was the story?

"You must've had some adventures, or maybe misadventures?" he prompted hopefully. "There's a whole lot that can getcha out in them California woods."

"So we're in California?" Mike asked excitedly. It had been a source of great speculation as they'd trekked through the forest. Everyone had guesses, but none of them had any way to know for sure exactly where they'd landed. They could easily have ended up on the other side of the planet, and it would have made just as much sense.

Clive let out a great guffaw of laughter. "My goodness young man, you must have been exceptionally lost indeed! Where did you think you were?"

Mike flushed as red as his hair, but his police instincts kicked in quickly enough. "Oregon," he replied, hoping they were far enough north that this wouldn't be too far-fetched.

Clive's eyebrows shot up, but he nodded. "You probably did start out in Malheur then. Is that where you folks started your hike?"

"Yes, yes it was," Mike stammered with a trace of relief.

"In more ways than one," Cameron added under his breath, unable to keep from smiling.

Clive let out another booming laugh and clapped a hand on Ephriam's shoulder, oblivious to the look the Elysian warrior gave him in return. "Well, if you aren't the luckiest sons-of-bitches around. There was a huge mudslide up in Malheur around a week ago. Could've taken all of you out."

"It very nearly did," Sherry muttered darkly.

The man's face paled in shock. "You were there?"

The companions froze in perfect unison, remembering how they'd ducked for cover in the frenzy of a rainstorm, the horrible, rumbling churn that had snapped them to attention, and the way the mountain itself had flown forward as if to swallow them whole.

Daphne came back with a giant platter, distributing plates of burgers and fries.

The smell hit first, and the salivation came a moment later. A second after that, the whole group was reaching, forgetting their captive audience and those pesky questions. It had been ten days in the woods. Ten days that had taken each one of them to the brink, then pushed them quite a bit further than that. They'd been so hungry for so long they'd ceased to notice.

*It's amazing how quickly a cheeseburger can fix that.*

"The mudslide wasn't as bad as the mountain lion," said Tavi, around a mouthful of burger. Brie looked at her, vaguely surprised to see the Elysian eating meat. Then again, hiking for so long through the California wilderness would make just about anyone abandon their vegetarian principles.

"The mountain lion? My gracious!" Clive exclaimed, slapping Ephriam on the back again. "You kids have been through it, haven'tcha?"

Brie stifled a grin, unsure what amused her more: the fact that he'd referred to their celestial counterparts as 'kids' or the fact that he couldn't stop smacking Ephriam. If he hadn't come bearing mooncakes, both offenses seemed likely to earn him an Elysian dagger to the chest.

"Well, don't fret anymore," Clive concluded. "Your luck is startin' to turn. Folks here in Mad River are a friendly, neighborly sort, and we'll get you fixed right up." He leaned forward curiously, taking a fry off Mike's plate. "Where did you say you were from?"

"Virginia," offered Sherry.

His eyebrows flew to his hair. "Virginia!" he exclaimed. "You're certainly a long way from home. Did y'all fly out to be with family while you watch?"

The friends exchanged a silent glance.

"Watch what?" asked Cameron.

Clive shot him a funny look, like he might be making a joke. When it became clear that wasn't the case, the man laughed. "Have you been living under a rock or something?"

"Um, kind of," Brie admitted. "We haven't had a signal in days."

Another funny look, one she didn't understand.

"I think I saw a stack of newspapers over there," Mike interjected, pushing to his feet. His eyes swept around the diner before landing on his friends. "He's right. We should figure out what's been going on these last few days. Make sure everything's, you know… normal."

Brie cringed as he swept across the diner, aiming for the stack of papers by the jukebox. Considering the man had been given formal training, it wasn't the smoothest line. But what was he supposed to say? They needed to make sure the mortal realm hadn't descended into apocalyptic chaos? Normal was a better choice. Normal would be fine.

Clive stared after him, looking uncharacteristically puzzled before his face cleared in sudden understanding. "Of course! You wouldn't know the date. Well, don't worry. Our TV gets a great picture here, and you can watch with the rest of us!" He grinned, gesturing at the packed diner. "Afterwards, my family has a guest house where you can stay until we figure out how to get you all home safe."

Brie smiled in return, touched. "That's very kind, but I'm sure we can manage," she answered. "Sherry can call us a rideshare, and we'll book a few rooms at the nearest hotel. I have points on my card, so we should be okay."

Right on cue, Sherry whipped out her phone, frowning at the screen. "I still have zero bars. Are you sure this place gets a good signal?"

Clive twisted in his seat, staring at the tiny device. "Of course. I mean, we have to jimmy the bunny ears every once in a while, but the picture always ends up coming in fine. What in the world have you got there?" he added, leaning closer in delight. "How new-fangled!"

The others glanced at him in surprise as Sherry followed his gaze.

"This?" she asked, waving it between them. "Not really. They came out with a new version last winter, but I'm not standing in those lines."

Mike slid into the booth beside her, a newspaper clutched in his hands. "Guys," he said under his breath, "something's not right here."

The rest of the table turned to him in surprise, but it was Clive who answered, swiveling around to see him square on. "I beg your pardon — I carried those in here myself. Helping to set up for the viewing, you know," he added conspiratorially to Brie. "The diner's been at it all week, unloading deliveries and stocking up on supplies. We didn't want to run out halfway through."

"The viewing?" she replied. "What are you—"

"The paper's fine," Mike interrupted with a trace of panic, "it's just not current. I'm looking for today's paper. This one's from July of 1969."

A ringing silence fell over the table, freezing everyone in place. For a few seconds, it didn't look like anyone could manage to break it. Then Clive leaned forward with a frown.

"Son, I don't mean to offend you," he began cautiously, "but you *did* say you folks were in a landslide. Did you happen to hit your head?"

Before anyone could answer, a voice rang from the back of the diner.

"Quiet! Everyone be quiet! It's happening!"

Clive jumped up from the table and stood at attention. Everyone fell silent and stared at the television screen.

The picture went fuzzy for a second, then resolved into a black-and-white image that was as familiar as it was utterly unfathomable at the same time. Brie's mouth fell open, and she gripped the table with both hands, leaning closer as the figure of a man descended a ladder and the voice of Neil Armstrong crackled across the room.

"That's one small step for man, one giant leap for mankind."

The diner was silent for a moment, then exploded into thunderous applause. People embraced, laughed, cried, and shouted back and forth. Confetti poppers erupted, and the air was filled with glitter and streamers. Someone started singing "The Star-Spangled Banner," and before five seconds had passed, nearly everyone in the crowd was singing along.

Only six people remained perfectly silent, frozen to their seats in shock.

It had seemed like a turning point. It had seemed like a *good* thing. They were literally out of the woods. They'd found a ceiling. They were feasting on burgers and fries. For a fleeting moment, it had seemed like their cosmically terrible luck might actually be turning around.

*And now?*

Brie stared at the television, her eyes glazing over.

*We're in more trouble than I thought.*

# CHAPTER TWO

## The Butterfly Effect

"How is this possible?"

The question rang out for the tenth time as Sherry paced the living room of Clive's guest house in a wild panic. The others had long since given up any hope of stopping her. At any rate, they couldn't stop asking the question themselves.

They had stayed at the diner, staring at their banana splits until they melted into ice cream soup, while the residents of Mad River celebrated the moon landing until they'd tired themselves out. Music had been cranking from the jukebox, which was suddenly eyed with new understanding, and the doors had been thrown open to welcome a fresh crowd of people from the town. When things finally started winding down, Clive and his wife Myrtle had driven them home in the bed of their pickup truck and left them on the porch of their guesthouse with a pile of blankets and reassurances that if they needed anything, just to holler. It was the kindest of gestures. Circumstances aside, it was downright lovely.

If they hadn't been having a collective panic attack, they could have enjoyed it.

"I mean, how is this *possible?*" Sherry asked again, in a strange pitch several octaves higher than normal. "I haven't even been born yet, and I'm here. How am I here?" This time, the question seemed to strike home, and she sank abruptly onto the couch beside Mike, staring into the ether with a horrified expression. She hadn't made it through the entire moon landing. A part of her had splintered before Armstrong made it all the way down the ladder.

*I don't know. But we are.*

It would have been an excellent time to think clearly. It would have been a terrific time *not to* have expletives screaming on a loop in her mind, but as things stood, Brie couldn't think of a single reassuring thing to say to Sherry. Every time the words rose to her lips, it became clear she was having a meltdown of her own.

"Look, it's fine," she started with false confidence. "It's fine. I mean, we've already been here ten days, walking around and everything, and we haven't disappeared yet. So maybe that's like a movie thing that doesn't happen when you actually time travel — which we apparently did. We time traveled." She slipped abruptly to the floor, holding her head in both hands. "Oh my God, we traveled through *time*. Cameron, how did this happen?"

As a rule, in times of interdimensional chaos, her eyes went first and foremost to her boyfriend. But for one of the first times, the lovely guardian angel looked as out of sorts as the rest. His skin was a shade lighter than most corpses, and his blue eyes kept flicking to the window like he might find the answer out there. If things were in a better state, she might have felt sorry for him. As it stood, she could only lean back silently against his legs and panic.

Ephriam seemed to feel differently.

"I'll tell you how this happened," he growled, glaring furiously. "*Somebody* was so focused on *where* we landed that he gave no consideration whatsoever to *when*. So here we are, trapped in a somehow even *more* primitive timeline with even *more* primitive beings. And now, in addition to navigating this ever-worsening vortex of interdimensional insanity, we have another problem: how to navigate through it without tangling the human timeline beyond all repair!"

Cameron stared at the ground and made no move to defend himself.

"Every single thing we have to do is now infinitely more impossible," Ephriam ranted on. "Travel. Expenses. Medical care for Tavi. Everything is *sixty years* more primitive than it had to be, and we were already counting on the kindness of these knuckle-dragging cavemen to get us to Jophial and fulfill our quest without our powers!"

"Hey—" Mike began to protest.

"*Cavemen!*" Ephriam thundered for emphasis, casting him a withering look.

Mike's jaw snapped closed as he abruptly decided to drop it.

It was quiet for a few minutes as each of them sat there in silence. It was never a good sign when one of the Elysians began to panic. The others had started setting their own internal anxiety barometers on a mortal versus immortal scale. It was Ephriam himself who'd steered them through the worst of the mountains, but here, within the safe confines of a guest house, the notion of an inadvertent time jump had clearly pushed him too far.

"What about the bugs?" cried Sherry out of nowhere.

The others turned to her slowly.

"What?" Brie finally asked, half-wishing she hadn't.

"The bugs!" Sherry cried. "What if we step on an ant or kill a butterfly, and then the wind patterns change, and our parents never meet, and we disappear like Marty Freaking McFly?" She reached the end of her breath, then dropped her head in her hands, letting out a dry sob. The others watched her cautiously like that might not be the worst of it.

"Why are you planning on murdering insects?" Ephriam asked incredulously.

"It'll be fine. We'll be *fine*," Mike insisted, trying to convince himself. "All I need is a DeLorean, a flux capacitor, and an old clock tower." He pulled his girlfriend close and rubbed circles on her back. "Doc Brown did it. So can I."

"But she's right!" Brie cried, ignoring his crazed expression and whirling to face the others. Cameron was almost catatonic, and Tavi was resting on one of the beds in another room, so her panic was directed at Ephriam. "We've been wandering for days. What if we *caused* that landslide in the forest? How many butterflies did that kill, Ephriam? *How many ants?*" She sucked in a breath. "How do we do anything here without ceasing to exist?"

The Elysian might have been in a rage himself, but he softened at her terror. "You needn't fear that, child. You should fear a great many *other* things, for example, Cameron's complete navigational ineptitude and Sherry's bizarre vendetta against butterflies, but on this one front, you are all safe."

Mike lifted his eyes with a fevered expression. "Explain," he demanded.

"Now that we are here, we have always been here," Ephriam answered simply. "The future version of you, the one you are and will again become, has always been here, in this guesthouse in 1969. Because this is your past now, it has always been and must always be so."

*Regardless of the bugs?*

The Elysian nodded as if this settled it.

"That... I don't..." Mike floundered a few seconds before bowing his head in defeat. "Yeah. Whatever you say."

Ephriam tried again. "This cannot interfere with the version of you that you have always been. It can only cause chaos for what you consider to be your future from your *future* point of present. Not from now. Well, not from this now."

"Ephriam?" said Mike.

"Yes?"

"Please stop."

Brie pushed to her feet, pacing distractedly across the floor, before coming to a stop in front of the large farmhouse window. The moon was high above them, glowing behind the branches of an old oak tree.

She stood there staring at the crescent until a dark cloud drifted over its surface, hiding it from view.

*They're up there right now,* she thought. *For the first time in our history, humans are walking on the surface of the moon.*

For a bizarre moment, she almost smiled.

Then, her pulse spiked with an incoherent shout.

"What is it?" In his concern for her, Cameron finally found his voice.

"They're up there right now!" she cried, pointing wildly out the window. "The astronauts! They're up there right now! *With Baal!*"

Mike's jaw dropped, and Sherry turned white as a sheet.

"They'll be eaten!" she cried. "They've probably already—"

"Don't worry about it," Ephriam interrupted dryly.

The others turned to him in shock.

"But NASA—" began Brie.

"Seriously," the Elysian insisted, rolling his eyes, "don't worry about it."

There was a moment of bewildered silence. Then—

"Oh, for God's sake, don't tell me you're one of *those,*" Mike snapped.

"One of what?" Ephriam asked.

Brie's eyes flew between them in confusion.

"One of those people who think the whole thing was staged by Stanley Kubrick and the U.S. Government," Mike answered. "This is *serious.* If we're concerned about changing the timeline, there aren't many things I can think of that would change it as drastically as, oh, I don't know, *Neil Armstrong being eaten by an ancient demon on national television!*"

The Elysian eyed him with a slight smile. "I said not to worry about it because the time jump occurred when we transported from the moon back to Earth, *not before.*"

"Oh…" Mike trailed off apologetically. "Sorry."

"Although," the Elysian continued, "I stayed at Kubrick's house for a spell in the mid-sixties. I can tell you that he had some fascinating set pieces stored in his basement—"

Cameron held up his hands, finally roused from his stupor. "Perhaps the humans have been through enough for one day."

Ephriam shrugged and sat on the couch.

"How can you be so sure?" asked Sherry. "How are you *certain* we were on the moon in our time and not in 1969?"

"Two reasons," answered Ephriam. "For one thing, there wasn't an Apollo space shuttle in orbit while we were up there. Although that doesn't necessarily prove…" he trailed off at Cameron's stern look. He coughed and continued. "And secondly, *I* helped us get up there. Amateur mistakes like *jumping decades into the past* are utterly beneath me. On our way back to earth? This was all Cameron." He crossed his arms over his chest in accusation. "We came to the past *after* luring Baal to the moon in your present."

"So you're completely sure we haven't just served up NASA's finest on a titanium alloy platter?" Mike asked, still shaken.

"Completely sure," Ephriam reiterated.

The humans let out a unison sigh of relief.

Brie turned back to the window, reaching absently for the pendant on her chest. When her fingers closed around the familiar stone, it pulsed faintly, almost like a recognition. She shook her head. "We aren't going to get anywhere debating this tonight. We need to rest. And shower," she added, glimpsing her reflection in the glass.

Nobody answered. Nobody had to.

Sherry and Mike wandered off to the bathroom, and soon, the sound of running water filled the guest house. Ephriam went to check on Tavi, leaving Brie and Cameron alone for the first time in…

*How long has it been?*

She watched him approach in the window's reflection, placing his hands on her shoulders and kissing the top of her head. There had been many such moments over the last few days. But they were always damp and shivering, and there were always people around. She leaned into him, reveling in his warmth. Their faces were reflected in the panes of glass, cool white in the moonlight.

After a moment, he broke the silence with the most unlikely of questions.

"Do you remember how mortified you were on the drive to Virginia," he began quietly, "when Mike pulled you over in his squad car?"

She turned to him, half-smiling despite herself. "I do remember. Vividly," she added.

He nodded, tracing his fingers along her neck. "You said you'd never gotten so much as a speeding ticket before."

"I hadn't," she replied. "Come to mention it, I guess I still haven't. You Obi-Wan Kenobi'd Mike's brain before he actually had a chance to smear my record."

There was a brief pause as her angel filed this away with a long list of other human peculiarities he would one day unravel. "I have no idea what you're talking about, but I'm glad you didn't get the ticket." He squeezed her slightly, dropping his eyes to the floor. "Brie, I can't remember a time in my life when I've screwed up so completely. I'm so sorry. I can't believe how bad this…" He trailed away, looking as lost as she'd ever seen. "I've never gotten so much as a speeding ticket, either. So to speak."

Her heart melted a little as she smoothed back his hair. Since the moment they'd met, her poor angel had held himself to such impossible standards.

*This must be hell for him.*

"Hey," she said, tipping his chin up to meet her gaze. "You saved us. You trapped Baal on the moon, and you got us back to Earth, away from civilization. You kept everyone safe." She lifted suddenly onto her tiptoes, pressing their lips together. He was still registering the contact when she pulled back with a smile. "And if this is the celestial equivalent of getting a speeding ticket, we can always memory-wipe Ephriam when he's distracted, like you did to Mike."

"*Oh, can you?!*" A voice sounded behind them.

The pair froze in surprise, then whirled around to see Mike standing in the doorway, his face a mask of betrayal. Their hands dropped, and she took an automatic step toward him, but his eyes flashed in anger, and she stayed where she was.

Cameron braced where he was standing, eyeing him warily. "Mike, it isn't what it sounds like——"

"All that time in the woods," the policeman fumed. "All that time in Elysium, and you never *once* mentioned that we'd already met? That you actually…" He shook his head, unwilling to say it. "*That's* why I thought I recognized you at our first dinner together. Because I effing *did*! And you let me go on and on, thinking I was crazy!" Cameron took a step toward him, but Mike stepped back. "And to think, I gave you my secret recipe for queso dip." He glared at the pair of them. "I *was* coming to tell you that the shower's free, but now I think I'll go back in there and run the hot water until it's gone. Have a pleasant friggin' evening!"

Without another word, he turned and stomped back into the bathroom.

The couple stared after him a moment before Cameron turned back to Brie, utterly deflated. "So, is there anything else I can mess up before we go to bed, or does that just about cover it?"

Brie woke at the crack of dawn to steal the shower before Mike's retribution could rob her of another opportunity to bathe. She and Cameron had fallen asleep leaning against one another on the couch, feeling too guilty to claim any of the bedrooms. She stole away as quietly as possible, trying not to wake him.

The bathroom was simple and clean, armed with a sparse vanity and a shower that heated with improbable speed as she stepped beneath the jets. Her body tensed a split second, then practically melted with relief. There had been moments in the woods when she'd thought she'd never get a warm shower again. There had been moments when she'd thought they wouldn't make it to the other side.

She had never been fond of mountains. As a child, they were the jagged edges of a world too large for her to comprehend, ominous shadows on the horizon that whispered of untamed wilderness and dangers lurking just out of sight. They were beautiful, but in the way that a predator's fangs are beautiful: sharp, deadly, and likely to tear you apart if you weren't careful. As the days dragged on, she'd become certain that the mountains felt equally ambivalent about her. The wilderness felt vast and indifferent to their struggles, and she'd never quite shaken the feeling that they were nothing more than ants crawling across a giant's spine.

And that was all before the mountain lion.

She'd never forget the way the beast had appeared out of nowhere, eyes glowing like embers in the twilight. She had been staring into the lens of Azrael's magnifying glass, trying to decipher its secrets, when she'd felt the prickling sensation of being watched. Lowering the glass, she'd found herself face to face with two-hundred-fifty pounds of muscle and teeth.

That's when she did the sensible thing and let out a scream.

She'd felt like she was dreaming when its hot breath blasted her face. But Cameron was there before her heart had the time to beat twice. Without hesitation, he'd thrown himself between her and the beast, arms flailing and voice rising in a war cry that echoed off the mountainside. The lion had startled, perhaps more annoyed than threatened, and retreated back into the forest, leaving them all trembling in its wake. The second it was gone, he'd rushed to her side and crushed her in his arms, checking her for damage, kissing her face all over, eliminating any doubt that Ephriam and Tavi might have had about the nature of their relationship.

Brie grabbed the bottle of shampoo Clive had been kind enough to provide and started massaging it through her long curls, shivering despite the steam.

If they were honest, it was Mike who'd saved them. It made her feel even worse that he'd found out about their initial meeting and memory wipe. He'd been their anchor, his uncanny foresight rescuing them time and time again. On their very first day, when he'd called for a lunch break around noon, they'd looked at him like he was mad. But then he'd built a fire, boiled river water, and produced sachets of dehydrated potato soup and instant coffee as if it were the most natural thing in the world. At that point, Sherry looked at him like he was the messiah and instantly proposed. His ensuing grin, plus the steaming bowls of soup, had revived their spirits, and they had set off again with renewed determination, hoisting Tavi onto their shoulders and marching south, following the light from Azrael's glass.

Tavi had been in a bad way since their encounter with Baal. She'd lost the ability to regulate her unique electrical powers, and drinking water, the one thing that might help heal her physical injuries, mixed poorly with the ill-timed shocks that still pulsed without warning through her body. At first, her injuries were so severe she could hardly walk. For someone so proud and fiercely independent, the makeshift stretcher they'd fashioned from pine boughs and Mike's emergency ponchos was a bitter pill to swallow. But there had been no other choice, and they had taken turns carrying her, each step a reminder of their shared burdens. By the second day, Tavi's resilience had shown itself in full force. She had insisted on walking, first leaning on Sherry and Cameron for support, then gradually finding her strength until she was marching alongside them, her face set in a grim mask of determination.

It was the only thing that had gone right.

The rest of their journey had been a cascade of minor disasters. They'd blundered through a thicket of poison ivy, their skin erupting in angry red welts despite Mike's attempts to warn them. Ephriam had eaten a handful of berries he swore were safe, only to spend the next few hours retching into the bushes while the rest of them eyed the remaining rations with increasing unease. Pine boughs had lashed at their faces, the trail had disappeared into a maze of underbrush, and every time Brie looked through the magnifying glass, the world beyond seemed no closer than before.

But the worst part was when the mountain *itself* tried to eat them.

It had started after an unexpectedly vicious argument over chocolate rations. Voices had risen in frustration and fear, their patience exhausted by the endless march that seemed to be taking them no closer to their goal than when they'd started. Brie could feel the tension rising like a storm and wasn't sure how much longer they could hold together. Rains came, torrential downpours that soaked them to the bone and turned the trail into a river of mud. They'd pressed on, heads down, barely able to hear each other over the roar of the storm.

Then came a low rumble, a sound so deep and resonant that it vibrated in Brie's bones. It had taken her a moment to realize that it wasn't thunder. She'd looked up in confusion, only to freeze in visceral terror.

The mountain was moving.

No, not moving — collapsing. A wall of earth and rock was tumbling down the slope above them, a deluge of mud and debris that was gaining speed with every passing second. Her heart had leapt into her throat, and she'd turned to shout a warning to the others, but the words were lost in the ear-splitting roar.

"Run!" Cameron's voice had cut through the chaos. He'd grabbed her arm and pulled her forward, his grip like iron. The others were already moving, their survival instincts kicking in as they scrambled to find higher ground.

Her feet had slipped in the mud, and her legs had burned as they'd raced for the safety of the trees. She could hear Sherry crying out in fear, Ephriam's voice urging her on, and Tavi's grunts of pain as she pushed herself beyond her limits. The world was a blur of movement and sound, and the ground trembled beneath them as the avalanche of earth roared closer.

They'd barely reached the shelter of a rocky outcrop when the mudslide thundered past, a torrent of earth and stone that swept away everything in its path. She'd collapsed against the rocks, her chest heaving as she gasped for breath. The others were beside her, equally exhausted, their faces pale with shock.

For a long moment, the only sound was the distant rumble of the mudslide as it continued its destructive path down the mountain.

"How the hell was the mountain lion, *not* the hardest part?" Brie had muttered to herself, the words slipping out before she could stop them.

She'd been echoing this phrase at least once every day since, still absolutely gobsmacked by the experience. Even now, she was unable to believe that she was recalling the event from the safety of a steamy guest bathroom. In the mountains, there were many times she'd genuinely thought she might not live to experience the blessing of modern amenities again.

*Not that they're modern,* her inner voice reminded her.

As it turned out, nothing in those woods was the hardest part.

Brie practically shoved Cameron into the shower after her. Her angel wanted to abstain in atonement for his sins against both Mike and the space-time continuum, but she sniffed him discreetly and insisted that this wasn't just for him — it was for all of their sakes. He begrudgingly obliged, and she walked outside to towel-dry her hair on the porch.

In spite of everything, it was a beautiful morning. The sun had broken free of the clouds that had caged it and was spilling, light and cheerful, over the eastern trees. The air was already warm and smelled of chimney smoke and pine. She dabbed the towel to her curls absent-mindedly, imagining for a wistful moment a simpler life, one where they blew off the celestial catastrophe and merely stayed in the guest house. She could get a job in town, sweeping up at the diner. Ephriam could find work as a lumberjack, setting off each morning with a dozen other surly-tempered men, toppling evergreens with his bare hands.

*Like a modern-day Snow White.*

"Hello there, Brutus." A familiar voice sounded behind her.

Her eyes snapped shut for a moment. Then she turned to see her best friend sitting in a chair near the door, legs crossed, and a single eyebrow raised, like a woodland Bond villain. If she'd been stroking a pure white cat, it would not have looked out of place.

Brie sighed, bracing for the worst. "Mike told you?"

"That you wiped his memory with your fun new angel friend to get out of a speeding ticket upon your first meeting? That you Men-In-Blacked my boyfriend-slash-fiance, depending on how seriously he took that moment by the river with the coffee? *Yes*, Brianna, he told me."

*Brianna, huh? This is worse than I thought.*

"I know." Brie sighed again. "I'm sorry about that. And Cameron is a wreck. I think Mike is the closest thing he's had to a best friend in… I don't even know how long. We didn't know who he was to you, Sher. Cam thought he was helping me."

Sherry steepled her fingers a moment longer before a smile tugged at the corner of her lips. A second later, she burst out laughing, rocking back in the antique chair until tears pooled at the corners of her eyes.

Brie took a step back, ready for anything. "This is a scary pream-ble—"

"Brie, look where we are," Sherry interrupted. "In a stranger's guest house, in a podunk town, in California, in *nineteen-sixty-freaking-nine*. So you blanked out my boyfriend to get out of a speeding ticket." She rose to her feet and gave Brie an unexpected hug. "Don't worry about it, babe. All's fair in love and traffic violations."

*Thank God!*

"You total scoundrel!" Brie clasped her in return, letting out a shaky laugh. "I thought you were serious. You're a problematically good actress, you know that?"

"I am. And I do." Sherry grinned. "But listen, don't tell Cameron everything's alright. Let Mike torture him for a while, okay? I mean, he did strand us in the past."

It was a rather generous way of capping things — like her boyfriend had lost his keys at the diner or accidentally overslept.

Brie nodded slowly, dabbing again at her hair. "Yeah, that's fair. Though he's being pretty hard on himself."

*In super helpful ways. Like denying himself showers.*

"Men," Sherry mused, settling back in her chair and patting the one beside her. "They don't need any help from us. Leave them alone for ten minutes, and they self-destruct."

Brie nodded wisely and sat down, turning her eyes to the distant field. "Just lighten up before he completely unravels, please?"

"Absolutely no promises," Sherry replied with a wink.

The sun had cleared the trees and pierced through the morning mist, spilling great sheets of light across the meadow. A bird was singing somewhere, hidden amidst the foliage. Now and then, she'd get a glimpse of it, the rustle of leaves or the flash of a crimson wing.

"We haven't talked about it yet, but what are we supposed to do next?" Sherry spoke tentatively, picking at a splinter on the railing. It was the question on all of their minds, but no one had yet been courageous enough to ask. "We don't have any money that'll be recognized in this day and age, no valid identification, no car, no one to call, and no idea where to go except to keep following that damn magnifying glass of yours to God-knows-where — the Hall of Jophial? Wherever and whatever the heck that is?" She stole a glance at Brie's pocket, trying to manage her frustration. "I swear, for a magical gift given to you by a freaking archangel, that thing has sure proved to be a wash. Kept us wandering around the wilderness for days, offered protection from precisely zero disasters, and the picture inside never even budged an inch. Always the same town. Always those weird-looking cars."

Brie pulled in a breath to answer, then let it out with a sigh. She wished she could contest this. She wished she could provide some helpful insight, but the truth was, she felt exactly the same. Azrael's glass had seemed like a godsend at first, quite literally — a divine artifact to help guide them on the quest King Enoch had entrusted to them. But after two days of following what they assumed was its "guiding light," only to end up increasingly lost in the woods, she'd started to lose faith in the celestial object. Even now, its weight in her pocket seemed more of a burden than a gift.

She gave Sherry her best theatrical shrug. "I don't know what to tell you. Maybe it's a prank." She pulled out the glass. "Some sort of celestial hazing that's gone too far."

Considering the fact that she'd woken up early and had yet to find any caffeine, she thought this was a downright hilarious suggestion. It was only Sherry's withering stare that made her pause. A few seconds passed, then a few seconds more. Her pulse began to quicken.

"A celestial hazing, huh?" Sherry finally replied.

Brie offered a tentative smile. "Too soon?"

Their eyes met a suspended moment before Sherry walked back inside. "I've decided I'm angry with you after all."

# CHAPTER THREE

## The Shadow in the Pages

Brie and Sherry stepped back inside the guesthouse, leaving the cool air of the patio behind. In the living room, Mike was sprawled across the couch, a heavy book open on his lap, his brows furrowed in concentration. The old tome looked out of place in his hands — ancient and weighty, its dark blue cover embossed with silver filigree.

"Still trying to decipher that?" Brie teased, plopping onto the armrest beside him and tossing him Azrael's glass. "You might need this."

It had become second nature during their time in the woods — Brie would use the glass like a beacon to guide their path until they could walk no more. Then they'd take a break, and she'd toss it to Mike. He'd spent hours pouring over the book Brie had taken from Elysium's library, looking for any information that might help them figure out how they were supposed to fulfill the mission given to them by Enoch: to find Jophial, the Angel of Wisdom and Understanding. The others had encouraged this. Sherry had massaged his back while she read over his shoulder. Ephriam and Cameron tried to help, along with Tavi, when she had the strength.

The only one strangely ambivalent about his efforts was Brie. She'd gotten it into her head that they needed to go to the Garden of Eden, a notion she couldn't defend but whose origins she could easily trace.

Enoch had told her back in Elysium that the only other person who might have any insight into her family's connection to her pendant was Elijah, the guardian of the Garden. She knew they had more pressing matters to deal with, but the idea had planted like a seed in her mind, and the sight of Mike trying so diligently to lead them in a different direction every day chafed at her soul on some deep level she didn't understand.

Mike smirked without looking up. "When else am I gonna read *The History of the Time Seas*? I figure this is the closest I'll ever get to an inter-dimensional travel guide."

Sherry sat beside him, cross-legged on the couch. "Yeah, but is it *good*? Are there any juicy betrayals? Forbidden love? Scandalous time-line paradoxes? Scathing one-star reviews of time itself?"

Mike sighed dramatically and riffled through the pages like he was shuffling a deck of cards. "Alas, still nothing of the sort. No intrigue. Just page after page of — ah!" He stopped suddenly and drew his hand away.

"What is it?" Sherry moved closer, alarmed.

"Nothing, just a paper cut." Mike squeezed the red line of blood curiously for a second before returning to the book. "Wait…" He frowned. The enormous tome had fallen open to a random section near the middle. "That's weird."

Brie glanced over his shoulder. "What's weird?"

Mike turned the book so they could see. Entire paragraphs were covered in black streaks, the ink blotting out words as if someone had tried to erase history itself.

Ephriam and Cameron appeared in the doorway, followed by Tavi. They'd been summoned by the sound elicited by Mike's papercut.

As soon as Ephriam caught sight of the book's page, he stiffened. "Let me see that." Mike turned the book toward him. Ephriam took two steps forward, his golden eyes narrowing. "This isn't age. This is deliberate censorship."

The humans looked at each other incredulously. "By who?" Sherry finally asked.

Ephriam's expression darkened. "By someone who didn't want certain knowledge of the Time Seas to be recorded."

Mike let out a nervous laugh. "That's… not at all concerning."

"Why wouldn't the Elysians be allowed to record something?" Brie asked with a frown. "What could be so dangerous about the Time Seas that it had to be classified?"

Cameron leaned in and scanned the page. "This section is supposed to be about anomalies of the Time Seas — things lost, things taken." He hesitated, pointing to one of the passages that was still intact. "This says there are entities that slipped between the cracks of time. Some say they were absorbed, others say they were devoured… and others say they became something else. Something no longer bound by time."

A prickle ran down Brie's spine. Something about those words itched at the back of her mind like she'd heard them before but couldn't remember where.

"Um, guys?" Sherry's voice was unusually small. "Look." She pointed at the edge of the book, where Mike's finger had sliced open on the page.

The drop of blood that had issued forth was trickling toward the center of the book. Not naturally, not pulled by gravity and physics. It writhed and wriggled like a raindrop on the side window of a speeding car toward the middle of the page. When it hit the very center of a redacted passage, it vanished as though sucked into the pages themselves.

Before anyone could respond, the air shifted.

A sharp breath cut through the silence.

The others turned to see what was the matter.

Tavi sat behind them, rigid on the edge of a chair, fingers twitching against her knees. Her eyes were unfocused, staring at nothing. Cameron and Sherry approached cautiously, trying to see what was wrong. Before they could reach her, the air snapped and turned cold.

A sound, like low laughter, rumbled through the guesthouse. The lights flickered.

For just a moment, Brie felt sick, like the moment at the top of a roller coaster before the first plunge. Her pendant glowed brightly on her chest and pulsed once, twice, like a heartbeat.

Then, the house lurched back to normal.

Only the sound of Tavi's shaky breathing filled the air. Cameron and Sherry rushed to her side to see what was wrong. She waved them aside. "I'm okay… I think I'm fine. I don't know what that was," she finished with a frown.

Ephriam snatched the book from Mike's hands, his jaw tight as he flipped through the pages to the redacted section again. After studying it for a minute, his face darkened. "This book hasn't just been censored."

Mike blinked. "Excuse me?"

Ephriam turned it toward them and pointed at the black streaks hiding the ancient words. Then he tilted it toward the light from the windows, and they saw it. Shimmering faintly, a black stamp within black ink was barely visible. They could only make it out when the light hit it just right — an intricate celestial sigil on the page.

"This is a concealment sigil," Ephriam said with a dire look. "Someone didn't just black out parts of this book. They locked something inside."

This revelation landed heavily on everyone in the room.

"Something that liked the taste of my papercut?" Mike asked in an unsteady voice.

Ephriam's eyes shot to Mike. "Where exactly did you get this?"

Mike's hand shook as he pointed to Brie. "She brought it home from the library in Elysium. I think…" He gave her an apologetic look as he finished. "I think she might have been a little drunk."

Brie swallowed as Ephriam's golden eyes shot to her, boring into her soul.

Thankfully, Cameron stepped in. "She wasn't drunk. Raphael dosed her with ambrosia — it wasn't her fault."

Ephriam's eyes remained narrowed, but he nodded slowly. "The question remains. Who gave this to you?"

Brie flushed red. "It's a little fuzzy, but it was either Raziel or Azrael. I think it might have been both."

Ephriam looked upset. "We have enough going on. We shouldn't be tampering with forbidden texts on top of—"

"Brie, you're bleeding!" Cameron interrupted, walking over and brushing Brie's hair from her shoulder in alarm.

She turned to a mirror hanging on a nearby wall, and sure enough, there was a trickle of blood running from just behind her earlobe down her neck. She frowned. "The back of my earring must've knocked into my neck in all the commotion. It's nothing."

"Maybe you shouldn't be wearing this thing." Her angel gently touched the earring Zadkiel had given her back in Elysium. "If it's so sharp that it—"

She pushed his hand away with a forced smile. "Cam, I'm fine. This is a fluke. After all, it didn't do this during a literal landslide. Go help look after Tavi."

Seemingly satisfied, he turned back to help with Sherry's examinations.

Brie turned back to the mirror and discreetly wiped the blood away. A rust-red smear remained. As she studied it, she saw the reflection of the book. In the mirror, it seemed to emanate a certain gravity — a darkness that hadn't been there before. Brie shivered and covered her neck with her hand.

*Better safe than sorry.*

Clive and Myrtle Emerson had never entertained such exotic visitors in their lives, and they were not about to waste the opportunity. Such moments were rare and would propel them to the epicenter of town gossip for years to come. By the time the six companions got to the main house, the table had been set and a meal laid out fit for royalty. Every country breakfast delicacy you could imagine was plattered high — pancakes, bacon, eggs, hash browns, waffles, and every jam and syrup in the Western hemisphere. Best of all, the smell of fresh-ground coffee wafted over the table like a fragrant, heavenly cloud.

The old couple saw them walking up the path and waved them over excitedly, heaping food onto plates before their guests could even sit down.

"Have a seat," Clive commanded cheerfully, "eat while it's hot."

The friends sat, alternating between thanking the couple profusely and warding off a hundred questions. A newspaper was lying open on the table, though no one seemed inclined to read it. Quite the contrary, Mike was deliberately averting his eyes, like the thing had personally offended him. Meanwhile, Myrtle was fussing over Tavi, who was tearing into breakfast like she hadn't eaten in a month.

"You poor, poor dears!" Myrtle kept tutting under her breath and shaking her head. "I can't imagine why some park ranger didn't manage to find you sooner — all that time in the woods. And Clive said you came *this close* to being eaten by a cougar! I can't imagine what you've been through. Here, sweetheart, have some more eggs." She delivered another giant scoop of sunshine-yellow scramble onto Tavi's plate.

The Elysian warrior flashed her a look that bordered on adoration. "Thank you, ma'am," she murmured, reaching for the coffee.

The woman batted her hand away gently, reaching for her mug. "Here, let me get that for you. Clive! Clive, didn't you tell me these poor young things were in a landslide?" She poured Tavi coffee before buttering her toast. "I can't imagine! Oh, but you must have been *terrified*! How did you manage to escape with your lives? And keep yourselves fed? And make it so far on foot?" She paused a moment for breath, looking overwhelmed just speaking of it. "I mean, my goodness, you must be a wreck. Here, dear, try the maple syrup. It's from Canada."

Brie smiled gratefully, watching from across the table. No matter the century, some things remained exactly the same. She'd met people like Myrtle before. The questions were solely for her own benefit, a compulsive and delighted summation of the drama. No doubt, she'd be spinning the same tales at church and around the diner for months to come.

"And what unusual clothes you have!" Myrtle eyed both the Elysian battle gear and the glittering fishing waders skeptically. She could usually find some small point to latch onto, but in this case, she was utterly bewildered. "Tell me, is that the new fashion? I can't keep up with the fashions these days. It always seems as though the skirts are getting shorter and the hair is getting higher."

"Don't threaten me with a good time," Sherry whispered.

Brie stifled a laugh.

"Well, now that you've managed to rescue yourselves, what are you folks going to do next?" Clive asked cheerfully.

The question snapped them back to earth.

They looked around at one another, at a collective loss. They'd barely had time to talk the night before, and most of that had been spent debating the moon landing and arguing about the existential safety of butterflies. At no point had they considered *next steps*.

It was Mike who finally answered. Granted, he took the time to knock over Cameron's coffee first. "Well, sir, we aren't really sure yet. Still trying to get our bearings." He flashed the couple a charismatic grin before glancing at the angel. "You should probably clean that up."

Cameron nodded with a flush, dabbing at his steaming pants.

"No rush, no rush at all," Clive said happily. "Though I expect you'll be wanting to call your folks back home to let them know you're alright. You can use the phone upstairs if you need to."

Brie glanced involuntarily at the ceiling, tickled at the idea of a landline.

"Thank you for that," Mike said politely, charming both of them with his sincerity. "Thank you for everything. I'm sure this hasn't—"

His eyes caught on the newspaper, and he forced himself to look. "Actually, may I read that when you're finished?"

Clive handed it over obligingly, and the others watched with amusement as Mike flipped past the black and white photograph of the moonwalk, murmuring under his breath and shaking his head in amazement every so often as he scanned down the page.

It was a quaint scene. Coffee was brewing, and a dog started barking at squirrels outside. Myrtle stood up and began washing the dishes. The television was playing in the other room. Talking heads were jabbering excitedly about the astronauts' daily schedule, mixed in with some local news and the odd commercial. Some of those had aged better than others.

*More doctors smoke this cigarette brand than any other…*

"Dear God," Brie muttered, watching from the table. She jumped when Sherry kicked her sharply, unseen by anyone else. "Ow! What, you maniac?"

Her best friend leaned closer, shooting a discreet glance at the Elysians. "Talking about future plans," she whispered, cupping a hand around her mouth, "I haven't worked out all the ethical questions yet, but full disclosure — if we end up stuck here for a while, I intend to make an absolute killing in the stock market."

Brie grinned, rubbing her shin. "Of course you are, you little capitalistic monster. This coming from the same girl who nearly fainted over the implications of a squashed bee. Of *course* you want to manipulate the stock market."

Sherry looked at her square on, utterly devoid of apology.

"Weldon, I've got a hell of a student loan to start repaying once we get back, not to mention the ninety years of therapy I'll need to help me recover from this time-jumping road trip with your first serious boyfriend. So pardon me for showing a little damn pragmatism."

There was a weighted silence.

"I'm sorry," Brie finally apologized. "It's hard to talk to you about pragmatism while you're wearing sparkly rubber waders."

A dainty hand smacked her in the face.

"What is that?" Cameron exclaimed, leaning suddenly past them. The others turned in surprise, but he was fixated on the television. "Somebody turn that up!"

The friends shared a bewildered look as Myrtle set down her dishrag and walked obligingly to the television, flipping up the volume.

"Cameron, what are you doing?" Brie hissed.

"Shh! Just watch!" He was standing now, staring excitedly at the screen.

It was a commercial. A stagecoach, pulled by Clydesdales, was trotting down a country road while a man with a rich newscaster's baritone talked about financial security and putting the customer first. Apparently, some bank in San Francisco had installed a new, state-of-the-art security vault, and the rest of the world simply *had* to know.

The friends looked at Cameron like he was crazy. It wasn't until the camera zoomed out and they saw the wide shot that they gasped and leapt to their feet.

It was the exact image they had seen a thousand times in Azrael's magnifying glass. The one that had almost seemed to taunt them as they'd trekked aimlessly through an unending redwood forest. How many times had they looked at it? How many times had they discussed what it might mean? But they'd clearly been wrong. The "weird-looking cars" weren't cars at all.

They were stagecoaches.

The ancient relic had been showing them the commercial for the bank.

Brie sat down hard, feeling like someone had knocked the wind out of her. The others were frozen in similar positions. Clive and Myrtle looked on with concern.

A moment passed, then Cameron turned to the couple with a wide grin.

"Mr. Emerson, is there any chance we could hitch a ride with you to San Francisco?"

# CHAPTER FOUR

## Roadtrips

Cool wind whipped through Brie's hair as Clive's truck bumped along the Pacific Coast Highway, sending her curls dancing behind her like a rebellious flag. Her hand slipped from Cameron's warm grasp, and she laughed, enjoying the rare moment of peace. When she leaned closer, he draped an arm over her shoulders, eyes twinkling in the sunlight as he gave her a little wink.

There were probably more direct routes to the city, but Clive had opted to value scenery over haste. That morning, after Myrtle had given them a basket filled with enough home-baked goods to sate an army, the portly man had loaded everyone into his truck, and they'd taken off through the forest, heading for the coast. Even on wheels, the woods were endless. Sunlight filtered in ethereal slants through the redwood canopy for over an hour before suddenly, after rounding one last twist in the road, the scenery broke wide open, and they caught their first glimpse of that endless Pacific blue. The sound was quick to follow — crashing waves pulsing through salted air. Everywhere they looked, light dazzled off the water, and waves met in a seamless embrace of earth and sky.

"I can't believe how beautiful it is," Sherry exclaimed from the backseat, leaning forward to get a better view. "No wonder my dad talks about this place like it's some sort of paradise. The mountains, the shore… it's like God decided to show off."

The Elysians smiled to themselves, probably armed with inside information.

It was Brie and Mike's first time in California. Sherry had been before, but even she had never seen the coast. She'd only been to the city to visit her dad's offices. Her father had made a fortune in a tech startup and, of course, had his roots right there in California. He'd met Sherry's mom on a business trip to Georgia, fallen madly in love, and was, for all intents and purposes, still in the middle of living happily ever after.

*Must be nice*, Brie thought, ignoring the sharp pang of envy.

She tried not to wonder how her own dad was doing. Living in the moment seemed to be the key to surviving her catastrophic adventure. Whenever she tried thinking past the present, things started to unravel.

She laced her fingers through Cameron's. "It's one of the most gorgeous places I've ever seen." She leaned out of the passenger's side window and squinted into the sunlight. "And I think this is the first time we've gone a full morning without some kind of disaster," she added, half expecting the sky to open up and rain frogs to prove her wrong.

"I wouldn't count your chickens yet," Sherry answered back. "We've still got plenty of time to be accosted by rogue seagulls or something equally weird. Knock on wood, and let's keep all that sunshiny optimism to ourselves, yeah?"

Brie bit her lip to keep from grinning. Sherry's mood had been swinging wildly between nature-inspired awe and obvious sulking all day, and it didn't take a rocket scientist to pinpoint the exact moment things had started to break down: it was when she'd laid eyes on the flannel.

Myrtle and Clive had brought their guests a box filled with church donations to rifle through for some new clothes. They'd meant this as a kind gesture, given that Mike and Sherry had been hiking in their water-proof, rhinestone-encrusted waders from the Guinea Jubilee for ten days, and both the odor and the fashion statement had become untenable. But when Sherry had held up the only clothes that were even vaguely her size, which turned out to be a pair of oversized work jeans and a red and black plaid flannel button-down, her face had contorted into a look of such abject horror, you'd have thought their lovely hosts were trying to murder her in cold blood. She'd managed to choke out a polite thank you, but now, as she picked a piece of red lint off the offending garment and flicked it out the open window, her face was stricken with a doleful look that clearly said, *I look like a lumberjack, and I'd rather be dead.*

"I wasn't trying to tempt fate, Sher—" Brie began, only to be cut off by the loud crackle of cellophane. Though Ephriam had chosen to sit on blankets in the truck bed rather than cram his towering body into the cab, Tavi had opted to stay closer to the picnic basket. The Elysian warrior had opened yet another bag of potato chips and started wolfing them down.

"She's like a vacuum," Sherry leaned forward and whispered to Brie, nodding toward Tavi. "I swear, I blink, and an entire bag of chips has disappeared."

"Maybe it's part of her recovery," Brie suggested.

"Or she's avoiding conversation," Sherry quipped.

"Or maybe," Tavi muttered without opening her eyes, "I'm conserving energy so I don't throw either of you out of this truck."

Sherry immediately sat back and folded her hands in her lap. "Noted." She picked at a hole in the too-large jeans. "Though at this point, the only thing I'm dressed for is a grisly roadside demise."

*And we're back.*

"I think you look perfect no matter what you wear, babe," Mike said bravely, taking her hand.

She turned to him with a martyred sniff. "You're very sweet. And very wrong. And if we ever get out of this mess, promise me you'll take me to Paris. I don't know what I'll need to wear to erase the memory of this, but I know it will be in Paris."

Mike nodded slowly, unable to restrain a smile. "Then, of course, that's where we'll go."

Cameron watched them fondly, leaning over to Brie with a whisper of his own. "I think Mike would sell his soul for a trip to Paris with her."

Brie nodded, watching them as well. "Let's hope it doesn't come to that." She stared a moment longer, then turned to him and asked in a low voice. "You sounded so certain back at the house, but you never said why. I get that the magnifier is leading us to the bank, but I don't see how that helps anything, aside from a rather ironic reminder that we don't have any money. We're going to get there, and then what? What are we supposed to do?"

He squeezed her reassuringly. "Trust me. I have a plan."

She nodded curiously and turned her attention back to Clive. "We really can't thank you enough for all the trouble you've gone to. This?" she gestured outside. "This is above and beyond."

"Not at all, young lady," he chuckled in response. "You might find this hard to believe, but not too much happens down in Mad River. It's exciting. And nostalgic," he added with a little wink. "It's nice to be around all this young love."

"I — I don't..." Brie stammered, shooting a quick glance back at Tavi.

At this point, she was confident the Elysians knew about the nature of her relationship with their prince. Still, somehow, during all their time in the wilderness, they hadn't had a chance to talk about it — which probably spoke to her terror about the repercussions of breaking one of Elysium's most sacred taboos. It was one of the only good things about getting trapped in the past and cut off from any contact with the celestial realm — for the time being, their secret was safe.

*But we'll have to figure it out eventually.*

*There are memory wipes and other Elysian censures on the table.*

"Besides," Clive continued, "I'll be the talk of the town, swapping stories with you fine folks. So keep your thanks to yourself. This is essentially selfish."

Brie laughed under her breath. "Selfish, right."

The trip was upwards of six hours, and Clive kept up a steady stream of conversation from start to finish, filling the truck with facts about the Bay Area's history and giving unsolicited yet highly welcome tips about the best restaurants in town. It was impossible not to like him. It was impossible even to try. When he suggested they stop for lunch at a place he knew on the route, everyone enthusiastically agreed, none more so than Tavi.

They stopped at a little place in Mendocino, which Clive referred to as "the last door on Ukiah Street." Truth be told, it didn't look like much at the onset — more like going to eat in someone's living room rather than in a restaurant. So it came as a surprise when, quite unexpectedly, the whole group proceeded to have one of the best meals of their lives. The family who owned the establishment served them personally, clapping Clive on the back and asking how the hell he'd been while eyeing his strange company with a curiosity they were too polite to voice. Desserts were served, and drinks were comped. By the time they clambered back into the truck, even Sherry had a decidedly sunnier outlook on things.

From there, it was a brief stop for gas, followed by hours of coastal scenery. Every now and then, Cameron would give Brie a soft squeeze on her knee or shoot her a glance that sent a tingle through her chest. She rested her head against him and gripped tight to his hand, letting her hair blow freely around them as her eyes lost themselves in the waves.

She might be drowning in questions, unable to see more than a few hours into the future, but whatever was coming, she knew one thing for sure: they would face it together.

That's when they saw it.

Enormous and elegant in its construction, a paint stroke glowing over the water, the color of a dusty sunset — the Golden Gate Bridge. The view was breathtaking — waves crashing against the shore, endless sky stretching above them, and the perfect blue of the Pacific glittering everywhere in a cast of dazzling light. And rising on gentle hills, as if swelling out of the Bay itself, the city shone in the late afternoon sun, a beacon welcoming the travelers.

"Now that is a gate," Cameron said quietly.

Brie couldn't help but agree as they passed over the iconic, rust-colored structure and entered the city itself — teeming with life and history.

A history they were now very much a part of.

It was utterly overwhelming. A symphony of music, traffic, shouts, and laughter rang out from every colorful corner of the city while the smell of the ocean mingled with street food, coffee, and marijuana. After more than a week lost in a forest with nothing to listen to except the wind, the birds, and each other, it was a sensory overload.

"Are you sure you're gonna be alright?" asked Clive for the tenth time. "I'd be happy to call in a favor or two, have a friend put you up for the night—"

"We'll be fine," Cameron answered reassuringly. "You've already done so much. I don't know how we can ever repay you."

"I actually had an idea on that front," Mike interjected, waving Clive forward. "Come over here for a second."

As the two men walked to the end of the street, the rest of their party turned and looked up at the towering facade of a skyscraper. Nestled halfway between Chinatown and Union Square, it was a forty-three-story building in the heart of the financial district that stood head and shoulders taller than everything else around it. A plaque on the wall outside identified it as the tallest building west of Dallas.

Sherry was the first to break the silence, which she did with her usual flair. "So what are we doing here, Cameron? Are we planning to rob a bank now?"

He flashed her a scandalized look. "Of course not! I wouldn't dream of such a thing. I happen to have an account here."

*Excuse me?*

The others turned to him with identical, incredulous expressions.

"You do?" Tavi finally asked.

"Well, it might be more of a box," Cameron answered with a slight frown. "I came here a long time ago, when I was a child, with my brother Ethan. We left a few things in a special box when this company was founded, and he gave me the key. I'd completely forgotten about it until I saw the name of the company on that television."

Sherry froze with a bracing look. "Hang on. We took a six-hour road trip from the relative safety of a small, friendly town to a huge city teeming with hippies and history we probably shouldn't mess with because you left a few things in a special box?"

There was a scathing pause.

Cameron looked defensive. "He said they would be valuable someday."

*Oh, holy hell.*

"Honey," Brie interjected tightly, "that's the sort of thing you might have *told* me instead of leaving it a happy surprise. How old were you when Ethan brought you here?"

Tavi chimed in simultaneously, "Your brother took you on a time jump when you were a *kid?* Did your father know about this?"

Cameron flushed and looked at the ground. "I was five. And… no, he didn't."

They all might have forgiven him. It might have been a cute story if Ephriam hadn't obliterated all chance of that the very next moment. He folded his enormous arms over his chest with his characteristic disapproving glare and asked, "And why did Ethan bring a five-year-old to San Francisco without his father's approval to put things in your special box?"

*Okay, it sounds worse the more times we say it.*

Cameron took a full ten seconds and turned an astonishing shade of scarlet before answering. "It was my birthday. I wanted to see a cowboy and pan for gold."

Brie looked heavenward.

*Lord, give me strength.*

*By which I mean, give me one hell of a right hook. I'm going to punch him in the face.*

She discarded the first three things she wanted to say, sensing they might bring about an inescapable end to the relationship. She discarded the next three things as well, sensing they would be covered by one of the others. In the end, she left it rather simple. "This was your plan?"

He flushed again, twisting his fingers together. "I mean, when you say it like that…"

"I could kill you with my thumb, you know," Ephriam interrupted.

Cameron cast him a frightened glance and raised both hands in a placating gesture. "Look, Ethan said that if I ever got in trouble, I could come here, use a special key, and open the box, and all my problems would be solved. And he knew a lot about Earth," he added quickly. "He could even *drive*." He set his jaw, doubling down. "I'm sure he was right. Why else would Azrael's glass lead us here?"

At that moment, Mike returned with Clive and saw everyone standing in a semicircle around Cameron, glaring at him like he was on trial for witchcraft. He paused a few seconds, glancing between them, before taking a deliberate step back. "Okay, so it looks like I missed something."

"I'd say so," Sherry answered bitingly. "We're pinning our ability to navigate this godforsaken decade on the mystery birthday present of a five-year-old."

Mike looked between them, searching for clues, but decided to roll with it. "I suppose that's not the weirdest thing that's happened lately. Anyway, Clive is going to take off, if anyone wants to say goodbye."

"Actually, is there any way you could wait here for a while until we finish up in there?" Cameron asked. "I'm not sure Tavi and Ephriam should join us."

As if the weapons weren't enough, nothing in the church donation box had come remotely close to fitting the warriors. They were wearing a combination of too-tight, highwater pants and the traditional Elysian armor they'd been stuck in since their battle with Baal. They glanced down at themselves before looking at each other. A pursed-lipped silence fell between them, but each seemed to think the other was the greater offender.

Clive gave them a knowing wink. "Not a problem. Why don't you young folks come with me? We can get a nice coffee," he added, to Tavi's obvious delight.

Before they left, Ephriam took a few steps closer, speaking low in Cameron's ear. "Whatever humiliation you imagine I will concoct for you as retribution for this ridiculosity, let me assure you — the reality will be twelve times worse." With that, he clapped the young prince on the shoulder, watched all the color drain from his face, then turned on his heel and followed after Clive and Tavi.

The others stared after him in silence.

"Doesn't mince words, that one." Sherry tilted her head appraisingly before glancing back at Cameron. "I wonder what he has in mind. I wonder if we could share notes."

Brie flashed her a look, trying to hold back a grin.

*Mean.*

Cameron took a deep breath and squared his shoulders, turning to face the others. They looked as bedraggled as he did, in a combination of their own wilderness-torn clothes and ill-fitting donation box supplements. There wasn't a hopeful expression among them. Every face was painted with the same mix of exhaustion and doubt.

"Listen," he began quietly, "I know it's a long shot. But you saw — the image on the screen was the same as the one from the glass. It can't be a coincidence. It simply can't." He turned to his girlfriend, willing it to be so. "Right?"

With a weary sigh, she slipped her hand into his, staring with a tired dread at the revolving doors. "If there turns out to be a bunch of confetti in that box, we're breaking up."

# CHAPTER FIVE

## Revelations

The lobby of the famous bank was a sea of bureaucracy floating on marble floors. It reminded Brie of the Great Hall of Elysium in a strange, far-less supernatural way.

*Same sense of intimidation.*

*Same sense that I don't belong here.*

She awkwardly pulled down her sleeve to hide one of the tears she'd received in the landslide. A single look at Sherry's stricken face said that she was constantly, painfully aware that she was still wearing flannel. That being said, the difference between the women had always been primarily focused on how they handled embarrassment. Brie tended to shut down and shy away, except when forced by circumstance to confront the issue. Sherry, on the other hand, refused to let it win and, in fact, refused to acknowledge its existence, choosing belligerent denial every time.

*Not sure which of those is more unhealthy.*

With a look that dared anyone to get in her way, Sherry marched up to the nearest desk and cleared her throat.

A bored-looking woman sporting a beehive and horn-rimmed glasses looked up with a complete absence of enthusiasm. "May I help you?" she asked, in a tone that indicated she'd rather be doing literally anything else. Her name tag identified her as Janet.

"Yes. Where is your VIP waiting room? My colleague needs to be assisted by your manager." She may have been dressed like a lumberjack, but the tilt of Sherry's chin and the arch of her neck could never allow her to be mistaken for, as she would say, "a commoner."

Janet raised an eyebrow. "We don't have one of those."

"Gracious, how do you get on?" Sherry replied with an obviously fake pseudo-accent and an air of scandal.

*Oh God. She's going British,* Brie thought. *This is going to be a disaster.*

"Actually, it's me who needs some assistance," Cameron interjected, cutting in front of Sherry. "I have a key to one of your special boxes, and I'm afraid I don't quite know how it all works. Is there anyone here who could help me out?" He flashed the teller his most blinding smile. The one that made it seem perfectly feasible that he'd grown up in a castle in the clouds. The one that had even his own girlfriend staring like her brain was on pause.

*How is he POSSIBLE? I like him even more with the hint of a beard—*

She shook her head to clear it.

*Focus, Brie. Stop ogling your boyfriend.*

*Janet is doing that enough for the both of us, anyway.*

Indeed, the dead-eyed bank employee had taken on a new attitude entirely, coming to life with an enthusiasm that had surely vanished from her personality fifteen years prior. She leaned over her desk, resting her chin on the back of her hand and smiling. "Well, that's another story entirely. Do you have an account number I can look up for you?"

"I'm afraid not, ma'am. I only have this." He took an ancient-looking wallet from his pocket and pulled out a tiny, golden key. Its handle was a thin metal strand twisted into an intricate pattern, and at the end sprouted three prongs, each carved into peculiar geometric shapes. A ribbon embroidered with numbers was tied to its end. "I was told this would be identification enough?"

A ringing silence followed his question. It stretched on a few seconds, then a few seconds more. At that point, Brie turned her eyes to the teller.

Janet had gone pale as a ghost.

Cameron frowned in concern. "Ma'am?"

The woman swallowed and, after a few tries, managed to say, "Let me get my manager. Please, make yourselves comfortable." The friends watched, baffled, as she sprinted away from her desk as fast as her clacking heels would allow.

*What the hell just happened?*

"Well," Sherry began slowly, "we've clearly triggered some kind of psychotic break in the woman, but if you ask me, the real shame is the waiting room. Here, at the tail end of one of the most fashionable decades in our nation's history, it seems I am doomed to do everything as stylelessly as possible. You pull out the key to a turn-of-the-century security box… and I am dressed for a hootenanny." Without another word, she slumped into the nearest chair to sulk.

Brie turned to Cameron, still thrown by this latest development. "Do you really think this will work?"

"I certainly hope so," he answered, raking back his hair. "My backup plan isn't what you'd call rock solid."

*As opposed to betting it all on a mystery key you got when you were five.*
*Fabulous.*

"It'll be alright," she replied with false confidence. "I mean, we'll figure it out," she amended. "Even if it isn't alright, we always seem to figure it out."

Just then, there was a commotion on the other side of the room. Janet and a short, balding man were hurrying towards them in the most comical powerwalk she'd ever seen, trailed by three men in suits and two security guards.

The friends clustered instinctively together, eyeing the entourage.

*Okay, maybe we won't figure it out.*

The balding man outpaced the rest of them, practically running up to Cameron with one hand extended while the other mopped sweat from his brow. From the look on his face, he simply couldn't get there fast enough, practically bursting until he seized the angel's hand.

"You must be Mister James," he cried, shaking fiercely. "Welcome! Welcome to our San Francisco branch. I'm Sal Huckabee, the manager. Please, please let me apologize for making you and your colleagues wait, sir. If we'd had any idea you were coming in today, of course, we would have made arrangements." The entire introduction was said in a rush of breath, and not for a single second did he stop shaking Cameron's hand. It quickly went past strange to comical, then back to strange again, as the handsome angel's cheeks colored with the hint of a blush.

"Not at all, Mr. Huckabee," Cameron said quickly, trying to put the man at ease. "We didn't have the opportunity to announce ourselves, or we would have let you know in advance." He pulled his hand away, discreetly wiping it on his jeans.

"Well, I can't tell you what an honor it is for all of us here. Frankly, none of us ever thought we would have the pleasure to—" The bank manager cut himself off suddenly as he laid eyes on the rest of the friends. "But where are my manners?" he gasped. "Please, come into my office. You can wait there while we get your papers in order. Is there anything we can get for you, gentlemen? Or you, ladies?"

Sherry perked up and answered without missing a beat. "Do you have a champagne bar?"

Twenty minutes later, the friends were sipping chilled champagne on leather sofas in a well-appointed private office. It was a welcome change of scenery, but the scene itself was somewhat familiar. Once again, everyone was looking at Cameron as if he was on a witness stand.

"Anything you want to tell us, buddy?" Mike asked with an amused smile.

It was a source of endless entertainment, how the powerful immortal reverted to a seven-year-old boy the second he was cornered, how the celestial composure vanished into blushing cheeks and stammered answers, how the prince of Elysium was suddenly unable to meet anyone's eyes.

Sure enough, Cameron shook his head faintly, glancing the other way. "Like what?"

*Forget the Seven. I'm going to kill him myself.*

"Like, why is he calling you Mister James?" Brie blurted, exasperated. "Why did he spend nine years shaking your hand? And why is he treating you like some visiting prince?" She realized the irony of her phrasing immediately. "I mean, sure, technically you are, but I can't imagine he's allowed to know that. Cameron, what's going on?"

In an unfortunate bit of timing, the door swung open, and Mr. Huckabee blustered through, carrying a stack of papers. "Here we are, Mr. James, for your signature. I apologize for the wait," he said for the hundredth time. "It's just so unusual! Such an honor. In fact, I've informed our CEO that you're here, and he's scheduling a flight out from Chicago to meet with you if you don't have any objection?"

*Excuse me?!*

"No, no objection," Cameron answered mildly.

"Our verifier should be here in a moment to examine your key. Now, obviously, with a deposit box this old, possession of the key itself is typically proof of ownership, as was stated in the terms of the original contract, which you can see here." He pulled a yellowed paper from the pile, placing it next to a modern copy of the same document. "As you can see, your box has been visited only two other times. Once, by your ancestors, when the bank was first established, and the account was opened, and once more, in 1919, by this individual." He placed a black and white photograph on top of the contracts. Cameron's face stilled as he picked it up.

Brie looked over his shoulder, and her breath caught. Next to a distinguished-looking gentleman wearing a tophat stood Ethan, grinning at them mischievously from the past. While he was nowhere near as formal as his companion, there was something inherently regal about him. Maybe it was the way he was standing, or the way he was smiling, or the fact that if he was Cameron's brother, he must also technically be a prince. She leaned closer for a better look. He was holding up two fingers to give the other man in the photo bunny ears.

"This must have been one of your ancestors," Huckabee mused, straining for a better look himself. "Keys like yours are typically passed from father to son, so I'm guessing your great, great, great grandfather may have opened the original account. Yours, in particular, is special because his original investment helped to make our bank a reality. Our founder always spoke with gratitude about a generous stranger who helped him get this place on its feet. I never dreamed I'd be meeting one of his descendants!" He let out another muted squeal, followed by a mop at his forehead with a handkerchief. There was a knock at the door. "Oh! That must be our verifier."

An old man whose name tag identified him as "Vassily" was escorted inside holding a briefcase. He nodded politely as he pulled out some documents and two stoppered glass vials. When he spoke, it was in a shaky voice. "Mister James, it is the policy of this bank to verify your safety deposit box ownership, not with traditional forms of verification, as your account predates such measures. As such, we must ask you a series of security questions. Do you want the rest of your party escorted outside?"

Cameron flashed a quick look at Brie before shaking his head.

The old man cleared his throat. "Question one: What is the real reason you were kicked out of the Elysian choir?"

Mike and Sherry immediately choked on their champagne.

*Seriously?*

The lovely angel stilled before his cheeks darkened to the color of burnt strawberries. He muttered under his breath, "Of course." He turned to the others. "I want to be very clear. If any of you tell Tavi or Ephriam about this, I will find a way to leave you in 1969 until your hair's gone grey. Do you all understand?"

The humans did their absolute best to maintain a straight face as they nodded.

Cameron turned back to the validator with a sigh. "I hit such a high note in a performance of *The Magic Flute* that it cracked Dad's favorite stained glass window."

Mike tried to swallow a laugh but ended up spitting out a small quantity of champagne.

He received a celestial glare. "And I suppose at the age of five, you were doing far more impressive things than performing one of Mozart's most stunning arias," Cameron scowled.

Mike held up his hands in surrender, using all the willpower he had not to grin.

The validator cleared his throat. "Question two: What is a griffin's favorite snack?"

Again, the friends leaned forward, breathless for an answer.

Cameron closed his eyes for a fraction of a second before lifting them like a martyr to the sky. "It's me."

The validator frowned. "I'm sorry, that's not—"

"It's a Little Lele sandwich," Cameron answered through clenched teeth.

Brie clapped a hand over her mouth.

*I take it back. Coming to the bank was a GREAT idea.*

The old man nodded. "Final question. Finish this poem: *Sleep now, little star. The sky will wait for you.*"

There had been a degree of levity in everything that had come before, but it vanished now. No sooner had the man started speaking than Cameron's body locked down — every muscle going perfectly still, as a host of tears sprang to his eyes. He drew in a silent breath, and without seeming to realize it, he reached for Brie's hand. She took it immediately, holding tight.

He answered in a quiet voice, like he was pulling the words from some inner place.

*"Sleep now, little star. The sky will wait for you. The moon will guide your dreams. The sun will guide you through. Sleep now, my brother. The night is safe and still. And if the world should call our names, we'll bend it to our will."*

It was utterly silent when he finished, every trace of mockery and amusement vanishing from the room.

The verifier nodded solemnly, lowering his sheet of paper. "The answers are all correct. May I see the key, please?" Cameron handed it over without a word, and the old man examined it carefully, writing down the numbers on the ribbon and rubbing the handle lightly across his black stone. After a moment, he unstoppered one of the bottles and released a drop of a chemical onto the stone. A few minutes later, he repeated the process with the other bottle. Then he turned with a serious expression. "The key is authentic, the possessor is verified. This is the legal owner of the box."

Mr. Huckabee let out a breath he must have been holding for a long time indeed, judging by the color of his cheeks. Without seeming to think about it, he reached again to shake Cameron's hand. "Mister James, I cannot begin to tell you what a thrill this is for me. Would you like to be escorted to your box now?" The lovely angel merely nodded, still trying to recover himself. "And would you like your friends to accompany you or remain here?" Cameron looked at Brie, and Mr. Huckabee understood. "Of course, the young lady may join you. Right this way, right this way!"

With a nod to Mike and Sherry, they were ushered through the bank's halls to an enormous, heavily guarded vault in the back.

It probably should have made more of an impact — the elaborate security precautions and towering archways — but none of it even registered. Brie was still spinning from that soft-spoken poem, still reeling at the look on her angel's face.

When they reached the vault, Mr. Huckabee retrieved a large steel box that looked older than the city itself before leaving them alone with a deferential bow.

The dimly lit room smelled faintly of dust and metal. Unable to help herself, Brie reached out to trace the sleek contours of the key Cameron held. His expression was unreadable — eyes focused, jaw tight. They stood before the safety deposit box like it was a sacred artifact, the thing that might save them.

The last tangible connection to Ethan.

"You ready?" she asked softly.

He nodded silently, but no part of him was in agreement. His eyes had darkened to storm clouds, and he moved reluctantly when he reached out his hand to insert the key. With a quiet click, the lock turned. The lid creaked open, and they both leaned silently forward.

A dazzling light spilled across their faces.

*Is that…?*

Her eyes widened in astonishment, reflecting the glow. The top layer of the box was a stack of gold bars, polished and gleaming, each one embossed with the Royal Mint seal.

Cameron lifted one tentatively, eyebrows arching in surprise. "Trust Ethan to go big," he muttered with a half-laugh.

Beneath the gold bars lay an old leather pouch. When he untied it, a cascade of rare, uncut gemstones spilled into his palm — sapphires, emeralds, diamonds, and a ruby the size of a tangerine. Each one sparkled with otherworldly brilliance, the kind of wealth that could buy countries and change countless lives. But it wasn't the gems that caught his attention.

At the bottom of the box was a folded piece of paper, yellowed with age. Cameron picked it up, his hands suddenly shaking. Brie stepped closer, watching as he carefully unfolded it. His eyes flickered across the page, and his breath hitched when he reached the last line.

"What does it say?" she asked gently.

Cameron handed it to her, answering in a voice thick with emotion. "He says he knew I'd need this one day. And he's right. He always knew me better than I knew myself."

Her lips parted uncertainly, but she could think of nothing to say. Instead, she turned back to the box, frowning faintly as she noticed a piece of cloth covering the bottom. Reaching in, she carefully unfolded it, uncovering two small gemstones — one a deep sapphire and the other a brilliant emerald — each glowing with an ethereal light.

He gasped. "These…" His voice cracked. "They're from the Gates of Elysium. Only the highest among the angels are granted these stones. They were supposed to be for Ethan's coronation."

Her eyes widened. "Ethan was supposed to succeed your father?"

Cameron nodded. "He was the eldest. My father always said it would heal many old wounds once he ascended to rule."

She considered this a moment, then looked at the gleaming stones. "But he left them for you."

Cameron nodded, his fingers brushing their smooth surfaces, blinking back the tears gathering in his eyes. "Yeah," he said softly. "He did."

They stood in silence, one brother's hand clasping treasures the other had left behind. It wasn't just the incredible worth of the gemstones or even the symbolism of the coronation jewels — this was Ethan's love, Ethan's faith, wrapped in the most priceless of gifts.

After what seemed like a long time, Cameron finally spoke. "We shouldn't keep the others waiting." He started to fold up the cloth and place the treasures back in the box when a final, ancient paper caught his eye.

He lifted it with a frown. "Now, what do you suppose this is?"

◆     ◆     ◆

*"Give him some space."*

*"I think he's coming around."*

*"Good thing he missed the flower pots."*

Brie and Cameron stood with their hands on their knees, leaning over the crumpled body of the bank manager. He'd been waiting to receive them when they stepped out of the vault, but no sooner did he catch a glimpse of the contents of the security box than he fainted dead away. The verifier appeared from nowhere, taking a compulsive step forward to help before deciding it was impossible to lift him. A receptionist had gone for smelling salts. They could still hear the sound of her high heels clattering frantically across the tile.

There was a feeble stirring before the man's eyes fluttered open. They took a second to focus before flying immediately to Cameron's face.

"Oh," he gasped, pushing onto his elbows. His glasses had fallen crookedly to the side of his face. "I'm so sorry, Mr. James. What must you think of me? It's just when I saw—"

"What did you see?" Brie interrupted, kneeling beside him. He was sitting up now, fanning weakly at the sides of his face. "Because there was a document in that box that I'm almost positive is—"

"The Magna Carta!" the poor manager exclaimed, swooning again at the thought. "You have a copy of the damn Magna Carta in your security box!" His head shook quickly back and forth, bathed in an ecstatic flop-sweat. "Pardon my French, but this is beyond anything we could have imagined. Do you have any idea what that document must be worth? And that's to say nothing of the gemstones! What *are* you doing, Vassily?"

The verifier looked up from the parchment with a start, one finger extended in the air, and a watchmaker's magnifying glass held up to his eye. His cheeks flushed with guilt, but he seemed unable to lower the glass. "Excuse me. It's just… it's absolutely remarkable."

"Don't touch it!" cried Huckabee, scrambling to his feet in a flurry of limbs and replacing the velvet cloth with painful care. Not until it was meticulously hidden from sight did he turn back to Brie and Cameron. "Sir, I fear we don't have the authenticators required to value such treasures in-house. I apologize for the delay, but it will take some time to arrange things. Is this acceptable to you?"

"Of course," Cameron answered quickly, looking predictably guilty to have caused the inconvenience. The box and all its priceless treasures hung loose in his hands. "I'm sorry again for surprising you with my visit. I can see now, it would have been better to have called—"

"Mister James," the man interrupted swiftly, "I am honored beyond words to assist you with your affairs. Where are you staying in the city?"

The couple looked at each other.

"Actually, we haven't…" Cameron trailed off uncertainly, "This whole trip was last minute, and we had a bit of a disaster getting here. We don't have anywhere lined up yet."

Huckabee's face broke into a relieved smile. This was a problem he could solve. "Then please allow me to make arrangements."

The angel smiled gratefully. "Thank you, sir. I appreciate it." His eyes flicked to the verifier. "Is there any way we could exchange some of the gold before we leave? I'm afraid we might need to purchase a few things to get back to our usual selves."

*A few hundred things, if Sherry has anything to do with it.*

"Of… of course," Huckabee answered, reaching into his pocket and pulling out a pair of white gloves with which to touch the gold bars. Even then, he hesitated, like the treasure was too great for mortal hands. "How many would you like to cash out?"

"I'm not really sure," Cameron answered hesitantly. "Four?"

The bank manager paused before continuing. "Very good, sir. And how would you like that?"

The couple exchanged a glance before Brie merely shrugged. "Ones and fives?"

# CHAPTER SIX

# The Fairmont

Half an hour later, armed with a suitcase full of cash and a belly full of champagne, Brie and Cameron, along with Mike and Sherry, met up with Clive and the Elysians at the outdoor tables of the cafe across the street. The trio raised their espresso cups in greeting as they approached, and Clive called out, "How did it go?"

*Mixed bag.*

"Far, far better than expected," Sherry answered cheerfully, less concerned with sentimentality than she was thrilled by their sudden change in fortune. "Mostly thanks to me."

Mike snorted under his breath, draping an arm around her shoulders. "Really saved the day, huh, babe?"

"I brought the charisma," she agreed with a warm grin.

"Is that right?" Clive exclaimed with a broad smile. "I'm glad to hear it! So you're all set, then? I can tell Myrtle that we don't need to fret and worry about you here in the city all by your lonesome?"

At that moment, a limousine glided around the corner, slicing through the slow-moving traffic before rolling to a stop at the curb. The driver got out and stood at attention, eyes looking straight ahead, wearing a neat navy uniform and a pair of starched ivory gloves.

Clive blinked quickly like he might be having a dream.

"We'll be fine," Cameron said with a smile, reaching into the brief-case the verifier had placed in his hands before leaving. "And Clive, there's something I want to give you and Myrtle for your troubles." A sudden glow fell over their faces as he pulled out a gold bar. "You fed us, clothed us, and helped us when we needed it most. We will never forget your kindness, truly."

Clive's jaw fell open as Cameron placed it in his hands. "This… this is too much!" he sputtered. "I can't possibly—"

"I insist," Cameron interrupted.

"Well, if you aren't the…" Clive swallowed, trying to control his emo-tions. "If you aren't the strangest, kindest folks I ever did meet. *Thank* you. Thank you very much!" He lifted the bar into the air, squinting against the sun. "Hot damn! I can't wait to see Myrtle's face when I tell her y'all were secret millionaires this whole time!" He let out a huge guffaw of laughter, startling the pedestrians walking next to him before heading back to his truck. "And you know what?" he called over his shoulder. "I won't forget about that company the nice red-headed feller told me about earlier. What was it again? Some kind of fruit — peach?"

"Apple!" Mike called back. "Don't forget, it's an apple!"

"I'll remember!" Clive gave him a thumbs up. "Hot damn!" With a jolly wave, he turned and headed down the pavement, vanishing into the crowd.

The friends stared after him for a few seconds in silence.

"Are you sure that's alright?" Brie asked, staring at the spot where he'd disappeared. "It isn't going to mess with the timeline to turn the Emersons into bajillionaires?"

Ephriam let out a frustrated humph. "I've already told you. You can only change the future from the future point of present, not that which you perceive to be—"

"Ephriam?" She cut him off. "Please stop."

Cameron stepped neatly in between them, gesturing toward the limousine. "Shall we?"

Brie's heart gave a little flutter. This was a wonderful side of her angel.

*The suave, debonair one.*

*The princely one, with the old-school gentlemanly manners.*

*The one I'd like to—*

"You never told us," Sherry interrupted her delicious train of thought. "Why did the bank manager keep calling you Mr. James?"

Brie's debonair gentleman flushed about thirty shades of crimson as every eye turned, once again, to him. He sighed and looked at his feet. "I had an obsession with Jesse James for a while when I was little."

"*For a while?*" Ephriam snorted.

"Please don't—" Cameron began with a pleading look.

"I pretended to be your pony for a year. You kept shooting the Elysian guards with finger guns, and you cried whenever they didn't pretend to die. *Tavianne bought you a hat.*" Ephriam shoved his way past his prince and into the limousine, cramming his enormous frame through the elegant doors while keeping up a steady recitation of incriminating memories. "You nearly killed Cong with your lasso, and Raphael had to spend two days reading up on giant tortoise medicine. You turned the Great Hall into something called the 'I Guess It's Fine Corral.'"

Cameron looked back to Brie. In a far more demure voice, he asked again. "Shall we?"

With a final, pitying glance, she sighed and climbed into the limo.

*So close. So close to being cool.*

*And yet so very, very far away.*

As the limousine driver went to have a quiet chat with the valet, Brie and Cameron stood outside the grand entrance of the Fairmont Hotel, its towering facade gleaming in the late afternoon sun. The rest of the friends were gathered behind them, still a little worse for wear from their unexpected time-hopping but starting to feel like they'd stumbled upon a change of fortune. Whatever damage they were carrying with them, the sight of the iconic hotel was enough to steal their breath.

"Wow," Brie murmured as she took in the grandeur. It looked like more of a palace than a hotel, complete with a gilded entryway topped with a hundred fluttering flags.

Sherry stepped forward and touched her arm. "I mean, *wow*. Look at those arches, that detailing! This place is a fashion show in marble."

"Are you sure this is alright?" Mike asked, glancing at the elaborate rooftop with a touch of nerves. "I mean, I've stayed in nice places before, but this looks like one of those spots they reserve for movie stars and angels."

Brie glanced reflexively at her boyfriend.

*We've come to the right place, then.*

Cameron gave him a reassuring smile. "Mr. Huckabee said the bank's owner arranged for this himself. It's definitely alright."

Mike returned his gaze coolly. "Well, you might need to remind me from time to time. Seeing as how I'm prone to *forgetting things*."

The angel's lips parted with a fresh apology, but Sherry was already flouncing between them, threading her arm through Mike's. "No need to say it twice, Cam. You're *preaching to the choir*."

Cameron fell terribly silent as the group walked inside.

Brie bit her lip to keep from grinning. Her expression shifted abruptly to awe once they passed through the entryway.

*Holy mother of Zeus.*

If the building had stunned Brie from the outside, it was nothing compared to what it looked like within. Chandeliers sparkled overhead, casting a soft light over the plush carpets and golden accents, while the sound of a tinkling fountain mixed with the strains of Chopin coming from a piano in the lobby. The noise of the city was immediately muted. She felt like she'd stepped into another world — one where time didn't matter, and wealth wasn't merely implied; it was draped across every surface.

"Well, this is certainly an improvement," she said under her breath, lifting her eyes to an oversized Monet hanging on the wall. "Not that I didn't enjoy our endless camping trip."

"Oh, come on," Mike teased. "You didn't like the cave? You know, the one where we found that family of bats?"

Sherry stared with wide eyes between them, feeling abruptly faint. "There were *bats* in that cave?"

A moment passed in silence before they started walking across the decadent lobby to the stately counter on the other side. A trio of men was conversing softly, but they stopped immediately at the friends' approach, glancing up with a uniform smile.

"Welcome to the Fairmont, sir," a concierge said formally, clearly unfazed by the group's disheveled state. "How may I assist you?"

Cameron gave a slight nod as if he checked into five-star hotels every day. "Um, I believe a Mr. Huckabee may have—"

"Ah, of course," the man interrupted, eyeing them with a flash of interest. "The special guests. I'll just need a moment."

As he picked up his phone and began a hushed conversation, Sherry sidled up to Brie, eyes dancing with excitement. "Just look at those velvet couches and the freaking stairs! The *stairs*, Brie. It's like something out of an old Hollywood film. Does the camera on your phone still work? I could drape myself over that banister and—"

"No draping," Brie said quickly, having been kidnapped into Sherry's impromptu photo shoots before. "We're here to rest, you loon, to *recuperate*. Not to go swooning on the veranda."

Sherry nodded distractedly, her eyes lit with a manic glow. "… drape myself all over that veranda—"

"Excuse me, sir?" The concierge's voice broke through the conversation as he set the phone down and turned to Cameron. "Here is your key. You're in the suites on the top floor — our finest. You'll have a panoramic view of the city and access to our private lounge."

Cameron nodded gratefully, reaching for Brie's hand. "Perfect," he said smoothly, "thank you very much."

A bellhop appeared, smartly dressed and eager to help. "Shall I take your bags?"

The friends froze in unison, glancing at their tattered backpacks — the ones that had survived a landslide, a cougar attack, and, of course, some pesky time travel.

"No thanks," Mike answered with a tight smile. "I think we've got it."

As they followed the bellhop to the grand elevators, Tavi looked suspiciously around the lobby, eyes darting from thing to thing, as her hand twitched involuntarily toward her blade. "This place feels… too soft."

"There's room service, Tavi," Brie coaxed, having already resolved to live at the hotel permanently, no matter the celestial cost. "You can order food from a menu, and they'll bring it right to the bedroom door. The only time you'll need to leave the bed is to *eat*," she stressed.

There was a contemplative silence.

"This is acceptable." Tavi stopped reaching for her dagger.

The group fell quiet inside the elevator, watching the rhythmic ding of the lights as they climbed floor after floor. When the doors finally opened, the bellhop shepherded them to an ornate hallway with gilded doors and thick carpeting. Silver-framed mirrors hung every ten feet or so on the walls, making the entire place feel like a Vienesse castle.

"This is it," the man announced, guiding them to a set of double doors at the end. He opened them with a flourish, revealing a suite so magnificent that even Sherry was momentarily speechless.

The space was enormous, with high ceilings and large windows offering a stunning view of San Francisco. The Golden Gate Bridge gleamed in the distance while the city itself stretched out beneath them like a sea of lights in a blanket of fog. A living room with plush velvet couches and a fireplace lay in the center of the area, while several doors branched off to the sides, leading to a series of luxurious bedrooms.

It was a far cry from the cave.

"Oh my God," Sherry breathed. "I could live here."

Mike nudged her. "Not forever. We still have a quest, remember?"

"Right," she said dismissively, her gaze locked on the extravagant crystal chandelier. "I remember that used to be really important, before we moved into this hotel."

The bellhop was still standing in the corner, unnoticed by the others, until Cameron reached suddenly into his pocket, remembering he was supposed to give the man a tip. The concept was there in theory, but the details eluded him. Unsure how much was customary, he ended up placing such a large stack of bills in the man's hand it could only register as a mistake.

The bellhop froze, waiting for him to correct it before slipping the money into his pocket with an incredulous smile. "Thank you, sir," he stammered in a daze. "Enjoy your stay at the Fairmont. And if there's anything you need, anything at all, please let me know." He pointed to his nametag. *Victor*. "Any time, day or night, just ask for me."

"Actually, Victor," Sherry began conspiratorially, "there is something." He nodded eagerly as she steered him toward the window. "Are you familiar with the film *Pretty Woman*?"

The young man frowned, rifling through his brain and coming up blank. "I'm sorry, miss, I don't believe I am."

"That was the nineties, babe," Mike said with a grin, realizing where this was going.

"Oh! Right, of course. Victor, are you familiar with the film *My Fair Lady*?"

The bellhop's face cleared in understanding. "The one with Audrey Hepburn? Oh, you bet, miss. My sister loves all her films. I must have taken her to see that one at least four times!"

"Excellent," Sherry replied, clapping her hands together, "so you understand the concept of a makeover montage. Here's what I have in mind…"

With that, she led the unsuspecting young man away, chattering like a Machiavellian overlord, while Mike trailed behind, chuckling under his breath.

The others stared after them for a moment before Tavi swayed abruptly and steadied herself on the door frame. Ephriam was beside her in a heartbeat, standing close in case she fell.

"She needs to rest," he said bluntly. "I also tire of these human interactions. I must be alone, deep in meditation with naught but my thoughts for company."

*That sounds like a ghastly place.*

Brie nodded, already used to his archaic way of speaking. "Go get settled in then. Let's meet back up for dinner later tonight. I think we could all use a few hours to rest and clean ourselves up."

The Elysian gave her a curt nod before helping Tavi down a hallway.

Things began to settle after he left. Brie's eyes drifted from the crown molding to the walk-in closet to the ivory figurines mounted by the door. An unexpected laugh bubbled out of her, catching a moment in her throat before spilling into the open. "I can't believe it." She shook her head with a dizzy grin. "I can't believe we just waltzed into the Fairmont Hotel looking like we fought a mountain lion and got away with it."

"That's exactly what we did. And stranger things have happened," Cameron replied, catching her lightly by the waist and pulling her close. They stared silently out the window, fitted against each other, the curve of his cheek resting lightly against her hair. A pair of gulls flew past, twining occasionally as they glided towards the open sky. "So, what do you think?"

Brie stared a moment longer, dazzled by the misty lights of the city, before twisting around to stare into his eyes. "I'm really happy that you're here."

It wasn't what he was expecting, and he didn't immediately know how to reply. He merely stood there with a little smile as she lifted to the tips of her toes and pressed their lips together. There had been precious few moments to indulge in such things since they'd left Virginia; considering everything they'd been through along the way, it had seemed inappropriate to try. But there, in the decadent privacy of their lofty suite, there wasn't anything stopping them.

With a sudden burst of speed, he lifted her off the ground and clasped their faces together, forcing open her lips as his fingers knotted in her hair. She gasped in surprise, then closed her eyes as the kiss deepened, stealing her breath and muddying her senses, leaving her spinning as he abandoned their usual caution and drew her even closer, slipping a hand underneath her shirt.

Her pulse spiked. Her blood was racing. Everywhere he touched, her skin was aflame.

There was a bed somewhere behind them. A four-poster extravagance she had clocked on the way in. He seemed to remember at the same time and started backing towards it, tripping over the thick carpet as they tangled together — heated, wanting, and impossible to contain.

*Is this actually happening?*

The question stunned and thrilled her at the same time. They had been dancing around this moment for too long, with too much pressure building up inside.

His tongue slipped into her mouth. Her legs hitched around his waist.

He hesitated. "Brie—"

The door burst open, and Sherry flew inside, the poor bellhop still trailing behind her as she rattled off a list of things. The couple detached unnoticed, breathless and panting. Sherry made a bee-line for the bathroom and took a single look at the tub before deciding it was better than the one in her own room.

"Dibs on the tub with the view!" she called, dismissing Victor with a fluttering wave of her hand. He vanished as Mike took his place, a pair of towels draped over his arm.

"I already called it," he teased, "you'll have to share."

Her voice echoed through the room. "Not my strong suit, but for you, darling…"

Brie and Cameron stared in silence as they disappeared into the bathroom, shutting the door behind them with a cheerful, "Don't wait up!" Ephriam had laid claim to the living room, and Tavi was undressing loudly next door, removing every piece of armor and dropping it onto the tile with a resounding *clunk*.

Brie and Cameron stood in the lingering energy of their interrupted moment, the buzz of adrenaline still thrumming between them. She let out a soft, breathy laugh, shaking her head. "Well, that was something. I… I don't think this is going to happen right now," She offered a bashful smile, still feeling the fading chills where his fingers had traced over her skin.

Cameron sighed, raking a hand through his hair as his shoulders slumped. "I swear, there isn't a single moment where—" He stopped mid-sentence when he looked at her, his frustration melting away in an instant.

Brie was barely holding back a yawn, her exhaustion catching up with her now that the tension had been broken. Her eyelids drooped. Her body leaned into his without even realizing it.

Cameron exhaled, the last of his irritation dissolving as he tightened his arms around her. "You're exhausted," he pressed a kiss to her temple. "And I'm an idiot for trying to keep you upright when you're about to collapse."

She hummed sleepily against his chest. "You're not an idiot."

"Debatable." He smoothed a hand down her back, his voice warm with amusement. "How about this — we order room service, get massages, and then actually sleep in a bed for once instead of on a cave floor. Sound like a plan?"

Brie pulled back just enough to look at him, her lips curving into a lazy smile. "I like the way you think, angel."

With one last lingering kiss, he pulled away and reached for the hotel phone, already scanning the menu for something decadent. Brie turned toward the window, her smile fading into something softer, something almost wistful, as she gazed out at the city stretching before them.

San Francisco glowed beneath the mist, the streets weaving like rivers of golden light. Somewhere out there, danger was still lurking, the mysteries of the Time Seas waiting to unravel before them. But for now — for just a moment — they were here. Together. Safe.

And for Brie, that was enough.

Later, they lay together in bed, the city's golden glow casting soft, shifting patterns on the ceiling. The world outside was vast and unknowable, full of unseen dangers and untold stories waiting to unfold. But here, in the hush of their suite, time had finally stilled.

Brie nestled against Cameron's chest, his warmth surrounding her, his steady heartbeat beneath her ear grounding her in a way nothing else could. His fingers traced slow, absentminded circles along her spine, the touch feather-light, soothing.

She exhaled softly, her voice barely more than a breath. "Sometimes it doesn't seem real," she whispered, "when I'm with you. Sometimes it feels like something I've imagined, like the spell might break, and I'll wake up in my bed."

He gazed down at her, brushing a curl away from her face.

"Do you want to wake up?" he breathed.

She stared a moment, then shook her head — bringing them together once more. No, she didn't ever want to wake up.

Give her the fantasy. Give her the dream.

# CHAPTER SEVEN

## Summer in the City

The next morning, Brie awoke to the loveliest of sights: her half-dressed angel sleeping with his arms around her, snoring softly onto the pillow, lips curved into a slight smile. Sunlight streamed through the windows, lighting them both in the glorious rays of the San Francisco dawn.

She traced his lips with her fingertip and felt something within her tug in longing. She moved closer, arching to press against him, lifted her chin, and tenderly, delicately, bit his bottom lip. His eyes flew open in surprise. Then he tightened his grip, pulling her even closer and rolling so he was above her, weight on his forearms, pinning her down and smoothing her hair from her face as he kissed her hungrily. He shifted his hips, and a quiet moan escaped her lips, muffled by their kiss.

*This is it. This is the moment.*

Her whole body thrummed in anticipation as he pulled back just enough to look at her the way all women want to be looked at.

Unable to contain herself, she thrust her hips up and to the side with surprising strength, reversing their positions in an instant. The sight of his perfect face haloed in chestnut curls on the pillow, his blue eyes staring up in surprise and delight, lit a fire somewhere deep in her belly. Deeper, even. She leaned forward, long curls curtaining around them as she kissed him. Her thighs gripped his hips, grinding their bodies velvet-soft against one another. His hands tightened around her waist. Her kiss swallowed the sound of his moan, but she felt its vibration shudder through her.

"Brie," he whispered.

"Shh." She kissed his neck. "We need to be quiet."

His body tightened beneath her. "Brie, I can't—"

"Yes, you can." Her voice was a jumbled murmur. Her tongue was too busy to properly form words. "I want you to."

But he paused, just for a second, with his hands on her shoulders. "No, Brie, I mean I—"

She stopped immediately, pulling back, still straddling him. Suddenly, she'd never felt more vulnerable or self-conscious in her life. She looked at him with huge eyes and tried to keep the tremor from her voice. "You don't… you don't want me to—?"

His eyes flew wide, and he sat up in an instant, pulling her closer and covering the rest of her question with a kiss. She tried to speak, and he kissed her harder. His tongue tangled with hers, pressing, testing, tasting, leaving her breathless with desire when he finally pulled away to answer her.

"Brianna Weldon, there is nothing under the sun I want so much as you."

A part of her melted. Another part of her locked her ankles behind his back and angled her hips so he wouldn't change his mind again.

"But," he continued, looking deep into her eyes. "I don't just want to…" He was momentarily distracted when she nibbled his lip. "Brie," he tried again, smiling. "Look at me. I want to give you everything you want — *all* of your desires. I just can't right now." He searched her face, willing her to understand. "I want to satisfy you in every way — not just this one. Is that… is that alright?"

She released her ankles with a defeated sigh and rested her head on his shoulder. "Are you sure?"

He held her tight. "I've never been so sure of anything in my life. But, you know," he went on, tipping up her head so they could lock eyes. "I can think of another way to pass the time. Something that might satiate you… for now."

His eyes twinkled, and she momentarily forgot how to breathe.

That's when a splash from the adjoining bathroom cut into their perfect moment.

This was followed by a peal of laughter layered over Mike's faint cursing.

"I can only hold my breath so long, darling," Sherry's giggles sounded from the bathroom.

A fist banged on the opposite wall. "Keep your primitive couplings to yourselves," Ephriam's voice thundered through the suite. "Some of us are meditating to ascend to a higher plane."

"Don't judge my methodology, you killjoy. I bet I'll get there faster!" Sherry shot back.

Brie glanced up at Cameron, who looked like someone had thrown a bucket of ice water on his soul. "She's your best friend," he muttered. "And murder is wrong."

Brie bit back a smile and kissed his neck. "I find it's helpful to keep repeating that."

Quieter this time, they came together again. He grabbed a fistful of her hair just at the nape of her neck. The motion of her hips became more rhythmic. Her body grew hot and flushed. Just as she was about to peel off her camisole, fate decided to step in again.

Somebody knocked at their door.

"For the love of God, Ephriam — *GO* to the higher plane. I can't name a soul that will miss you," Cameron shouted, burying his face in Brie's chest as she tried to stifle a laugh.

"Oh… sorry, never mind." Tavi's voice was faint but unmistakable.

"Wait! Hang on." Brie practically leapt off of him and raced to the mirror to fix her hair.

Cameron haphazardly tried to make the bed, an effort which consisted mainly of throwing pillows at the headboard. He perched on the corner of the bed, legs crossed, trying and failing to act nonchalant when Brie gave up on her tousled mane and threw open the door.

"Tavi!" she exclaimed far too brightly. "What can we do for you? Wait — are you okay?"

The Elysian was white as a sheet. "Can I come in?"

"Of course," Brie stepped aside.

Tavi came in without so much as casting a glance around and sat down heavily beside Cameron. His face grew grave with concern. "Tavi, what is it? What's happened?"

It took her a minute to collect herself. She sat at the edge of the mattress, her back unnaturally straight, fingers drumming soundlessly against her thigh. The warm golden glow of the morning light softened her expression, but Brie could see the tension in her jaw, the way her lips pressed together. It was an alien expression on her — the warrior who had faced down horrors without flinching, whose measured calm had been their rock since this nightmare began.

The Elysian warrior exhaled slowly, almost as if she had to remind herself how. She didn't look at them right away, instead studying the city beyond the window, her dark brows pinched together.

"I haven't been feeling like myself."

The words were quiet but unshakable. No embellishments. No dramatics. Just a simple truth laid bare, and yet, it might have been the most alarming thing she could have said.

Brie's stomach knotted. "What do you mean?"

Tavi finally turned her gaze on them, and Brie almost wished she hadn't. The golden flecks in her irises, so familiar and warm, were fainter now. Duller. As if something was dimming her from the inside out.

Cameron stepped forward instinctively, concern darkening his expression. "Tav, what's going on?"

She let out a quiet breath through her nose. "I don't know. That's the problem."

Brie lowered herself onto the edge of the bed, feeling the weight of what Tavi wasn't saying settle over her like a lead cloak. "Tavi, you're one of the strongest people I've ever met. If something's wrong, we need to take it seriously. Tell us everything."

Tavi flexed her hands against her knees. The leather of her gloves creaked softly. "It started after we left Virginia. At first, I thought it was just exhaustion or the weight of everything that happened. But it hasn't gone away." She hesitated as if reluctant to say the words aloud. "It's like I'm… not all the way here. Like there's something just beyond my reach, something pressing in at the edges." She exhaled sharply. "I feel wrong."

Brie exchanged a glance with Cameron, her pulse ticking up. They'd all been through hell, but this was different. This wasn't just grief, or trauma, or the weight of their journey. This was something else.

"You need to rest," Cameron said. "Maybe—"

Tavi shook her head. "Rest doesn't help. I wake up feeling the same. Or worse." She paused, as if weighing whether to say the next part. "And sometimes, I think I hear things. Just… whispers. Like something is calling me, but I don't understand the language."

A chill passed over Brie's skin. She swallowed hard, forcing her voice to stay steady. "Have you told Ephriam?"

"No," Tavi admitted. "I don't want him to worry. He has enough to deal with."

Brie reached out and took her hand, squeezing gently. "Tavi, this isn't just something we can ignore. If something's happening to you, we need to figure it out before it gets worse."

The warrior let out a slow breath, her grip tightening around Brie's in return. "I know. That's why I'm telling you."

Cameron knelt beside them, his expression serious. "We'll figure it out. Whatever this is, we won't let you face it alone."

Tavi looked between them, something like gratitude flickering in her dimming golden eyes. But beneath it, Brie could see something else.

A fear Tavi would never name.

And Brie had the sinking feeling that whatever was happening to her was only the beginning.

Then Tavi exhaled, forcing herself to let go of whatever was weighing her down. A faint, tired smile flickered across her lips. "Cameron's right. I should get some rest."

She pushed herself up and made her way to the bed, easing onto it with more effort than Brie liked. Within moments, she had curled onto her side, her back to them.

Brie and Cameron lingered, watching her for a beat longer, both lost in a sense of foreboding. Cameron's gaze met Brie's, the concern in his eyes mirroring her own.

Brie forced herself to shake off the heaviness. She turned toward the door, then glanced back at Cameron with a small, weary smile. "Come on, angel. Let's get some coffee."

Brie inhaled deeply, taking in the strange combination of patchouli, ganja, and salt air permeating the streets of Haight-Ashbury. Their concern for Tavi was great, but they couldn't have asked for a better distraction than the city. Every corner of San Francisco seemed to offer something unique — from the sleek lines of the financial district, to the sugar and brine of the pier, to the constant churning party of the Castro.

Her guardian angel walked beside her, eyes wide as saucers, holding her hand and soaking in the ambiance of this technicolor world. They could have walked for days and not seen everything. The swirling patterns of psychedelic murals on the walls, the strumming of guitars from every porch, and the general buzz of the city all thrummed around them — coaxing them further and further from their own reality to a place where things were lighter and more manageable, where they could be a little more free.

"Well, I feel wildly out of place." She laced their fingers together as a man walked past in a top hat and a cape, a tiny grey kitten perched on his shoulder.

Cameron merely smiled, giving her a little squeeze. "Business as usual."

A group of young hippies ambled past them, singing. All but one were sporting bare feet. One glanced over her shoulder as they walked past, offering Brie a flower with a serene smile. She accepted it awkwardly and tucked it into her hair, lifting the tips of her fingers to the petals.

"Scratch that," she whispered, "I'm definitely blending in, fully embracing the aesthetic."

He chuckled to himself, giving the blossom a secret sniff. "Totally inconspicuous. I shall try to blend in as well."

*Good luck!*

It didn't matter where they went or when — her boyfriend stood out like a sore thumb. He might as well have been glowing for how well he blended into the human experience. At least three people on the boisterous street were wearing some version of a scuba suit, yet it was her Elysian prince who was drawing eyes.

"Loosen up on the grammar a bit," she suggested, resting her head in the hollow of his shoulder. "I'm not sure anyone around here says 'shall.' Try to pepper in some slang."

Cameron frowned thoughtfully and nodded, reading the graffiti on the wall behind her. "Whatever you say, daddy-o."

*I've made a horrible mistake.*

They passed a group of musicians sitting on the steps of a coffee shop, strumming their guitars and nodding to the rhythm of the city. One of them, a curly-haired kid, grinned and raised a peace sign as they walked by.

"Hey man, you new to town?" he asked, clearly in no hurry to get an answer. "Far out!"

"Indeed, my good man," Cameron answered warmly, nodding at the others. "Utterly far out." He let the words hang impressively, casting a secret look at his girlfriend as they continued wandering up the street. "How am I doing? Convincing?"

"You sound like a time traveler trying to impress a hippie," she teased, knotting her fingers in the side of his coat. "But don't worry. I'm convinced."

Their laughter rang above the city as they strolled the lazy blocks — delighting in every new interaction as they lost themselves in the magic of the day. The music swelled and receded like a familiar tide, carrying them along the pavement. They wandered aimlessly, eventually coming to a stop beneath a neon sign flickering above a small music shop.

*The Sound Well.*

"Let's check it out," Cameron suggested, already heading toward the door.

Inside, it smelled of incense and aged vinyl. Rows of records lined the walls, and in the corner, a shaggy-haired man in a knitted poncho sat tuning an acoustic guitar. He gave them a glance, but even when his eyes landed on their shabby, ill-fitting clothes, he didn't seem to care. This was Haight-Ashbury, after all; everyone looked like they could be someone, and no one looked like they wanted to be found.

As they browsed the eclectic collection of musical instruments, miniature Buddha statues, and assorted drug paraphernalia, Cameron leaned over to Brie and whispered, "I feel like I'm about to join a magic circus or be inducted into a commune."

"May I interest you in some tarot cards and free love?" she whispered back with a smile, nudging him playfully and fanning out a deck of colorfully illustrated occult symbols. "Maybe we'll catch a glimpse of the future. I could check my voicemails."

He snorted with laughter but took the cards from her hands and placed them deliberately back on a shelf, having slightly more experience with the celestial repercussions of such things.

They continued wandering through the shop, trailing their fingers over the classic vinyl, until she noticed a cluster of gig posters near the register. They were hand-written and demanded attention, drawing her closer as the brightest of them caught her eye. It was for that very evening, advertising a performance at an exclusive dinner club. Free drinks and good music.

The headliner was someone named *Little Stevie Wonder*.

She gasped, tugging at Cameron's sleeve. "Do you see that?"

He raised his eyebrows. "Are they referencing a child?"

"Hang on a second." She turned to him slowly, assessing that enchanting face in a whole new light. "You've never heard of Stevie Wonder? Cameron, what exactly do you listen to in Elysium?"

He shrugged as they headed to the counter. "The heavenly choir, mostly," he replied.

The cashier perked up immediately, flicking the top of the poster. "You dig Stevie?"

"All my life," she replied enthusiastically before checking herself. "I mean, ever since I heard about him. He's playing tonight?"

The guy grinned, thick braids framing the sides of his face. "Private gig at one of the fanciest clubs in town. Exclusive crowd."

Most days, both would have been prohibitive statements. But between their moon field trip and the time travel, her perspective had somewhat changed.

She turned to Cameron, hoping against hope. "Do you think we could actually see him perform?"

He looked at her in amusement. "What's so special about this child?"

"He's Stevie Freaking Wonder," she cried, throwing up her hands. "He's a blind musical genius who plays piano like he was touched by God. *Superstition? Isn't She Lovely? Signed, Sealed, Delivered?*" She ticked them off her fingers. "He's a superstar. Watching him now would be like seeing a comet right before it ignites."

Her angel smiled to himself, eyes catching the sun from outside. "Sounds like one of Pahalia's projects."

"What's Pahalia?" she asked.

"He's the Angel of Virtuosity. Every so often, he pops up to Earth when he finds what he calls a 'worthy vessel.' Your Wonder Child sounds like he might be one such soul." He paused, casting a look at the cashier. "And he's playing tonight," he repeated casually. "Do you happen to know a way we could gain entry to such a performance?"

The man blinked. "You mean get tickets?"

"I do," Cameron nodded.

"Nah, man — I'm not in the business. You'd need some serious dough to get into a place like that. And even if you had it, that thing's been sold out for months." He smiled in apology.

*Damn right, it has — because he's Stevie Freaking Wonder.*

"Surely something can be done," Cameron pressed, flashing that particular smile that left the people around him breathless. "A number you could call—"

"It's alright," Brie interjected, placing a hand on his chest. "It's sold out." She flashed a parting smile at the cashier. "We'll try again in another couple of decades."

# CHAPTER EIGHT

# Mister Wonder

After a leisurely lunch at the pier, at which Cameron declared clam chowder in a bread bowl to be one of the most brilliant and innovative inventions that humans had ever contrived, Brie decided she'd had enough and could use a bath. No sooner had they gotten back to the hotel than they were greeted by a squeal at a pitch usually reserved for canines. Their heads snapped up in alarm as Sherry dashed into the room, arms overflowing with what had to be a hundred shopping bags.

"Look what I *found*!" she exclaimed, dropping them dramatically onto the bed. "San Francisco has *everything*."

Mike appeared in the doorway behind her, clutching a banana daiquiri like it was the only thing keeping him alive. He was swaying slightly from the drink, undeniably exhausted, but a single look at Sherry and his face lit with a tired grin. "I carried all of these," he declared, equal parts proud and tipsy. "Up a thousand urban mountains and back again, I carried them."

Brie raised an eyebrow, no idea why she was surprised. "You went on a shopping spree in 1969?"

Cameron walked up behind her, smiling in spite of himself. "I wonder what this will do to the global markets," he mused.

It was softly spoken, but the response flew back at him as if he'd been shouting. Both Mike and Sherry turned to him with icy glares.

"If it bothers you too much, I suggest you *forget* it," Mike snapped.

Sherry struck a threatening pose behind him. "If you presume to think that I'm going to walk around this city in *flannel* for *one single minute longer*…?" She trailed off dangerously, leaving the others to imagine it for themselves. "I don't care what year it is — I'm a fashion emergency. The Dow Jones will simply have to adjust. And by the way, I didn't go shopping. *We* did." She tossed the briefcase full of the remaining cash at his head. "Thank you for your contribution."

Instead of defending himself, Cameron wisely retreated into the hallway. All things considered, it could have been worse. And it was best to weather those kinds of storms from behind several sets of locked doors.

Brie shot Sherry an exasperated look and was rewarded with a wink. "What?" Sherry said. "He wiped Mike's memory, Brie. If he produces another suitcase full of money, we'll call it even. Now, get over here this instant!" She waved her over with a euphoric smile. "Donation Box couture be damned. Prepare to be massively upgraded."

Brie couldn't help but laugh as she began pulling out various items: everything from casual cashmere to shimmering evening gowns, with fitted jeans, shirts, and sharp suits for the men. In addition to the ensembles themselves, there was a cache of coordinating accessories sure to help them blend into the most sophisticated of establishments with ease.

By now, she knew better than to ask how Sherry was certain it would all fit. Her best friend had a habit of sizing people up the moment she met them, both figuratively and literally. She was hardly ever wrong.

"I know we said the last time was the *last* time," Sherry began with a roguish grin, holding up a blood-red cocktail dress. "But are you up for a little dress-up?"

About thirty minutes later, the door swung open, and the Elysians stepped into the room. While the others had been delighting in the city, they'd taken the opportunity to catch up on some long-awaited rest. No sooner had they come through the door than they took a quick step back, staring in acute disorientation at the chaotic storm of fabrics and accessories.

Ephriam kept his distance, watching with a trace of alarm as Sherry attempted to clasp a deadly-looking choker around her neck. "I do not wish to overstep, but I'm fairly sure those are meant to kill you." He turned as the door opened again, and Cameron walked into the room. "I assume this is part of your plan?" he asked dryly. "Or are we just making things up as we go?"

The handsome angel regarded him cautiously, lingering at the door. "This wasn't exactly my idea," he replied, "but you may consider it phase two." Without another word, he picked up a freshly purchased suit jacket and tossed it into the Elysian's hands. "On that note, I've taken the liberty of making us plans for the evening. Could everyone get dressed in… the shiniest things Sherry purchased? I believe those will prove most appropriate." He eyed the sequined gown that Brie was holding up like she'd netted a large fish. "I think," he added with a frown.

"Why you…" Sherry narrowed her eyes and stalked toward the poor angel like he was something she'd decided to eat for dinner. A horrible silence fell over the room, crackling with tension before her face broke with a beaming smile. "You darling, darling man!" she finished, smacking him cheerfully. "Now *that* is how you apologize for memory-wiping your best friend. With lavish displays of remorse and groveling." She patted him once on the cheek before turning back to the room. "Right. Lots to do. Cam, what's our timetable?"

Brie bit hard on her lip, refusing to laugh.

*Cam?*

The lovely angel froze like it might be some dastardly trick before recovering himself enough to speak. "Th-The long car will be here to pick us up at seven."

"Seven — I can work with that." Sherry graciously didn't mock him for failing to correctly name the limousine.

Tavi ventured another step into the room, picking up a stunning silk gown with a frown. "This looks terribly impractical."

Sherry gently wrested the garment from her hands. "It's not meant to be practical. You're not *fighting*, darling. You're blending seamlessly into the glamorous world of late-sixties San Francisco nightlife."

The words were delivered in such a swoon that the Elysians glanced at Brie for assistance. Having been swept up in her best friend's escapades before, she merely shrugged her shoulders at the warriors with a smile. "The fight's already over," she said, picking up a pair of stilettos, "we lost."

The air was warm, but a salty breeze stirred up from the ocean when the friends arrived at the club later that night, looking like they'd stepped out of a fashion magazine. The men wore sharp suits. Sherry looked gorgeous in a daring, backless dress, and Tavi had stopped growling long enough to be wrestled into an elegant, rose silk A-line that was meant to drape to her knees but looked like a mini-dress on her stunning, tall frame. Brie was resplendent in a floor-length gold gown that paired uncannily well with the earring Zadkiel had given her back in Elysium.

Cameron had kept an air of suspense on the way over, but now that they'd arrived, it was impossible to keep the secret any longer. The club was a local haunt, decadent and exclusive, but every inch of the windows was plastered with the same poster.

*Little Stevie Wonder.*

A single look and Sherry's knees buckled like she would faint. In the time it took them to make it from the limo to the door, she must have asked every variation of the same question:

*"It's not actually him, is it? It can't possibly be him, can it?"*

Brie gripped her angel's arm so tight he laughed and tried to ease her fingers off. By the time they made their way past the unending line and inside the club itself, she had worked herself into a frenzy. "Celestial shenanigans aside, how did you make this happen?" she asked, eyes darting around the room. It was simple but elegant, draped in velvet curtains, with chandeliers casting warm, intimate light across the tables. It was the sort of place where one could imagine Frank Sinatra sipping martinis in the corner. "This is *insane!*"

Cameron merely shrugged, eyes twinkling in the soft light. "You know. Celestial shenanigans."

"Seriously, man," Mike began, fidgeting a little in his designer suit. "This is above and beyond. I don't know how you always…" He trailed off, shaking his head. "Thanks."

The Elysians were merely impatient, the historical significance utterly lost on them. It cheered them slightly to see a bar, but that was the extent of things.

Their mortal companions couldn't have been a greater contrast. Brie whispered excitedly as they were led to their table. "This is *so* surreal. And we're right near the stage?"

Her angel flashed a grin, looking uncharacteristically young. He pulled out a chair and waited for her to sit. "Just act natural. Pepper in some slang." His eyes twinkled as he bent over and gave her an upside-down kiss.

As they settled in, the lights dimmed, and the crowd hushed. A young man, not yet in his twenties, took the stage with a small band. Her heart skipped, and she leaned closer, bracing her hands against the table.

There he was — Stevie Wonder, not yet a legend, but already on his way. With a cool confidence that would only grow more polished in the years to come, he sat down at the piano and began to play. A hush fell over the room as every person in the audience watched in silent rapture, feeling themselves transported to a slightly different state of mind. His fingers danced effortlessly across the keys as his voice filled the room, soulful and smooth, performing songs Brie recognized but not the ones that would make him famous. A waiter brought them drinks, and the companions listened, rapt with attention. It was a generous set, and the crowd applauded wildly as the band finally set down their instruments and promised to return.

"Here's when we kidnap him, right?" Brie said practically, watching from afar. "So he can join our gang of celestial crime fighters and play a little music on the side?"

Tavi crushed an ice cube between her fingers as Ephriam leveled her with a cool glare. "Don't ever call us that again," he said flatly.

*That's a definite yes!*

Brie looked around in amazement before flashing Cameron an adoring glance. "I still can't believe you did this."

Her angel flashed a casual smile, leaning forward and pressing their foreheads together. "It matters to you? You want this?"

Her eyes welled at the corners, and she nodded. "Yes, very much."

He flashed a bewitching smile, leaning his lips to her ear. "It might cost you later," he whispered.

Her mouth fell open in surprise. He never talked like that, *never* played like that. If anything, he was meticulously gentlemanly — like he was trying to remember the knack of it, like he was used to spending time alone.

*I forget that sometimes. He's new to this, too.*

She jolted back to the present to realize he was still staring with a slightly puzzled expression, given that she'd yet to respond. Her cheeks flamed red.

*Say something, Weldon! Say something brilliant!*

"It might cost *you* later," she stammered.

An empty silence fell between them.

*IDIOT!*

His face was a perfect blank. She stared slightly to the side of his head. It made the whole thing worse that it happened in the gorgeous nightclub decades in the past.

When their eyes met, she could only manage to look defiant.

*Chased by demons. Now this.*

It was a problem only Stevie Wonder could fix.

The friends drank, laughed, and danced the night away. Even the Elysians set aside their eternal composure and joined in the fun. After singing an encore, and then another after that, Little Stevie Wonder retired for the evening and a house player took his place. The companions left the dancefloor and settled back around the table, watching the candles burn low, reflected in their drinks. They were tired, but for once, it was a good tired. For once, the demons that hunted them were temporarily held at bay.

"Arafel would have loved this. Though she'd never have agreed to wear a gown," Tavi added with a wistful smile, dipping her fingers into the flame. She'd been quiet for most of the night, and she spoke softly now, missing her friend back in Elysium, staring towards the stage with a peculiar expression. "I can see why people are drawn to this time. It feels important."

Cameron leaned forward, resting his arms on the table. "I think that's the magic of it. There's something about being in a place and time like this — right before everything changes. You can feel it in the air."

"Maybe it's the music," Brie mused, leaning her head against his shoulder. His arm came up at once, tucking her inside. "But I think it's the people. Everyone here feels like they're on the verge of something big, standing together on the brink of some great future."

Mike raised his daiquiri. "To the future," he toasted, wrapping Sherry under his arm. "To getting back there as quickly as possible and never getting lost in time *again*."

The glasses clinked, and Cameron muttered under his breath.

"There's a chance that last part was meant for me."

The lights in the club dimmed even further as the house band settled into a groove for the night. Despite the late hour, they didn't show any signs of stopping. Quite the contrary, the liquor was flowing, the people were dancing, and they were just getting warmed up.

The evening's enchantment settled into yet another memory they would never forget, becoming yet another story that no one back home would ever believe.

"This city," Brie said softly, "is full of magic."

It was in the air. She could breathe it. It was so thick she could feel it, almost *see* it. A near-tangible thing, like a glowing spell that had fallen over—

"Brie, what's going on with your purse?"

She snapped back to attention and looked down to see Sherry frowning at the gilded clutch that matched her outfit. Now, it was beaming from within, with golden shafts of light spearing from the clasp and seams.

Without thinking, she reached out and opened it.

*Well, I'll be damned.*

The picture in Azrael's magnifying glass had changed.

# CHAPTER NINE

## Goodbye Golden Gate

Their exit from the nightclub could not, in good conscience, be characterized as graceful.

Brie had never been more relieved that Mr. Wonder couldn't see her as she was when the entire group tried in vain to encircle her and hide her magically glowing handbag, then scuffled out the door as quickly as possible. They weren't any less conspicuous back at the lobby of the Fairmont when she accidentally dropped her purse, and blinding light spilled out like she was smuggling a tiny star. It didn't help lower their profile when Ephriam shouted something in Elysian, and Tavi reflexively drew a dagger she'd been hiding God-knows-where.

Back in their suite at last, Brie took the incriminating glass from her purse and set it on the coffee table.

During their time in the woods, she'd gotten used to it. The glass looked like a normal, if stylized, object — something that wouldn't have looked out of place on an office desk until she held it up to her eye and saw its beam of light, presumably guiding them in the direction they were meant to go. Nobody else could see it. It had never lit up with enough force to scandalize a nightclub or a hotel lobby before.

Now, a projected image shone from its lens, bright as a sunrise. It shimmered in the air, then sharpened, filling their luxurious San

Francisco suite with a hologram of dazzling, foreign light. The air in the room shifted. The scene on display was epic in scope and undeniably beautiful but not comforting. Sun-baked cliffs soared from an expanse of orange and gold sand that looked like the sunset itself had taken up physical form and residence on Earth. Patches of stubborn vegetation and what looked like the remnants of an ancient ruin lay nestled within a crescent-shaped canyon carved into red stone.

It looked like another world.

Somewhere very, *very* far away.

Tavi sucked in a breath and leaned over Brie's shoulder, eyes narrowing in recognition at the desert landscape.

"I've seen this place before," Ephriam muttered, staring at the image. His voice held the weight of someone who wasn't thrilled about revisiting old memories.

"You and Tavianne both, by the looks of it," Brie said cautiously, having learned to heed the immortals' warnings and cues. "Care to enlighten the rest of us?"

Tavi's lips twitched. "That is the Valley of the Moon."

Brie turned to her slowly before skewering Cameron with a hard look. "Listen, I am very committed to our cause, but if we need to go back to the moon? I'm out. Find somebody else with a different ancient necklace. I am *out*."

"It isn't the actual moon," said Ephriam. "It's Wadi Rum. The edge of the Arabian desert in southern Jordan. It's called the Valley of the Moon because of its otherworldly beauty."

"Oh!" Brie let out a relieved breath. "Well, that sounds better."

"Yes, it's very cozy if you know where you're going, have a guide, and plan extensively. If you don't have, say, any of those things? It's still a great place for a vacation if you enjoy nearly dying in a desert," Tavi said with a mirthless grin.

*I hate your jokes.*

"We've been there before. It is a beautiful country, and the people of Jordan are perhaps the loveliest in all the world. But the price of such beauty is no small measure of danger. Wadi Rum is not a forgiving place," Ephriam said, breaking the silence with the confidence of someone who had seen enough in his long life to be weary of seeing it again. He leaned forward, his sharp, golden eyes tracing the landscape with concern. "The desert is filled with ancient forces and relics from the wars of the Nephilim. Some say the intersection of the mortal plane with the divine lies hidden deep within the heart of the desert. Also, Tavianne had a spot of trouble there when we last visited."

There was a weighted pause.

"What sort of trouble?" Sherry finally asked, tearing her eyes from the spectacular hologram.

Tavi heaved a weary sigh. "I got chased by a cursed camel."

Brie blinked, putting the magnifying glass down on the table. "I'm sorry, what now?"

"It was hilarious," Ephriam smirked.

"It was a mess," Tavi corrected, fidgeting uncomfortably in her dress. "The whole mission was botched from the start. We were investigating rumors about a horde of wraiths terrorizing the local Bedouin tribes when all of a sudden, this crazed dromedary launched itself straight at me, making a noise like you wouldn't believe. Ephriam had to break an ancient seal, we ran for a mile, and I had to throw my best dagger into the thing's face to get away."

*Typical Tuesday in the ancient desert.*

"Don't forget the part where it spit fire," Ephriam added casually, doing his level best not to smile.

Tavi threw him a look, fingering the edge of her blade. "And then we had to go back to rescue the infernal animal because, well, it was a fire hazard, and anyway, it wasn't the poor thing's fault." She shook her head, looking highly inconvenienced by the whole thing. "They're sweet, gentle creatures, and I couldn't leave it in such a state. But it was a complete disaster. Do you have any idea how difficult it is to perform an exorcism on a camel during mating season?"

Another heavy silence followed this remark.

"No," Mike answered mildly, "I can't say that I do."

Sherry let out a long, slow breath, massaging her temples. "Great. So, we're heading to an ancient desert filled with fire-breathing camels and possibly a horde of wraiths. This is exactly how I wanted my week to go."

Cameron flashed her a secret look, standing quietly in the corner. "Maybe we don't *have* to go," he suggested casually. "I mean, we don't even know if the magnifying glass is pointing us there on purpose. It could be a mistake."

*A mistake?*

Brie glanced at him, unsure what to say.

"Divine artifacts don't make mistakes," Ephriam said without missing a beat.

The lovely angel shot a pleading look around the group, his expression one of mild panic. "We have options. We don't *have* to launch ourselves straight into the fire. Why would it point us there, anyway? What are we hoping to find?"

"I think I know," Brie answered quietly. Every eye locked on her as she stared at the glowing desert and set her jaw. "It has to be the gateway to Eden."

A ringing silence fell over the room.

Ephriam alone looked open to this interpretation of the sign. "Explain," he said curtly.

She started slowly. "I know we're supposed to be heading to the Hall of Jophial, but the truth is, we have no idea how to get there without access to the Time Seas. But the glass is still leading us somewhere, and I think I know where, and I think I know why." She stared around at the expectant faces of her friends and continued. "Back in Elysium, Enoch said that the only other person who might know something about my pendant, Elijah, is in the Garden of Eden. Ever since he mentioned it, I've had this feeling tugging at me. Azrael's glass started showing us clues when we were put in a position where we *have* to find a place where the physical world intersects with the divine. Enoch said Eden is one of those places. And Ephriam just said that Wadi Rum is one of those places, too."

One look at the Elysians' faces told her it was true.

She continued. "We haven't had any luck with that cursed book, have we? We're no closer to fulfilling the mission Enoch gave us and finding Jophial. We're still completely cut off from Elysium, and without access to its energy, Tavi isn't healing the way you are, Ephriam. We need to get somewhere we can help her. In fact, to do *anything* we need to do — heal Tavi, find Jophial, even get back to Elysium, we need to find a place like that. None of it's possible while we're stuck in the human world, and none of you have any Elysian powers to get us back. We need a *door*. I believe Azrael's glass either shows you where you want to go or where you need to go. And I think…" She tugged on her earring nervously. "I can't explain exactly why, but I just *know* that it's Eden."

"But you *don't* know," Cameron said softly. "It's a guess. A guess that puts you — puts *us* — in very real danger." He looked at her with such pain and passion in his eyes, it was as if he'd said the words out loud: *If anything happens to you, I will never be alright again.*

She considered this quietly before answering. "I hear you. And you're right. But… there's a special word for optimistic, unconfirmable guesses that require some sacrifice, though, isn't there?" The pendant shone brightly, half-hidden beneath the folds of her dress.

The others were silent, but Sherry gave a wry smile. "Faith."

Brie nodded. "Exactly."

Her best friend took one look at Cameron's desperate, frustrated face and clapped an unexpected hand on his shoulder. "I feel you. I hate it when she's right."

"Look, we don't have to go right away," Brie continued, trying to make it sound like less of an impending disaster than it surely was. "We still have to meet the CEO to cash in some gold and…" she took a deep breath and shook her head incredulously, "figure out what to do with the Magna Freaking Carta. Then we'll figure out how to get over there and deal with whatever comes up. Fire-breathing camels? Excellent. Mating season? Perfect."

Cameron shifted uncomfortably, rubbing the back of his neck. "You're really dead-set on this? Trading invaluable treasures for cash to carry around with us and traipsing halfway across the globe to follow the clue of a deranged librarian? Wouldn't it be smarter to keep a low profile? Be a bit less conspicuous? Stay here?" His eyes were still pleading with her.

Brie raised an eyebrow. "I think we passed the threshold of inconspicuousness some time ago. We need the money, Cam. Whatever's waiting for us in Jordan, we can't face it broke. We're going to need resources, equipment, and probably a lot of bribes."

*Perhaps something to repel camels.*

"Good point," Sherry agreed, popping a bubble of gum she'd somehow acquired. "Nothing says 'let me pass through your demon-riddled desert' like a fat wad of cash."

Ephriam crossed his arms. "Money will only take us so far. We'll need more than that to navigate the Wadi Rum."

Brie gave him a sidelong glance. "Then it's a good thing we've got you to handle the local cursed animal population." She held that piercing gaze only a moment before bowing her head with a sigh. "Though right now, it feels like we're the ones who've been cursed, and we're bringing all the bad luck with us."

"You aren't cursed." Mike shot her a friendly grin, the kind that had been indispensable to bolstering the group's morale during their decade-hopping ordeal. "It's just a long series of unfortunate coincidences."

*Title of my memoir.*

"That's right, love," Sherry added helpfully. "Coincidences that result in celestial battles, near-death experiences, and usually someone yelling, *'Brie, why did you touch that?'*"

"Enough." Ephriam's voice cut through their bickering like a whip. "We keep our meeting with the CEO, handle the gold to fund this misbegotten quest, then head for the airport." Cameron looked like he was going to interrupt once more, but Ephriam cut him off. "I, too, would prefer to leave it be and find a different way back into Elysium to deliver the humans to their own time. But we find ourselves stranded without the benefit of powers, supplies, or options. And we would be foolish to ignore the gifts of Azrael."

Cameron hesitated, then nodded grimly.

"I have a few logistical questions," Mike ventured tentatively, compartmentalizing the word *Eden* to the back of his mind. "How do you propose we actually get there? A plane is a nice idea and all, but we have no passports or valid forms of identification. This might be 1969, and I'm sure airport security is a far cry from what we're used to, but it still does, you know, exist."

The group looked temporarily stumped before Sherry answered. "Money talks." All eyes swiveled to her as she gave Mike a sweet smile. "Haven't I taught you anything, darling? When in doubt, throw money at the problem until it goes away. This CEO tomorrow — I assume he'll be traveling in a private plane?"

A smile broke over Brie's face as comprehension dawned. "Sherry, you are a genius."

"What am I missing here?" asked Cameron.

"I do not understand," added Ephriam with a scowl.

"We won't be flying commercial," Brie said with a grin. "We'll be commandeering some wheel's up service, courtesy of our new best friend, the banking executive."

"As it should be," Sherry concluded with a satisfied nod. "Now, out of your evening wear, everyone. Looks like we have a big day ahead of us tomorrow. And if past experience is any indication, we'll need all our wits about us to field whatever impossible thing happens next."

After a few hours of restless sleep, the group gathered their things and bid a reluctant farewell to the luxurious confines of the Fairmont Hotel.

"Goodbye, room service that costs as much as my mortgage," Sherry whispered. "Goodbye, beds that feel like clouds and towels softer than my—"

"Honey?" Mike gently unpeeled her fingers from the coffee table. "You need to let go now."

Ephriam was the only one who didn't seem even slightly nostalgic. "Time to leave."

The hotel staff were unreasonably chipper from the perspective of a group about to leave on a mission that would likely result in an international incident. As they reached the lobby, the bellhop ran over to Sherry with a wave. "Ma'am, the concierge took care of that little issue for you. Here's the key to your new storage unit." Sherry took the key gratefully as he flashed a smile and handed her a receipt. "Heading to the airport?"

Sherry nodded, casting a last, longing look at the elevator doors as they closed behind them. "That's the plan. And Victor, we've talked about this — *don't* call me ma'am."

"Right, miss. Sorry, miss. Old habits. Traveling light, I see," he remarked, eyeing their suspiciously small amount of luggage. "No souvenirs?"

"Just emotional baggage," Sherry sulked before turning to Cameron. "When we get there, introduce me as your business manager and then say as little as possible." She whipped out a compact mirror and touched up her lipstick. "I was born to play this role."

Half an hour later, their small party was in the CEO's spacious, glass-walled office. The view of the city spread out beneath them, sunlight glinting off skyscrapers and casting shadows over the bustling streets below. The executive, one Mr. Coldridge, was a tall, slim man with precisely styled gray hair and an air of restless efficiency. He sat across from them, eyes darting between Cameron and the stack of gold bars and rare jewels on his desk.

"These items," Mr. Coldridge began, each word cautiously measured, "are remarkable. And clearly authentic."

Cameron nodded thoughtfully, hoping he wouldn't be asked any more specific questions. "Rare, unique, and extremely valuable."

The CEO gave a tight smile, nodding appreciatively as he examined one of the jewels. "You've been carrying around an impressive fortune. Under our very noses, no less."

"And your famed discretion is no small part of why we're here," Sherry replied smoothly, with a hint of a British accent she'd developed on the ride over. "We would like to take this business relationship a step further than selling the items. Sir," she added, letting her voice dip conspiratorially, "our interests require us to travel in order to obtain certain acquisitions."

"Oh?" The CEO's interest was piqued. "You're investors, then?"

"Indeed," Sherry cut in, her voice low and persuasive. "And let's just say that one of those assets, one that will most certainly benefit from your bank's backing, lies in a particular region of the Middle East. But, you see, time is of the essence, and commercial flights don't exactly align with our operational standards."

The CEO studied her, his brow furrowed. "Are you asking for transportation?"

Sherry's face softened into a practiced look of mild embarrassment. "I don't suppose your organization has a corporate jet? This would be a substantial acquisition, and sensitivity is paramount. Of course, the bank would be adequately compensated."

Mr. Coldridge hesitated, casting a wary glance between them. Brie gave Cameron a nudge, prompting him to lean forward, arms resting lightly on his knees. "You know as well as we do that some transactions can't be delayed," he began in a careful, sincere tone. "If you arrange something for us, it will benefit both parties. The faster we close on this, the sooner your bank receives a frankly outrageous sum of new assets to manage."

Brie could practically see the executive's mind weighing his options, working at breakneck speed as he considered their proposal.

Finally, he set the jewel down, fingers tapping a slow rhythm on the desk. "I can arrange something. You'll need to return the jet within the week. We have other clients who rely on it."

"Absolutely," Sherry replied, her voice smooth as silk. "Your generosity won't go unacknowledged, I assure you."

The CEO's lips curved into a smile. "I'll have my assistant make the necessary arrangements."

They left the bank a few minutes later, each of them astounded by their sudden change of luck. Mike was practically bouncing, wrapping an arm around Sherry's shoulders. As usual, he was as proud as he was legitimately afraid.

"How did you do that?" he whispered into her ear. "Babe, you're amazing!"

Cameron alone was quiet, casting suspicious glances at the sky. "Something feels off."

Sherry gave him a sidelong glance. "You always think something feels off."

"No, this time it's worse," he replied. "This went way too smoothly. I'm telling you, this can't last," he muttered as they walked out of the bank with what was probably enough money to purchase a small country. "Something's going to go wrong."

"Maybe we've used up our bad luck," Brie said optimistically, which earned her a withering look from Sherry.

"Darling," she said with a sniff, "I approve the sentiment, but let's be honest — you are the human embodiment of bad luck. If you sneeze, someone's house will explode."

"Exaggeration," Brie replied, but it wasn't very convincing.

"We cashed in some gold and made some luxurious travel arrangements, Cameron," Sherry said, adjusting her sunglasses as she checked her reflection in a shop window. "We didn't steal the Mona Lisa."

"Just the Magna Carta," muttered Cameron.

"Look," Sherry said, gently taking Brie by the shoulders and steering her along. "We've already been chased by demons and ended up decades in the past. What else could possibly go wrong?"

# CHAPTER TEN

# Trouble in Transit

Brie had known — *known* — that getting through security at the air-port was going to be a nightmare. She didn't share Sherry's absolute confidence that their access to a private plane would wholly shield them from airport security measures, and as it stood, they had no tick-ets, no IDs, and were carrying a small arsenal of Elysian blades.

What she hadn't anticipated was just *how* ridiculous the situation would get.

San Francisco International Airport, circa 1969, was a strange place for a group of Elysians and time-displaced humans on a quest to find Eden, yet somehow they almost managed to blend in.

Almost.

"This place is a nightmare," Cameron muttered, looking around at the lines of frantic people, the crying children, and the general feel-ing of stress that permeated the air. As he watched, an off-duty pilot spilled a coffee down his shirt and let out a deafening curse.

Ephriam gave him a withering look. "It's a port of travel, not a bat-tlefield. Pull yourself together."

"Remember," Sherry whispered as they approached the terminal, "we're a completely normal group of friends catching a private flight to Jordan. A perfectly typical Tuesday."

"Oh, yeah. Perfectly typical," Brie replied, adjusting her oversized sunglasses and the wide-brimmed hat Sherry insisted made her look less conspicuous. "Except that Ephriam's carrying a sword, Cameron's got at least three concealed knives, and Tavianne's probably packing enough hardware to start her own militia."

Tavi snorted knowingly like this didn't even come close.

"That's the sort of thing that would concern me if we were flying commercial, but we aren't. And good thing, too — we'll need those for the next time Tavi decides to get into a tussle with the local wildlife." Sherry replied.

Ephriam shot her a look. "Discretion is the better part of valor. Let's try not to get flagged before we even make it to the gate."

"Did anyone bother to confirm the 'private' part?" Cameron muttered, glancing at the bustling crowd around them. He was clearly nervous but was doing his best to keep his usual cool intact. "For all we know, the CEO changed his mind and rerouted us to, I don't know, a cargo plane."

*That might be easier. They might not care about the blades on a cargo plane.*

"Relax," Sherry replied crisply. "The CEO confirmed everything this morning. We're expected. So, let's all act like we belong here. Think expensive thoughts. Look down on the commoners. Project luxury."

In spite of the tension, Brie couldn't help but smile. Her lovely best friend had been saying the same things since they were in the fourth grade.

As they passed the main terminal, she found herself struck not only by the absurdity of their situation but also by the moments of surreal normalcy peppered amidst it all. Here they were, a ragtag band of warriors, exiles, and celestial beings, wandering through an airport like tourists on their way to the beach. Sunhats and chewing gum. Perfectly average.

"What's the worst that could happen?" Sherry added, flashing a devil-may-care grin that immediately made Brie's stomach tighten.

"We're flying private. We aren't even going through security. Just relax — everything's going to be fine."

"Please don't tempt fate," Brie hissed, practically begging. "With our luck, we'll end up in a holding cell before we even reach the runway." When Cameron shot her a pained look, she relented and did her best to be cheerful. "I'm kidding. It's going to be fine. We just have to get through the terminal and grab some snacks, and we'll be on our way to Amman. Easy."

*But you know better, don't you, Weldon?*

*You know exactly what those are: Famous last words.*

◆ ◆ ◆

"Excuse me, sir. Is this your bag?"

The security officer's voice was so level, so measured, that for a brief moment, Cameron thought everything would be okay.

"Yes," he replied, trying to exude an aura of innocence. "But we're flying private today, so it's fine. Sherry said so."

The officer didn't look convinced. "That isn't how any of this works, sir. Who is Sherry?"

Cameron swallowed, trying hard to keep his rising anxiety from showing on his face and pointing a finger at the woman in question. "She's my… business manager."

The officer took one look at the woman wearing the ridiculously oversized hat and sunglasses and the two seven-foot-tall giants standing next to her, then fixed the Elysian prince with a dead-eyed stare. "I'm going to need you to step over here for additional screening."

"What? Why?" Cameron stammered. "What's wrong with my bag?"

The officer ignored him and unzipped his pack. After a moment, he replied. "You're carrying six knives, three throwing stars, and what appears to be a battle axe."

*A battle axe?!*

Brie bit the inside of her lip, vowing to kill him with it.

"Oh, right." Cameron's face drained of color. "Those. Uh, those are—"

Before he could even attempt an excuse, Ephriam strode up, looking entirely unbothered. "You should have mentioned the weapons," he said coolly as if this were a completely normal conversation to be having at an airport.

The officer raised his eyes to Ephriam's near-seven-foot height and lifted an eyebrow. "Are you all traveling together?"

*Damage control!*

Brie stepped quickly between them, flashing a calming smile while frantically thinking on the fly. "Yes, we are, but it's a… ceremonial thing. The weapons are part of a — a cultural exchange program."

The officer blinked at her. "A cultural exchange program?"

"Exactly," she said, straight-faced. "Very important to our heritage."

"And what heritage would that be?" he asked.

Six answers flew back at him simultaneously: "Dutch," "French," "Aramaic," "Irish," "Gypsey," and "I don't see how that's any of your business."

He gave them a cool stare. "Would you like a minute to decide?"

Sherry stepped up next to Brie. "We're historians, you see, so it's really all of them. The weapons are replicas. Educational. Totally not lethal."

The officer tilted his head. "Really?"

He set Cameron's pack down next to Tavi's, eliciting a sharp clinking sound, then immediately began to examine her bags, his movements professional and efficient. "Ma'am, are you aware that weapons are not permitted, even on private flights?"

The Elysian sighed loudly, her patience fraying. "I'm trying very hard not to be offended by this entire exchange. These artifacts are *traditional.*"

The agent's skepticism was palpable. "Is that so?"

"Absolutely," Ephriam cut in smoothly. "In fact, it's customary to carry these specific items as part of our culture. It would be insensitive to travel without them."

The agent looked unconvinced, yet it was difficult to deny that there was something quite different about the towering people in front of him. He cast a silent look at a co-worker.

For a moment, it seemed like they might be able to talk their way through.

Then, the agent picked up Mike's bag. He must have felt something because he immediately froze. "What's in here?" he demanded.

*Good question.*

Brie felt a pang of dread as the policeman shifted uncomfortably, his face reddening. "Nothing special. Personal items. Um, I mean ceremonial. I mean… cultural?"

The agent raised an eyebrow. "If you could open the bag, please."

Reluctantly, Mike unzipped the bag, revealing his police sidearm resting on his belongings.

The agent's expression hardened, and he looked up slowly. "More artifacts?" Without waiting for Mike to reply, he grabbed him by the arm and shoved him against the wall. "Sir, step back and keep your hands where I can see them!" he barked, reaching for his radio. "I need backup in the private terminal, Code Blue!"

"Wait, wait, that's not necessary," Brie began, trying to maintain a rational tone as she stepped forward. "This is all a misunderstanding. The weapon is ceremonial! Symbolic!"

"The weapon is a firearm, ma'am," he glared.

"A ceremonial one!" she insisted.

The agent ignored her, keeping a firm grip on Mike's arm as he barked more commands into his radio. She could see backup amassing in the distance, alerted by the commotion and already making their way over.

Mike had never looked so scandalized in all his life. "But I'm a policeman!" he cried in a strange, strained voice. "This can't be happening!"

The color drained from Brie's face. "If anyone has a Plan B, now would be the time!"

Ephriam's face was unreadable, growling as he surveyed the situation. "We don't have time for this."

That's when Sherry elbowed her way past the Elysian warrior and stood before them with the energy of a bull about to charge. "Stand aside!"

Before anyone could respond, she pulled something from her pocket—a pouch of Elysian freeze spells, enchanted by King Enoch himself, given to her before they left Elysium. She took out one of the smooth, blue-glowing orbs and hurled it straight at the officer. It burst on the back of his uniform, and a sphere of ice-blue energy rippled out like a supernatural bubble, freezing time for everything within a ten-foot radius… including Mike. And Sherry.

None of the others said anything for a moment, simply staring dumbfoundedly at the scene: Mike frozen in embarrassment, the officer in anger, and Sherry, a living statue of triumph.

After a moment of shock, Ephriam let out a curse in his native language that needed no translation, and all hell broke loose. He raced forward, grabbing the agent's arm and forcing it away just enough to make him release Mike. Cameron grabbed Mike as he fell awkwardly, unable to move so much as a muscle to help, though his eyes darted around in silent panic. Ephriam picked up Sherry and tucked her gracelessly under his arm like an ungainly statue before barking a simple command.

"Run!"

Tavi was already moving, grabbing their bags and sprinting through the terminal with the practiced agility that came from years of dodging both mortals and supernatural beings alike.

The group tried not to scatter, ducking and weaving through the maze of corridors and security checkpoints, trying desperately to keep their wits as the scene erupted into chaos around them.

"Left!" Cameron called out, veering toward a hallway marked *Authorized Personnel Only.*

Without hesitation, they followed him, skidding around corners and dodging bewildered employees as they made their way deeper into the restricted area. Sherry's feet banged against a corner as they made a particularly sharp turn.

"Careful! She'll never forgive you!" Brie yelped.

"I'll never forgive *her*!" Ephriam shot back.

"This is insane," Cameron panted, glancing over his shoulder as running footsteps echoed behind them. "We're going to get caught."

"Not if we move fast enough," Ephriam replied, "A goal now immeasurably more difficult thanks to your helpful friend." He glared at Sherry's paralyzed form and frozen though she was, there was no mistaking it — Sherry glared back. "We just need to find the right hangar and get to that jet."

"Small problem," Brie gasped, holding onto Sherry's sunglasses she'd rescued from the floor. "We don't know which plane it is."

Ephriam grimly set his jaw. "Leave that to me."

"What are you going to do?" she cried. "Charm them with your angelic glow?"

"No," he answered, eyes narrowing. "I'm going to do something even better."

"An air traffic control tower?" Brie couldn't stop her voice from taking on a panicked, shrieking quality as the renegade companions looked out of a security window at the building spiring from the tarmac. "How are we… how are you… Ephriam, *how*?"

Ephriam scrutinized the structure. "We need the tail number. That's how we find the plane."

"Can't we just take any plane?" Cameron asked.

"You think every plane in this airport has enough fuel to get all the way to Amman without stopping?" Ephriam fired back. "We can't simply stop somewhere to refuel once we're airborne. We can't afford to attract attention."

Brie's eyes widened. "Ephriam, I think that ship has sailed."

"Irregardless," he replied. "It's our best chance. If we can get into the tower, we can grab the tail number and the plane's location."

"How do you know all this?" Brie asked suspiciously, straightening Sherry's sunglasses on her friend's frozen, furiously glaring face.

"Ephriam," Cameron interjected grimly, "they are going to *shoot* you. They are going to shoot us all. I cannot begin to guess what kind of security we might be up against in there. We'll never make it to the top."

"No," Tavi mused, lifting her eyes upward, "not if we take the stairs."

Ephriam nodded knowingly.

"Well, how else would you…?" Brie trailed off, looking like she deeply regretted asking.

"I'll need Tavianne's help," he replied. "We have scaled more difficult peaks than this."

"But she's injured," Cameron said softly. "Have you ever done it while she's hurt?"

Ephriam gave a stoic shrug. "Do you have a better idea?"

Brie and Cameron crouched low behind a stack of crates, a safe distance from the towering structure, watching with breathless anxiety as two figures scaled its exterior.

Brie squinted, barely able to track as Ephriam and Tavi moved at a terrifying pace, climbing the smooth cement walls with a coil of rope and an alarming disregard for gravity. They looked like ghosts against the foggy windows, a glimpse of shadow here, a flash of movement there. Part of her marveled at how easily they defied every rule of basic physics and self-preservation. The other part of her? She couldn't tear her gaze away or stop the feeling of dread curling in her stomach.

"I think I've officially lost the ability to be shocked," she whispered as Ephriam clung to a ledge using far too few fingers. Tavi was already several feet above him, moving with the ease of someone who did this sort of thing as regularly as the rest of them made coffee. Only once did she falter — the slightest hesitation that made the rest of them hold their breaths. By the time Brie sent up a prayer for assistance, she had already continued to climb.

Cameron let out a long breath. At this point, he was equally horrified and impressed.

A strange sound tore Brie's attention from the Elysian's ascent, and she turned to the stiff figures of Sherry and Mike, which stood frozen at awkward angles facing each other. "What was that?" Brie asked as if they could answer her.

Sherry's eyes flashed at her in fury as her petrified form let out an incomprehensible but clearly outraged grunt once again. "*Uuuuhhhh-hhnnnnnggg!*"

"Oh! Sorry," Brie apologized, understanding immediately and turning her frozen friend to face the action.

The Elysians approached the top and paused, suspended just below the main window of the control room. Tavi flashed a quick signal, then both she and Ephriam punched the window with shocking force. The glass fractured before raining to the ground. By the time the pieces landed, Ephriam and Tavi had already swung into the tower.

Cameron looked a bit sick. "I'd say they've got about ten seconds before every guard on shift is up there."

"Better hope that's all they need," Brie muttered. Her stomach churned as she scanned the area for armed personnel or sirens. At this point, she wouldn't be surprised if the lot of them were karmically punished with a battle axe.

For a suspended moment, everything went eerily quiet. Then came the noise. A crash — a brutal, jarring clang that reverberated through the air, followed by a series of muffled shouts.

"Here we go," Cameron muttered as they strained to listen.

The sounds of struggle grew louder: more crashes and what sounded suspiciously like someone toppling a row of filing cabinets. Brie winced as she imagined the chaos inside, the meticulously arranged papers flying through the air, the wide-eyed terror on the faces of the poor control officers who'd been tasked with a routine shift, only to have it end in a battle with two highly dangerous supernatural warriors.

"Should we… I don't know, go help?" Brie asked tentatively.

Cameron shook his head. "We'd only compound the chaos. Besides, it sounds like they're holding their own."

She looked doubtful. "It sounds like they're losing ground to a security team several times their size."

At that moment, a sharp, shattering sound split the air, and they ducked reflexively. Immediately, the world went silent again.

"Did they… did they win?" Brie whispered.

Two shadows emerged through the broken window — one after the other, sliding down the rope they'd rigged to the tower's top floor. Ephriam reached the ground first. Tavi landed beside him a moment later, flashing a far-too-bright smile before they sprinted full-tilt back to the group.

"Did you—" Cameron began, but Ephriam cut him off with a glare.

"Hangar," he shouted, grabbing Sherry around her petrified waist and hoisting her under his arm. "Now."

Tavi shot Brie a grin. "That takes me back." She grabbed some of the packs and inclined her head toward the far end of the tarmac, where the white nose of a private jet gleamed inside a hangar like a watch in a jewel case. "Shall we?"

A group of men emerged from the base of the tower, their shouts barely audible over the pounding of Brie's heart as they pointed directly at the group and started chasing them down.

Even Tavi faltered. "I think we shall." She took off down the tarmac.

"We're about to have company," Cameron muttered, picking up Mike's statue-fied form as the sound of footsteps echoed in the distance.

With Mike tucked under one arm and Brie clinging to the other, their feet flew over the pavement as her hair whipped out behind them. Her floppy sun hat threatened to dislodge entirely, but she caught it with a manic hand, pinning it to her head.

The plane's gleaming white nose drew closer with every step. The guards had spotted them — that seemed inevitable. They were still at some distance but closing fast.

The group reached the hangar a few moments later, skidding to a stop on the slick concrete. Of course, it was only then that Brie realized the obvious problem:

*Who's going to fly the plane?*

"Hey guys…?" she ventured.

But they were already moving.

Tavi flew up the stairs and into the cockpit. As the Elysian started flipping switches, the engines roared to life.

*Oh. She's going to fly it.*

Ephriam was next, struggling with Sherry like a piece of oversized luggage. He vanished for a moment once he managed to get through the door, then reappeared a second later. "Pass that one to me!" he shouted, and Cameron obligingly passed Mike up the stairs.

*We are never going to hear the end of this.*

Brie stood in a daze on the tarmac, shaking her head.

"This is officially the worst plan we've ever had," she declared, climbing the stairs and attempting to yell over the engines.

"Correction," Ephriam said, stepping over Mike's prone form on the floor and eyeing the overhead bins for a dangerous moment before shoving Sherry into the bathroom. "This is the best bad plan we've ever had."

As the jet began to taxi toward the runway, Brie couldn't help but laugh. A high, tenuous, hysterical laugh, like a child's toy whose off-switch had been disabled. This might be one of the more dangerous civilian activities she'd ever gotten involved with, but they'd survived worse.

*Haven't we?*

No less than two dozen men raced toward them, yelling and waving their arms to signal them to stop. Brie took a single look and ducked inside the plane. Cameron was close behind her but, somehow, stalled, fumbling frantically with his briefcase.

"Cameron!" she cried, whipping around in exasperation. "What are you doing? Get on!"

Tavi started to taxi down the runway without any regard for the Elysian prince's safety. Brie tried to call out to stop her, but her words were lost in the roar of the engines.

"Cameron!" she screamed again. "Come on!"

Her angel finally got the clasp loose and triumphantly pulled out an enormous stack of bills before snapping the case shut again and leaping wildly onto the departing stairs. When he got to the top, he leaned out, calling to the brigade of people chasing them and throwing the cash into the air. The draft from the engines caught the bills, blowing them in a flurry toward the baffled staffers.

"I'm sorry!" he shouted. "We're so, so sorry! I hope this covers the damages—"

Ephriam pushed past Brie, grabbed Cameron by the front of his shirt, turned, and threw him backward into the cabin. Then he reached one enormous, muscled arm down and heaved the staircase up, creating a seal and latching it shut. He whirled on his friend. "I swear by all the Heavens — if an ancient demon doesn't do us in, your renegade conscience surely will."

Without further ado, they lifted off into the brilliant sunlit sky, San Francisco shrinking beneath them as they soared toward their next adventure in Amman.

It was official. They were airborne, and they had stolen a plane.

"Next stop, Jordan," Tavi said over the intercom, a pained grin on her face. "I hope you all enjoy the in-flight service."

"So that's it then. We've committed Grand Theft Aviation. We're officially international criminals now." Cameron sank low into his seat with a defeated expression.

"Technically," Brie said consolingly, "we were probably already on several watch lists."

"Yes, but not in this decade." Cameron let out something between an exhalation and a groan and put his head in his hands.

Brie sighed. "I swear if we make it through this alive…"

"You'll what?" Ephriam asked, glancing at her.

"For a start, I'll never let you plan our trips again."

They fell into a shell-shocked silence, the hum of the engines drowning out, for however brief a moment, the insanity they'd just survived. Brie settled into a seat and closed her eyes, mind whirling in a state of complete disbelief.

*Just be grateful you pulled it off.*

*For now, we have a plan.*

*For now, we're okay.*

The bathroom door slammed open, and everyone turned as Sherry emerged, fists clenched and seething with wrath. She stalked over the still-frozen form of her boyfriend, tripping slightly, and claimed the best seat in the cabin before decreeing through clenched teeth: "I want to be crystal clear about this: *I* saved the day, and we shall *never* speak of this again." She shot blazing glares at everyone, daring them to dissent, then asked, "Now, does anyone know where the snack cart is?"

# CHAPTER ELEVEN

## Altitude

Tavi was in the cockpit, looking far too relaxed for someone who'd just stolen a plane as if the action had made her feel like her old self again. The rest of the friends sat scattered throughout the luxurious cabin, each in varying degrees of disbelief, relief, and irritation.

"So," Sherry began, eyeing Ephriam over the rim of her sunglasses as she fastened her seatbelt. "Am I the only one wondering how our resident angels here know how to steal and fly a private jet without so much as breaking a sweat?"

Brie, who had been flipping through an in-flight magazine essentially titled *Luxury Real Estate You Could Never Afford,* raised her eyes. "Actually, that's an excellent question. Care to enlighten us, E?"

Ephriam, who was gazing out the window with an unruffled calm that only a being of divine origins could pull off, turned his head slightly. His golden eyes glinted with a mischievous light. "Divine knowledge," he said simply.

"Right," Sherry replied, drawing the word out as though she were trying to wrap her mind around the concept. "So, divine knowledge includes bypassing airport security. Someone should really get the Pentagon on the line."

Ephriam's shoulders lifted in an effortless shrug. "Adaptability is a gift."

Tavi's voice crackled over the intercom. "Arafel and I learned for fun once humans started messing around with flying machines. You should've seen DaVinci's face when we busted up his birch-branch model. Cameron knows a little, too, though I've never once seen him land anything successfully."

"Truer words were never spoken," Ephriam added, shooting Cameron an icy stare that made her angel flush scarlet.

Mike chose that moment to sit bolt upright, the effects of the Elysian freeze spell having finally worn off. "I object to the theft of this plane in the strongest of terms!" he shouted.

The others turned to him and stared before Ephriam jerked his thumb over his shoulder and replied, "There's a parachute in the back if you want."

"Oh good, you're awake!" Sherry ignored both comments. "Be a darling and mix up a couple of daiquiris. Wait, make it a pitcher. I am entirely too sober for this. I think I saw a bar back there somewhere."

Brie sighed, tossing her magazine onto the empty seat next to her. "Count me in. And listen, Mike, I'm right there with you. But options were fairly limited after you tried to take a gun from 2016 through airport security in 1969. Rather lacking in subtlety, sir. Mix up those drinks."

Mike hauled himself off the floor, muttering under his breath, but obediently made his way to the bar.

"The sheer tonnage of felonies we've committed over the past hour is, frankly, staggering." Cameron shifted in his seat with a resigned sigh. "At this point, the *only* thing keeping us from being shot out of the sky by karma itself is sheer divine intervention."

The intercom crackled to life with Tavi's voice once again. "Or the fact that I am rather expertly flying under every radar system between here and the Atlantic. Think of it as our personal cloak of invisibility."

Sherry leaned into the aisle, giving Tavi an approving nod. "Props, Tavi. Way more useful in a crisis than Mr. 'Divine Knowledge' over here."

"You wound me," Ephriam replied dryly, though there was a hint of a smirk tugging at the corner of his mouth. "This is how you repay me for hauling your petrified body through an international airport? Anyway, I'll have you know I'm quite capable in many fields."

*Carpentry, braids, interdimensional catastrophes.*

"Oh, I bet," Sherry deadpanned. "I'm sure all the demons quake in fear when you whip out your ability to lecture them into submission."

Ephriam's smirk grew a fraction wider. "Only the lesser demons. The smarter ones have learned to avoid me altogether."

Before Sherry could fire back, Cameron raised his hand, looking genuinely troubled. He nodded toward the window, where dark clouds were gathering in the distance, and called up to the cockpit. "Tavi, are you certain it's alright if we fly this low? There's something about those clouds I don't like."

She yelled back, "We might hit a spot of turbulence here and there, but trust the process, kid. We'll be okay."

*Famous last words. Again.*

"You probably just think that because the last time we saw ominous clouds, they turned out to be the ancient, demonic embodiment of Gluttony, and it tried to eat us all alive," Sherry chimed in, waving him off. "Besides, feeling vaguely doomed is your natural state. We'd have to worry if you *didn't* bring an aura of anxiety with you to the function. Thank you, dear," she added as Mike handed her a cocktail. He humphed in reply and handed Brie one as well before snatching Azrael's glass away in return and taking the seat next to Sherry.

But Ephriam cut in, his voice unusually grave. "Cameron's right to be cautious. This isn't merely a beautiful place we're going to. It's a cradle of history, and it holds primeval power — cursed cities and ancient beings that don't take kindly to visitors."

Brie rubbed her temples, feeling the beginnings of a headache. "Perfect. All I want is one whole week where I don't have to worry about being torn apart by something. Is that really so much to ask?"

"No promises," Tavi's voice chimed in over the intercom. "But on the bright side, we're making good time. We'll be in Amman by sunrise, assuming, of course, that our jet-setting felonies go unnoticed. I've got us flying low and off the major flight paths. Sit back, relax, and try not to think about how many international laws we're currently breaking."

◆     ◆     ◆

Hours later, Brie had almost managed to fall asleep when a sudden lurch jolted her awake. She rubbed her eyes blearily, heart pounding as her mind raced through a thousand potential reasons for why the plane had dipped so abruptly.

Ephriam, who sat nearby and looked like he hadn't so much as blinked during the entire flight, gave her an appraising look. "A little turbulence. We'll get there just fine."

"You say that like it's a good thing," she mumbled. "I'd rather be up here than down there, facing whatever ancient horror is waiting for us."

"Practicality is good," Ephriam replied with a slight smile. "Cowardice, on the other hand, does not become you."

"It's hardly cowardice, Ephriam," she retorted. "It's called realism. Huge difference."

Sherry let out a soft snort. "I'd say it's self-preservation, with a side of 'We'd really rather not get eaten.'"

*Yeah, that fits.*

From across the aisle, Cameron, who had spent most of the flight buried in a guidebook about the Jordan Valley, looked up, his face pale. "I read up on the area. It's not exactly friendly terrain. Quite a few legends about things that don't like to be disturbed."

"Fantastic," Sherry said, crossing her arms. "And why would we disturb them? Subtlety is our strong suit, after all. Like when we, you know, *stole the plane.*"

Brie let out a groan, wondering if it was possible to simply stay airborne until the end of time. "Could we stop dwelling on that? I'm sure there are plenty of other terrible—" Her stomach somersaulted as the cabin tilted sharply once again. She gripped her seat, knuckles turning white. "I really, really hate flying."

At that moment, the snack cart rolled cheerfully down the aisle.

"Ooh, snacks!" chirped Sherry, snatching a bag of pretzels as it rumbled past. "Praise be to the gods of junk food."

Cameron shot Brie a sympathetic look. "If it's any consolation, if we flew higher, we might get shot at, and you might hate getting shot at more."

"Both are terrible," she replied, clenching her teeth as the plane banked again, throwing them all against their seat belts. "In case I haven't said it already, *everything's* terrible."

The cart rolled back the other way, raining a trail of peanuts.

Brie gripped her seatbelt, a silent prayer running through her mind. Her eyes flashed to Cameron, those chestnut locks whipping around his face. Sometimes, it was still hard to believe he was real. Now, it felt like something threatened to take him away every moment of every day. Today, it was this. Tomorrow, it might be fire-breathing camels.

*If we live to see tomorrow.*

"Are you catastrophizing?" Sherry called from across the plane.

Brie wrenched her eyes from the carpet, death-clenching her jaw. "Excuse me?"

"You're catastrophizing, aren't you? I can feel you all the way from here." Sherry bounced hard with the plane but kept a fixed smile. "Quit moping around, Weldon. We can handle a bumpy ride. You make accommodations for a private plane," she added.

Brie threw a look at the ceiling, fighting down bile.

"I wasn't catastrophizing," she said through gritted teeth, clutching the arms of her chair. "It's not a stretch to say, after everything that's tried to kill us lately, it would be a real shame if a simple plane crash was how we died."

Mike shot her a silent look, holding tight to his seatbelt.

"It won't be a plane crash that does me in," Sherry said, her eyes fixed on the window with a steely determination. It will be a dragon, or a sorcerer, or a hypoallergenic yak — something with flair. And even then, I'll find a way to beat it."

Brie snorted despite herself, forgetting, for a moment, that there was a decent chance they were about to fall out of the sky. She flashed her friend a sideways look.

*She's distracting me.*

"A hypoallergenic yak?"

Sherry's eyes widened to sudden attention. "Did I never tell you about that dream?"

At that moment, Tavi's voice crackled over the intercom. "Everyone can breathe again. Just a patch of rough air — nothing we can't handle."

Sherry threw her arms up in victory while Mike slid unnoticed to the ground and silently kissed the floor. Ephriam said something to Cameron in a language that had died with the Romans, and both of them laughed. Brie tried to smile along, but her pulse couldn't settle.

*Safe. For now.*

The cabin lights dimmed, and the rest settled back, closing their eyes and trying to get some rest as the plane droned on. Brie tried to do the same for a while, then leaned against the cool window, watching the clouds skim past.

*It's so peaceful up here. Why can't it just be peaceful?*

A peanut hit her in the face.

She looked over in surprise.

Sherry shot her a grin. "Want to talk about it?"

Brie offered a tired smile. "Is it that obvious?"

Sherry shifted to face her, softening her tone. "To me? Definitely."

Brie let out a slow breath, staring at her hands. "I can't shake the feeling that this is somehow bigger than what we signed up for. And Sher, we signed up for a hell of a lot." She met her friend's gaze. "When we started this whole quest, I thought we'd find some answers, close a few old doors, and hopefully pass this whole responsibility over to somebody immensely more qualified. But now? It feels like we're in over our heads. And *alone*. I mean, when did *quest* even become a valid part of our vocabulary? How? Why? And, why *us*?"

Sherry tilted her head with a thoughtful expression. "If it helps, you're not alone in feeling that way. I think we've all sensed it. The stakes are higher, and every turn feels like it's pushing us closer to some edge."

"Exactly." Brie sighed, glancing out the window again. "Plus, I feel like I'm missing something important — like there's a piece of the puzzle just out of reach. And I'm afraid that when I finally figure it out, it's going to be too late. I can't even say too late for what."

Sherry leaned forward, resting her chin in her hand. "It's okay to be afraid, Brie. You're human — or close enough to human for it to count. None of us know how this is going to end. But we're doing it for a good reason. And we can all rest safe in the assurance that none of us are doing this alone."

Brie's throat tightened. "I know that. But I think that's what scares me most — knowing that if something goes wrong, I'm putting everyone else at risk."

"None of that, now. Look," Sherry took another peanut from her snack pack and closed one eye, aiming her flicking finger at Brie's face. "This group? We chose this. Every last one of us knew what we were getting into when we joined you, and we're not exactly the 'sit back and relax' type. Can you open your mouth?"

Brie obliged, shutting her eyes a fraction of a second before a peanut hit her in the forehead.

Sherry continued as if nothing had happened, lining up another peanut. "So, let us carry this with you, okay? A burden shared is a burden halved. Or whatever Coco Chanel said."

Brie let out a short laugh. "I don't think it was—"

"All wise things were said by Coco Chanel," Sherry interrupted with a solemn nod.

Brie smiled, the weight on her chest loosening a bit as the next peanut glanced off her ear. "Thanks, Sherry. You know, if you weren't such a magnificent trauma nurse, you'd probably have a brilliant career as a psychologist if you wanted it."

Sherry looked at her, aghast. "Brianna, promise me you'll never say such a thing again. I have a reputation to maintain."

Brie bit back a grin when she was struck by a random thought. "Sher, what was that bellboy talking about before we left? Why did you rent out a storage unit in 1969?"

Sherry settled in her chair and opened her magazine with a self-satisfied smirk. "If you think I'm going to let all of that vintage couture go just because we need to travel to an ancient desert to find a mythical garden and fight a demonic camel, you're out of your mind. Everything's in storage, and it's all paid up for the next fifty years."

"Naturally." Brie let out a laugh, leaning back in her seat. The jet's engines hummed softly, and for the first time since they'd taken off, she felt herself begin to relax — a little.

They sat in comfortable silence. After a while, Brie somehow managed to drift off, closing her eyes and allowing the exhaustion of the day to take her.

She'd managed a few hours of dreamless sleep before she woke to a sky beginning to blush with the rosy fingers of dawn. Mike was hunched over, reading something, and Sherry was asleep beside him, resting in a tangle of affection and fatigue. Cameron and Ephriam were up near the cockpit, talking to Tavi and rifling through their backpacks filled with snacks and magical Elysian artifacts.

*This might be the strangest and most dangerous situation I've ever been in.*

*But at least I'm here with the best people I know.*

Ephriam let out an oath in Elysian.

Brie sighed.

*Well, "people" might be a stretch.*

She leaned back in her seat with a soft smile and rested her forehead against the cool window, gazing out at the lightening sky as the moon started to fade and the new morning sun cast its warmth over the landscape below. The hum of the jet's engines and the steady altitude gave her a momentary sense of security.

A flash of movement caught her eye, and she turned her attention back to Mike. Only then did she realize what he was reading. Only then did something register as being truly wrong.

He was hunched over *The History of the Time Seas*. His fingers pressed against the aged, leathery pages as if he were trying to feel the words themselves.

Brie unbuckled her seatbelt and made her way over to them. Mike didn't even look up. As she approached, she saw what had gripped his attention — the book was reacting to him. The ink rippled like water, shifting and curling as though it had a will of its own.

"Mike?" Brie said cautiously.

Sherry woke up and rubbed her eyes. "Babe?" she asked sleepily. "What is it?"

He still couldn't manage to tear his eyes away. "I think I found something," he muttered. "Or… something found me."

Sherry frowned. "That's not ominous at all."

Mike finally tore his gaze from the book, his face unusually pale. "Look at this." He turned the book toward them. The words had rearranged themselves, forming sentences that hadn't been there before.

Brie leaned in, reading aloud through Azrael's glass.

*"The lost are never truly gone. Those who tread the edge of time leave echoes, marks upon the sea. When called, they return to become the One."*

The ink shifted again, forming a new line.

*All things marked must be retrieved.*

Brie's breath hitched. "That doesn't sound good."

"No kidding," Mike muttered. "And that's not even the best part — I swear this page was blank before."

Sherry narrowed her eyes at the book. "You know what? I don't trust creepy, self-editing tomes. Maybe we should just put it down and—"

Before she could finish, the ink spread outward like black veins. The air around them seemed to pull, distorting for the briefest moment, like something unseen had brushed against the edges of their reality.

A slow, unsettling chill crept up Brie's spine. *Marked…*

She didn't know why, but she suddenly felt like something had just *seen* them.

Sherry made a command decision, reached over, and slammed the book shut. She snatched it away from her boyfriend with an irritated glare. "Michael Mitchell, we are standing in a glorified metal lobster, ten thousand feet in the air, propelled forward by nothing but flammable liquid and modern magic. Stop playing with cursed objects. Make yourself useful and whip up another round of daiquiris."

The policeman looked truly chagrined for a moment before deciding she was right and making his way back to the bar.

Sherry kept up the pretense of irritation until he'd turned away, then caught Brie's eye with a frightened expression that made her look suddenly very young. She swallowed. "So, what do you say — ignore this and start praying to the powers that be that we just get there in one piece?"

Brie lifted her shoulders in a *You've Got Me* gesture. "It's as good a plan as any."

Sherry nodded firmly as if this settled it, stashed the book on Mike's seat, and picked up a fashion magazine. She started thumbing through it ferociously, wrinkling the pages and belligerently trying to look interested.

Brie made her way back to her seat.

*It's just a book.*

*If we just stop reading it, it can't do anything to us.*

*Right?*

At that moment, she happened to look out the window at the plane's wing.

The glowing, red eyes of a wraith stared back at her.

# CHAPTER TWELVE

## Wraiths on a Plane

For a solitary moment, Brie froze perfectly still.

Suddenly, she was sixteen again, staring into those same bloody eyes, watching as an identical creature reached a shadowy hand into her mother's chest, stopping her heart and destroying her world. Tavi had told her more about them when they'd been lost in the woods — they were creatures that thrived in the liminal spaces between the living and the dead, predators that fed not on flesh but on fear and despair. And now, one of them was perched on the wing of their plane, staring at her as if it knew her as if it had been waiting for this moment its entire withered life.

For a few seconds, neither of them moved. The wraith tilted its head curiously as if amused by her silence. Then, without warning, it surged abruptly forward, its wispy, skeletal fingers stretching out, preparing to tear the metal straight off the plane.

Brie exploded back to life.

"Wraith!" she choked, whipping around to Sherry.

Sherry didn't even look up from her magazine. "That's a funny name for a drink. What's in it? Gin? Something exotic?"

Brie seized the arm of her chair in a death grip. "There's a wraith on the wing," she hissed. "A real one. Staring at us."

Sherry lowered her magazine and looked out the window before turning back to Brie. "You've been sleep-deprived for a while now. Perhaps it's time for another nap."

Brie's eyes flew back to the window. The wraith had vanished. She scanned the horizon, looking for any trace of it, any movement in the swirling morning air, but the wing was empty.

Sherry looked wary but sympathetic. "Brie, that book freaks me out too, but there's nothing there. Now, I love you, but if this is about your fear of flying, this isn't the time to—"

Before she could finish her sentence, the plane jerked violently to one side. The cabin lights flickered, and a distant, eerie screeching sound filled the air.

Brie's heart leapt into her throat.

*I've heard that sound before.*

"That," she gasped, pointing toward the window, "is not my imagination."

Sherry went very still before nodding once in agreement. "Point taken."

Brie was already unbuckling her seatbelt. Before she could even get to her feet, the plane lurched again, rattling the overhead compartments.

Mike appeared, sloshing around another pitcher of frozen bananas and booze, looking around in confusion and alarm. "Babe, what's going on?"

"Your study habits have come back to bite us. We've got company," Sherry muttered. "And it's not the friendly kind."

They didn't need to warn Ephriam. By the time Brie and Sherry reached the cockpit, he was standing on high alert, assessing the situation.

"They're here," he said simply.

"You don't say," Sherry hissed, casting a petrified look at the ceiling. "What gave it away? The ghostly wailing or the fact that we're about to drop out of the sky?"

Cameron appeared next to Ephriam, his face a shade paler than usual. "I hate wraiths," he muttered.

Mike materialized out of nowhere and put a protective arm around Sherry. "This isn't the first time you've encountered these creatures. There was that time back in Virginia, too. Why can't Sherry and I see them?"

"They're invisible to humans. You're not supposed to," Ephriam answered, casting Brie's pendant a look.

"You don't *want* to see them," Cameron added. "They look like…" He trailed off with a shudder. "Bad things children dream about at night."

Brie threw him a silent look.

*Welcome to my childhood.*

There was a gasp and a curse from the cockpit.

"They're going for the engines," Tavi's clipped voice sounded over the intercom. The plane dipped as she aimed the nose down to reach an even lower altitude. "If they take out the turbines, we'll be down in minutes."

"Wraiths don't usually attack randomly," Ephriam mused, his eyes flickering as he scanned the cabin. "Either they've been ordered to attack us, or they're drawn by something — or someone. And Brie's pendant is shielding her, which means—"

Tavianne let out a strangled scream.

The plane banked violently.

The sudden lurch sent Brie's stomach tumbling. Her hands shot out, gripping the nearest seat. Shouts of alarm filled the cabin. The overhead compartments rattled, and a few of their bags tumbled onto the floor.

In the cockpit, Tavianne sat rigid, her fingers twitching against her knees. Her eyes were unfocused, staring at nothing.

Sherry unbuckled and raced toward Tavi. Cameron was reaching around her to take the controls, trying desperately to steady the plane. Ephriam tried to squeeze his enormous frame into the cockpit to see what was wrong.

It all took less than a minute.

Then, everything became much, much worse.

The air snapped. Reality buckled.

The windows shuddered as an unnatural pressure filled the cabin, warping light and bending the world's edges. Brie's ears popped as if she'd been plunged into deep water. Something appeared in front of the cockpit windows where Tavi had been blankly staring. A patch of air rippled like fabric being pulled too tight directly in front of the plane.

And something moved behind it.

A figure of living shadow, stitched together from darkness, its form unstable — as if it couldn't decide what shape to take. The place where there should have been a face flickered in and out of existence. Where its eyes should have been, there was nothing but a void.

The creature spoke.

Not in English. Not in any human tongue.

The sound somehow coiled through the cabin, as though the shell of the plane did nothing to hinder it. It was foreign and ancient, syllables woven from a language that felt older than time itself.

Ephriam inhaled sharply. "That's the tongue of the High Angels," he said in a hushed voice. "It hasn't been spoken since before the Fall."

"You mean like… Lucifer's fall?" Brie's blood ran cold.

The creature moved. And yet, it didn't — it was like everything else, even time itself, was bending toward it. The plane felt like it was levitating completely still, hovering in the air, surrounded by wraiths. The rest of the world whipped around it at shocking speed.

Brie felt her stomach drop.

"What the hell is that?" Sherry shouted.

The thing warped and pulsed into too many shapes to count — some human, some like a giant serpent, some like a flock of birds trying to shelter from a cruel wind. Then, its head tilted as if listening. Its mouth — if it could be called a mouth — stretched open.

*"Marked…"*

The voice was layered. Distorted. *Wrong.* It sounded in Brie's head, not her ears.

Tavianne gasped. Her hands flew to her chest as though something inside her was responding. Her body jerked like a marionette, caught in some unseen force.

The thing *laughed* — a dry, scraping sound.

The lights flickered.

Cameron moved on instinct, grabbing Tavi's hand and wrenching her around. "Tavi!" he yelled. "Come back to us right now!" He tried desperately to wrestle her out of the captain's chair. Ephriam helped, lowering her to the ground as Cameron took her place. Tavi's breath came in short, ragged gasps, fingers clutching at her shirt as if something inside her was burning.

Mike had raced back to his seat and was gripping the book, frantically flipping through the ancient text. "There's gotta be something else in here. Some way to—" He stopped abruptly, landing on one of the only uncensored passages at the end of the blacked-out chapter. He froze. "Wait."

Ephriam spun toward him. "Mike, *don't!*"

Mike's eyes flew over the ancient text. "This says there's a way to bind something to the Time Seas. To send it back."

Brie felt a wave of nausea roll over her. "Mike, you don't even know what that means—"

Ephriam moved to stop him. "That's a *binding phrase!* If you don't know exactly what you're dealing with, you could send *yourself* through instead!"

But Mike was already reading the passage aloud, sounding out the Elysian words as best he could, finishing strong, shouting the unfamiliar word at the thing that had invaded their space.

For a moment, nothing happened.

Then, the air *fractured*.

Through the patch of broken air, Brie saw beyond the sky to an endless, storm-ridden ocean of fractured time, shifting and breaking. Within its depths, she caught glimpses of things moving. Watching. *Waiting.*

Tavianne collapsed.

The entity let out a shriek as its form began unraveling. It fought back, its amorphous body resisting, clawing, screaming. The moment stretched, the tension unbearable. Then, with a final, guttural howl, it was ripped from existence.

But the plane was already lost.

The final blow had been struck. They were falling.

Fast.

And a dozen wraiths still swirled around the plane, their twisted, shadowy faces no longer laughing.

Blind to every other concern, Ephriam rushed to Tavi's side, speaking in Elysian, trying to revive her. Sherry, ever the triage nurse, turned in a slow circle, assessing the damage, before coming to a stop facing Cameron. He was pressing buttons, seemingly at random, and pulling up on the controls with all his might — an action that was leveling them out far slower than any of them would have liked.

Sherry swallowed. "I have a fun and exciting question. Can anybody else fly the plane? Anybody who's ever, literally once, successfully landed one?"

Mike's hand shot up into the air. "Oh! I used to do that on PlayStation all the time!"

Sherry pinched the bridge of her nose. "I'd say you've done enough, don't you think?"

A metallic screech came from outside the window.

"It won't matter if we can land if those wraiths rip up apart while we're still in the air. We need a plan!" Brie stared around in fright. "Does anybody have any ideas? Anything at all?"

Sherry's eyes flew wide. "Wait, I have something!" She held up a small pouch and opened it, pouring the remaining Elysian freeze spells into her hand.

Ephriam lunged toward her before he could stop himself. "Careful!" he barked, gingerly placing the orbs back in their pouch. "Remember what happened the last time!" He ignored Sherry's ensuing glare and continued. "I agree we don't have another choice, but precision is key. We'll need to avoid hitting the plane itself or we'll plummet like a stone." He shouted toward the cockpit. "Cameron, can you get this thing on auto-pilot?"

Cameron didn't answer, just threw an incredulous look behind him. "I'll see what I can do, but give me a minute."

Ephriam took his meaning. "Right. Brie, you help me take the front door, then I'll take the rear." He wrestled Tavi into the front seat and buckled her in as quickly as possible before giving Brie a handful of the freezing orbs. "You two," he barked at Sherry and Mike. "Clear this cabin, get in the back, and get ready to help me. And hold on to something."

They obeyed and started hurrying to the back of the plane, picking up their fallen supplies as they went, thrusting them back into their packs and out of the way.

A high-pitched screech sliced through the air, like something tearing through metal.

Brie could feel the pressure in the cabin shift. Her ears immediately plugged, and she yawned quickly, trying to reopen them.

*We don't have much time.*

"We need to hurry," she said hoarsely as Ephriam placed two hands on the bar holding the door in place.

"Yes," Ephriam agreed. He gave her an indecipherable look before adding, "Don't fail. And don't die."

The plane shuddered again, this time so violently that Brie had to grab onto the nearest seat to balance herself. They pitched abruptly downward at an alarming angle, dropping altitude and cutting through the dawn when they saw them. At least five wraiths were hovering just beyond the wing, matching the plane's speed. Their smoke-like forms swirled. Every few seconds, one would swoop closer, claws tearing at the metal as they sought to breach the engines. Their lips were pulled back. Brie could have sworn they were laughing.

"They're on the wings!" she shouted over the roaring chaos.

Cameron shouted from the cockpit. "We're almost low enough to open the doors."

"We'd all better hope so," came Ephriam's less-than-reassuring answer. "Because it's now or literally never. Everybody hold on." In the back, Mike threw Sherry into a chair and buckled her in.

Ephriam turned back to Brie. "Here goes nothing. On three, two, one!"

He opened the hatch, and all hell broke loose.

It felt as if a hurricane filled the plane within the space of a second. Ephriam fought against the rush of air and lobbed the first orb out the door. It collided with the nearest wraith. Instantly, the creature froze mid-motion, its shadowy form suspended in time, and disappeared. "One down," he shouted, already preparing the next orb.

Cameron fought his way out of the cockpit. Glancing behind him, Brie saw that he'd used his belt to tie the controls into position. He stood beside Ephriam. "I've got this," he shouted. "Go get the other wing!"

Ephriam nodded and handed him half the remaining freeze orbs before wrestling his way through the insanity to the back of the plane and opening the emergency hatch.

The storm inside the cabin became somehow infinitely worse.

Within a minute, Ephriam took out two out wraiths on the other wing. Brie, Sherry, and Mike watched breathlessly as the lethal game of celestial paintball took down five more until only two remained, one on each wing. Cameron's aim was spot on, and another wraith froze in place and disappeared into the sky behind them.

The Elysian prince turned with a triumphant look, but his face fell when he saw the expression on Ephriam's face. "What is it?" he shouted over the roar.

All heads turned to Ephriam as he told them, "I'm out."

A lone wraith remained on the wing. Its mouth twisted in a horrific approximation of a smile as it reached a skeletal hand to the metal and tore off a strip as easily as one tears paper from a notebook.

A cloud of fuel poured forth.

"Oh my God!" screamed Sherry. "What is that?"

A vapor trail misted out from the torn wing. Particles of jet fuel caught the early morning light, shimmering like rainbows in the sky, a toxic constellation spelling their doom.

"How do we get to it now?" Brie screamed.

"I'll go," Ephriam said grimly, looking out as the wraith continued peeling metal strips from the plane.

"Don't be ridiculous!" Sherry shouted. "You'll be killed!"

"Better me than all of you," he fired back. "Once it gets bored, that thing will open up this cabin like a tin can and make a meal of you all. Somebody get me a rope."

"Not on my watch, sir. Stand aside." All eyes turned to Mike, who shoved his way to the open hatch. "Everybody, sit down, strap in, and *hold on*." The others took one look at his face and obeyed. Cameron buckled Brie in next to Tavianne, whose eyelids were just starting to flutter, then buckled himself in as well.

Before anyone truly had a chance to question Mike, he clutched the nearest seat for dear life, aimed a flare gun at the shimmering fuel, closed one eye, and fired.

The explosion was deafening. The shredded wing blew into a million pieces.

The plane jerked to the left. The remaining wing was perpendicular to the ground for a heart-stopping moment before the jet rolled completely upside down. Brie's hair hung below her. Cameron gripped her hand in silent terror. Mike was on the ceiling, attempting to claw his way into the seat next to Sherry. Tavi suddenly regained consciousness and let out a stream of oaths and curses. But the one who had Brie truly frightened to the marrow was Ephriam. She'd never seen the Elysian warrior scream before.

In a last-ditch effort, with a final screeching expletive, Tavi ripped off her seatbelt, clawed her way across the cabin's ceiling and into the cockpit, and pulled on the controls with all her might. The plane flipped right-side up.

A thunk behind her told Brie that Mike had landed back on the floor, while the steady stream of curses in front of her told her that Tavi was tying herself back into the captain's chair. Her stomach lurched as the plane began plummeting to earth. The engines sputtered twice and then died, leaving them in an eerie silence, except for the sound of wind whistling through the cabin like a reed in a hurricane.

They were going down.

"How long before we hit?" Brie shouted, though she wasn't sure she wanted to know.

"Minutes." Tavi wrestled the controls, a vein in her neck straining as she tried desperately to pull the nose up, to no avail. "Brace yourselves. This is going to be ugly."

Cameron practically crushed Brie to his chest, wrapping his protective arms around her, stronger than any seatbelt.

Brie's mind raced. They were crashing — really crashing. Not some metaphorical fall; this was actual, plummeting-to-your-death, ground-rushing-up-to-meet-you, crashing.

Ephriam yelled over the roar of the wind. "Tuck low and brace. If we're lucky, we'll survive."

"*If we're lucky?*" Sherry repeated, her voice several octaves higher than usual.

"Focus," Ephriam shouted. "It's about survival now. Nothing more."

Tavi attempted to glide as the plane continued to drop, the wind howling around them as they fell toward the vast expanse of the Jordanian desert. Brie squeezed her eyes shut, gripping Cameron so tightly her fingers ached.

The earth seemed to gain speed as it rushed up to meet them until suddenly, it was there.

"Hold on!" Tavi shouted.

The plane shuddered, and with a violent crack, its belly hit against one of the columns of granite that spired from the desert. A terrible metallic screech ripped through the air. Brie felt her heart drop as she saw Sherry, Mike, and Ephriam clinging to the seats near the emergency exit at the rear. The walls around them ripped apart, and their half of the plane tore away with a sickening, shredding sound.

"Sherry!" Brie screamed as her friend's face disappeared into a cloud of dust and flying rock, mouth open in a cry she would never hear. If it hadn't been for Cameron holding her thrashing body close to his own, Brie would have jumped out after her.

The front half of the plane dipped into a canyon, and the ground flew up to meet them, a blur of sand and rock.

The last thing Brie remembered was a sensation of weightlessness as the plane slammed into the earth. A blinding white energy burst from her pendant, encircling them all in a sphere of star-bright light.

Then everything went black.

# CHAPTER THIRTEEN

## Exodus

Brie was floating.

At first, she thought it was the eerie weightlessness of falling, that breathless space in the seconds before the inevitable crash. But this was different. The panic wasn't there. Instead, there was a quiet stillness, as though the universe had pressed pause, allowing her to drift, suspended in the void. She couldn't tell if she was dreaming or trapped in some half-conscious limbo. The sensation was strangely serene, like a reprieve from the chaos.

And then, slowly, her surroundings began to change.

A soft light seeped into the darkness, not the harsh, glaring light of reality, but something warmer, more welcoming. It enveloped her, cradling her like sunlight filtered through the leaves of an ancient tree. The air was fragrant, carrying the scent of flowers she couldn't name but felt she'd known all her life.

She blinked, her senses slowly returning.

*Where am I?*

She sat up as the landscape came into focus — a lush, untouched forest clearing bathed in golden hues. It felt ancient and timeless like a place that had existed before the world knew names for things. The trees towered above her, branches swaying gently in a breeze she couldn't feel. After a moment, she heard the splashing sound of water against rocks and turned to see the waterfall from her childhood, her family's favorite spot.

From the shadows between the trees, it appeared.

A fox.

It padded toward her silently, its paws leaving no mark on the earth. The creature was both familiar and strange. Its fur caught the light, shifting between deep auburn and silver as it moved like it was woven from the essence of dusk and dawn.

But what stood out most were its eyes.

One was a striking green, the color of life and growth, like the deepest part of a forest after rain. The other was a piercing blue, bright as the clearest sky, but cold — unnervingly so. They seemed to carry entirely different energies — one warm and inviting, the other distant and sharp.

The fox stopped a few paces away, locking its gaze onto hers. It studied her with a depth that no animal should possess, its head slightly tilted as though assessing her.

"You need to wake up."

Brie froze, heart, skipping a beat. The fox had spoken. Its voice wasn't a sound in the air but something that resonated inside her mind, like a thought not entirely her own but one she recognized all the same. It was smooth and vibrant, young and old at the same time.

"I'm dreaming, right?" she whispered, though the words felt heavy, as if speaking them anchored her to this place.

The fox's mismatched eyes narrowed slightly as if it found her question quaint, amusing. "Does it matter?" it replied. "Dream, vision, reality — they all converge in the end. What matters is that you are needed. *I* need you to wake up."

Brie shook her head, confused. "Who are you? Where am I?"

The fox took a few graceful steps closer, the soft grass parting under its paws. "You're asking the wrong questions, Brianna Weldon," it said cryptically. "But for now, you may call me an old friend. One you've yet to meet."

Her mind struggled to make sense of this, but something about the fox's voice soothed her racing thoughts. There was something undeniably familiar about it, as though this creature had been with her all along, watching from some distant place she couldn't quite see.

"You've been asleep too long, Brianna," the fox continued, its tone growing more urgent. "The others will need you soon. And, I must find you."

"Find me?" she echoed. "Aren't you already here?"

The fox's eyes gleamed. "Not in the way that matters. Not yet. There are places we must go — places hidden from even the oldest of minds. And you and I, we must walk together to reach them."

She shook her head, dazed. "What places? Where are you trying to take me?"

The fox turned, its eyes shifting toward the trees as if looking at something she couldn't yet see. "The *Garden.*" As he spoke, the world around them shifted again. The trees stretched taller, their trunks becoming impossibly wide, their branches thick with leaves that shimmered. And beyond the clearing, just past the forest's edge, a new sight appeared — gates. Tall, majestic, wrought from gold, and gleaming with an ethereal light.

Brie's breath caught in her throat. The gates stood impossibly high, entwined with vines that bloomed with flowers, unlike anything she had ever seen. Beyond them gleamed a soft radiance as though the very air on the other side was filled with something ancient and pure.

"You must find it. We must find it." There was a slight edge to the fox's voice, one she hadn't noticed before. "I cannot hold this form for long."

She could feel something shifting within her, a deep pull toward the gates, like some unseen force was drawing her forward. "What's beyond the gates?" she whispered.

The fox looked at her, eyes gleaming in the light. "That is for you to discover. But be warned — every step toward the Garden brings you closer to what you seek, and to what seeks you."

Her blood ran cold. "What seeks me?"

The fox didn't answer immediately. Instead, it took a few steps back, fading into the shadows as the light began to dim. "Wake up, Brie," it whispered, its voice like the rustle of leaves in the wind. "Wake up, or you will never reach the Garden, and neither of us will ever be saved. And tell him—"

She reached out a hand to the fox, trying to keep them together.

"Tell who?" she called. "Tell him what?"

"Wake up!"

The gates grew hazy, dissolving into the air. The light dimmed, and the ground beneath her feet began to slip away. The peaceful warmth of the dream ebbed, replaced by the cold, hard sensation of reality clawing its way back.

Brie woke with a sharp gasp, her body jerking upward as if pulled from deep water. The oppressive heat of the desert slammed into her all at once, along with pain — a sharp, insistent ache in her ribs. Her head pounded like a hammer on stone. The last few moments were a blur: the wraiths, the explosion, and the wounded plane's sickening drop to the desert floor.

For a second, all she could hear was the ringing in her ears, the world around her reduced to harsh, scattered light and distorted sounds. But as her senses slowly began to recalibrate, the reality of their situation began to settle in.

They'd gone down.

Her heart stuttered.

*The others.*

She scrambled to her feet, ignoring the burning protest of her muscles as she forced herself to move. The desert seemed infinite. Dunes rose like waves in every direction. Enormous rock formations and cliffs jutted from the sand. But it wasn't the endless labyrinth that held her attention — it was the debris. The wreckage lay scattered across the ground like pieces of a broken puzzle, smoke rising in thin, dark tendrils.

It struck her suddenly, with the force of a comet.

*That isn't enough debris.*

She sucked in a breath of punishingly hot air as she realized she was only looking at the mangled remains of the front of the plane. The back was nowhere to be seen.

Her breath came in short, desperate bursts as she scanned the desert, her eyes wild.

*Where are they? Where's—*

"Cameron!" she screamed, voice raw and hoarse. "Sherry! Anybody!"

No response.

Her heart hammered in her ears as panic seized her. She couldn't lose them. Not after everything they'd been through. They couldn't just—

"Brie!" a voice called out, ragged and urgent.

She whirled to see Cameron stumbling through the wreckage, coughing violently, his face streaked with dirt and sweat. A wave of relief surged through her, but it was immediately followed by a burst of fear.

*What about the others?*

"Cameron!" She rushed toward him, grabbing his arms as soon as they were close enough to touch. His skin felt too hot like he'd been standing too close to a fire. She grabbed his chin without thinking, checking the dilation of his eyes. "Are you okay? Have you seen the others? They could be—"

"I'm fine," he cut her off gently. He started to say something else, then registered the grip of her fingers. "What are you doing?"

"I'm…" She trailed off, slowly lowering her hand.

*What am I doing?*

*What the hell is happening right now?*

They had been in a plane crash. Her bones were still trembling.

She couldn't see the rest of her friends.

"Cam, I don't…"

The angel was shaken to the core, but he grabbed her with surprising strength. In hindsight, perhaps he was catching her. A few seconds went unaccounted for before she found herself standing in his sudden grip. His eyes were bright as ocean jewels in the desert sunlight as they locked onto hers.

"We're going to find them, Brie. I promise." His gaze flitted over her forehead, clouding with concern. "But you need to slow down. You're hurt."

*I don't care.*

"I don't care." She shook her head, wiping manically at her face with the back of her hand. There was a pain budding in her shoulder. A trickle of blood ran down from behind her earlobe, where Zadkiel's gift had pierced into her neck. Her bottom lip was sliced. "I have to make sure they're okay. They have to be okay."

The words were looping in her mind, catching on a rhythm. Her knees locked into place, and suddenly she was standing, suddenly she was walking — or *trying* to walk. A stabbing pain shot down from her hairline, and she thought she might be as hurt as Cameron said.

*They have to be okay.*

Her angel held up his hands, ready to vanish her pains in a moment, then suddenly remembered himself and lowered them back to his sides. A shock of betrayal jolted through him like a slap from on high, and for a solitary moment, every part of him went still.

Then he drew in a breath and reached for her hands instead.

"We're going to find them," he said softly, "you and I, together."
He dipped his head, catching her gaze. "We're going to find them
together, Brianna. And this is going to be alright."

She clutched onto his fingers, fighting the hysteria rising in her chest.

"But how could it be? In the whole desert…?" Her voice choked
silent, cracking with the heat and the dust. "I can't breathe in this.
Cam, I can't—"

"No, no," he shook his head calmly, never breaking her gaze. "We're
not going to do that right now. Right now is when we pull together.
Right now is when we find them."

She stared over the smoldering heaps of rubble in the distance, nodding without actually hearing. Her lips were muttering a silent mantra.
He stepped into her line of sight.

His beloved had devoted her life to battling death on a daily basis
in a hospital, and that was before she'd signed up to play celestial
chess against the fates. But it was a different thing entirely — to
plummet out of the sky, falling like a rock from the heavens. Fortu-
nately for the girl in question, this wasn't his first time battling death,
either.

"Brie," he caught her gaze, "this is when we find them."

She gripped at his sleeves, desperate for it to be true, and pulled in
a breath, finding her footing. "They need us."

Their hands entwined as he answered her. "Yes, they do."

The heat was unbearable.

Brie thought she'd educated herself from the snippets of Cameron's
book she'd stolen glances at on the plane. She'd known it was going to
be hot. It was the desert.

But this? This was something else entirely.

"We need to slow down," she panted, grabbing weakly for Cameron's shirt as they trudged across the scorching sand. "I can barely see where I'm going."

It wasn't just the temperature; it was the disorientation. With every step, the ground swam dizzily in front of her. Granted, that might have been the head wound.

She was trying not to think about that too much.

An arm wrapped suddenly around her waist, tipping her back upright as she began to lose balance. Since the moment they started looking for the others, Cameron had been glued to her side.

"Let me carry you," he urged softly, the same as he'd done a dozen times before.

She shook her head without looking, trudging onward into the sun.

"You can't carry anybody. Your arm basically got pulled out of its socket. And besides," she threw a murderous look at the sky, "it would only make things hotter."

They carried onwards, searching the debris for anything that might resemble their friends. After seeing the destruction of the first few piles of wreckage, they'd each secretly amended their initial parameters to include anything that resembled pieces.

*How could they not be in pieces?*

They'd been torn out of the sky by monsters who made ribbons of their plane.

They'd spoken less and less after each empty search, forcing themselves painfully toward the next pile. But the sun was scorching in the sky, and those steps were getting more challenging. Each one in the thick sand felt like wading through a swamp.

*Just a little bit further. We'll find something at the next one.*

"My arm is fine," Cameron said yet again, forbidding it to be otherwise. There had been a frightening tear, followed by a nova of pain, but it was nothing that a little stroll through the desert couldn't cure. "You're stumbling more with every step, Brie, let me help you—"

"Look!" she interrupted, pointing wildly. "I see something!"

It was barely there — a hint of fabric, the sole of a boot. It wasn't until they rounded a bend in the canyon that she could identify the half-buried figure beneath what might once have been a cockpit.

"Tavi," she breathed, her heart lurching. She sprinted forward, falling to her knees beside the scorching metal. She was afraid to shake her. She didn't know where to touch — every inch of her was covered in blood. "Tavi! Tavi, wake up!"

The Elsyian's face was deathly pale, her lovely features arranged into an expression of restful sleep. With a sickly look of dread, Cameron reached down to take her pulse, then jerked his hand back again as a current of electricity shook them both from the inside out.

"Oh my God!" Brie gasped, leaping backward. "Well, at least we know she's alive."

Alive, but clearly not in a good state. Not only was she drenched in the blood of what looked to be the world's most violent head wound — half of her body was still trapped under the plane.

"No, no, no," Brie muttered, hands shaking as she tried to pry off the metal. It seemed an impossible task. "Cameron, help me!"

He was already beside her, his bruised fingers gripping tightly as they heaved together, straining against the weight. After what felt like an eternity, they managed to lift it enough for Brie to pull Tavi free, dragging her a safe distance away as Cameron let go with a gasp, and the wreckage let out an ominous creaking sound.

Brie looked down at the unconscious Elysian, afraid to touch her. Tavi had been having trouble controlling her electricity since their collision with Baal, but the head wound had taken things to another level. Every time she managed to settle, she'd convulse once again, losing more and more blood each time.

"Tavi," she whispered, throwing caution to the wind and cradling her friend's head in her lap. "Come on, please wake up."

Cameron knelt beside them, his hand resting on Tavi's forehead.

"She's alive," he said softly. "But barely. And she's not going to last long if we don't get this bleeding under control." He was already stripping off his shirt, pressing it against the wound. When the electricity came again, he braced against it with a hissing breath.

Tavi stirred weakly against the pressure, her eyes fluttering open. She blinked a few times, disoriented, before her gaze focused on Brie. "Oh!" Her voice was pained and hoarse, but her face broke into a beautiful smile. "Thank God. It's you."

"Tavi!" Brie cried, nearly breathless with relief. "Yes, yes, it's me. Are you alright? You've got us all so worried."

"Of course I'm alright. Never… better." Tavi slumped down again with a grimace before lifting a tentative hand to her head. For a split second, she merely looked surprised before glancing up again with an apologetic smile. "Guess he got me pretty good, didn't he?"

Brie froze in confusion. "Who do you mean? Who got you?"

"That new recruit. I tell him every time…" Tavi tried once more to sit up. "*Every* time, not to use the edged lance when we spar, but he never listens." She closed her eyes and brought a hand to her forehead. "Fetch me some of that potion, won't you, love? The one I hate — the one that tastes like tin." She made a face. "And don't tell Raphael I needed it. That man needs no encouragement."

Brie sat very still, staring at Tavi with a look of dread.

Tavi's eyes fluttered open, and she smiled with a puzzled look. "What is it, Arafel? Oh!" She interrupted herself, clapping eyes on Cameron for the first time. "Kid! By the stars! What are you doing here? Your father will be—" She broke off with a blank look and fell silent, before turning back to Brie. "Arafel, do you think you could bring me some of that potion? The one I hate? But don't tell Raphael I needed it. It'll just go to his head." A jolt of electricity shook through her, leaving her in a daze. "Arafel?" she asked again.

"Y— yes, of course," Brie said quickly, flashing a tight smile. "I'll go get it. Just hang on a minute, alright?"

Tavi gave a weak smile. "I'm not going anywhere."

Cameron stared, silent for a frozen moment, then shifted his friend into a sitting position, resting her against what was left of the cockpit. "Is that any better?"

She nodded, putting on a brave smile, which cracked the moment she tried to sit up straight. She slumped back, caught her breath, then pointed an accusatory finger at Cameron as though seeing him for the first time. "Kid! What are you doing here? You need to go talk to your father right away. And if you see that new recruit, tell him that if I ever learn his name, he's in a lot of trouble."

Brie swallowed hard, fighting back tears. "Absolutely," she said, reaching for Cameron's wrist. "We'll tell him." Without another word, she pulled him a few paces away before turning desperately. "What should we do?"

"I have no idea." Cameron's face looked exactly the way she felt. Shaken to the core. "The pendant?"

Brie's hand shot up to the stone hanging from the chain on her neck. As soon as her fingertips touched it, her hope ran cold. After the battle with Baal, when it had healed her friends, it had been warm to the hand. Right now, even in the desert heat, it felt like ice.

But it was still their best shot.

She nodded and walked back to Tavi, who smiled at her, puzzled. "Back so soon?" the Elysian asked. "I wasn't sure if we had any."

"Sorry," Brie replied, "but do you mind if I try something real quick?"

"Of course."

Brie came close and held her pendant to Tavi's temple, bowing her head and praying ardently for healing. After a couple of minutes, Tavi pulled away with a painful laugh. "Listen, I appreciate the thought, but this is a strange time to be giving me jewelry."

Brie's hands dropped to her side. "No, of course. Silly of me. I'll go fetch Raphael's potion now."

She walked back to Cameron in time to see a flash of genuine panic before he carefully cleared his face. "We need to stabilize her," he said, his voice low but controlled. "I think if we try to move her now, it'll make things worse. And we need to keep her cool."

*Cool. Right.*

Brie looked around at the endless desert and the radiating off the sand. Even in the shade, it was easily over a hundred degrees. "How do we do that out here? We don't have water, we don't have—"

"Give me a minute." He ducked inside what remained of the cockpit, scrambling through the twisted metal and ruined controls before emerging again, triumphantly holding up one of their battered backpacks. "We have this." Cameron rummaged inside and pulled out a small, sleek flask. He unscrewed the cap and handed it to Brie. "Thank God Mike packed our bags," he said with relief. "Always prepared."

She took the flask, hands shaking, and poured a small amount of water onto her hands. She dabbed it on Tavi's forehead and tried to cool her down. The action felt futile in the scorching heat, but it was something. Tavi closed her eyes.

"I think I should stay with her," Cameron said quietly. "She seems to… I mean, she knows me as myself right now. You'll need to find the others." He pointed to the nearest sand dune, a veritable mountain with a surface that shifted in the wind like water under a breeze. "Get to the top and look for reflections, anything that could be metal or glass."

She nodded and took a step, but his hand flashed out to grab her.

"And if you start feeling dizzy or faint, you're going to call for me," he commanded quietly, holding her gaze. "You're going to shout my name until I find you. Swear it."

She nodded again. "I swear."

Another jolt of electricity rippled across Tavi's body, and Brie handed back the flask, straightening the tattered remains of her clothes.

"I'll be quick," she promised. "Just keep her stable."

He flashed a weak smile, trying not to shake. "Simple as that."

The climb felt endless. Every step through the sand was more difficult than the last, as the heat pressed down like a physical weight. Every twenty feet or so, she stopped, took off one sneaker and then the other, and poured a full cup of desert back onto the dune. Then, she'd start the process over again. At times, it felt pointless, but she forced herself to keep moving, summoning the strength through sheer force of will.

*I'm going to find them.*

She finally reached the summit, panting and coughing, the arid desert wind sucking all moisture from her throat as she steadied herself to look around. She'd always imagined the desert as a vast, flat expanse filled with nothing but sand and relentless sun as far as the eye could see. Instead, she was looking at an intricate pattern of granite cliffs, some with passages in between, jutting out of the rolling mountains of sand. Everywhere there was even a hint of shade, plants grew. She recognized white broom, yarrow, and wormwood from a hazy recollection of a children's book about different habitats on Earth. But as fast as the images came, they faded in the light of her obvious problem:

*If it were flat, at least I'd be able to see them.*

*How am I supposed to find them in all this?*

There were too many canyons, too many twists and turns in the rock, the dark side of too many dunes to explore. If one of the others was hurt like Tavi, she might never get to them in time to help. She turned this way and that, desperate to glimpse anything that seemed out of place.

*Nothing.*

Without a better idea, she took a deep breath and started yelling at the top of her lungs, calling out names.

*Nothing.*

There was only the echo of her own voice bouncing off all that gorgeous desolation and coming back to her empty.

*Please, please let them be alive.*

*Please help me find them.*

She pulled in another breath, prepared to shout again, but just when despair threatened to strangle all hope and reason, she saw it: a glint of sunlight off metal. With a strangled cry, she started racing toward it, waving her arms and half-slipping into the sand. When she reached level ground, she took off, sprinting toward the light, hope propelling her forward at a speed that defied her human frame. She reached the place where she'd seen the reflection, only to find a twisted metal shard sticking out of the sand like a flagpole that had long since lost its banner. Raising her eyes, she saw the tail end of the plane scattered in pieces and a familiar figure half-hidden in the wreckage.

"Ephriam!" she shouted, recognizing him as she got closer.

He didn't stand, just turned toward her, scowling but composed as always, golden eyes flashing in the harsh sunlight. "You're alive," he called back dryly, as if surviving a plane crash was a minor inconvenience. "That's surprising."

"Well you commanded me to survive," she snapped, sharper than she intended. Satisfied that the surly Elysian was alert and responsive, she shouted, "Have you seen Mike and Sherry?"

He nodded toward a nearby rock formation. "I heard their voices over there."

Brie's chest tightened as she reached him. "Why haven't you gone to them?"

He casually gestured down at his leg. She looked down and gasped. The Elysian had tied a makeshift tourniquet above a twisted pole of metal that impaled him straight through his thigh.

"Oh my God, Ephriam! Hold still." She knelt to examine the wound. "Under normal circumstances, I'd say we should leave this in, but in light of the whole pendant with healing powers thing, it might be okay if we—" She jerked back suddenly, clapping a hand over her mouth. "What the hell are you doing?!"

Without batting an eye, he'd reached down and unceremoniously yanked the metal from his leg. Glowing blood gushed forth and pooled on the sand. His expression barely changed. If it weren't for a slight grunt, she would never have known anything happened at all.

"Damnit, Ephriam, of all the — don't move!" She leaned close and repeated the procedure that she had used after the battle with Baal. This time, the pendant warmed under her hand as she pressed it to his skin and prayed. Before her very eyes, his leg knit itself back together, the muscles and fascia reweaving themselves in a macabre dance. She took her hands away and let out a deep sigh of relief when his thigh appeared whole and intact. Then she punched him in the arm, a decision which hurt her hand more than it so much as fazed him. "Ephriam, you would be a *terrible* trauma nurse. Never remove what's impaling you!"

He ignored her, eyes narrowed as he scanned the horizon. "We need to regroup. If we don't start moving soon, the heat will kill us before anything else does."

"I know," she said, wiping sweat from her brow. "But Tavi's hurt."

He shot her a sharp look. "How serious?"

"Very," she admitted, thinking back with a shudder. "She was in the cockpit, and I'm worried she took the brunt of it. Cameron's trying to stabilize her. Ephriam... She thinks I'm Arafel. And the pendant wouldn't help."

He looked shocked for a moment, absorbing her words before his expression steeled once more. "We'll need water, shade, and a way to signal for help. There must be something we can use."

She swallowed the panic that threatened to rise. They were stranded, injured, and exposed in the middle of the desert, but Ephriam was right — they had to survive.

There was no other choice.

◆    ◆    ◆

Brie walked beside Ephriam, every breath a struggle against the oppressive heat. They moved quickly, scanning for any sign of life. She could feel the tension building within her, the gnawing worry that they wouldn't find Mike and Sherry in time.

"There." He pointed toward a crumpled section of the cabin.

She squinted against the harsh light and saw movement — two figures, stumbling toward them. Sherry was the first to come into view, covered in dust, features creased with fatigue. Beside her was Mike, limping slightly, his face pale but determined.

"Sherry! Mike!" Brie called out, breaking into a run.

Sherry looked up, eyes widening in relief as she called back. "Oh, thank God, you're alive. For a minute there, I thought we were the last two idiots standing." Brie threw her arms around her best friend, dizzy with relief. Sherry immediately winced. "Easy. I'm pretty sure my ribs are being held together by hope and sarcasm at this point."

Brie pulled back, gaze shifting to Mike. "Are you okay?"

He gave a weak smile, having already made up his mind not to scream. "I've had better days. But I'll live."

"Everyone's alive," Ephriam interjected. "For now. But we need to regroup. Tavianne is injured, and we don't have much time before this heat takes us down."

"Cameron's with her over there," Brie added, nodding over her shoulder at the dune she'd just scaled. "We need to get back to them."

"Right," Sherry muttered, brushing the dust from her clothes as best she could. "Let's get moving. Before anything else decides to fall out of the sky."

◆    ◆    ◆

They made their way back through the scattered remains of the plane, gathering what was left of their packs along the way. When they finally reached the small patch of shade where Tavi lay, Cameron was still beside her, hand resting on her shoulder as he spoke quietly in their native tongue. He looked up as the group approached, face lighting up with relief. "You found them." He reached for Brie's hand. "I knew you would."

"How is she?" Brie asked, giving his palm a squeeze and nodding to the woman by his side.

"Hey, love!" Tavi's face lit up when she saw Brie. "I was just telling the kid about that time we raced chariots in Antioch. Do you remember that?"

Brie knelt beside her, forcing a smile. "Remind me."

"Well you cheated, of course! Mounting a Z3 motor onto an ancient Assyrian chariot. You gave it a steering wheel and hooked up the horse trailer you'd stolen from that rancher in Montana! Ephriam, come on — you remember, don't you?"

Ephriam knelt beside her, too. His smile did not reach his eyes. "Arafel pointed out that nowhere in the rules was it stipulated that the horses needed to be pulling the chariot, and thus won on a technicality."

Tavi raised a hand in a *come on now* gesture and flashed Brie a grin. "You are a knave, a cad, a thief, and a hooligan to boot. I don't know why I put up with you."

Sherry covered her mouth as Brie attempted to smile in return. "I suppose I just don't deserve my luck."

The weight of the comment hung heavy on the moment, until Ephriam reached out and grabbed Tavi's hand. "What about the time you tricked her into bringing home a pocketful of sea snakes and failed to mention the surprise inspection?"

Brie turned away, swallowing in a fruitless attempt to dislodge the lump in her throat. She left the Elysians talking and walked back to the others. Sherry and Mike looked on, unsure what to say.

"It's getting worse," Cameron said, voice tinged with worry. "If we don't do something soon…"

Sherry nodded gruffly. "We will. First, let's see what we have."

Mike heaved a conjoined pair of luxury cabin seats out of the sand, righting them and sitting down heavily. He winced as he examined a tear in his pants. Brie could see the skin beneath was bruised and swollen. Sherry came over to examine it as he spoke. "We collected as many of these as we could find." He gestured to the small pile of ragged packs beside him. "I think we got them all, but I'm not sure how much survived the crash."

Brie reached for one of the bags, her hands trembling slightly as she unzipped it. Inside was a medley of supplies: basic first aid, a few bottles of water, protein bars, a handful of emergency blankets, and the gifts they'd been given in Elysium. It wasn't much, but it was something.

"Water's going to be the biggest problem," Cameron said, inspecting the other bags. "We've got enough for a day, maybe two, if we ration carefully."

The reality of their situation was sinking in. They were in the middle of the Jordanian desert with limited supplies and no immediate way out. They hadn't filed a flight plan, and nobody knew where to look for them. Even if somebody was looking, it would doubtless be to arrest, interrogate, and incarcerate them.

Most pressing of all, Tavi needed more than a first-aid kit.

"What about the gifts Enoch gave us?" Mike asked suddenly.

Brie's heart lifted slightly at the thought. Enoch had been adamant about preparing them for the unknown. His gifts, wrapped in celestial magic, had been part of that preparation. She reached into her backpack, pulling out an intricately carved wooden box. A symbol of Elysium, a spiral of light and wings, was engraved on the lid. She opened it with a sense of reverence. Inside were several objects, each emanating a soft, otherworldly glow. "Enoch said these would help us when the time came." Her fingers brushed over the contents as she remembered.

Sherry leaned over, peering into the box. "I hope one of those things is a hospital with a premiere neurological wing. Or a five-star hotel with room service."

Brie couldn't help but smirk despite the tension. "I'm afraid not. I still have Azrael's glass, and besides that? The best I can do is two mostly empty crystal vials, a key, that God-awful book, a weird animal horn, and…" She stilled before pulling out the most incriminating thing she could think of. "Your one remaining Elysian freeze marble."

Sherry's face drained of all color with a look of pure dread as she reached in and picked up the blue-glowing orb.

Ephriam's ears perked up, and he turned slowly to skewer her with a flaming glare. "You had another one?" His voice was absolutely venomous.

Sherry pocketed the orb and backed a few steps away, looking for all the world like a cornered rabbit. "It must have fallen out. I didn't know—"

"*We blew up a plane!*" Ephriam snarled, flexing his biceps.

Tavi tilted her head, puzzled. "When did you do that?"

"Wait, that's not all!" Brie interrupted, desperate to redirect the frankly dangerous energy permeating the scene. "There's also…" She pulled something from the box and held it up to the light. "Um, there's also Mike's dead stick."

Mike's face lit up with renewed hope. "Let me see that!" he said, snatching it from her hand and holding the tiny, desiccated twig up in front of his face at eye level. "Oh, Brie, you've buried the lead. This is going to save us all."

The others stared at him blankly.

"Well, that's it. He's lost the plot, he's round the bend. It took a lot to get us here, but we finally broke Mike." Sherry shook her head and took his hand, patting it reassuringly. "Don't worry, love. As soon as we get out of this mess, we'll get you all fixed up."

"Sweetheart, you don't understand," he said patiently. "Don't you remember? They're grapes that will grow *anywhere*." He looked around at their blank faces triumphantly.

Brie nodded and said in a soothing tone, "That's wonderful, Mike, but we probably don't have time to wait for grapes to grow right now, seeing as how we're actively dying of heat stroke with limited water and no rescue in sight."

Mike narrowed his eyes at her. "Are you disrespecting my stick?"

*Tread carefully.*

"Am I — n-no, I wouldn't — Mike, is that a metaphor?" Brie sputtered.

He let out an exasperated sound and rummaged through his pack, grabbing his flask, which contained a large percentage of their precious water reserves. He marched a few paces away and adjusted the mangled remains of the cockpit frame above him so the metal beams cast broken, cross-hatched patterns on the sand beneath his feet.

Sherry came to stand beside Brie as they watched his bizarre antics. "Well, it isn't the nervous breakdown I thought we'd be dealing with, but the man's entitled."

Brie nodded silently in agreement.

It wasn't until Mike knelt, jammed the dried stick into the sand, unscrewed his flask, and started pouring their precious water reserves out over the obviously dead plant that anyone even thought to start running toward him, yelling for him to stop.

Their cries were cut short when a cracking sound split the air. The water sank into the earth without leaving a trace of moisture on the surface. For a horrible moment, nothing happened. Then, all of a sudden, the stick sprang to life and started growing, leafing, thickening, duplicating itself. It rose like a geyser of life from the dunes, twisting and blooming, greening as it went. When it reached the bizarre structure Mike had created with the jet's remains, it twisted around them, and they saw he had improvised an arbor. Before their eyes, the vine produced tiny clusters which ripened into huge, beautiful bunches of deep purple grapes before giving one last shudder and standing still.

Mike raised his arms over his head in victory before turning with a smug look. "Never disrespect the stick!"

The company rested beneath the shade of the grape vines, gratefully nibbling its fruits and apologizing to Mike whenever the mood struck. Brie carefully uncorked the vial containing the remaining ambrosia, pouring a few drops of the glowing liquid into a flask and handing it to Tavi. The Elysian warrior drank it and let out a soft sigh, her body relaxing slightly as she reached for yet another bunch of the celestial fruit.

Cameron was talking quietly with Ephriam. "It's only a few flasks and blankets. I wasn't sure it was feasible, but the vines will help enormously."

"It's more than we had before," Ephriam replied. There was an edge of approval in his voice. "We can make this work. Lucky for the short one," he added, glaring at Sherry.

Brie sat down to join them and nodded. "We need to make a plan. We can't move Tavi right now. I can't tell if she's confused, hallucinating, or delirious, but all signs point to a serious head injury. Plus, I don't think we'd get far in this heat."

Cameron glanced at the sun, its scorching rays beating down on the dunes with unforgiving intensity. "If we move during the day, we won't last long. The heat will kill us before we can get anywhere."

"Then we move at night," Ephriam said simply as if the decision had already been made. "We try to protect ourselves during the day, rest while we can, and travel when it's cooler. We grow the vines for shade and water, we stay hydrated, and we allow Tavi to rest."

Brie's mind raced, the weight of responsibility heavy on her shoulders. But as she looked at the group, the exhaustion etched into their features, the resolve in their eyes, she knew they didn't have a choice. "We wait until nightfall, and then we move."

The heat bore down as the sun climbed higher, but the vines' protection kept the worst of it at bay. Tavi was resting, her breathing steadier now, thanks to the healing ambrosia. Mike, Cameron, and Sherry sat in the shade, sharing sips of water and trying to conserve energy.

Brie stood with Ephriam, staring out at the horizon. The desert stretched on forever, an endless sea of sand with no sign of help in sight. But they couldn't afford to lose hope.

"We'll make it," Ephriam said resolutely, his eyes fixed on the distance. "One step at a time."

Brie echoed him. "One step at a time."

# CHAPTER FOURTEEN

## Myths and Mirages

As a pale moon rose over the Wadi Rum desert, the group trudged forward over endless terrain. The air had lost the sun's searing heat, but the chill of the night did little to relieve their exhaustion.

Tavi had woken up strong enough to walk, but the damage to her mind was another matter entirely. Ephriam had hardly left her side, and she leaned on him heavily.

Brie clutched Azrael's gift, the ancient glass casting its hologram of flickering light into the dusk. She told herself it was enough to guide them, ignoring the creeping doubt.

In the darkness, the desert was magnificent and terrifying in equal measure. By day, it was a blinding expanse of white-gold, impossible to stare at directly. But by night, the sand softened to a velvet black, streaked with silver as moonlight reflected off its surface. Towering cliffs of red sandstone rose in the distance, carved by centuries of wind and time into shapes so surreal they looked like something out of a dream or a nightmare. Shadows pooled at their bases, dark and impenetrable, as though hiding ancient secrets.

Brie paused as they crested another dune, her breath catching at the enormity of it all. "It's beautiful," she whispered, forgetting for a moment her parched throat and aching body.

"Yes, it is," Cameron replied, coming up beside her. His eyes moved over the desert with a reverence she rarely saw. "But it's indifferent. It would bury us all without a second thought."

She felt the truth of his words in the stillness around them. The desert felt alive, but not in a comforting, nurturing way like a forest or meadow. It was a fierce, untamed spirit, filled with a dangerous kind of beauty.

Looking closer, she noticed faint tracks of creatures that had come and gone across the sand, marks left by the night's elusive inhabitants. Small, delicate footprints led to tiny plants, half-buried and coated with fine dust. Their resilience was astounding in this unforgiving place. Every so often, the flicker of a lizard or the glint of an insect caught her eye.

"Do you think we'll make it out of here?" Sherry asked, breaking the silence.

Brie glanced back at her friend. Despite the fear lurking in her heart, she felt a sudden surge of confidence. "We have to," she replied.

*I'll find a way, even if I have to carry us out of here.*

But the desert seemed to mock her resolve. A wind picked up, sweeping over them like a ghostly whisper, lifting grains of sand that sparkled under the moonlight before they lashed across her face, abrasive as glass. She winced, as in that instant, she was reminded how fragile they were, how insignificant against the sheer scale of what lay before them. She caught sight of strange, twisted rock formations ahead, shaped like massive arches and pillars by eons of erosion. One looked disturbingly like the skeletal remains of a creature long forgotten, its stone ribcage jutting upward. The shape loomed over them as they approached, casting long shadows that stretched like claws across the ground. She shivered though the air was warm.

Suddenly, a low rumble echoed across the dunes, a sound that rose from the depths of the earth itself. Her heart raced as they all glanced around, searching for the source. There was nothing — only the vast, endless landscape, as still and silent as before. Brie couldn't shake the feeling there was a presence watching them, lurking beneath the surface.

"It's the earth shifting," Ephriam said, though his voice betrayed his unease. "The desert plays tricks on the senses."

She didn't answer.

Tavi, who had been silent for some time, suddenly staggered and clutched Brie's arm. "Arafel, we've got to get back," she whispered, voice trembling. "He will come for us here. I know you can feel it. He can sense us. He'll find us."

Brie felt a deep dread as she met the woman's feverish gaze.

For days now, Tavi had been slipping in and out of delusions, mistaking Brie for her best friend, left behind in Elysium — Arafel. From time to time, Brie managed to gently remind her who she was, but lately, Tavi seemed less willing to let go of her illusions. At this point, Brie didn't know if it was kinder to bring her back to reality or to play along.

*She doesn't know where she is,* Brie reminded herself, holding her friend's hand tightly. *What would you want her to do, if the situation was reversed?*

"Tavi, it's me. Brie," she said, trying to smile.

But Tavi's grip tightened, her eyes glassy. "I'll protect you," she vowed in a strained voice. "I won't let anything harm you."

Brie placed her hand over Tavi's. "I know. Let's keep moving, okay?"

They pressed on.

Their dwindling supplies and the celestial grapes were their only respite from thirst and hunger. When they set out each night, Mike would take a cutting from the vines he'd grown the day before. When they stopped to rest, he'd plant and water the fresh cutting, and the spectacular vine would grow magically before their eyes once more. The Elysian fruits seemed to supply them with all of their nutritional needs. Without them, they would surely perish.

Mike never asked to use Azrael's glass again. They never mentioned the book he carried in his pack, shooting suspicious glares whenever they happened to glimpse it.

"I feel strange," Sherry said abruptly one night as they were about to set out again.

"What do you mean?" Cameron's voice was wary.

"I don't know. Just tense," she muttered, glancing uneasily at Brie, then back at Mike, whose hand she held tightly. "I can't quite put my finger on it."

Brie felt it, too. Like the whisper of something sinister, a cloud hung in the air. A cloud that gave no shade but clung to her thoughts, subtly twisting them. The longer they walked, the worse it became. She felt inexplicably annoyed when Ephriam slowed his pace to help Sherry or Tavi, even though she knew it was the right thing to do. She scowled involuntarily when Mike and Sherry held hands and didn't receive the fleeting look of disapproval from the Elysians she'd come to expect herself when Cameron held hers. Each of them started keeping a wary distance from the others, their trust fraying.

*It's the thirst,* she silently reassured herself. *We're all exhausted.*

"It's the thirst," Mike said, his voice cracking as he unknowingly echoed her thoughts. "Just stay focused."

But Brie had the uncomfortable feeling that neither thirst nor exhaustion was entirely to blame. She clenched her jaw, willing herself to shake it off, and pressed forward, leaving deep footprints in the sand as they headed into yet another long night.

The friends wandered for days, barely resting save for the fleeting sleep they managed during the oppressive heat. Their desperation rose with each passing hour. Even the beautiful moments — the gleaming stars, the occasional green of an oasis plant, the gentle sound of a night breeze — were tinged with dread.

They were alone, and yet, not.

Every so often, they felt it: an unnatural tremor beneath their feet, like something moving through the earth below. At times, shadows flit in the corner of their vision, large and looming, only to vanish when they tried to focus. Cameron's brow was constantly furrowed, his hand resting on the hilt of his blade, while Ephriam's eyes perpetually roved the darkness.

Finally, on the fourth night, Sherry froze in place as they reached the summit of a small dune. "There's something out there."

They all squinted into the moonlit distance. At first, Brie saw nothing but the expanse of sand and distant rock. But then, a flicker of movement. A massive, shadowy figure lumbered in their periphery. It was there, then gone. "What do you think it is?" she asked.

Cameron shook his head. "I don't know. But it's big. And it's hunting us."

Two more days passed in the same pattern. They marched at night, searching high and low for the image projected by Azrael's glass, or at least some sign of civilization until they could march no more. When the sun rose, they took turns keeping watch in pairs while the rest fell into whatever sleep they could manage in the crushing heat.

That afternoon, Cameron and Brie sat side by side on a summit overlooking a view of the Wadi Rum. They sat in silence, lost in their thoughts. After a while, she threw him a sideways glance, studying his profile as he scanned the horizon. The sun cast sharp shadows across his face, accentuating the lines of his jaw and the intensity in his eyes. She'd grown so used to his presence, his quiet strength. It felt strange to think there had been a time when they hadn't been together. Yet, in moments like these, she felt the gulf between them — the prince of Elysium, bound by duty, and her, a human tangled up in forces far beyond her understanding.

Just as she was about to speak, something caught her eye atop a nearby dune. She squinted, heart pounding, as the shape became clear: the silhouette of an enormous lion, its form outlined against the bright sky. It was massive, the size of a pickup truck, and its fur gleamed dark as ink. She could see its muscular shoulders, the curve of its spine, and the intense focus of its gaze as it stared directly at them.

"Cameron," she whispered, not daring to look away. "Do you see that?"

They both sat frozen, staring at the creature. It stood perfectly still, like a statue, its dark shape blending into the shadows of the sand. Then Brie blinked, and it was gone.

Cameron exhaled slowly. "It's been stalking us. Sometimes, I think it's only watching out of curiosity. I didn't want to tell you before I was sure." He gave a short, mirthless laugh. "I've been trying to convince myself it's a mirage."

She shivered. She'd been plagued by the feeling they were being hunted for days. "I think I'll join you. If there are supernatural lions in the desert, I don't want to know."

He nodded, still staring at the spot where the beast had stood. "Whatever it is," he turned back to her, his expression softening. "There's a reason it hasn't attacked us yet."

"I'm all ears," she said.

"It must sense the presence of a superior predator protecting his mate." Her pulse quickened as his fingers intertwined with hers, his thumb tracing circles over the back of her hand. The touch was warm and grounding. Suddenly, the vast emptiness of the desert seemed to fall away, leaving only the two of them. She tightened her grip as their eyes met.

*How did we end up here? Sitting beneath the same sky?*

A silent understanding blossomed between them. Slowly, he lifted his other hand to trace the line of her jaw and the curve of her face. His touch was impossibly gentle, like a whisper across her skin.

"Brie," he murmured, his voice low. "I would protect you with my last breath. No matter what dangers come, no matter what we face, I'll be by your side."

A warmth spread through her, fierce and overwhelming. She felt as if she were standing on the edge of a precipice. Yet, she couldn't help but trust. She searched his eyes for something she couldn't yet name but desperately wanted to find.

"Even if I don't make it easy?" she asked softly, gesturing around the impossible landscape. "I'm obviously a series of catastrophes waiting to happen."

He smiled and leaned in, pressing a soft kiss to her lips. "Lions and all."

Their fingers entwined as the sun continued its relentless climb across the sky. Her heart ached with bittersweet longing, and she wondered if he felt it, too — the impossible beauty of a moment shared, fleeting and precious, in a world that seemed intent on keeping them apart. For the first time, she allowed herself to believe that there was a chance for them — if they could only survive the trials that lay ahead.

When night fell, the company began their ritual once again — checking their weapons and supplies, hoisting their packs heavily onto their backs, and trudging, exhausted, into the unknown. The night stretched endlessly on, their fears mingling into a haze that numbed their senses. But tonight was different. Tonight, the rumbling sound grew louder, closer, and more persistent until there was no ignoring it.

"Maybe we should stop," Sherry suggested, glancing at the sand nervously. "What in the ever-loving hell *is* that?"

Ephriam paused, then shook his head. "Keep moving," he commanded, adding under his breath, "there's no other option."

They continued, instinctively moving closer together, stopping every so often as the noise swelled louder.

*I don't like this. Something's coming.*

Without warning, the earth beneath them erupted, sending them scattering in all directions. Brie flew backward and tumbled down a slope. When she finally stopped, her vision swam as she struggled to get to her feet.

Then, she saw it.

It wasn't a lion.

A gigantic scorpion, its exoskeleton glistening black in the moonlight, loomed before them, its stinger poised high. It clicked its pincers menacingly as it advanced on the group. They scrambled for their weapons, but its massive tail whipped through the air, forcing them to dive aside. They clawed their way up the sides of the canyon, finally coming together again at the mouth of a cave high above the sandy ground.

"No!" Sherry shrieked, wild-eyed and spitting sand. "Absolutely not!"

"That's a scorpion," Mike panted, white as a ghost. "A scorpion as big as my apartment."

"It's worse than that," Ephriam replied, his gaze steely. "That's an Ushumgallu, a creature of ancient legend. A guardian of the desert."

"What's it guarding?!" Sherry cried.

"The desert itself," answered Tavi, far too demure given the circumstances. She pulled one of their last remaining protein bars from her pack and took tiny bites, struggling to swallow. "I suppose it must see us as a threat. I don't know why. If this is a battle, it's clearly winning."

"That isn't helpful!" Brie said through gritted teeth as she clutched her pendant, mind racing as she tried to think of a way to outmaneuver the creature. She edged to the mouth of the cave, Cameron by her side. The scorpion, or Ushumgallu, was stabbing its pincers at the base of the canyon walls immediately below them. But as she raised her gaze to Cameron, a fresh horror appeared.

There was another beast.

To their left, clinging to the side of the canyon wall, a massive figure was outlined in the shadows. It took another few steps toward them, moving with a reptilian undulation that struck fear into her heart. The lion-headed creature was stalking toward them, its dragon-like body covered in dark fur, its fanged maw bared in a snarl. Its eyes glistened with malevolent intelligence as it watched them, shoulders hunched in anticipation.

"And what the hell is *that*?" Sherry screamed in sheer terror.

"A manifestation of the worst luck in the world," muttered Mike.

"An ancient beast," Ephriam corrected in a low voice. "A descendant of the Nephilim that somehow survived the flood. I do not know how it escaped our notice over the centuries."

They had no time to react before the scorpion lunged upward again, snapping at Mike and barely falling short. He stumbled backward, deeper into the cave, shouting a warning as he dodged a disturbingly large swarm of bats. The sound of beating wings began as a murmur but rapidly grew to a roar. An enormous, erratic-looking cloud of the creatures began to form deep within the heart of the cave while the six friends huddled near the entrance. Meanwhile, the lion-headed monster clawed its way ever closer, ignoring the scorpion altogether, its eyes gleaming with hunger.

"Can I freeze it?" Sherry asked in a panic, pulling the last glowing sphere from her pocket.

"I fear if we leave the cave to freeze one, it will afford the other the opportunity it needs," Ephriam answered in a clipped voice. Brie could practically see a thousand scenarios, a thousand ways to handle this, spinning behind his eyes. She could also see each possibility being dismissed. His clenched jaw and protective stance betrayed what he would never say aloud — he didn't see a way out of this.

For a heart-stopping moment, she was absolutely certain they were all about to die.

Then, an idea sparked in her mind. "Cameron, get the scorpion closer to the cave!" she shouted.

"Closer?! Have you *completely* lost your mind?" screeched Sherry.

Brie continued. "If we can make them fight each other—"

Cameron nodded, catching on quickly. "Ephriam! Mike! Lure that lion thing over here!"

Without questioning, Mike flung himself from the cave's opening and started waving his arms wildly, taunting the nightmarish creatures. The scorpion climbed higher, pincers snapping furiously, while the lion-headed beast let out a terrifying growl and prowled toward them, closing the distance. The pounding of their enormous feet against the canyon walls vibrated through the ground and into the air, further enraging the bats.

"Sherry!" Brie shouted. "Help me block the entrance. At the last possible second, we make a run for it — the same path that the lion is on now!"

Sherry's mouth fell open in astonishment as she understood. "That's never going to work—"

"It's the only thing I can think of! If you have a better idea, I'd be thrilled to hear it!" Brie yelled back.

Her best friend hesitated, then locked arms with Brie and Tavi as they blocked the horde of bats from escaping the mouth of the cave. Leathery wings flapped against their backs, and Sherry let out a whimper of despair as one became briefly tangled in her hair. Mere steps ahead of them, Mike baited the two monsters outside.

*Come on, just a little bit closer…*

Finally, with one last push, the scorpion lashed out in frustration, its tail whipping dangerously close to the mouth of the cave. The tip of its stinger came so close to Mike's face that it seemed to pass by in slow motion, leaving a thin ribbon of phosphorescent poison trailing through the air behind. The lion at last took notice of the scorpion and spared it a passing glare before turning back to its prey with a rumbling growl. It reared back on its haunches, preparing to pounce, as the scorpion gathered its strength in a terrifyingly similar motion.

Both monsters leapt toward the cave at the same moment.

"Now!" screamed Brie, and all six companions dropped flat to the ground.

The bats that had been massing behind them burst forth into the moonlit sky. Hundreds, maybe thousands of flying bodies slammed into the lion, changing its trajectory midair so it began to fall away from the canyon wall toward the leaping scorpion. The gigantic creatures collided with a sickening thud, followed by a vengeful, feral cry. Before a full second had passed, both beasts reoriented themselves to turn on each other in retaliation. The lion roared at the scorpion, sinking its fangs into the creature's armored body. The scorpion fell backwards and thrashed in fury, its stinger lashing wildly as the two monsters locked in a deadly struggle. The canyon echoed with ghastly sounds as the last of the bats cleared the cave in a cloud of silver and black.

"Now!" Brie shouted again, grabbing Cameron's hand. "Run!"

They sprinted along the path the lion had taken, toward the top of the canyon, as fast as they could without falling. Rocks rained down as their feet slipped on the sandy granite formations. Behind them, the sounds of the brutal fight filled the night air, a cacophony of snarls, hisses, and the sickening crunch of an exoskeleton breaking under the force of claws and fangs.

There was a moment when they thought they'd gotten away. But just as they reached the summit, an inches-thin sliver of rock next to a nearly-sheer dropoff on the other side, Sherry stumbled, her foot slipping in the loose gravel. She spun around, pale with shock, and raised her hands as if saying goodbye before falling into the canyon.

Without thinking, Mike launched himself after her, grabbing her ankle in midair.

This started a chain reaction as, in the space of a heartbeat, the rest of them leapt from the ledge, grabbing onto one another until Ephriam alone had a hand on the face of the cliff. He held on for the barest moment, before his grip slipped and they fell together in a tumbling, screaming tangle of limbs and terror.

It was Sherry who saved them — Sherry, who had been the first to fall.

In a moment of either inspiration or desperation, she reached into her pocket and crushed the blue Elysian freezing orb.

A shimmering barrier materialized around them. For a few bizarre minutes, they floated suspended as if in a bubble, halfway between the cliff and the ground, unable to talk, unable to move, unable to help themselves or each other, simply staring down at their impending doom.

The celestial barrier popped like a soap bubble in the wind, and they plummeted the last several meters, hitting the earth below with a bone-jarring impact.

Brie's vision darkened as pain radiated through her body. She gasped, struggling to stay conscious as she looked around. Her friends lay motionless nearby. She ached from the fall, and her mind struggled to come back to life.

As her vision began to fade, she saw a figure standing over her — a man cloaked in flowing white robes, his face weathered by the desert winds. Around him were others, their forms shrouded in shadows, speaking in a language she didn't understand.

"No… please…" she tried to talk, but the words were a mere whisper, swallowed by the night. A moment later, her eyes fluttered shut, and the world turned black again.

# CHAPTER FIFTEEN

## Oasis

Brie stirred slowly, her senses sluggish, as if surfacing from a deep, dreamless sleep. The world around her was warm, quiet except for indistinct voices and the occasional rustle of fabric. The scent of wood-smoke, herbs, and something sweetly-spiced filled the air, grounding her in the present.

She hurt everywhere, a dull, persistent throb that reminded her of their fall — of the monsters, the cliff, and the terrifying final plunge. So it had really happened, she was feeling the evidence of it. But what in the world had happened next?

*Where am I?* she thought, struggling to focus.

Blinking against the soft light, she realized she was lying beneath a canopy of richly patterned fabric on a cushiony surface. The sun streamed through the edges of the cloth, casting intricate shadows on the ground. When she shifted, a quiet groan escaped her lips.

"Brie?" Cameron was beside her, his hand resting lightly on her arm. Relief washed over his face. "You're awake."

She turned her head toward him slowly and deliberately. His features came into focus: messy hair, the hint of a bruise on his jaw, and intense blue eyes brimming with concern. He looked exhausted but unharmed.

"Where are we?" she managed to croak.

"A Bedouin camp," he said. "Their scouts found us after the fall and brought us here. You've been out for hours."

She let the words sink in, her gaze drifting to the space around them. It was a spacious and inviting tent, its walls adorned with vibrant textiles and rugs. Through the open flap, she glimpsed the camp beyond: more tents, people moving gracefully in traditional robes, camels tied to posts, and children playing near a fire pit.

"The others?" she asked, stomach clenching in sudden panic.

"They're fine," he reassured. "Tavi's getting medical care, Sherry's resting with Mike, and Ephriam's — well, being Ephriam."

She smiled at that, though worry still gnawed at her. "Tavi, her injuries—"

He hesitated. "They've done what they can. She's stable, but their doctors say there's something else — something deeper they can't heal. They don't know what it is."

Before she could respond, a man stepped inside, wearing a flowing white robe edged with intricate embroidery. His dark eyes held a kind expression.

"You are awake," he said in a rich, melodic voice. "Thanks be to God."

Cameron rose to his feet, bowing his head slightly. She tried to follow suit, wincing as she sat up straighter. The man smiled and gestured for her to remain seated.

"My name is Khalid," he introduced himself. "I am the sheikh of this camp. You and your friends are safe here. Rest, and we will see to your needs."

Unsure what else to do, she murmured a quiet thank you, flushing awkwardly under the sheikh's gaze. There was a reverence in the way he spoke, as though he knew more about them than he was letting on. When his eyes flickered to Cameron, she noticed the subtle shift in his demeanor — deference, like he was addressing an elder or a visiting dignitary.

*Or royalty*, she thought, *from somewhere in the clouds.*

"We have returned your items," the venerable man continued, gesturing to a tray Brie had failed to notice earlier, on which rested their gifts from Elysium. On the carpet beside it sat Cameron's backpack, containing a fortune's worth of American dollars and priceless gems from at least two planes of existence. "Your companions are well, for the most part," Khalid continued. "Our physicians have done what they can for the injured one. But there is a wound beyond our skill to mend."

Brie's heart sank, having guessed this already. "What do you mean?"

Khalid hesitated, his expression unreadable. "The wound is not physical. Something lingers within her, unseen. It must be healed by greater hands than ours."

She shook her head, confused. "Do you mean greater skill?"

"Yes," he replied. "And also, greater hands."

Before she could press him further, he inclined his head and stepped out of the tent, leaving her with a thousand fractured questions swirling in her mind.

Some time later, after drinking a full flask of water and three cups of tea at Cameron's insistence, he finally, begrudgingly, stopped pestering her long enough to facilitate her escape from the tent. She stood outside, squinting against the dazzling sunlight, as the camp buzzed with life around her. The air was filled with the sound of laughter, the clinking of metalwork, and the bleating of goats. She stretched, feeling the ache in her muscles, but it was a good ache — the kind that reminded her she was still alive.

The second she emerged, Sherry appeared out of nowhere — racing toward her and wrapping her in an enormous hug. "Oh, thank God," she whispered. "Brie, I'm so sorry."

Brie hugged her back, mystified. "Sorry for what?"

"I set that freeze thing off when we were still so high above the ground. If I'd waited—"

"Sherry," Brie interrupted. "Are you seriously apologizing for saving all of our lives, wrong?"

Her best friend blinked. "When you put it like that—"

Brie held a finger to her lips and kissed her on the forehead. "Well, thank goodness, you lunatic. Don't let it happen again."

Mike, who had followed close behind his girlfriend, chuckled quietly. "I've been saying the same thing for hours. Not to any meaningful effect."

"Where's Tavi?" Brie asked, deciding to change the subject.

"She's resting," Cameron answered, walking up behind them. "The doctors said she needs quiet."

"Quiet, in this place?" Mike gestured around the bustling camp, where children darted between tents, women carried woven baskets, and animals grumbled in their pens. "Seems optimistic."

Ephriam joined them. "We must be as gracious as our hosts, if such a thing is possible. We owe them our lives, and beyond that — we do not know how much of what transpired on the cliffs they saw." As the others stared back in fearful comprehension, he continued. "I have no power to alter mortal memory at this time. We must proceed with caution."

Before anyone could respond, Khalid approached, his robes whispering elegantly over the ground as he walked. He smiled warmly. "At last, you are all awake, God be praised. Might you permit me to show you around?"

"That'd be great," Brie answered, returning his smile.

As they followed behind him into the heart of the camp, winding their way through the bustling tents, Sherry's curiosity got the better of her. "Your English is perfect," she began. "How did you learn it?"

Khalid turned, his smile widening. "When I was a boy, I was fortunate to study the languages of many cultures — English, French, Farsi,

Latin. My family believed that the knowledge of words, is the knowledge of worlds." Sherry nodded, clearly impressed, but Khalid's eyes sparkled mischievously as he added, "It is a peculiarity of the English and Americans to study only their own masters — if they study at all."

Mike let out a bark of laughter. "Fair enough."

"Hey!" Sherry objected, though she couldn't help but grin. "Some of us have read plenty of foreign authors."

Khalid inclined his head. "Then you are among the wise," he said smoothly, soliciting a smiling blush.

The camp unfolded before them like a vibrant tapestry. They passed groups of women in stunning embroidered gowns, covered in intricate designs of red, gold, and deep blue. Some worked at looms, fingers deftly weaving delicate patterns, while others carried pots balanced gracefully on their heads. The women greeted Khalid warmly, their laughter ringing like bells as they exchanged friendly banter in Arabic.

Brie was transfixed by the beauty and elegance, unable to keep her eyes in a single spot longer than a second.

They turned a corner and nearly stumbled into a herd of goats shepherded by a young boy no older than ten. The boy whistled sharply, and the goats obediently trotted aside, clearing a path. Mike, grinning ear to ear, crouched down to examine the animals more closely.

"Look at these guys!" he said, reaching out cautiously to pet one as it brazenly tried to eat his shoe. "They've got more personality than half the people I know."

Unimpressed, the goat bleated loudly in his face and attempted to nibble the buttons off his shirt.

As they continued, a group of children began trailing behind them, giggling and whispering among themselves. One of the braver boys darted up to Mike and tugged on his sleeve, pointing at his bulky backpack. Mike crouched down, unzipping a small compartment to reveal a handful of wrapped candies he'd been rationing for the group.

"Want some?" he asked, holding one out. The boy's face lit up, and the entire gaggle of children soon crowded around him, eagerly accepting the treats. Mike handed them out with exaggerated flair, earning peals of laughter from the kids.

Ephriam, who had been standing stiffly at the back of the group, watched the scene without a shred of expression. But every now and then, Brie saw the corners of his mouth twitch.

"You're enjoying this," she said quietly, sidling up beside him.

"I am doing no such thing," he replied gruffly, though his eyes followed the children.

They passed a row of tents where men sat cross-legged on rugs, heads bent over ancient star charts and manuscripts. Khalid gestured toward them. "Our scholars," he explained. "Here, we study not only the history of our own people but the wisdom of many cultures. Philosophy, astronomy, medicine — all knowledge is welcome here."

Brie was struck by the quiet dignity of the scene. As they passed, one of the men glanced up and nodded respectfully before returning to his work.

"I didn't expect…" Sherry began, then trailed off, searching for the right words. "I guess I didn't expect to see this much—"

"Sophistication?" Khalid raised an eyebrow, a hint of amusement in his expression. "And why not? Did you think the desert was only dust and camels?"

"No!" Sherry said quickly, flushing. "I just didn't think—"

"You *didn't* think," Ephriam muttered, earning a vicious glare in return.

Khalid chuckled, diffusing the tension. "Many believe the same, but the desert has always been a cradle of wisdom. Its people must live in harmony, both with the land and each other. That harmony breeds understanding. The underpinnings of your modern chemistry and mathematics are based on principles discovered in Arabic lands during what your ancestors would call your 'Dark Ages.' We built hospitals while Vikings fought Danes for control in the British Isles. In the early caliphates, such times were marked by inventions that allowed us to map the stars, perform surgery, and brew coffee."

Sherry stopped dead cold.

The rest of the group turned to see what was wrong, but she appeared to be in a place beyond their reach. With eyes that suddenly occupied most of her face, she stepped closer and asked in a reverent whisper, "Your people invented coffee?"

Khalid nodded. "Of course. We make the finest in the world."

For a split second, she was too overwhelmed to speak. Then her voice thickened, and her eyes welled with unshed tears. "Khalid, your people are a reflection of the divine."

The man let out a hearty, sonorous laugh. "Would you like to sample some?"

"Sheikh Khalid, there is literally nothing in this world I would like to do more."

Without further ado, Sherry abandoned the rest of the group and locked arms with her new best friend while Mike followed behind, trying hard not to laugh.

They approached a pen where a group of men was saddling some camels. One of the animals let out a long, disgruntled groan, shaking its shaggy head as if to protest its fate. Mike pointed. "That one reminds me of Ephriam for some reason."

Cameron turned to him with mock solemnity. "They have much in common. Both are loud, stubborn, surprisingly strong, and their constant companion is a distinctive odor."

The group erupted into laughter, even Ephriam letting out a soft snort.

As the tour continued, Brie felt a sense of peace begin to settle over her. The camp was more than a safe haven — it was a world filled with unique warmth, culture, and community.

When they reached a tent slightly larger than the rest, Khalid pulled aside the thick canvas flap, and they settled down around a beautiful, octagonal table inlaid with bone. A woman dressed in fine, dark silks walked in with a tray of little intricately carved cups surrounding a silver carafe. She bowed and slipped into a back room amidst the group's murmurs of thanks.

As he poured, Khalid laid out a plan. "Tomorrow, I shall take you to our local market so that we may replenish your supplies. Tonight, I invite you all to be my honored guests at a feast to celebrate your safety."

*Seriously?*

"That's incredibly kind," Brie began tentatively, "but you've already been so generous, I can't imagine putting you through any more trouble—"

"It is no trouble," he said, raising his hand. "Hospitality is among our most sacred virtues. You must come, and you must have a marvelous time. I insist."

A lump rose in her throat as she flashed a watery smile. "It's our honor, sir."

As the friends sipped what was indeed the finest coffee they had ever tasted, a small miracle began to happen.

They began to relax.

As the sun dipped below the horizon, the camp came alive with the sounds of evening — laughter, music, and the crackle of fires.

Brie sat cross-legged, her gaze fixed on the flames as she listened to her friends' voices and enjoyed what was, far and away, one of the most delicious meals she'd ever had in her life. Plates of slow-cooked lamb and beef, so tender they nearly fell apart at the touch of a fork, were surrounded by an array of dips: creamy hummus drizzled with golden olive oil, smoky baba ganoush flecked with garlic and lemon, and a fiery red harissa that made Mike's eyes water. Glass after glass of rich, sweet tea was poured, the amber liquid warming their throats and lifting their spirits.

Tavi had managed to join the group for the evening meal. She was pale, leaning back against a pile of cushions, with a distant expression on her face. She ate continuously, in such quantities that, at one point, Sherry quietly asked Brie if they should stop her out of respect for their hosts. Brie considered it, then shook her head. Whatever Tavi was doing to keep herself going, she should be left to do in peace.

When their bellies were full, Mike suggested they take turns telling campfire stories. Sherry turned to Ephriam with an inquisitive look. "You mentioned you've been to a place like this before. Something about fire-breathing camels and cursed cities. Surely, you must have a tale or two."

"First of all, don't call me Shirley." He raised an eyebrow as his lips quirked into a smile, and the others laughed. "The desert and I are old acquaintances. I spent years wandering lands like these, seeking knowledge."

"What sort of knowledge?" Mike asked through a mouthful of food.

"All sorts," Ephriam's voice took on a reflective tone. "All cultures have stories, and only a fool thinks themselves above the acquisition of their wisdom. Once, I came across a place called Ubar — the Atlantis of the Sands, some called it. A city swallowed by the desert, its ruins barely visible among the dunes. Our Elysian scholars say it is a place that changes its face. Even travelers who have managed to avoid it once may not be able to do so again. Our scrolls say it is cursed, that those who enter will never return."

*Of course, you decided to visit.*

"And?" Brie asked, intrigued despite herself.

The Elysian chuckled. "I returned, clearly. But the stories weren't entirely false. The air in that place was oppressive. It felt wrong. I was called away before I could discover why."

"Why were you called away?" asked Mike.

"There was an urgent matter at the Elysian court which required my attention." Ephriam shot a glance at Cameron. "Someone had stolen the sacred gems from the gates of Elysium on the eve of our youngest prince's birthday."

Cameron blushed scarlet and shot a guilty look at his backpack but said nothing.

"Let's hope this desert isn't hiding any more cursed cities," Sherry muttered. "Though it would be just our luck."

Brie sat back with a sigh, unable to disagree.

*Just our luck.*

Night settled quietly over the camp. The companions were invited to join the Bedouins around a central fire, where the tribe's families had gathered. The flames danced in the breeze, and the air was filled with the low hum of conversation, laughter, and the sweet-sounding notes of an instrument being plucked somewhere in the background.

It was impossible to keep defenses up against such warmth and hospitality. Sherry leaned against Mike, eyes half-closed, while Tavi sat propped up with pillows. Cameron remained close to Brie, watchful as ever, shooting her tender glances in the firelight.

A woman entered the circle with a quiet grace. Her robes were deep indigo, adorned with embroidery that shimmered in the firelight. Lines of wisdom etched her face, and her eyes shone with a timeless energy that reminded Brie of their gracious host.

"This is my sister, Mariyah," Khalid said, introducing her to the companions. "Our most cherished storyteller."

The woman bowed graciously. "You are welcome here," she said in a lovely, musical voice. "Tonight, I will share with you a tale — a tale of the desert, of shadows, and of the unseen."

The children darting around the fire grew still, their wide eyes fixed on the storyteller. Even the adults quieted, leaning closer to the fire as if the story would unfold in its glow.

Mariyah's gaze swept over the group, her words carrying a rhythm that seemed to pull the night closer. "Many years ago, there was a young man of the tribe named Idris. He was bold and curious, often wandering beyond the safety of the camp. One night, under a sky much like this one, he strayed too far into the heart of the desert, where the sands grow wilder and the creatures less forgiving."

Brie leaned forward slightly, caught in the cadence of Mariyah's voice.

"Idris carried with him nothing but his courage and his wits, but neither was enough when he came upon a beast — a creature of nightmare. It had the head of a lion, but its body had scales like a serpent, with claws sharp enough to carve through stone and eyes that burned like embers in the dark. The air grew heavy with its presence, and Idris knew he was trapped."

The companions froze, remembering the monster to perfection.

The firelight flickered, shadows playing across Mariyah's face. "Just as the beast was upon him, a voice called out. A woman stood atop the dune, her robes flowing like water in the moonlight. Our stories tell us her eyes held the light of the stars, and upon her chest, a stone shone as if lit from within. She raised her hand, and the beast froze, unable to move. Idris watched as the woman stepped between him and the creature."

Mariyah's smile softened, and Brie felt an unexpected warmth spread through her.

"The woman spoke softly to the beast, and though Idris did not understand the words, he could feel their power. The creature levitated into the air and flew into the desert as if thrown. Idris, still trembling, asked the woman who she was. She smiled and told him, *'Your people helped me once — for you, perhaps in the distant future. Return to your tribe, and remember this kindness, as I have always remembered yours.'* With that, the mysterious woman disappeared."

Mariyah's gaze swept over her listeners, lingering on each of the companions in turn. "Idris returned to his people and never forgot the strange woman's words. He carried her wisdom with him for the rest of his days, teaching his children, and their children, to respect the desert and the unseen beings who dwell within it and to offer help freely to all strangers in need."

The storyteller sat back, hands resting lightly in her lap. "It is said that the woman and those like her still walk these sands, watching over travelers who lose their way. If you are fortunate, they may guide you back to safety. But only if you remember to walk with respect."

The fire crackled. Even the children were quiet, their faces shining with wonder. Brie felt a strange sense of comfort settle over her, though she couldn't shake the feeling that the elder's words carried more than just a lesson.

They felt like a prophecy.

After the story, Brie wandered away from the fire, her thoughts restless, and found herself near the edge of the camp, staring up at the sky. She stood alone, arms crossed tightly against the chill of the desert. The stars sparkled above her, brilliant and unyielding, their light spilling over the dunes like scattered jewels. The vastness made her feel small — insignificant, even — but that was a relief in its own way. Here, beneath the infinite expanse, the weight of her responsibility felt like it might dissolve into the night.

*Eden,* she thought, the word a whisper in her mind.

It sounded like a promise, a place so mythical it felt impossible to believe it could be real.

Yet, they had to find it. Something inside her knew that it was true.

Her fingers instinctively sought the pendant resting against her chest. Its cool surface warmed beneath her touch, a reminder of its power, and the burden that came with it. She pulled it from beneath her shirt, holding it up to catch the moon's light. The ancient glass glinted as though mocking her doubts.

Her shoulders sagged with a quiet sigh.

*Why me?* she thought. *Why did it have to be me?*

The pendant had been her mother's before her, and its significance had always been a mystery shrouded in pain. She wanted to throw it away, to rid herself of the responsibility it carried — but she knew she couldn't. The pendant wasn't merely a relic. It was a part of her, of whatever destiny she had been thrust into without consent.

She reached into her pocket and pulled out Azrael's magnifying glass, its polished surface cool against her palm. No matter how many times she saw it, the object was strange and mesmerizing, its weight heavier than it should have been. Holding it up, she positioned the lens over the pendant and angled it toward the desert.

Light spilled across the sands like the ghost of a map half-forgotten by time. The hologram shifted and twisted into the same landscape it had been showing them since a lifetime ago in the Fairmont Hotel — the same red crescent carved into the earth.

She lowered the glass, letting the projection fade into darkness.

"Are we even close?" she whispered into the vast silence. Her voice sounded small. "Or are we just wandering blind?"

The only answer was the rustle of the wind, tugging at her hair and the edges of her clothes. She closed her eyes and took a deep breath. Cool, sharp air filled her lungs, but it didn't ease the knot of anxiety in her chest.

She dropped the magnifying glass back into her pocket and tucked away the pendant.

*We have to keep going,* she told herself.

The thought felt more like a plea than a command.

*For Tavi. For everyone.*

The sands whispered underfoot as she turned her gaze back to the stars. They were beautiful and remote, indifferent to her struggles, yet something about their constancy was comforting. As much as she wished for an escape, she knew she couldn't run from this. The burden was hers to bear, whether she wanted it or not.

*So then, I'll bear it.*

A sigh escaped her lips, carried away by the desert wind. She stood frozen, caught between the immensity of the task ahead and the faint hope that maybe, just maybe, they would find what they were looking for.

She heard footsteps behind her and turned to see Cameron approaching.

"Couldn't sleep?" he asked softly.

She shook her head. "Too much to think about."

He reached for her hand as both their heads tilted back to gaze at the sky.

"It's beautiful out here," she said. "Peaceful."

He looked down with a peculiar smile. "Your ability to find moments of gratitude in the midst of the storm is…"

"Incredibly irritating?" she guessed with a wry look.

He gave a low chuckle. "Inspiring and endearing," he finished. "And timely. Peace, in places like this, is always fleeting. We should enjoy it while we can."

She turned to him, searching his face. "Do you think we'll make it? To the Garden? To whatever's next?"

"We will," he said firmly. "I'll make sure of it."

His thumb traced circles over the back of her hand, and her heart skipped a beat as his other rose, brushing lightly against her cheek. His touch was featherlight, so painfully tender that little tears sprang to her eyes.

"You don't have to do it all alone," she whispered, her voice catching.

His gaze locked with hers. "Since I first met you, Brie, I have never been alone."

For a fleeting moment, the world fell away, leaving only the two of them standing together under the infinite expanse of stars.

# The Bazaar and the Bandit

Tavi's soft breathing was the only sound in the tent as the healer adjusted the cushions beneath her. She stirred slightly but didn't wake. Her brow furrowed even in sleep. The tribe's healers had tried everything they could think of to wrestle her mind back into the present, back to reality, but to no avail. She was slipping further and further away. Now, she mistook Brie for Arafel every time they spoke. Sometimes, she'd have entire conversations with people who weren't there.

Brie watched her for a long moment before stepping outside into the morning air.

The others were waiting, standing near a tray of tiny, steaming cups surrounding another enormous silver carafe. Ever the gracious host, Khalid handed one to Sherry, who took it eagerly while Mike sniffed his cup with suspicion. Hints of cinnamon and cardamom wafted through the air, adding an exotic twist to the group's favorite beverage.

"Coffee is a gift," Khalid explained, motioning for Brie to help herself. "It sharpens the senses and clears the mind."

Mike took a cautious sip. His eyes flew wide. "Oh, my goodness!"

"It's strong," Cameron said, suppressing a smirk as he sipped from his cup with practiced ease. "But you'll get used to it."

"Strong?" Sherry exclaimed, already reaching for a second cup. "This is just warming up. You should see the espressos I've had back home."

Khalid chuckled, watching in amusement as Sherry drained another cup with gusto. "Perhaps, but moderation is key. Too much will leave you buzzing like a locust."

Sherry raised an eyebrow, clearly unfazed, and proclaimed. "Buzzing is fine by me."

After what the Bedouins would later describe as an unhealthy amount of caffeine — though Sherry looked like she could have handily put away several more shots — the group set out for the bazaar.

Khalid led them away from camp to a well-worn road that wound its way through a series of dunes. Before they knew it, a market sprawled before them like a kaleidoscope of color and sound, nestled in the shadow of an ancient sandstone ridge. Tents, stalls, and rows of more permanent structures packed tightly together, and the air was alive with the hum of conversation, laughter, and the occasional clinking of metal.

"Welcome," Khalid said with a sweeping gesture, "to one of the jewels of the desert."

The first stall to catch Sherry's eye was overflowing with silks, their vibrant hues catching the sunlight like stained glass. She let out a delighted gasp, diving into the display with an enthusiasm that made Brie wince on behalf of the vendor. "This one!" she exclaimed, draping an indigo scarf over her shoulders. "No, this one!" She swapped it for a silver wrap that glinted like moonlight. "Or this one?" A deep blue scarf replaced the silver in an instant.

"You know, you can get more than one," Brie pointed out with a grin.

"Don't tempt me," Sherry replied, spinning around to face the seller, who was watching her with a bemused expression. "How much for all of it?"

"Sherry," Brie chided, amused.

Sherry shrugged, holding up a delicate bracelet inlaid with tiny gemstones. "Maybe it's time for a new look. Silks, jewels, something more elegant."

Mike, standing nearby, let out a laugh. "I don't see how you could possibly be more elegant, sweetheart. But I do think that wearing a floor-length gown while trying to navigate the desert might stretch even your powers of gracefulness."

She shot him a mock glare. "Careful, or I'll make you carry my shopping again."

They left Sherry haggling over scarves and jewelry as Mike steered them to a stall displaying various weapons. Daggers, scimitars, and long spears adorned the vendor's table, their polished blades gleaming in the sunlight.

"This," Brie said, picking up a curved blade with a ruby-encrusted hilt, "is what I'm talking about."

"You wouldn't know what to do with that," Ephriam replied, his tone dry as he examined a smaller, more practical dagger. "It's decorative, not functional."

"It's intimidating," she retorted, holding it aloft. "And that's half the battle."

"Spoken like someone who's never fought a real battle," he said with a scowl.

In a fortunate bit of timing, Mike brought him a strange, whip-like instrument and asked about it. Brie discreetly bought the showy blade anyway before abandoning her friends to their more professional armament discussions.

Cameron stood nearby, ignoring their banter as he scanned another stall lined with jars and vials of herbs and powders. He leaned toward the vendor, speaking quietly in Arabic.

"What are you looking for?" Brie asked, stepping closer.

"Anything that might help Tavi," he said. "Medicines, folk remedies, anything."

Ephriam joined them, glancing at the selection with a hopeful eye. "The Bedouins are skilled in herbal medicine. They may have something that could ease her pain." It didn't matter what else was going on — Tavi was never far from his mind.

In a few minutes, the group moved deeper into the market. They finally stopped at a food stand, where the scent of spices and grilled meat was impossible to resist. Plates of dried fruits and nuts, baked cheeses and meats in flaky pastry, and fresh flatbread were laid before them, along with small bowls of hummus, yogurt, and tangy pickles.

"This," Mike declared, taking a bite of cheese in crispy phyllo dough, "is the best thing I've ever eaten. Hands down. It isn't even close. Everything else is in a race for second place. Honey," he turned to Sherry. "We should move."

"It's divine," she agreed, grabbing another bite. "Why doesn't all food taste like this?"

"Save room for the rest of your meal," advised Khalid. "These are merely appetizers."

Brie's gaze drifted across the marketplace as the others laughed and chatted. Her attention caught on a small figure standing in the shadows near a tower of woven baskets. It was a boy, no older than ten, his clothes dusty and worn. A scarf partially obscured his face, but his eyes stood out — one green, one blue, bright and piercing even from a distance.

She froze, the bite of food forgotten in her mouth. There was something unsettling about the boy. She couldn't look away.

*I've seen him before. But that's impossible. It's literally impossible. I'm not in my own country. I'm not even in my own decade.*

"Brie?" Cameron's voice broke through her thoughts. He followed her gaze, frowning. "What is it?"

She shook her head slowly. "I don't know. It's that child."

His face went blank. "What child?"

She tilted her head in frustration. "You know, the…?"

But when she looked back, he was gone.

The table was a feast for the senses, a symphony of colors and textures. Flatbreads arrived in baskets, warm and pillowy, perfect for scooping up the fragrant stews and tangy sauces. Bowls of rice were laced with threads of saffron and bursts of pomegranate seeds, each bite a blend of sweetness and spice that lingered on the tongue. Brie couldn't help but marvel at the complexity of flavors, each distinct yet perfectly balanced. She'd spent the better part of her youth tooling around the eateries of Georgia with Sherry, and nothing on the eastern seaboard even came close. The meal ended with plates of honey-soaked baklava, layers of crisp pastry, and crushed pistachios that crunched and melted in the same bite.

Sherry leaned back, sighing contentedly as she popped the last piece of baklava into her mouth and licked a sticky finger. "Tavi is going to be sorry she missed this."

Brie opened her mouth to respond but froze as she felt a slight tug at her side. She turned just in time to see a flash of movement — a small figure darting away from the table. Instinctively, she patted her pocket. For the first time in months, she felt nothing but empty fabric.

"Azrael's magnifying glass!" she gasped, springing to her feet. "It's gone!"

Cameron was up instantly, eyes narrowing as he followed her gaze. "Who—?"

"There!" She pointed, catching sight of the boy she'd seen earlier, weaving effortlessly through the crowd.

The group scrambled to their feet, knocking over chairs in their haste. The crowd watched curiously, but they were already on the move, racing forward as the boy disappeared into the maze of the bazaar.

The market was alive with sound and color, but Brie could only focus on the boy's retreating figure, his small frame slipping between the stalls like a shadow. She ran, pushing her way through the crowd, ignoring the startled cries of vendors and shoppers alike.

"Stop!" she shouted, though she knew it was futile. The boy was quick, his movements fluid and precise, as though he had done this a hundred times before.

Cameron and Ephriam were close behind her, their longer strides helping them close the distance, while Mike and Sherry brought up the rear. Vendors shouted in protest as the group upset baskets of spices and racks of colorful scarves, calling back desperate apologies.

The boy turned sharply, disappearing into a narrow alley. Brie followed without hesitation, her feet skidding slightly on the packed sand. The alley opened into a small courtyard, but the boy was already climbing a stack of crates, quick and nimble as a cat.

"Up there!" she called, pointing as she tried to catch her breath.

Cameron was the first to react, leaping onto the crates and scaling them with ease. The boy darted over rooftops, his bare feet silent against the wooden planks. Her angel followed, but the boy anticipated every move, slipping just out of reach every time he closed in.

On the ground, Brie and Ephriam rounded a corner just in time to see the boy drop from the roof, landing lightly in the middle of a bustling spice market. He took a second to get his bearings, then dashed away, scattering piles of turmeric and cinnamon in his wake.

"Ephriam, go left!" she shouted, veering right to cut off the boy's escape. The Elysian nodded grimly as he sprinted into the crowd.

The boy glanced back, his mismatched eyes glinting with mischief, and she felt a flash of frustration. He was toying with them, deliberately leading them on a wild chase. But there was something else in his gaze — something that stole her breath.

He darted around a corner and into a small shop at the far end of the market. She skidded to a stop outside the door, chest heaving. Cameron and Ephriam caught up a moment later.

"Inside," Cameron growled.

They entered cautiously, eyes scanning the dimly lit space. The shop was cluttered with shelves of scrolls and ancient books, the air thick with the scent of incense and dust. The boy stood in the center of the room with his back to them, twirling Azrael's magnifying glass between his fingers like a rockstar with a drumstick. He tilted his head slightly and grinned.

"Got you now," Ephriam growled, lunging forward.

The boy made no attempt to dodge. Instead, as Ephriam tackled him, his body simply evaporated, vanishing into thin air. The warrior landed hard on the floor, clutching the space where the boy had stood.

"What the—" Brie began, her voice trailing off as she stared at the empty space.

Ephriam sat up, holding the magnifying glass triumphantly. "Got it," he said, handing it to Brie. His tone was even, but his eyes betrayed his annoyance. "Hold tight to this, now. I don't know what that was, but it's over."

"Thank you," she grabbed it with relief, unfolded it, and checked the glass for damage as its now-familiar hologram filled the store.

Someone gasped, and she whirled around, closing the glass tight in her palm.

An older gentleman, presumably the shopkeeper, appeared from a back room and stood behind the counter. He stared at Brie, face pale as a sheet, with wide, frightened eyes.

"What's wrong?" she asked, darting a fearful look at Cameron. "Did he see?"

The man pointed a trembling finger at Azrael's glass and started speaking in Arabic so quickly she couldn't have followed even if she'd understood the language. At that moment, Sherry, Mike, and Khalid burst through the door.

Their host took one look at the shopkeeper and strode over to him.

"What is it?" she gasped. "What is he saying?"

Khalid convinced the old man to sit on a nearby chair, where they shared a hushed, hurried exchange before turning to the rest of the group with a grave expression. "He says the artifact you carry does not belong in any mortal hands. He says…"

He drifted off. It was the first time Brie had seen the sheikh look troubled.

*Or afraid.*

"What does he say?" prompted Ephriam softly.

Khalid drew a breath and continued. "He says if it is here, two things have broken. A sacred seal, and time itself. He says if the key is here, the sky is a spiderweb of cracks waiting to break apart. And whoever holds this key," he locked eyes with Brie, "is themselves the epicenter of the destruction."

# CHAPTER SEVENTEEN

## Secrets in the Starlight

*A spiderweb of cracks.*

Brie remembered as if it was happening now — Baal's monstrous face as it broke apart the Elysian sky with an evil grin, and wraiths poured through the jagged fractures into the celestial kingdom like a black tide.

It had looked just like a spiderweb in the sky.

Like when you hit a glass plate, and it splinters before shattering.

"Brie? Brie, what do you think?" Sherry's anxious voice snapped her back to reality.

Brie walked over to her friends, who had gathered in a tight huddle near the back of the shop. Their faces were a study of conflicting emotions — worry, confusion, and an edge of panic.

"What do we do?" Sherry hissed, her gaze darting between the shopkeeper and the door as if calculating the fastest escape route. "He saw. He knows. And he's told Khalid. I'm sure the entire tribe will know soon. We can't stay here!"

"I don't think there's anything we *can* do," Cameron answered quietly. "Normally, Ephriam and I would simply modify the memories of this event for the safety of all those involved, but…" He trailed off at the look on Mike's face, cleared his throat, and continued. "But of course, that would violate the sanctity of their free will, and I would never invade a mortal's privacy that way. Ever again," he added hastily as Mike shot him another glare.

"We could saddle up and make a run for it," Sherry suggested, half-serious.

"That might be the kindest course of action," Ephriam muttered. The tension in his voice undercut his usually commanding presence. "Anything else risks dragging the entire camp into danger, and that would be a very poor way to repay the generosity of our hosts."

Mike scratched the back of his head, looking uncomfortable. "I'm not sure you're right about that." The others turned to him, surprised. It wasn't often he and Ephriam disagreed on matters of strategy. "Not that running isn't a fantastic option and all. I mean, look how well we've fared so far," he shot a pointed look around the group, and Brie found herself flushing. "But maybe we should try talking this out first. You know, words. Diplomacy. I've heard good things. Works wonders sometimes."

Sherry turned to him. "You want to give the unvarnished truth to a guy who nearly fainted at the sight of that thing? Not to mention, I thought it was forbidden for humans to know about Elysium at all. They put Brie through a whole court-martial about it. As I recall, there was interdimensional kidnapping involved." She shot Ephriam an acid look.

"I don't see what more these people could possibly do to earn our trust," Mike answered quietly. "And I'm not keen to keep wandering through the desert subsisting on nothing but grapes again, with no idea where I'm going and no end in sight. I have an extremely beautiful woman to protect, and I don't think that plan will keep her safe."

*That's hard to argue.*

Ephriam took a moment to reply. "Mike, you are far from wrong. But the fact remains that the secret of Elysium's existence is paramount. It could put these lovely, trustworthy people in grave danger to know of our world. Would you have me put them at risk to mitigate the risk to Sherry?"

Mike faltered and stayed quiet.

Brie's thoughts churned as the others argued, but she said nothing. She could feel the tension rising with each passing second, a pressure that made the air in the shop seem stifling despite the open windows.

"What are you thinking?" Cameron asked, his voice cutting through the mayhem like a lifeline.

She shook her head. "No matter what we do, there's no easy way out of this."

"Easy? No. Direct? Maybe. There's a corral full of camels right outside the bazaar. We could pick up Tavi on the way and make for the hills," Sherry said. Her tone was dry, but she shot Mike a soft look. "I appreciate your concern, but I am, in fact, tougher than I look."

Before anyone could respond, Khalid cleared his throat, drawing their attention. The shopkeeper still sat on a low stool, dazed but no longer panicked.

The sheikh stood tall and composed, hands clasped lightly before him. "If you wouldn't mind," he began mildly, "delaying your plans to steal our camels and make a run for it — toward certain doom in the desert, I might add — I would like to propose a meeting. The six of you and our tribal elders. We have much to discuss."

The group froze, their collective guilt at being overheard rendering them momentarily speechless. Sherry opened her mouth, perhaps to protest, but Brie beat her to it.

"Of course, Khalid. We'll be there," she said simply, tucking the magnifying glass back into her pocket. She kept her voice calm though her heart pounded.

Khalid nodded serenely. "Good. I'll go to the camp and arrange everything. I'll also send someone to escort you back. For now, enjoy the bazaar." His lips quirked into a knowing smile. "And please, no camel theft. The desert is far more forgiving with a guide. Besides, I have serious doubts about your collective abilities to mount, let alone control, the beasts."

As he turned to speak with the shopkeeper again, Brie exchanged a glance with Cameron. His expression mirrored her own — barely contained apprehension. Whatever Khalid had to say, it seemed they had no choice but to listen.

*No smart choice anyway.*

*Though Sherry's right — we could always take our chances with a cursed camel.*

The tent where the council convened was large and ornate. Lanterns hung from a central beam, casting long shadows that danced like living things. The air was thick with the scent of frankincense.

The companions sat cross-legged on soft cushions, stiff with tension. The council members formed a semi-circle before them, their faces weathered with time and wisdom. Khalid and the shopkeeper sat at their center, their expressions watchful. Next to them, Mariyah leaned slightly forward, dark eyes alight with curiosity.

"You have honored us by coming," Khalid began. "This council is a place of truth. What is spoken here will not leave these walls. We would like to know who you are and what has brought you to the sands of Wadi Rum."

Brie shifted uncomfortably. The others exchanged uneasy glances, caught in the same reluctance.

"It's complicated," Cameron answered, his voice carefully neutral.

"Most truths are," Mariyah replied softly, hands resting lightly in her lap. "But we are not here to judge. We are here to understand."

Sherry cleared her throat. "Look, it's not that we don't trust you. You've been so kind. We can't talk about it; we're not allowed to talk about it. It's classified."

Mike snorted softly. "Darling, that makes this sound like a bad spy movie."

Mariyah's gaze swept over the group. "You are not simply from another place. You are out of sync in a different way. I can feel it." Her words tugged at a truth they had tried so hard to keep hidden. "You are not of this time, are you?" she asked abruptly, ending the charade.

The air grew heavy with anticipation. Brie's pulse quickened as all eyes turned toward her. Slowly, she nodded, the motion feeling like an irrevocable step forward.

"We're not," she finally admitted. She hesitated momentarily before pulling her pendant free, allowing it to rest against her shirt. The ancient stone caught the lantern light, casting an ethereal glow.

The council murmured in wonder. Khalid's expression remained unreadable, though his eyes lingered on the pendant with keen interest.

Brie reached into her pocket, withdrawing Azrael's magnifying glass. She placed it carefully on the rug before her. The object felt imbued with an unspoken gravity. Taking a deep breath, she looked at the council. "This is going to sound impossible. But it's the truth."

With that, she began to speak despite the fear curling in her stomach: about the wraith attack she'd survived, how Cameron had appeared and saved her, and how they'd been searching for answers and running from danger ever since. She told them about her showdown with Greed and the revelation that she had enemies more powerful than she'd ever imagined. When Ephriam coughed and shot her a meaningful look, she stopped short of using the word archangels. She described the battle with Baal and how they'd saved a whole town at great personal cost, how Tavi hadn't fully healed, how things had just gotten worse in the California forests, and finally, how their pursuit of answers had led them to not only another place but another time.

The words spilled out like water breaking free from a dam, and as she spoke, the tension in the air shifted. The council listened in rapt silence, their expressions ranging from astonishment to solemn understanding. Mariyah's gaze never wavered from Brie, as though she was finally piecing together a puzzle whose existence she had long suspected.

When Brie finished, it was silent, save for the crackle of the lanterns.

Khalid spoke first. "Your story is extraordinary," he said quietly. "And it explains much."

"You believe us?" Sherry asked in astonishment.

He smiled faintly. "Only the ignorant fail to believe in the extraordinary. The world is filled with things beyond comprehension. Your journey is one of them." One of the council members said something in Arabic, and the sheikh nodded and leaned expectantly forward. "You spoke of visions — a place shown to you by this artifact." He gestured toward Azrael's magnifying glass. "I assume it is the same thing we saw in the bazaar. If it does not trouble you, the council would like to see it."

Brie hesitated and turned to Ephriam for approval. The thought of revealing the hologram in this sacred, intimate space made her heart quicken. An unspoken question shone in her eyes — *May I show them?*

Ephriam and Cameron shared a glance as the answer became apparent — there was no use holding back now. Ephriam gave her a subtle nod.

Taking a deep breath, she opened the glass and angled it toward the center of the tent. She tilted its surface, and a shimmer refracted into a pale, shifting image. The council members leaned in, speaking in hushed tones as the projection grew and solidified with an otherworldly glow. The picture that emerged was the same place the companions had seen time and time again — a red-stone, crescent-shaped canyon encircling a sunken area filled with half-hidden structures they could barely discern.

The room fell into awed silence, the light of the hologram reflecting in the wide eyes of the council members. Mariyah placed a hand over her heart, her lips moving in what Brie guessed was a silent prayer. Even Khalid, usually so composed, looked deeply moved. Beside him, the shopkeeper pointed at one of the cliffs in the hologram's background and spoke to the sheikh in rapid Arabic. Khalid nodded without breaking his gaze.

Ephriam's anxiety was palpable. "Do you recognize this place?"

Their host nodded slowly with a troubled expression. "Yes, we know it well."

Brie's breath caught. "You do?"

Mariyah answered. "It is the entrance to Ubar. The cursed city beneath the sand."

*Of course it is.*

*Perfect.*

A ripple of unease spread through the companions. Brie's eyes flicked to the hologram, studying the image with a newfound wariness. Ephriam had mentioned something about this — Ubar, the cursed city that could change its face. The name alone made her stomach twist.

Brie didn't want to ask, but somebody had to. "Ephriam, isn't that the place you told us about? The one place we definitely, absolutely do not want to visit?"

Ephriam didn't blink. There was a chance he'd forgotten how. "That would be the one."

Sherry cleared her throat. "Well," she said, trying for levity, "at least our luck is holding."

There were a few half-hearted chuckles.

Mariyah nodded. "Your quest has guided you here for a reason," she said. "It seems the desert is not finished with you yet."

*No, it seems not.*

"What do you advise?" Cameron asked.

Khalid exchanged a glance with Mariyah before turning to the group. "Prepare for what lies ahead. The place you seek is impossible to find by the stars alone. Without a map and a guide, you would wander the dunes forever."

"Does such a map exist?" Ephriam asked grimly.

"As it happens, the very shop where your thief led you in the bazaar today contains the only copy known to our people. The thief who, if

I'm not mistaken, did not simply disappear after leading you there —
he vanished."

The shopkeeper chimed in, speaking in Arabic, and withdrew a
long, brass cylinder from a box by his side. Unscrewing one ornately
carved end, he pulled out a tightly rolled parchment and spread it on
the rug before them.

The friends momentarily forgot to breathe as they leaned in to look.
The image was exactly the same as the one from Azrael's glass.

Bordered by helpful star charts and miniature physical maps of the
region, the red-stone crescent, rendered in ancient paints and pig-
ments, stared back at them from the scroll.

"I can't believe it," Brie shook her head. "I can't believe it's real."

The sheik's eyes locked, unblinking, onto hers. "It seems that forces
beyond our understanding guide your path. It is our honor to assist
you on your journey."

Mariyah and the rest of the council nodded in approval. Khalid
clapped his hands together twice, and three young people appeared
out of nowhere with trays of sweetened tea. The sheikh passed these
around as he spoke. "Then it is decided. Tomorrow, we will gather
supplies and form a caravan to take you to your destination."

Brie looked up sharply. "We can't possibly ask such a thing of you.
You have already shown us more kindness than we can ever repay."

The sheikh merely smiled. "One does not refuse dancing lessons
from God. And you are not asking — we are insisting. Tonight, please
rest and allow us to tend to your needs. And rest well," he added, his
dark eyes settling again on Brie. "I suspect this may be the last safety
you'll see for some time."

The still-stunned friends accepted the fragrant tea and lifted it to
their lips in a chorus of gratitude when Sherry suddenly stopped. "So,
wait — who the hell was that little pickpocket in the market today?"

Mariyah paused. "This is an interesting question. If he truly vanished, as you have said, he would seem less like a child and more a

spirit. And spirits are not to be trusted. Some bring mischief, some wisdom, and others disaster. Though this boy seems to have given you aid, be wary the hidden motives of the hidden heart."

Sherry stared over her ornate teacup, somehow more confused than before.

Ephriam summed it up with a growl. "I'm not sure who, or what, that kid was. But somehow, I know he's going to be a problem."

# CHAPTER EIGHTEEN

## The Caravan

The first rays of dawn stretched across the desert, painting the world in hues of amber. The Bedouin camp was a flurry of motion, camels groaning their objections as their handlers secured supplies to their saddles. Brightly woven bags and brass-bound chests were stacked with practiced efficiency, the rhythm of preparation reflecting the tribe's deep familiarity with the desert's demands.

Brie stood near the edge of the camp, arms crossed against the early morning chill as her gaze wandered over the horizon, where the dunes rose and fell like frozen waves. Somewhere out there lay the cursed city of Ubar — and beyond that, she hoped, Eden. She clutched the pendant hanging from her neck, the stone warm against her palm. It felt heavier with each passing day, as if the weight of their journey had seeped into it.

"Brie," Cameron said softly, stepping up beside her. "We're ready."

She nodded and released the pendant. Cameron held her hand as they made their way back to the camp. She stole a sideways glance at his face. His blue eyes caught the morning light, and she smiled softly to herself.

*He'll be there with me. Every step.*

The others were already gathered, their postures varying from excited to resigned. Mike was attempting, and failing, to mount his camel. The animal, a particularly cantankerous creature with a lopsided hump, let out a deep grunt and sidestepped just as he swung his leg over its back. He landed with a thud in the sand, eliciting a loud bray from the camel and a smattering of laughter from the Bedouins. He blushed as red as his hair and laughingly shook his fist at the beast. "You did that on purpose, you overgrown carpet!"

Sherry clapped her hands, her tone laced with amused, mock encouragement. "You're a natural, babe. They'll be writing songs about your grace any day now."

"I have other skills," he grumbled, brushing sand from his clothes. He tried again, this time managing to climb aboard with an awkward scramble that earned him another disgruntled huff from the animal. "See? Easy."

"Looks like Jerry's warming up to you," Sherry quipped, patting the animal's neck as she passed.

"Jerry?" he asked, frowning.

"Yeah. He looks like a Jerry. Don't you think?" She grinned, ignoring his exasperated expression as she mounted her camel with inexplicable ease.

"How the hell did you do that?" he asked suspiciously.

"Riding lessons!" She shot him an airy smile. "What else?"

Brie couldn't help but chuckle at their antics as she settled onto her own mount, the leather saddle creaking beneath her when she turned to cast a final look at the camp. People waved from every corner, smiling as if they were parting as old friends. She lifted a hand in return, wondering if she would ever see them again.

With a sharp command from Khalid, the caravan began to move.

The rhythm of the camels' steps blended with the rustle of the wind as they wove their way through the shifting sands. The rising sun burned away the morning chill, and the desert stretched before them in endless waves of gold.

Brie clung to the reins, her gaze fixed on the horizon.

Somewhere out there, their destiny awaited.

*Ready or not, here we come.*

The sun burned high and unrelenting from above. The caravan moved steadily, its rhythm broken only by a camel's occasional groan or a circling bird's distant cry. Dust rose in swirling clouds beneath their feet, clinging to their clothes and dampening their spirits.

Brie adjusted her scarf against the wind, her attention drifting to the group ahead.

Mike and Sherry rode side by side, smiling and talking in low voices. They leaned toward each other at a precarious angle so Mike could plant a kiss on her lips, and Sherry laughed, bright and easy.

There was an inexplicable tightening in Brie's chest.

*What's wrong with me?* she thought, biting her lip.

There was no reason for the irritation prickling beneath her skin, no need for the flare of jealousy. Sherry had been nothing but supportive. And she was happy for Sherry and Mike — happy that they'd found each other.

*But it must be nice*, a bitter voice chimed in her mind. *Hugging and kissing in the open like that. No judgemental glares from the Elysians to haunt them and keep them on edge. No celestial taboos in the way of their future together.*

She shook her head slightly, trying to clear it.

*Brianna Weldon, that is your best friend. Snap out of it.*

Still, the warmth of their affection felt like a splinter lodged in her mind, pushing things off-kilter no matter how hard she tried to keep them steady.

Ultimately, she forced herself to look away, clutching the reins tighter.

"You doing okay back there?" Sherry called, glancing over her shoulder. Her tone was light, but there was a hint of concern in her eyes.

Brie nodded quickly, plastering on a smile. "Yeah. Just tired."

Sherry slowed her pace to fall into step beside her. "I get it," she said quietly. "It's been rough. And Tavi's got us all worried."

Brie flinched at the mention of Tavi, guilt flooding her heart. "Yeah," she agreed, eyes flicking to the covered stretcher strapped between two camels, protected near the center of the caravan. Their injured friend lay within it, pale and still. It struck Brie that the whole contraption looked like a tomb.

"She'll make it," Sherry said, voice firm with determination. "We're going to find the help she needs. We have to."

Brie nodded, her throat too tight to speak. She glanced ahead at Cameron, who had turned back to look at them. Their eyes met briefly, his expression unreadable before he returned his focus to the horizon. She sighed and allowed her eyes to drift as well.

They were in for a long road.

By the third day, the desert's toll was becoming evident. The companions spoke less, their energy spent enduring the heat and the endless monotony of sand and stone. Even Mike, who usually filled silences with jokes or complaints, had grown quiet, his usually jovial demeanor tempered by the unyielding landscape.

It was late afternoon when the group stopped to rest beneath a cluster of rocks offering sparse shade. Khalid distributed their water carefully while the others merely collapsed, exhaustion setting in. Mike stretched with a groan, pulling off his boot and pouring out about a quart of sand. "I bet I could fill an Olympic-sized swimming pool with what I've emptied from my shoes this past week."

Ephriam, seated nearby with his arms crossed, shot him a sharp look. "You think it's funny?"

Mike blinked, caught off guard. "Um, no? Just making conversation."

"Perhaps you should spend more time focusing on what lies ahead and less time making pointless observations," the Elysian snapped in an unusually harsh tone.

The group froze, the tension palpable. Brie glanced between them, alarmed by the sudden hostility. Even Khalid, who had been quietly observing, tilted his head slightly as though weighing Ephriam's words.

"Alright," Mike said, holding up a hand peacefully. "I was only trying to lighten the mood."

"It's a distraction," Ephriam muttered, rubbing his temples. "We can't afford it."

Brie opened her mouth to intervene, but Sherry beat her to it. "Everyone's tired," she said firmly. "Let's take a breath before we start tearing each other apart."

Ephriam stared at her a moment, then simply turned away. Brie exchanged a glance with Cameron, who shook his head subtly.

Something was shifting among them, and it wasn't just exhaustion.

That night, the camp was quiet save for the wind and the sound of the Bedouins tending to the animals. The companions gathered near a small fire. Tavi lay nearby on a pile of cushions, eyes closed and breath shallow.

"She hasn't said a word," Sherry whispered. "Not since yesterday."

"She's saving her strength," Ephriam snapped. He knelt beside Tavi, adjusting her blankets with the care of someone grasping for control in a situation that allowed none.

Mike leaned forward, elbows resting on his knees. "You think she's even aware of what's going on?"

"She's aware," Cameron said quietly. "Even if she can't show it."

Brie's heart ached for the fallen warrior. The once vibrant, quick-witted woman seemed like a shadow of herself, her light dimmed by whatever wound she'd suffered in their battle with Baal, made worse by their recent plane crash and endless travels. Brie looked down in betrayal at the pendant around her neck. Its warmth was a cruel reminder of how little she could do.

Khalid watched the group with a thoughtful expression. His silence was patient, as though waiting for the puzzle pieces to fall into place. She caught his eye briefly, but he said nothing, inclining his head slightly before turning back to the fire.

As the days passed, the group's unrest grew harder to ignore. Small tensions flared into brief arguments, and moments of silence felt heavier, more charged. Brie caught herself snapping at Sherry over nothing, her irritation evaporating almost as soon as it came. She saw it in the others, too — in the way Ephriam avoided Mike's eyes, and how Sherry's usual cheeriness felt brittle around the edges.

Khalid remained an enigmatic presence, his quiet observations giving nothing away. She wanted to ask what he thought of them — of their fraying and strained camaraderie — but the words died on her tongue. She was embarrassed and angry, and a whole mess of other things that had seized upon her that she didn't fully understand.

She looked out over the endless landscape and couldn't shake the feeling that the sands whispered secrets only the wind could hear.

The lantern in Brie's tent flickered softly, sending light dancing across the canvas walls. She probably should have been resting but instead sat cross-legged on her blanket, the pendant resting heavily in her palm. She turned it over and over, absentminded, lost in her thoughts.

*Are we doing the right thing?*

*Is this journey leading us closer to salvation — or ruin?*

*What if Cassius was right, and Azrael should never have entrusted this to me?*

The tent flap rustled, and she looked up sharply. Cameron ducked inside, his broad shoulders brushing against the narrow opening. There were dark circles beneath his eyes, but he looked as awake as she was. He scanned her tired face, looking for clues.

"Hey," he said gently, kneeling beside her. "I wanted to check on you."

She let the pendant fall. "I'm fine," she said, too quiet to be convincing.

He tilted his head. "Are you?"

She sighed, shoulders slumping. "No," she admitted. "I don't know what's happening to us. I think we're on the right track — I can feel it — but at the same time, it's like we're falling apart. Like the closer we get to Ubar, to Eden, the more fractured we become."

His brow furrowed. Over the last few days, he'd noticed the same thing. Just that evening, Mike had given him a shove for stepping on his coat. "Do you think it's the stress? Everything we've been through?"

The words she wanted to say stuck in her throat, but when she looked up at Cameron, his patient expression coaxed them free. "It's more than that," she said quietly. "I think… I think I'm jealous."

His eyebrows lifted in surprise. "Jealous? Of what?"

She hesitated again, then blurted it all out, words tumbling over one another in a rush. "Of Sherry and Mike. Of their relationship. It's perfect. Their love isn't forbidden. There aren't celestial forces standing in their way. They just *have* each other, without all these consequences hanging over them."

Her voice caught, and she ducked her head, blinking against the sting of tears.

"Sherry's always had all the luck," she whispered. "She has this big, successful, loving family. No tragedy in her past. No dead mother. And now, she has this perfect relationship at the perfect moment, with nothing stopping her from being happy — well, nothing except me.

And here I am, sitting in a tent, feeling jealous of my best friend. The same woman who's *risking her life to help me*." Her voice cracked on the last word, and she clenched her jaw, willing herself to stay composed. "What kind of person does that make me?"

Her angel didn't answer immediately. Instead, he moved closer, reached out, and took her hands in his, gently tugging her toward him. She looked up, eyes glistening, as he leaned forward and wrapped his arms around her.

*I needed this — more than I knew.*

When he finally pulled back, his hands cupped her face tenderly. Their eyes met for a split second before he leaned in and kissed her. Not a tentative kiss, but one filled with longing, heat, and an urgency that sent her heart racing. His lips pressed against hers, and everything else faded — the weight of the pendant, the uncertainty of their journey, the gnawing envy inside her.

When he finally pulled away, his voice was low and husky, his breath warm against her cheek. "If it makes you a terrible person," he said, "I'm just as guilty. Because I'm jealous, too." Her eyes lifted in confusion as he traced the line of her jaw. "I'm jealous of every person who's ever gotten to hold you. Every person who's ever touched you. Every second of your life that wasn't spent with me." His hand moved to the back of her neck, gently massaging. She closed her eyes as he gathered a fistful of silken curls at the base of her head and pulled lightly, tilting her head back. "From the moment I saw you, I've been aching — down to my soul — to be able to say, 'She's with me.'"

His words were a confession, raw and unfiltered. They sent a warmth to her core. Before she could respond, he kissed her again — deeper, hungrier, as though he were pouring every ounce of pent-up longing into that very moment.

Her hands found his shoulders, fingers curling into the fabric of his shirt as she leaned into him. Their lips parted beneath each other, and the air between them charged with electricity.

His hands slid down her arms, leaving a trail of fire in their wake.

The lantern flickered as they came together. There was little talking after that.

Brie lay on her side, her back pressed against Cameron's chest. His arms were wrapped around her, his breathing slow and rhythmic, the warmth of his body chasing away the desert's chill. For the first time in what felt like forever, the weight of their journey had lessened, replaced by a fragile sense of peace. The pendant still lay heavy against her skin, but it felt more like a part of her now — a burden she could bear as long as he was beside her.

He shifted slightly in his sleep. She turned just enough to see his face, relaxed and unguarded, the lines of worry smoothed away.

*How can any single person be so lovely?*

She closed her eyes, matching her breath to his slow rhythm. Sleep beckoned, soft and insistent, but as she began to drift, a sudden gust of wind rattled the tent. Her eyes flew open as the faint patter of sand followed, grains brushing the canvas like a whispered warning. And, so quick that she might have imagined it, a tremor shook the earth, like a traveling earthquake passing directly beneath them.

*Please, let that not be real.*

Another gust came harsher this time. Her heart quickened as she stared at the walls, illuminated by the lantern's glow, as shadows danced wildly in the shifting wind.

The desert was waking. And it carried no promise of peace.

# CHAPTER NINETEEN

## The Wrath of the Sands

Within a minute, the wind rattled the tent in earnest. Sand hissed against the fabric, and the entire structure shook ominously. Brie sat bolt upright, the blanket pooling in her lap.

Cameron stirred beside her. His eyes flew open as he quickly registered the scene. "It's starting."

Her heart pounded as the wind grew even stronger, the faint scratching of sand rising to a constant rasp. She scrambled to her feet, gripping the edge of the tent for balance. "We need to check on the others," she said urgently, straightening her clothes.

"Wait, Brie——" he began, but she was already untying the flap.

The moment she stepped outside, the storm hit her with the force of a battering ram. Wind whipped around her in a swirling chaos of grit and noise, flinging sand in every direction, stinging her exposed skin and blinding her. She stumbled forward, arms raised to shield her face, but the sand found every opening, scraping against her cheeks and filling her nose and mouth.

*This was a terrible idea.*

Panic clawed at her as she tried to turn back, but her footing slipped on the shifting ground. Before she fell, strong arms wrapped around her from behind, lifting her off her feet.

Cameron's voice cut through the deafening howl.

"Inside. Now."

He pulled her back to the tent, his body shielding hers as the sand lashed at them mercilessly. The moment they ducked inside, he dropped the flap and tied it tightly, securing every fastening with precision. She coughed, her throat raw from inhaling the grit, as he turned his attention to her. "What were you thinking?" he demanded, his hands moving quickly to dust the sand from her clothes and hair.

"I wasn't," she admitted, coughing again. "I just need to know they're okay."

His hands stilled, then resumed their work, gentler this time. "They're fine," he said firmly. "These tents are built for this. But you—" He shook his head, his expression softening. "You don't need to throw yourself into the line of fire at the first sign of trouble."

"What about Tavi?" she whispered hoarsely.

"There's nothing we can do until this passes," he replied. "Then we'll do whatever we must."

She nodded but couldn't tear her attention from the tent flap as the storm outside raged louder. Despite Cameron's best efforts, wisps of sand found their way around the fastenings and collected in little mounds near the doorway. He grabbed two scarves, handing one to her before wrapping the other around his own face. They huddled together, pulling the blanket over them like a shield. The wind screamed, animalistic in its ferocity.

She pressed closer to her angel, trembling. He held her protectively, his breath warm against her scarf-covered cheek as he whispered, "I've got you."

Sand battered the walls relentlessly at such a deafening pitch, it felt like the desert itself was trying to claw its way inside. The idea of being buried alive flit through her mind, dark and insistent. "Do you really think we'll be okay?" she asked, her voice barely audible over the wind's roar.

His hold tightened. "Yes," he said fiercely. "We'll get through this. Together." He pressed a kiss to her forehead. "Just try to get some sleep."

She closed her eyes, trying to focus on his words and the rhythm of his breath, but what little sleep she managed was fleeting and troubled. At one point, she jolted awake as a quake rippled through the ground beneath them. She held her breath, eyes wide in the darkness, as a low, rumbling sound reached her ears — a terrible, guttural laugh that seemed to come from deep within the earth.

*What the hell is that?!*

Her pulse thundered in her ears. Her hands gripped Cameron's shirt as the laughter faded as quickly as it had come. The ground stilled, and silence returned, broken only by the storm's relentless howl.

"It's just the wind," she whispered to herself.

But deep down, she wasn't sure she believed it.

Cameron stirred beside her, sensing her unease even in his sleep. "Brie?" His voice was heavy with exhaustion. "What is it?"

"Nothing," she said quickly. "It's nothing."

He pulled her closer, his warmth a barrier against her lingering fear. She nestled against him, mind restless, even though her body begged for sleep.

And so it went, for hours and hours.

When the first light of dawn seeped through the top of the canvas walls, the wind finally began to die. Slowly, maddeningly slowly, the storm eased, its roar fading to a whisper.

She opened her eyes, exhausted, as the last flurry rattled the tent.

Then, abruptly, it stopped.

She had never, in all her life, been so grateful for silence.

"Thank God," she breathed, looking at Cameron. "It's finally over."

He nodded, eyes scanning the walls as though half-expecting the storm to return. "For now," he said softly. "But we'll see what it left behind."

Brie fumbled with the ties of the tent flap. When she managed to open them, a cascade of sand spilled inside, forcing her to pull back with a gasp. "Oh no," she muttered.

Cameron was already moving to her side. Together, they carefully pulled back the canvas to reveal a solid wall of sand pressed against the tent. Only a faint streak of sunlight filtered in from the top.

"We're buried," she gasped in disbelief.

"Not entirely," he assured her. He grabbed a nearby blanket and fashioned it into a makeshift shield. "We need to dig our way out."

They worked side by side, hands plunging into the sand as they carved out a narrow tunnel toward the light. They moved quickly, adrenaline driving them. Within moments, her arms burned with effort, and sweat mingled with the grit clinging to her skin.

After what felt like hours, they broke through. Sunlight flooded in, and she squinted against the brightness as she emerged from the suffocating confines of the tent. She looked around to get her bearings and let out a reflexive gasp. The camp was a chaotic expanse of half-buried tents and scattered supplies. Only the tiniest peaks of canvas were visible. The Bedouins were already hard at work, unearthing their people and belongings with an efficiency that spoke to centuries of resilience.

Cameron climbed out behind her, brushing his clothes. "We need to check on the others."

She nodded, watching as a group of camels shook their fur. "Let's find Khalid first."

They made for the central tent, where the sheikh was issuing instructions to a group of his people. His collected demeanor stood in stark contrast to the disorder around him. His movements were sharp and efficient as he directed the rescue efforts.

"Khalid!" Brie called, rushing towards him.

He glanced over his shoulder, greeting her with an unlikely smile.

"You survived," he declared. like it was quite the thing to have done before breakfast.

She let out a shaky laugh. "We did, indeed. How can we help?"

The man looked over the scattered remnants of the camp. "Your offer is appreciated, but we have our methods. Go check on your people." He gestured toward a partially uncovered tent near the edge of the camp. "Mike and Sherry are in there. They will need help."

They followed his direction and found a similar mess of sand spilling over the edges of a canvas. Muted voices told them they were in the right place.

"Keep digging!" came Sherry's muffled cry.

"We're almost there!" Mike's voice rang out.

"We're here! We can hear you!" Brie called, dropping to her knees in relief.

"Brie?" Sherry shouted back. "Thank God. Took you long enough!"

Brie stifled a smile. "We had to dig our way out ourselves. Are you two alright?"

"I'm *buried*, hon. I've been better," came the dry reply.

"We're fine," called Mike.

"Speak for yourself. I'm all for exfoliation, but this is ridiculous," Sherry retorted.

Cameron and Brie joined the effort, using their hands to scoop away the sand. Within minutes, Sherry's head popped out, her hair a wild, sand-covered mess. Cameron and Brie took her arms and dragged her the rest of the way. Once she was free, she immediately rolled onto her back, panting and covering her eyes with one hand.

Brie knelt beside her. "How are you doing?"

"When we get out of this, I'm going to soak, for a week, in a *vat* of the most expensive lotion money can buy," came the unhinged yet somehow inevitable reply.

Brie patted her shoulder. "That's the spirit."

Mike surfaced a moment later, coughing and shaking sand from his clothes. "I used to be a beach person," he muttered. "I know the Irish aren't supposed to be, but I always loved it. Now? If I never see sand again for the rest of my days, it'll *still* be too soon."

The four friends struggled to catch their breath. They could only brush away so many disasters before they started to catch up.

The moment she could manage it, Brie struggled to her feet. "Let's go find the others."

Cameron was already on the move.

The desert had completely engulfed the medical tent. Ephriam was already there, his normally-composed face drawn with worry as he clawed with his bare hands.

"She's inside," he said tersely when they approached. "I can't get through fast enough."

They joined his efforts immediately, their combined strength carving a narrow path to Tavi. The moment they touched the canvas flap, Ephriam yanked it open in a display of sheer determination and crawled inside, vanishing into the darkness. While the others continued throwing armful after armful of sand behind them, Brie followed him in, her breath catching at what she saw.

Tavi lay motionless on the pallet, her face pale and her breathing shallow.

Ephriam knelt beside her. "She's alive," he said slowly. "But I can't wake her."

After extracting the fallen warrior, the group gathered in tense silence, watching as Ephriam adjusted her blankets and tried unsuccessfully to give her water. It seemed she might stay asleep, but then her eyes fluttered open, unfocused and wild.

"Arafel?" she whispered.

Brie leaned closer. "I'm here."

The Elysian's voice was strained. "We have to go. We're in danger."

Brie froze. "What danger, Tavi? What are you talking about?"

But Tavi didn't seem to hear. Her eyes were wide now, filled with a desperate urgency. "We have to tell the king. He'll know what to do. Arafel, please — they're coming."

"Tavi, it's okay," Ephriam soothed, trying to keep his voice even. He placed a hand on her shoulder. "You're safe. Just rest."

For a moment, it seemed his words were enough. Tavi's breathing slowed, and her eyes began to close. But just as the tension in the room started to ease, they snapped open again, wide and unseeing. She spoke, and her voice had changed — it was deeper and resonant with something unnatural.

"He is almost here."

The words hung in the air like a physical weight, chilling Brie to her core. Then Tavi's body went limp, her head falling to the side as if the effort had drained her completely.

The silence that followed was heartbreaking.

Brie looked at Ephriam. "What does that mean?" she asked with a shaking voice.

He didn't answer.

Outside, the Bedouins worked steadily, their voices carrying over the dunes, but the group was motionless inside the tent, Tavi's ominous declaration echoing in their minds.

It was a testament to the Bedouin's unmatched skills that the caravan recovered from the sandstorm and was back on the move within hours.

That afternoon, the sun hung low on the horizon, bathing the desert in blinding light as the caravan reached the top of a rocky ridge. The camels moved slowly now, as though they sensed a shift in the air. Brie pulled her scarf tighter around her face, the chill of the descending night biting against her skin despite the lingering warmth of the day.

Khalid raised a hand, signaling a halt. The tribe members spoke softly among themselves as they dismounted, their eyes fixed on the vast expanse of shadowed dunes stretching below. Brie followed their gazes. Her breath caught as she saw it—

*Ubar.*

Nestled within the red crescent-shaped canyon they'd been searching for since San Francisco, the ruined city sprawled across the desert floor. Towers leaned at precarious angles, their once-proud spires now ancient and crumbled. Massive stone arches jutted from the ground, carved with symbols visible even from the ridge. The city seemed to breathe in the shifting light, shadows rippling like living things across its surface.

"Well, that's gotta be it," Sherry said in a flat, subdued voice.

Khalid nodded, his expression grave. "The lost city of Ubar," he said. "Known in your stories as the Atlantis of the Sands. A place cursed by the heavens and swallowed by the desert for its sins."

Brie stared at the ruins. Even from this distance, they radiated an aura of unease, their silence louder than the howl of any storm. The air seemed heavier here, thick with something she couldn't name.

"This is as far as we go," the sheikh continued. "The living have no place within those walls."

*Yeah, I'd like to head back, too.*

Brie was about to half-seriously suggest this when Ephriam stepped forward and spoke, rigid as a statue, backlit against the desert sun. "We don't have a choice. If that place holds the answers we're searching for, we have to go."

Khalid nodded. "The caravan will remain here until dawn. We will ensure you have what you need, but we will not follow you into Ubar.

Be wary," he continued. "The sand does not lie, but it often hides truths better left buried."

Brie forced herself to swallow the lump in her throat. "Thank you," she managed weakly. "For everything." She could say it for a hundred years, and it would never be enough.

Khalid inclined his head, then gestured for the Bedouins to begin setting up a temporary camp at the edge of the ridge. The group watched as the sun dipped lower, the shadows of Ubar stretching across the desert like reaching hands.

"We'll set out at first light," Ephriam said, breaking the heavy silence. "We need to be ready."

As the group turned back toward their camp, Brie couldn't shake the feeling that they were being watched. For a brief moment, she thought she heard something — a low, distant rumble that seemed to be coming from the ruins themselves.

She froze, heart pounding, but the sound faded as quickly as it had come.

"Did you hear that?" she asked softly, turning to Cameron.

Before he could answer, Tavi let out an unsettling giggle. "The city is waiting," she whispered with a feverish smile.

Brie swallowed hard. She didn't ask Tavi what she meant.

She wasn't sure she wanted to know.

# CHAPTER TWENTY

## The Cursed City

Dawn broke reluctantly over the desert. The sun cast pale, diffused light across the sands as if hesitant to fully illuminate what lay ahead. Ubar loomed dark and foreboding against the horizon. The city seemed shrouded in shadow, defying the sun. The air was heavy with the weight of what was to come, and the camp was quiet, save for the low sounds of the Bedouins preparing for their departure.

The companions stood together near the edge of the ridge. Khalid and Mariyah walked over to their group. She carried a small bundle in her arms.

"This is where we part ways," the sheikh said in a solemn voice. "You go where we cannot follow."

Brie nodded, ignoring the tightness in her throat. "We wouldn't have made it this far without you," she said.

He inclined his head. "It has been our honor."

Cameron walked up beside them and pulled a small, wrapped parcel from his pocket. With the greatest deference, he handed it to the sheikh. "Please accept this token of our most sincere gratitude," he said quietly. "We will never be able to repay your kindness, but it will gladden our hearts to know you have this gift."

Khalid accepted the offering with a slight bow.

Mariyah stepped forward, holding out the package in her arms. "We have prepared supplies for you," she said, unwrapping the cloth to reveal carefully tied parcels of dried meat, nuts, and flatbread, along with small vials of a clear liquid. "These will sustain you for the journey ahead."

Brie took these with trembling hands. "Thank you," she whispered. "For everything."

Mariyah smiled, her gaze lingering on Brie. "You carry a great burden," she said softly. "Take heart, and do not give in to doubt or despair. The sands will test your resolve. But the Divine One does not entrust such burdens to those who are unequal to the task."

Brie nodded. "Mariyah, I will never forget you."

The woman gave a slight, knowing nod. "Inshallah, our paths will cross again."

The companions approached the rest of the tribe as they dismantled the last of the camp. The air was thick with unspoken farewells, and everyone seemed subdued as they helped load their supplies.

"This feels final," Sherry observed, watching the Bedouins work.

Cameron replied, his gaze fixed on the ruins in the distance. "They're not simply leaving us behind. They're staying out of harm's way."

Sherry let out a soft snort, shaking her head. "Smart choice."

*My thoughts exactly.*

The Bedouins began to gather around them with solemn faces. They approached one by one, some offering quiet blessings, others simply nodding as they passed. The companions returned the gestures, overwhelmed with gratitude.

As the tribe prepared to leave, Khalid held back a moment longer, his dark eyes scanning the group. "When you no longer need them, simply let the animals go. They will find their way back to us. And remember what we have told you — Ubar will challenge you in ways you cannot imagine. Trust only your purpose. Nothing else is real."

Brie's brow furrowed. "What does that mean?"

The sheikh hesitated, his gaze lingering on her pendant. "It means that the city is not merely a place. It is a reflection — a mirror. And mirrors can deceive as easily as they reveal."

His words hung cryptically as he turned and mounted his camel. Mariyah followed, casting one last glance at the companions before pulling her scarf over her face. The Bedouins began their descent from the ridge, moving single file, their silhouettes growing smaller against the vast expanse of sand.

The friends stood silently, watching until the last figure disappeared over the horizon.

"Well," Brie finally managed. "This is it."

She turned to the others, her eyes roving over their weary faces before settling on Tavi, who sat slumped in the saddle Ephriam had carefully prepared for her. Her pale face was a stark contrast to the warm tones of the desert, but her breathing was stable for now. She was still wearing that eerie, delirious grin.

"Are you ready?" Cameron asked, stepping up beside Brie.

"No," she admitted. "But we have to go anyway."

With a collective nod, they turned toward Ubar. It loomed ahead, its stark skyline silhouetted against the pale light of dawn, waiting — its secrets buried beneath the sand, perhaps along with something far worse.

They began their descent toward the cursed city, their gracious host's warning echoing through their minds.

*Trust only your purpose. Nothing else is real.*

Ubar rose from the sands like a fever dream made solid, its fragmented towers and half-buried arches clawing skyward as though defying their own decay. As they approached, the city distorted in the wavering heat. Its jagged edges blurred into shapes that seemed to shift with every step. Brie couldn't tell if it was her eyes or the city playing tricks on her, but the effect was deeply unsettling. She shivered, though the sun still beat down with unrelenting heat.

"It looks alive," Sherry said, her voice uncharacteristically soft, her usual quipping humor replaced by wide-eyed apprehension.

"It's a mirage," Ephriam muttered, though his tone lacked conviction. "It plays tricks on the eyes."

"Yep," Mike said under his breath, "this feels fine. I'm sure the cursed city will welcome us with a gift basket and a firm handshake."

Sherry snorted, her laughter sharp and brittle. "Don't forget the warm cookies. Maybe they'll throw in a scented candle, too. Speaking of gifts," she turned to Cameron. "What was in that package you gave Khalid?"

This brought a smile to his lips. "A ruby," he answered.

"Ah." They rode a few paces before Sherry found the words to follow up. "That thing was the size of—"

"About the size of my fist, yes," he cut her off cooly, raising an eyebrow as if challenging her to critique him.

Instead, she gave a satisfied nod. "Sounds about right. Should cover the damage to the bazaar, with enough left over to buy a country or two." She tilted her head sarcastically, adding, "I will, however, accept no further commentary about the extravagance of my shopping excursions. Ever." She gave her camel a nudge and trotted up to ride beside Brie. "How are you holding up?"

Brie nodded absently, her gaze locked on the towering columns at the city's entrance, their surfaces etched with symbols that writhed under the shifting light. She could make them out better now — serpentine figures coiled around humanoid shapes, their eyes staring blankly into the void. The details were exquisite, the craftsmanship impossibly fine, but something about them made her skin crawl. She gestured in their direction. "It feels like they're watching us."

"They probably are," Sherry muttered, her eyes darting nervously. "This place is giving me major 'run the other way' vibes."

Tavi let out a soft chuckle, still slumped over her camel. It wasn't the light, airy laugh Brie remembered from happier days. This one was darker, as if the Elysian had heard the punchline of a joke no one else understood. "Do you hear them?" Tavi asked suddenly, her voice carrying a singsong quality. She didn't wait for an answer. "The whispers. They're everywhere. So much to say, but none of it for us."

"She's been like this since the storm," Sherry murmured, worried.

Brie forced herself to ask. "Tavi, what whispers?"

The warrior tilted her head, her glassy eyes fixed on nothing in particular. "The ones in the stone," she said simply. "They've been here longer than you've been alive. Longer than anyone. And they're very, very hungry."

Everyone deliberately chose to ignore this, but they all paused when they reached the entrance to the ruins. Brie's pendant felt heavier and hotter than ever as if even the ancient stone was reluctant to cross the threshold. She glanced at Cameron. He didn't say anything, but his hand rested heavily on the hilt of one of the daggers they'd purchased at the bazaar, and his expression was set with grim determination.

On an unseen signal, they rode together into the shadow of Ubar.

The air changed instantly. The bright sun seemed to dim, and an indistinct hum echoed through the ruins, like the remnants of a melody just out of reach. It was the kind of thing that would send anyone with a shred of common sense and a choice running for the hills, but the companions rode slowly onward. The camels' eyes darted nervously, and their hooves sank reluctantly into the sand as they plodded deeper into the unknown.

The air rippled around them as though the heat of the desert had seeped into the stone, bending light and sound alike. Brie blinked, her vision swimming. It felt like her head was submerged underwater, her surroundings warped and muffled.

Then the world snapped back into focus, and she froze.

Sherry stood ahead of her, radiant in a flowing emerald gown, a delicate crown perched atop her head. Her hair caught the light as if spun from pure sunlight, and she smiled, effortless and captivating. She stretched her arms wide, and Brie realized she was surrounded by her adoring family and others as well — a crowd whose faces turned to her in admiration and love.

Brie's breath caught as she saw a vision of herself there too — lost in the crowd, dressed in plain, muted tones, her hands empty, her presence invisible. The crowd ignored her, their cheers and applause reserved for Sherry alone. The sight hit her like a punch to the gut.

"Brie?" Sherry's familiar voice broke through the illusion, and the scene wisped away like smoke in the wind. "Are you okay?"

Brie blinked, heart racing, the oppressive heat of reality slamming back into her senses. She whirled around to see the real Sherry behind her, face full of concern and clothes covered in dust.

*What the hell just happened?!*

The vision was gone, for she realized now that's what it was.

*Answer. She's waiting for you to answer.*

"Yeah," Brie lied. "Just dizzy."

Sherry's frown deepened, and she said nothing. Her attention had been drawn to something else. Her expression unraveled into something uncharacteristically vulnerable.

Brie turned to follow her gaze and froze again. There was a shadowy figure standing at the edge of the ruins. It was wavering but unmistakable.

*That's me.*

She was dressed in armor, leading their group with purpose and poise. Her pendant shone brilliantly. She was confidence incarnate — a resplendent vision of leadership and the promise of tomorrow, guiding a group of adoring friends and followers.

Before she could blink, the vision evaporated.

She turned to Sherry in astonishment. "Sherry, what was that?"

"Nothing," Sherry said quickly, sharper than usual. Her expression had hardened, and her lips had thinned to a tight line. She shook her head as though trying to dislodge the image and kept pushing forward.

Brie pulled in a breath, about to call to the others, but they were having troubles of their own. Ahead of them, Mike's mount stumbled to a stop. His face was pale, his usual grin replaced by something closer to fear.

"Mike, what—" Brie started, but he waved her off.

"It's nothing," he insisted, though his eyes told a different story.

Her stomach churned. Something was wrong — something more than the oppressive atmosphere of the city. These felt like more than mere mirages; they were visions. They had to be. She glanced at Ephriam, hoping for reassurance, but she was shocked to see that his expression was dark — those bright golden eyes were fixed upon Cameron in a simmering rage.

With a feeling of dread, she followed his line of sight to see her angel, but not as he actually was. In Ephriam's vision, Cameron stood taller, his shoulders draped in a regal mantle. A crown of silver adorned his head. His expression was serene and commanding as if the weight of authority rested on him easily. Ephriam clenched his fists, his jaw tight.

"Ephriam?" Brie asked in a small voice. "What is this?"

He shook his head without looking at her. "Pay these tricks no mind," he said stiffly. "This is what Khalid and Mariyah warned us about. Remember our purpose. Nothing else is real."

His words made an impression on the group. There was a general straightening of posture and squaring of shoulders. Mike nodded and marched forward with renewed energy.

But Brie remained uneasy, feeling that they had been shaken more deeply than anyone was prepared to admit. The weight of the city pressed on them all, its invisible tendrils winding into their minds and pulling at their most profound insecurities. She looked from one companion to the next, their expressions betraying the tiny cracks forming beneath their composure.

Only Tavi seemed unaffected. She moved with a strange, carefree affect, her body swaying slightly as if to music. Her lips curled into a troubling smile, her pale face eerily calm despite her weakened state. Every so often, a soft laugh escaped her, low and unsettling.

"Tavi, are you okay?" Brie asked, not because she expected an answer but because she didn't know what else to do.

The Elysian turned her head slowly. "Oh, I'm wonderful," she said in a dreamy, lilting voice. "It's so funny, isn't it?"

Brie hesitated. "What's funny?"

The woman didn't answer. Instead, she pointed at the nearest column, her hand trembling with unspent energy. "They like us," she said, her voice dropping into a conspiratorial whisper. "They think we're delicious."

# CHAPTER TWENTY-ONE

## The Descent

The air grew heavier, thick with the weight of centuries-old secrets. The carvings in the ancient stone became more intricate, telling fragmented stories that swirled and twisted under Brie's gaze. She reached out instinctively, moved by some strange compulsion, her fingers hovering inches from the surface of one of the etchings.

"Brie, don't!" Cameron's voice rang out sharply.

She froze, then turned to find both Cameron and Ephriam staring at her with expressions of alarm. Cameron moved closer, his hand hovering near his sword as though the carvings themselves might lash out at any moment.

"Do you have any idea what you're looking at?" Ephriam asked, his voice urgent. "This isn't mere decoration. These symbols are old — older than most civilizations. It's best to leave them well alone."

Brie dropped her hand, swallowing hard. "What do they mean?"

Ephriam exchanged a look with Cameron, and then they launched into a story that felt like it belonged to another world.

"Ubar was once a thriving trade hub," Cameron began, gesturing toward the crumbling remains of a marketplace in the distance. "It was called the Atlantis of the Sands, a jewel in the desert that connected kingdoms through the incense trade. But it was also a city of excess.

Greed and Gluttony ruled here, along with the rest of the Seven. And its human leaders sought power at any cost."

Ephriam picked up where Cameron left off. "According to Elysian records, the Nephilim struck a bargain with the rulers of Ubar. They offered the city untold riches in exchange for the humans' loyalty and worship."

She frowned, fighting back a rising sense of dread. "What kind of worship?"

Cameron's expression turned grim. "The kind that required blood. Sacrifice. Entire families were given over to feed the Nephilim's insatiable hunger for power. The city prospered, but its people suffered."

Ephriam gestured toward the carvings. "These symbols? They're not just art. They're a record of what the Nephilim demanded. This one," he pointed to a pictograph of the city surrounded and ensnared in enormous serpentine coils, "is a warning. It's Leviathan."

Her stomach churned. "What is that?"

"One of the Seven. You humans call him Envy." Ephriam was grinding his teeth so hard she could hear it from paces away. "Whoever in the city chose to stand opposed to the Seven, Leviathan swallowed them whole."

Sherry chimed in. "What happened to the city?"

"The Elysian Council intervened," Cameron replied. "They sent a host of angels to destroy the Nephilim and bury the city beneath the sands, but with a caveat. Ubar was left as a warning, a place imbued with the souls of all who had transgressed within its walls, cursed to never truly die, bound here by these runes to an eternity of watching."

Mike's brow furrowed. "But why would the entrance to Eden be in such a God-forsaken place? Surrounded by these… whatever they are?"

"The entrance to Eden never remains in one place for long," answered Ephriam. "It is unfixed in both time and space to keep it hidden from friend and foe alike. Why it should choose to appear here is as much a mystery to me as to you."

"Great," Mike muttered, his voice dripping with sarcasm. "So we're casually strolling into a city that's basically the world's worst haunted house."

Sherry elbowed him lightly. "At least we're not alone. We've got a city's worth of zombie-stones and Tavi's running commentary to keep us entertained."

Tavi laughed, her head tilted back as she pointed at the carvings.

"They're laughing at us," she said. "They think we're hilarious."

This was met with dead silence — the group simply continued into the shadows.

As they reached the central plaza, Brie felt the atmosphere shift again. The ruins closed in around them, and the shadows grew darker despite the midday sun. The carvings became grotesque, depicting serpents entwined with human figures, faces twisted in ecstasy and despair. Her pendant burned even hotter, searing her chest. "Does anyone else feel that?" she asked.

Cameron frowned. "Feel what?"

"It's—" she hesitated, searching for the right words. "It's like something's pulling me. Toward the center."

As if on cue, Tavi pitched forward, clutching her chest. Ephriam leapt off his mount and was at her side in an instant, lowering her to the ground as her breathing grew labored. The rest of them dismounted quickly. Before they could even grab hold of the reins, the camels scattered, racing back to the open sand and the safety of the tribe.

Brie stared after them for a split second in dismay before rushing to her fallen friend.

"Tavi?" She knelt in a burst of panic. "What's wrong?"

Tavi's lips moved, but her words were barely audible. Ephriam pressed a hand to her forehead. "She's burning up," he said tightly, shifting to a better angle. "Whatever's happening here, it's accelerating her condition."

Brie felt a wave of frustration crash over her. "It's the city, isn't it? *It's* doing this to her."

Tavi's eyes fluttered open, and for a fraction of a second, she sounded like herself. A broken version of herself, but the woman they knew and loved all the same. "Arafel," she rasped. "He is here. You have to stop it. Before it's too late. They are coming."

"Who?" Brie whispered urgently, crouching beside her. "Who is coming?"

A crackle of electricity rippled over the Elysian before her lips curved once more into that unnatural smile. "You'll see."

With that, she passed out cold.

The group pressed on. Ephriam and Cameron carried Tavi between them, wincing when her random shocks of electricity jolted through their bodies. They reached the plaza's center a few minutes later, and all their momentum stopped.

"Now what?" Sherry asked, throwing up her hands.

"I have no idea," admitted Brie. "There's got to be something here."

"Why? Because your magical necklace told you so?" her best friend snapped viciously.

Brie stared back at her, stunned, as Camron placed a quiet hand on her shoulder.

Within the space of a second, every ounce of rage drained from Sherry's face, leaving it the color of soured milk. She shook her head quickly, looking mortified. "I'm sorry," she said softly. "I don't know what that was. I'm just… it's so hot." She sank onto a nearby bench and hung her head. "I wish there was something I could do," she added quietly, kicking at the sand. "Feels like it's always you leading the way."

She took off her backpack and heaved it onto a nearby rock.

It immediately began to sink into the earth.

With a wild squawk, Sherry leapt to her feet and snatched her bag, backing away as the rock rose to its original position once again.

Everyone froze in shock before Brie cried, "Sherry, you're a genius!"

Sherry blinked twice and pivoted flawlessly. "As I was saying," she replied smoothly, "I'm basically in charge here, and you'd all be lost without me."

Mike hid a chuckle as he and Ephriam wasted no time finding a rock of similar weight and heaving it onto the trigger. As it began to sink back into the earth, a spiral of light-colored cobblestones sank with it, revealing a sunken courtyard at the base of a winding set of stairs.

The process took only a few minutes, leaving Brie just enough time to wonder if this was a trap and conclude that even if it was, they had to go in anyway. "This is it," she said, trying to project confidence despite the nervous flutter in her stomach. "We have to go."

The others must have undergone a similar thought process, as by the time the stairs gave a final thud and stopped moving, they stood up with matching, stoic expressions, hoisted Tavi and their supplies onto their backs once again, and started to climb down.

The steps were carved directly into the stone, their edges worn smooth by time. The light from the courtyard reflected into the depths, illuminating the way forward, and a series of glowing stones lit the staircase. The walls were etched with ancient symbols, their meanings long forgotten, pulsing with a phosphorescence Brie had only seen in British-narrated documentaries about coral reefs or deep caves.

*This is utterly surreal.*

The stairway seemed endless, a dreamy sort of endless, until suddenly, it stopped. They passed below an arch that led to a wide hallway. Brie paused, her pendant shining brighter now, its light matching a faint pulse emanating from somewhere in the distance. As they marched on, the oppressive heat gave way to something cooler, reverent in its stillness.

The stone walls grew lighter until they finally emerged into an underground canyon deep beneath the city. It was impossible, stretching farther than the eye could see. The air was crisp and clean, carrying a hint of an unidentifiable fragrance — something ancient and untouched.

Brie looked up, and her breath caught in her throat. Above them, a ribbon of light flowed in hues of silver and gold, its surface rippling as though caught in a gentle current. Patches of an endless sky appeared, filled with twinkling stars. It was awe-inspiring and completely disorienting like the heavens had folded inward to guide their path.

"Is that a river? In the *sky*?" Sherry asked in a hush.

Nobody answered. Nobody knew what to say.

The path twisted and turned, the stone beneath their feet smooth and cool. Ethereal light shone from above until, at last, the canyon widened into a vast clearing, and there it stood.

A tree.

It rose from the center of the clearing as though it had grown directly from the heart of the earth. Its bark shimmered with an otherworldly luminescence. Its canopy stretched high, disappearing into the light above as if the tree was drinking from the celestial stream. At its base, massive roots spiraled outward, forming natural arches and alcoves. They seemed to pulse, alive with the same energy that coursed through the canyon. Nestled among the roots was a pool of crystalline water, its surface so still and clear it mirrored the canopy above. The air around them grew lighter and buoyant like they were stepping into a space untouched by time.

"You were right," Cameron said in a hushed voice. "I should've believed you. I've heard stories since I was a boy… That *has* to be the entrance to Eden."

Without another word, Ephriam and Cameron touched their fingers to their foreheads and bowed in their Elysian sign of respect.

Brie's pendant grew brighter with every step. The tree hummed in response, its energy resonating with hers. For one perfect moment, everything else — the fear, the exhaustion, the doubt — vanished. All that remained was the light, the tree, and the promise of what lay beyond. Her heart was beating like a drum. The pendant shone like a newborn star.

Cameron reached for her hand, his face awash in the exquisite light. "What do we do?" she asked.

He shook his head. "I've never been here before. I have no idea. Ephriam?" He turned to his friend and immediately tensed.

Brie turned and saw the Elysian staring back the way they'd come, in full battle stance, nostrils flared, sword drawn. "What is it?" she asked, afraid of the answer.

"There's something else down here." He rotated in a slow circle, every inch of him rigid as a blade. "Something old. Something dangerous."

The group froze before instinctively encircling Tavi, searching in every direction for the source of his dread.

But the attack came from the one place they least expected.

# CHAPTER TWENTY-TWO

## The Shard of Betrayal

A tremor rippled through the ground beneath them, subtle at first. Within seconds, it built to a frenzy. Waves of earth tossed the group around like sailors on a storm-ravaged ship. The force of it roused Tavi back into consciousness.

Before anyone could draw a breath, yell, or come up with a plan, it stopped. The sound that followed wasn't thunderous — it was worse. Low, guttural laughter echoed off the canyon walls. It didn't come from a single direction but emanated from everywhere at once in a cruel, mocking chorus.

Mike drew his gun. "Tell me someone else hears that," he muttered desperately.

"Who...?" Sherry shook her head, voice cracking in the silence, all bravado stripped away by the primal fear that gripped them all. "What is that?"

Ephriam's hand tightened around his sword, standing ready.

"It's aware of us," he said, his words clipped. "It's been aware of us this whole time."

The laughter deepened, shifting into something that felt more like metal grinding against stone. Brie winced, her hands flying to her ears as the vibrations coursed through her. The whole canyon resonated with the sound, amplifying it until it was unbearable. The air thickened with a pressure that made it difficult to breathe. "It's the city," she cried. "Or the canyon. Or—" She broke off, unable to find the words.

Ephriam turned his head sharply, nostrils flaring as though he were scenting the air. His expression hardened. "No," he said. "It has to be him. Leviathan."

The name sent a chill through the group, their fear solidifying into something sharper, more tangible.

Tavi, who had remained unconscious and unnervingly quiet, suddenly laughed — a sharp burst of mirthless glee that sent ice racing through Brie's veins. "I told you," she said, her voice high and strange. "He's coming. He's already here."

The tremors returned, shaking the ground beneath them in violent surges. Brie staggered, reaching instinctively for Cameron. The laughter grew until it was impossible to tell whether it was coming from Tavi or the canyon itself. Then, all at once, her manic laughter stopped. Her body jerked as though a puppet's strings had been yanked taut. Her head snapped back, and her eyes rolled upward, turning a stark, unnatural white. A crackle of energy rippled over her skin, sending bursts of sparks snapping and arcing into the air around her.

"Tavi!" Brie shouted in a panic. She tried to step forward, but Cameron held her back.

"Tavianne, stop!" Ephriam bellowed, reaching towards her until a burst of electricity drove him back. "You must—"

Before he could say another word, her body convulsed, and a blinding bolt of electricity erupted from her chest and shot outward, a searing tendril of energy that struck the cavern's walls. A deafening crack split the air as chunks of rock and sand rained down from above.

The force of the blast hurled everyone backward, slamming them into the ground. Brie's breath was knocked from her lungs, the impact jarring every bone in her body. Stars danced in her vision. Her ears rang with a high-pitched whine that drowned out everything else. She blinked rapidly and struggled to regain her bearings before turning toward Tavi.

She froze at what she saw.

The lovely warrior stood in the center of the blast radius, arms outstretched, alight with residual energy. The air around her shimmered with heat and static, distorting her figure like a mirage. Her eyes, still white, shone with a fierce luminescence. And then she spoke — not in her own voice, but one that was dark and reverberated in the marrow of their bones.

*"You cannot stop what is already in motion. He is here."*

As the last word echoed through the cavern, the energy around Tavi dissipated, and she collapsed like a marionette with its strings cut. Ephriam was the first to recover, rushing to her side and checking for a pulse. "She's alive," he called. "But barely."

Brie forced herself to her feet, shaking. "What was that?" she asked, terrified.

There was a fleeting pause.

"A warning shot." Ephriam looked around like he was ready to murder the canyon itself. "It's toying with us. We can't stay here — we have to find a way into Eden."

It was deathly quiet now, save for the whisper of the wind. The chain around Brie's neck felt heavy, digging into her skin. The pendant throbbed urgently but gave her no direction, no clear sign of what to do. "There's nothing here!" she shouted, her voice raw with frustration.

"There has to be," Cameron stared up at the impossible branches and the canopy high above. "The tree must be the key. Otherwise, it wouldn't be here."

Mike paced a short distance away, growing frantic. "If it's the key, how do we open it? Do we knock? Say *open sesame*? What are we supposed to do?!"

"Maybe we climb it?" Cameron asked, still staring upward.

Sherry stood with her hands on her hips, glaring at the tree as if sheer force of will could unlock its secrets. "Try using the pendant."

Brie clutched it in her hand. "I don't even know how this thing works!" she admitted, tears of frustration stinging her eyes. "It's never done anything like this before!"

They went back and forth, searching frantically for some clue. Ephriam knelt beside Tavi, his face grim. He pressed his hands to her temples, lips moving in an Elysian prayer that Brie couldn't understand. "Stay with me, Tavi," he implored in a broken voice. "You don't get to leave us like this."

She didn't respond. Her breathing was shallow, her body unnaturally still, as if whatever force had taken her was holding her right on the edge of life.

Sherry broke away from the group, crossing the clearing to Ephriam. She tried to speak softly so as not to disturb Tavi, but panic laced her voice. "What are we even up against here? What exactly is Leviathan?"

"He's an eater of cities," he replied softly, never looking away from Tavi. "He devours everything in his path — stone, steel, souls. He leaves nothing behind but sand and silence."

Sherry swallowed hard but pressed on. "What can we do to stop him?"

Ephriam sat there a moment, then lifted his head. His eyes were dark with something none of them could name. "You don't stop Leviathan," he said simply. "No one does."

The group fell silent, his words cutting through the frantic energy like a knife. It was like their strings had been cut as well, leaving them wobbling on their own.

"He isn't like the other Seven," he continued softly. "He has no agenda anyone can discern. No human form. He has but one sole purpose: to take away whatever gives you joy. Not because he wants it. Not because it gives him any pleasure. He is not like Baal — he has no desire to consume. Not like Mammon — he has no desire to possess. His only aim is that no one *else* should have anything good. If he can't have it, *no one can*. He is a being wholly divorced from the warmth of divine love."

The others shuddered, but Ephriam wasn't done. "I saw him once. He came upon an army in the heart of the desert — thousands of warriors armed with weapons forged by the finest smiths of their time. They had built a fortress, high and mighty, thinking it would hold him back." He shook his head. "He swallowed them whole. The city, the soldiers, the fortress. All of it. And then he dove beneath the sands and disappeared for an eon."

The hair prickled on the back of Brie's neck. "Then our only hope is to get into Eden," she whispered. "Before he comes back."

Sherry stared hard at Tavi. At first, her expression was simply distraught, but something else crept in. Suspicion. A tiny line creased the center of her brow. "Wait," she said slowly. "This doesn't make sense."

"What doesn't?" Mike asked, still pacing.

"Leviathan," she said, eyes narrowing. "If he's the one doing this, why is he coming after us now? Just because these were his stomping grounds once, forever ago? We've been here for days. Why now? And why Tavi?"

Brie's heart sank as the pieces began to fall into place. She looked at Tavi, her breath catching, her mind flooded with memories from the past few weeks, now cast in a different light. Her visions and hallucinations. That sing-song lilt and eerie smile. "She hasn't been herself," she said softly. "Not since…"

"Since Virginia," Cameron finished in a hush.

Mike frowned. "Wait, what are you saying? That this isn't Leviathan?"

"When we were on the plane, that creature we saw — it said somebody was 'marked,'" Brie hesitated. "And Tavi… She's been different. Irritable. Moody. And always eating. Eating like she couldn't stop. Like a part of her would starve if she stopped." She looked around at their horrified expressions. "What if we missed something? Ephriam said that anywhere even a sliver of him remains, the rest of him can follow. We've all been assuming that the vacuum of space would be enough to hold him — that the only way for him to get back to Earth would be through the Time Seas, and he couldn't even do that because they're in a different plane of existence than the physical world. But we're here now. At the entrance to Eden. At an intersection between those planes. And somehow, he's done it — he's eaten his way back."

The words hung in the air as the group turned slowly to Tavi.

"It's not Leviathan," Brie finished. "It's Baal."

Before anyone could respond, Tavi's back arched as if she were being pulled upward by a cosmic rope. Ephriam leapt back, pale with shock, as she rose to her feet. Her movements were jerky and unnatural, like a doll in the hands of a wicked child.

Her head lolled to one side with a horrifying smile as she turned those glowing white eyes to Brie. The voice that spoke was filled with malice.

"You're clever," it said, dripping with mockery. "But not clever enough."

Brie staggered back, reeling in shock.

*Baal.*

The figure that had once been Tavi lifted its head and laughed. The sound echoed through the cavern like shattering glass. "He has waited. Gobbled and torn his way backward through the ages, searching for this moment. And now," Tavi's face twisted with a cruel grin. "You're all going to burn."

The sand around them exploded upward, a sudden and violent eruption that tore through the clearing like a hurricane. Brie threw up her arms to shield her face, but she could barely keep her footing as the savage force of it threatened to knock her down.

From the swirling sand emerged shards of metal shaped like lampreys — hundreds, no, thousands of them — glinting silver and sharp as razors. They hovered in the air like predatory fish, their sleek forms glinting with an unholy light. The swarm surged and shifted, forming fluid shapes that moved with a terrifying, alien intelligence. Brie's ears filled with a cacophony of grinding, gnashing, and chittering — a sound so overwhelming it set her teeth on edge.

The shards encircled the group, separating them in an instant. Each one was cut off from the others, isolated in pockets of swirling metal. It moved like a living wall, flowing around their bodies in waves, sometimes rising to their chests, sometimes up to their chins. Brie could see only the terrified faces of her friends as they stood frozen in place, surrounded by the swarm. It encircled her as well, swirling around her waist like a metallic tide. She stumbled backward, her breath coming in shallow gasps as it closed in, so close she could feel their unnatural chill.

"Cameron!" she screamed, but the chaos swallowed her voice. "Mike! Sherry! Ephriam!" She tried again, but her pleas couldn't reach them. The swarm cut through everything — air, sound, hope.

Her eyes darted wildly around the clearing, searching for anything that could help, any way to break through the swirling mass. Her gaze landed on Tavi, still standing at the center of the chaos, her body rigid and her face twisted into that unnatural grin. Behind her, the shards began to shift and condense, forming a new shape.

A face.

It was enormous, heinous, and painfully familiar. A face that Brie had seen in her nightmares — the sharp, angular features, the hollow eyes that gleamed with malevolent light. A gruesome mouth twisted into a smile filled with jagged, metallic teeth.

"What do you want from me?" she screamed.

The face hovered above Tavi like a dark halo, and when it spoke, it did so with a mix of their two voices, a layered and monstrous sound.

"What do I want?" Baal repeated, voice dripping with condescension. Tavi's lips curled, mirroring the expression of the swarm behind her, and she raised a hand, gesturing toward the massive tree. "Isn't it obvious? We're at the gates of Paradise. I want you to let me in."

The swarm swirled faster, the shards glinting menacingly in the dim light.

She turned, her gaze darting toward the tree, then back to Baal. Her heartbeat pounded in her ears. Her pendant burned like fire against her skin.

"I don't know how!" she shouted, voice breaking. "I don't know how to get in!"

The response was immediate and merciless. The shards around Ephriam flashed brighter, swirling downward with deadly precision. His scream tore through the air as he lifted his hand, blood gushing from where three fingers had been severed. Elysian blood splattered the ground, its light dimming as soon as it hit the sand.

"Ephriam!" she cried, ragged with terror. She tried to run to him, but the swarm surged upward, cutting her off. "No, no, please!" she screamed, whirling back to Baal. "I don't know the way in! I swear, I don't know!"

Baal tilted its head, the shards that formed its face shifting like liquid metal. "How disappointing," it said, cold and mocking. "Perhaps one of your friends will know."

*No!*

The shards flashed again; this time, they swarmed around Sherry and tightened. Her scream was high and piercing as she clutched her shoulder a second later. Blood streamed between her fingers. Brie caught a glimpse of her stricken face before the swarm closed around her again.

She turned back to Baal, shaking violently from head to toe.

"Please. I'm not lying to you. I don't know how!"

The swarm surged around Mike and Cameron next, attacking in a sudden dive and leaving a chorus of bloody screams in its wake. Again and again, while Brie shouted her defenses, they moved in an unpredictable pattern, toying with their victims from above.

"What can I do?" she finally begged. "What can I give you to make this stop?"

Baal laughed, a grating, metallic sound.

Tavi's lips moved in unison with the face behind her as it spoke. "What can you give me? You have nothing I need, child. Nothing except…" The voice trailed off, and Tavi's terrifying white eyes fixed on Brie's chest. "That."

Brie's hand flew to the pendant, clutching it tightly. The warmth of it pulsed against her fingers like the beat of a second heart. "You want the pendant?" she whispered.

Baal's grin widened. "As I said. Clever girl."

Her mind blanched in panic, every fiber of her being screaming that this was wrong, that she couldn't trust Baal, that giving up the pendant would be a mistake she could never undo. But the screams of her friends drowned out every rational thought. She looked desperately at the chaos, barely able to see them through the swarm.

"If I give it to you," she began, holding it up, "will you let us go?"

The swarm went still, and a terrible silence fell over the clearing.

"You would give it to us freely?" Baal asked.

She couldn't speak. She simply nodded, her throat too tight to form words.

Tavi raised her hand, her movements slow and deliberate. Her fingers curled, palm outstretched, controlled by that horrific, invisible force.

"Yes," Baal answered, voice thick with triumph. "Give it to me, and all of this will end."

The pendant shone more brightly than ever, its opaline surface swirling with colors that danced like trapped galaxies.

Brie stared into its depths, desperate for answers, for a way out — finding nothing.

Baal resumed his assault on her friends, diving in merciless bursts and leaving the ground bloody in his wake. Sherry's whimper of pain somehow cut through all the horrifying noise, and Brie's heart broke as she heard Cameron's panicked gasp as blood poured from his mouth.

She lifted the chain over her head, eyes glistening with unshed tears.

"Please," she pleaded in a broken whisper. "Let them go."

The shards instantly stilled, freezing in place. The canyon fell into eerie silence, save for Brie's ragged breathing.

Tavi moved forward with that terrible, jerking gait, limbs twitching, pulled by those invisible strings. Her hand shook excitedly as it reached for the pendant.

But the second she touched it, everything happened at once.

A blinding white light erupted from the stone, so painfully brilliant it imprinted on the canyon walls. Shadows stretched long and sharp, every detail of the scene frozen in stark relief.

Brie's eyes shone with the same unearthly radiance that had overtaken her in Virginia. Her body was beaming, and her veins were filled with liquid fire.

Tavi was thrown backward, crashing into the sand so forcefully that a small crater formed beneath her, sending shockwaves rippling through the ground.

And the shards of Baal exploded outward with such violent speed they were flattened into silence against the canyon walls.

The light faded, and Brie collapsed to her knees, gasping for breath. Her vision blurred. Both hands were shaking. With a strangled cry, she scrambled over to Sherry's crumpled figure. Her limbs were limp and tangled, and her skin was deathly pale. There was a hole in her shoulder, dark and smoking, the edges burned black. Brie ripped off her sleeve, pressing it desperately against the wound.

"Sherry, wake up," she begged. "Please. God — please wake up."

Her attention shifted to Cameron. He was crumpled on his side, blood pooled beneath him. Her stomach lurched as she saw the jagged tear through his torso.

"No," she cried. "No!"

She turned toward Ephriam and choked back a sob. His left leg was gone from the knee down. Glowing Elysian blood seeped into the sand all around him.

Mike was barely visible, slumped in a crimson pool.

But the worst was Tavi. Her limbs splayed away from her body at impossible angles. With a broken cry, Brie scrambled over to the Elysian's side. On closer look, her skin was tinged with blue. Her lips were parted, her eyes glassy and unblinking.

Brie frantically put two fingers to her neck to check for a pulse. Nothing. She pressed her ear to the warrior's chest, praying for a heartbeat, even the slightest breath. Nothing.

*Nothing.*

She pushed shakily to her feet in the dead silence. It felt like she was filling with water, swelling to the brim. Then she started screaming.

"Somebody help us! Somebody! Anybody! *Please!*"

The only response was the worst one possible.

The shards of Baal twitched.

She froze as the swarm began to reconstitute itself, rising from the sands in a deadly tide. The shards flowed together, twisting and coiling like serpents, forming once more into the enormous, nightmarish face. The grinding, tearing sound returned, louder and more terrible than ever. The face swelled even larger, looming over them all, blotting out the sky. It rose higher still, a horrific counterpoint to the light sparkling behind it and the magnificent tree guarding the gates of Paradise. The mouth opened wide, and it dove, coming to devour them whole. Brie screamed and threw up her arms to cover her face, still clutching the pendant.

It was in that moment, when hope seemed forever lost, that it happened.

A rope of lightning-white energy burst from the pendant's stone, striking the tree's canopy high above. Where it struck, there were no sparks or fire. No shower of destruction. Instead, the energy was absorbed into the trunk itself, veining downward in sudden illumination until it reached the base.

It outlined a pair of magnificent doors.

At the same time, a wave of blue light surged outward from the point of impact, placing itself directly in the swarm's path like a luminescent barrier.

There was a low, shifting sound. The doors in the tree, imbued with the energy of her pendant, suddenly opened outward from the middle of the dazzling trunk. The crack of brilliant white light grew wider, spilling into the canyon. The face of Baal stopped its death dive and twisted to look as a figure appeared, bathed in heavenly radiance. His armor gleamed. His wings spread wide, shimmering with iridescent hues, and in his hand, he held a flaming sword, its blade a cascade of molten fire. He stepped into the canyon, and the doors snapped shut behind him.

Brie recognized him from the painting hanging over Cameron's childhood bed.

The Archangel Michael.

# CHAPTER TWENTY-THREE

## The Archangel's Intervention

The air around Michael shimmered, charged with an energy so profound it made the very atmosphere feel alive. His presence was a force of nature — glorious and perilous, a storm contained within his majestic form.

"Baal!" His voice was thunderous. The ground trembled. The light of his flaming sword cast even other lights into shadow. "You have no claim here. By the will of the Most High, I banish you!"

The shards of Baal's metallic horde wavered, but his face twisted with defiance and rage. "You cannot banish me, Michael." The swarm swirled faster, their grinding and gnashing rising to a keening pitch. "This place has known my touch. These sands are mine!"

With a deafening roar, the swarm forgot about the mortals and surged toward Michael, a silver tidal wave of death and destruction hurtling downward faster than sound. It seemed inevitable that it would crush him. There was no way to stand against such a thing and survive.

Then Michael moved.

To call it speed was to do it injustice. He didn't simply move faster than Brie's eyes could follow — he moved outside of time itself as if minor trivialities like cause and effect held no sway over him. One moment, he was standing still, sword raised; the next, the shards of Baal were splitting apart, each one slashed by the blinding fire of his blade.

It was a thing of wonder.

The sword blazed with celestial fury, its light cutting through the darkness like the first rays of dawn after an eternal night. The heat radiating from it was blistering, unbearable, and yet it carried with it a sense of assurance, an unspoken validation.

The light was unyielding, incorruptible. The light could never be undone.

The shards of Baal ignited on contact, exploding into flame before melting into writhing ribbons of liquid darkness. The archangel was as deadly as he was impossibly precise, each strike cleaving order into the chaos. He moved with a grace that was both terrifying and beautiful, every motion a testament to divine power.

As Michael struck another blow, Baal's metallic visage twisted, contorting into a mask of calculated malice. The writhing black ribbons of his fallen shards began to coalesce, folding inward — thickening, solidifying. A moment later, the massive face dissolved.

What rose from the sands was far worse.

To look at Baal in his corporeal form was grotesque: a towering figure of morbid obesity that defied the very laws of nature. His bloated flesh glistened like molten metal, dark veins pulsating beneath the surface of his mottled skin. His eyes, burning pits of crimson, locked onto Michael with a ravening hunger that was both physical and something far greater.

Michael scarcely had time to react as Baal lunged, the ground quaking beneath his weight. Despite his monstrous bulk, the demon moved with terrifying speed, feral and unpredictable. A clawed hand struck like a thunderbolt, its force sending shockwaves through the canyon. Michael parried with his sword, their collision erupting like a nova. The air rippled with the clash of divine and corrupted energies, the impact reverberating like a celestial drumbeat.

Brie watched in horror as the two beings fought, their movements blurring into streaks of light and shadow. For the first time, she felt a flicker of doubt. Baal's strength was overwhelming, his attacks relentless. Each strike of his claws left scars on the earth as his ravenous growls split the air.

A voice boomed out like an earthquake.

"Do you even remember us, Michael?" The sound was pure venom. "Do you remember how it began? How we, your siblings, were cast out for daring to create, for daring to aspire to the divine?"

Michael blocked another strike, meticulous and controlled. "You were cast out for corrupting creation," he answered in a clear, calm voice despite the fury of the battle. "You twisted what was pure. You sought to make yourselves gods."

Baal let out a guttural laugh, his massive body moving with surprising agility as he evaded a strike from that flaming sword. "Twisted?" he sneered. "We gave them free will. We gave them the fire to forge their own path! And what did you do, Michael? You smothered it. You told them to kneel, to obey, to live in fear of the Most High's wrath."

The next strike forced Baal back.

"You gave them power," Michael replied, pacing forward, "but you demanded their worship in return. You bound them to your will, enslaved them to their desires. You called it freedom, but it was nothing more than servitude under a different master."

They clashed again, blistering and impossible.

"And what of your servitude, Michael?" Baal spat. "You, the favored son, the ever-loyal soldier. Do you not tire of bowing to a Creator who gives so little in return? Who watches as His beloved children suffer and die?"

The archangel's sword met Baal's claws in a hailstorm of fire and light, the impact shaking the ground beneath them. "You see suffering because you create it," Michael answered, his voice unwavering. "You see injustice because you thrive on it. You cannot comprehend the light, Baal, because you have buried yourself in darkness."

The demon howled in rage, his massive frame shuddering with the force of his fury.

"Spare me your sanctimonious platitudes!" he thundered. "You do not understand what it is to be cast out, to be stripped of everything! You have never known the agony of being denied your rightful place in the cosmos!"

Michael paused as if the deadly battle was merely something happening amidst their conversation. For the briefest of moments, something like pity flashed across his face.

"You were not cast out because you were unworthy. You were cast out because you chose pride over purpose. You chose to corrupt rather than create. The Most High's love was never denied to you, Baal. You denied it to yourself."

There was another feral scream, this one unlike any that had come before.

"Enough!" Baal roared. "You are not my judge, brother!"

With a speed that belied his massive form, the demon streaked forward, claws outstretched, mouth gaping open as if to devour the archangel whole. But Michael was ready. He dodged the attack with effortless grace, his flaming sword spinning in a brilliant arc.

Time seemed to slow as the blade struck. It pierced Baal's bloated torso, the fire of divine justice spreading through his form like wildfire. There was an earsplitting scream as his body began convulsing in the devouring flames. The corrupted flesh melted away, collapsing into writhing black sinews of liquid evil that twisted and shrieked before seeping into the earth.

As quickly as it started, the fight was over. The ground beneath them stilled. The oppressive weight of the demon's presence lifted. Michael lowered his sword, its fire dimming to a soft glow. His eyes scanned the canyon for any lingering danger before he sheathed the blade with a satisfied clang.

*He killed it. He just killed it.*

Brie's legs buckled, and she collapsed to the ground as she struggled for breath. Her heart couldn't seem to catch its rhythm. Her eyes shot to the crumpled bodies of her friends, her stomach twisting at the sight of their broken, bloodied forms.

"Help…" she rasped, unable to give it any strength. She forced herself to her feet, staggering toward Michael. "Please, help them."

The archangel turned to her for the first time, staring with an indecipherable expression. His eyes locked on hers, and for a split second, she thought he might refuse. Then he nodded curtly, striding across the ground.

He knelt beside Sherry first, his hand hovering over her shoulder. A soft glow emanated from his fingers, and the gaping wound began to close, the charred flesh knitting itself back together. A second later, the bleeding stopped as her breath gradually steadied.

Brie let out a muffled gasp, covering her mouth.

*Thank God!*

With an easy grace, the angel moved from one person to the next, giving them the same quiet stare before healing each wound with a touch of his magical fingers. The laceration in Cameron's stomach vanished in a halo of golden light. A thousand ghastly cuts and bruises erased themselves from Mike's skin.

When the archangel got to Ephriam, a sudden noise broke the stillness.

Brie turned sharply, her breath catching in her throat.

Tavi lurched upright like someone had pushed a button, her movements strange and unnatural, that terrible light still glistening in her eyes.

"No," Brie whispered, shaking her head. "Tavi, no…"

With an incoherent shout, the Elysian launched herself at Michael, drawing a blade from nowhere and raising it high above her head. He turned just as her shadow fell over him, lifting a hand between them. Like something from a dream, she froze mid-air as though time around her had stopped.

"She didn't mean it," Brie gasped, seized with a sudden terror. "She's just—"

But the archangel made no attempt to draw his blade. Instead, he walked forward, examining the woman with a slight tilt of his head. After a few seconds, he nodded.

"Ah, a stowaway."

*What?*

His fingers touched together as he muttered a quiet incantation. The words were beyond Brie's understanding, yet there was a gravity to them, irresistible as the tides. Tavi's body convulsed, and there was a movement beneath her skin.

Something had hidden there.

Something that was trying with all its might not to leave.

Michael stepped closer, drawing it toward his palm, until something metal, no bigger than a splinter, burst forth in a spray of blood.

He caught it midair, crushing it to powder in his hand. By the time his fingers opened, it had already blown away in the wind.

Tavi collapsed, falling limp toward the ground. He caught her easily and swung her lifeless body onto his shoulder, but to Brie's surprise, he made no attempt to heal her. Her blood flowed freely down his back.

"You'd better come inside," he said abruptly, surprising her with the sudden informality of his tone. "Give me your key."

Brie blinked at him, utterly bewildered. "My key?"

She held out the pendant, thinking it was a good guess.

He sighed and shook his head. "Put that thing back on. Not that key — the other one."

For a few seconds, nothing happened. Then, he pointed to her pocket. Bewildered, she shoved her hand inside. He waited as she drew out Azrael's magnifying glass and handed it to him in a daze.

With practiced hands, he twisted the handle, pressing a tiny gemstone embedded in its base. The handle clicked and opened to reveal a delicate, intricately carved key.

*How? This whole time?*

"I *told* Uriel the humans would never understand it," he said sanctimoniously. "That I'd seen the moment myself, and they *didn't* understand it. 'But look at DaVinci,' he said. 'They aren't all the same. And even if they don't understand, humans always fiddle with shiny things. They're bound to figure it out.' Now here I am, playing out the scene I've seen a thousand times, with yet another ape who can't even tell when a key is a key."

With a shake of his head, Michael swept toward the base of the tree, holding the key high. There was a mighty creak as one of the branches reached down, taking it from his hand and inserting it into a hidden lock within the trunk.

The tree opened once more, revealing a radiant portal of light.

Michael tossed the key back to Brie, who watched numbly as it hit her in the chest and fell to the ground. The archangel sighed and picked it up himself, slapping it into her palm. "Follow me. Can you do that?"

She nodded through a sea of unspilled tears.

Michael directed the branches to gather up the rest of her friends. They descended from above and coiled gently around their bodies, cradling them carefully in the flowering boughs as they carried them past the threshold. The light from the miraculous tree washed over her as she stumbled after the archangel, following him inside. The tree closed gracefully behind them, smoothing into seamless bark, leaving no evidence of a door behind.

There was no one left in the canyon to hear it — the roar of fury that rose from the sands and split the desert sky.

# CHAPTER TWENTY-FOUR

## Eden

Brie staggered forward, her vision blurred with tears and exhaustion.

Above her stretched a sky so vast it felt infinite, painted in shifting hues of violet and sapphire. Wisps of light drifted through the air like living constellations, their patterns ever-changing. Even the ground was shimmering. It was alive, she realized. Everything was alive in a way that transcended her understanding. Plants glowed in colors richer than anything she'd seen, their movements subtle but unmistakably deliberate. Trees stretched upward, their branches twining together and sparkling like starlight.

It was like stepping into a reflection of the human world — one so impossibly perfect it defied reality. She felt as though she had been flipped upside-down, her body floating somewhere between the stars and the earth.

But none of it mattered. Not the radiant colors, not the celestial sky, not even the overwhelming sense of peace that emanated from every corner of the Garden. All she could see were her friends. Sherry, pale and limp. Cameron, barely breathing, covered in dried blood. Ephriam, with his missing leg and fingers. Mike, broken and unmoving.

And Tavi.

"She's dead," she choked out, stumbling toward Michael. "Let me see her. My pendant… maybe I can… oh my God, she's really dead."

The archangel continued moving gracefully forward, Tavi's body draped over his arm.

Brie struggled to follow. She barely noticed the figure that stepped out from the shadows of a towering tree. He was ancient in a way she couldn't define, commanding yet serene, his face lined with wisdom rather than age. His long robes swished around his ankles, woven from fibers that shimmered like water flowing beneath the moon.

"Michael, you are late." His voice was fathomless.

The archangel gave a short bark of a laugh. "Time doesn't matter here, Elijah. As always, the only thing pressing me is you."

The name barely registered, and as the friends were deposited gently on the ground, Brie fell to her knees beside Sherry. "Please," she begged, clutching her friend's hand. "They won't wake up. None of them will wake up."

Elijah turned to her, his dark eyes filled with something she couldn't name. He stepped closer, studying her for a long moment before glancing at Michael. "The chambers?"

Michael nodded. "The chambers."

There was a little pause, then Elijah turned his eyes to the tree. It towered above them, its branches a perfect mirror of the tree at the Garden's entrance. Its roots twisted downward, disappearing into the starlit pool below. From its branches hung enormous, cocoon-like structures, each one translucent and glowing with an inner light. Not just glowing, pulsing — beating like hearts in perfect rhythm.

One by one, Michael picked up her friends and carried them to the tree, lifting his head in greeting as the pods unfurled and lowered at his approach. They opened with a soft sigh, petals spreading wide to reveal an interior lined with luminous, brilliantly white fibers.

He gently placed each of her friends inside, watching as the petals slowly closed, encasing them within the protective shells. The last was Tavi, broken beyond all hope of repair. The tree nestled each of the shining white pods against its bright roots, protecting them like a womb. But it handled Tavi's with extra care, slipping her pod into the crystal water at its base.

Brie watched, riddled with fear and helplessness. "I didn't even get a chance to say goodbye," she whispered to no one.

*What if that's the last time I see them?*

*No. Absolutely not. Don't think like that.*

"They'll be okay," she turned and spoke loudly before losing even that tenuous grip on hope. "Won't they?" she finished in a small voice, lifting her eyes to the stranger, unsure whether it was a question or a plea. "Please, tell me they'll be okay."

Michael threw her a silent look, but Elijah's face held a gentle expression.

"They will heal," he said, calm and reassuring. "The chambers will restore them."

She shook her head, eyes swimming with tears. "How do you know? How can you be sure?"

He regarded her with a steady smile. "This is the Tree of Life," he said simply. "Its gifts are eternal. But you must trust it."

Michael nodded, walking to her side. "Now you."

She recoiled on instinct, shaking her head. "No. I'm fine. I'm not hurt."

"You are not fine," he said flatly. "You can barely stand."

She stumbled backward, clutching her pendant. "I can. I need to stay awake. I need to—"

"You need to rest," Elijah said gently. He placed a hand on her shoulder with a grounding touch. "You've carried a heavy burden. It's time to let it go. Just for a while."

She shook her head again, but her body shivered with exhaustion. "I can't. I have to—"

"Michael," Elijah said softly.

The archangel reached out, brushing his fingers against Brie's temple. The touch was light, almost tender, but it carried a weight she couldn't resist. A wave of warmth and calm washed over her, and within the space of a moment, her vision began to blur.

"No," she murmured, her voice slurring. "Please, I—"

"It is a kindness," Elijah said.

Her knees gave out a moment later, and Michael caught her easily. She felt herself being carried, head resting lightly against his chest. She barely registered the soft hum of the chamber opening or the white light that surrounded her as Michael placed her inside. The last thing she heard before drifting away was Elijah's voice, hazy and distant, like a lullaby.

"Rest now, child. You have done enough."

Brie's first sensation was warmth — not the stifling heat of the desert, but a subtle, all-encompassing warmth that seeped into her skin and bones, filling her with an overwhelming sense of safety. Her eyes fluttered open. At first, she couldn't remember where she was or what had happened. The air was sweet and fragrant, like flowers she couldn't name. For one fleeting moment, the world was perfect, and she didn't care.

That moment ended quickly.

With a jolt of panic, memories began to rush back — her friends, the attack, Baal's laughter, Michael.

*Tavi.*

She pressed her hands against the glowing walls around her. Their gentle pulse matched the rhythm of her heartbeat. She pushed her hands against the curved surface, her breath shallow. "Let me out," she whispered, her voice hoarse. She pressed harder against the walls. "Let me out!"

As if in response, the cocoon hummed softly. Its petals began to unfurl, folding back with a sigh. Cool, fresh air rushed in, carrying with it a thousand indescribable scents — sweet, earthy, sharp, and soothing all at once. She blinked as the sparkling light of morning flooded her vision, momentarily blinding her.

She stepped out hesitantly, bare feet sinking into the soft, luminous grass. Behind her, the chamber closed and was lifted upward, its stem-like branch withdrawing it back into the canopy of the Tree. She stood, disoriented beyond words, and tried to take in her surroundings.

The Garden stretched out before her, a tapestry of impossible beauty. The ground beneath her feet was covered in grasses and moss whose colors constantly shifted as if catching the light of an unseen sun. Flowers of every imaginable shape and hue bloomed in profusion, some as large as her head, others so delicate they looked like spun glass. Trees towered high above her, their leaves whispering softly in a language she couldn't understand.

A lion with fur like spun silver lay beside a lamb, its massive paws tucked beneath it as the smaller animal nuzzled against its side. A herd of antelope grazed nearby, their horns twisted like vines. A cluster of dragonflies hovered overhead, translucent wings painted with rainbows. A short way past, a massive, serpentine creature coiled lazily around the base of a tree, scales glinting with the colors of a stormy sky.

She pressed a hand to her chest, trying to remember how to breathe.

"This can't be real," she whispered. But the grass beneath her feet, the sweet air in her lungs, and the thrum of life all around told her otherwise.

"Real is a matter of perspective," said a voice behind her, smooth and lilting, like music.

She spun around, eyes widening in surprise.

It was an angel, clearly, but it wasn't like any angel she had ever imagined. The being's form shifted and flowed like a living watercolor, its edges blending and swirling as though painted by an artist's brush. Its face was ever-changing — male, female, old, young, and everything in between — never settling on a single appearance for longer than the blink of an eye. Wings spread from its back, but there weren't any feathers. They looked like vast, shifting canvases, a swirl of vibrant hues that melded and danced like oil on water, moving constantly, creating new shapes and patterns that seemed almost alive.

"Who... what are you?" she asked, tripping over the question in her wonderment.

The being tilted its head with an amused expression. "I am Morpheus," it answered in a voice that seemed to echo from far away. "The Angel of Dreams. And you, Brianna Weldon, are far from dreaming."

She stared in dizzied shock. "I don't understand."

Morpheus stepped closer, the ground beneath its feet blooming with flowers that vanished as quickly as they appeared. "You are in the Garden of Eden," it said simply. "A place shaped by belief as much as by creation. What you see here exists because it has been dreamed, because it has been imagined and remembered. Dreams give form to what might otherwise be forgotten."

She nodded, trying to understand. "Where are my friends?"

"They are asleep. Their healing process should not be interrupted."

"So, what am I doing here?" she asked, fearing the answer.

"You are here because you belong here," Morpheus answered, its voice softening. "For now." Without another word, it turned and glided gracefully through the Garden, motioning for her to follow. She did so without question. They passed by trees laden with fruits that gleamed like gemstones, their sweet fragrance filling the air, and paused by a stream with waters so clear they seemed invisible except for the rippling light that danced on its surface.

"This is a place of beginnings and endings," Morpheus said. "A sanctuary for those who carry the weight of creation and destruction alike."

She paused, hesitant to reply. "I don't understand what that means."

Morpheus turned to her, its ever-changing face serene. "You will. In time."

They continued on a little farther and stopped beneath a tree whose branches were woven with golden vines. Morpheus reached up and plucked a single, glowing fruit.

"Here. Taste."

She took it hesitantly, feeling profoundly uneasy about the concept of eating fruit in this particular garden. Yet the second she bit into it, a burst of sweetness filled her mouth — like sunlight and honey, and something she couldn't yet name but instantly craved. The weight on her soul lifted, and however briefly, she felt truly alive.

Morpheus smiled. "Good," it said. "You'll need your strength for what comes next."

She swallowed, the sweetness lingering on her tongue. "What comes next?"

Morpheus didn't answer. Instead, it gestured onward to the vast expanse of the Garden stretching endlessly toward the sun. "Come. There is more to see."

The glade where Morpheus led Brie felt like the heart of the Garden, an intimate pocket of serenity carved from the infinite majesty surrounding it. In the center lay a still pond, its surface so clear and undisturbed that she hesitated to call it water. It mirrored the heavens above, reflecting the branches of the Tree of Life as they twisted and stretched, their luminous leaves merging seamlessly with the stars. Beneath the surface, the roots formed an intricate web, a perfect inversion of the tree above, as though two worlds touched and met in this sacred place.

She knelt at the edge of the pond, her reflection rippling as the air moved around her. The pendant on her chest grew warm, its opaline light echoing the energy that seemed to emanate from the glade itself. She traced its surface absently, her thoughts a tangle of exhaustion, fear, and wonder.

"Do you see it now?" Morpheus's voice was like something out of a dream. "The balance between what is above and what lies below?"

She glanced at the being, its form swirling with colors and shapes she could barely comprehend. "I don't know what I see," she admitted quietly. "It's beautiful, but it feels so fragile. Like it could all break apart at any moment."

Morpheus tilted its head, the hint of what might have been a smile flitting across its face. "Fragile things endure because they adapt," it said. "Strength comes not from being unbreakable, but from bending without shattering."

She stared at the water, feeling heavy as a stone.

"What if I've already bent as far as I can?" she whispered. "Lost as much as I can stand? I keep searching for clarity, and all anyone ever brings me are questions and riddles. I'm *afraid*."

Morpheus's wings unfurled, their kaleidoscopic colors reflecting in the water like living light. "Courage is not the absence of fear," it said gently. "It is the choice to face it, again and again, even when you falter."

She shook her head silently, eyes welling with tears. "Morpheus, I don't know why this is happening, and I don't know what I'm supposed to do."

The angel leaned down. Its features stilled, becoming something almost human. "You will," it promised. "When the question is asked, when the moment comes, you will choose. And you will not choose alone."

Before she could respond, Morpheus began to fade, its colors blending into the glade until it was gone, leaving her alone by the pond.

*How utterly lovely... and wildly unhelpful.*

*Angels.*

Brie shook her head and turned as a figure approached. Elijah moved with a serene grace. His face was kind, lined with wisdom, but free of the weariness she had seen in so many others. His dark eyes sparkled with quiet humor as though he carried the weight of eternity lightly, even playfully.

"Ah, there you are," he said, his voice warm and unhurried. "I wondered when you'd find your way to this spot. It's one of my favorites."

She rose to her feet, wiping her palms on her shirt. "Elijah," she said, the name feeling both strange and familiar on her tongue.

He smiled. "At your service," he said, bowing his head slightly. "And you are Brianna Weldon." He studied her face thoughtfully, with intelligent, shining eyes. "I've been looking forward to this moment for longer than you know."

She frowned curiously. "How long is that?"

"A few millennia, give or take," he answered.

*See, that's the kind of response that takes more peace of mind than it gives.*

"I'll be happy to tell you about it," he continued, "Though I imagine you're less interested in me and more concerned about your friends."

Her chest tightened. "Are they okay?"

He gestured behind him, where the Tree of Life shone in the distance. "They are in the Tree's care," he said. "And the Tree has never failed those who trust it."

She swallowed, the knot in her stomach loosening slightly. "And Tavi?"

His expression shadowed, the humor fading. "All I can say is, things happened just as they were meant to."

Her heart skipped a beat.

She'd heard that expression before. Once, what felt like a million years ago.

When Cameron told her what had happened to her mother's soul.

Her mind went completely blank.

She didn't remember sitting down, but the next thing she knew, she was on a moss-covered log, with Elijah beside her, aware that he was speaking, though she couldn't decipher any words.

"What are you saying?" she interrupted him, bewildered. "She isn't dead. That isn't… she is not dead. She's my friend," she added, as though this might tip the scales.

Elijah regarded her quietly before repeating what he'd been trying to say for five minutes. "We placed her in the care of the Tree of Life itself. She hasn't returned. Her spirit has moved on. I know of no force in Heaven or on Earth, short of the Divine itself, that can bring her back."

She shook her head, first in disbelief, then in defiance.

"Show me," she demanded. "I can do it. I've done it before. Show me where she is."

Elijah said nothing, merely stood, and began walking back to the Tree. She followed him, her footsteps too loud, too harsh for the softness of the Garden.

She didn't care.

*I can save her.*

*I saved Rashida. I can do it again.*

When they reached the Tree, she marched with furious determination up to the edge of the impossible pool at its base before realizing that she didn't know what to do. The four pods that housed the rest of the group were still clustered amongst the roots, thrumming with that brilliant white light. But it wasn't until she stared into the pool's depths that she saw it — Tavi's pod, deep beneath the waters, emitting only the faintest trace of dark, amber light.

As she watched, the amber light flickered and went out.

Instinctively, she knew.

She fell to her knees. "It can't be true," she whispered. "She's too strong, too good. It can't be true." She looked down, her hand curling around her pendant. "I don't understand any of this," she said, utterly defeated. "Why her? Why me? Why any of us?"

Elijah stepped closer, placing a hand on her shoulder. It was a grounding touch, like standing on solid earth after a storm at sea.

"Questions are seeds, child," he said. "Plant them, and the answers will grow when they are meant to. I've had visions of more futures than I could ever count, and in none of them were you responsible for what happened here today. Please, for now, trust that you are here for a reason. The Garden does not make mistakes."

"But I do," she whispered. She gazed at the amber pod. "Tavi… I'm so, so sorry."

She leaned over the pool, her pendant swinging from its chain, when a single tear escaped and slowly rolled down her cheek to fall perfectly onto the ancient, opaline stone. She bowed her head, brokenhearted, as the tear fell from the pendant into the pool itself. "I love you, Tavianne."

The ancient prophet stood respectfully by as she struggled to compose herself to no avail. Eventually, he intervened. "Come, child," he said softly.

She allowed herself to be led away.

Neither of them saw the way her tear started to glow when it touched the waters of Eden.

Neither saw when the entire pool lit up, a brilliant, blinding white.

They wandered in silence for a bit, heading back in the direction of the Dreaming Glade, till they came upon a pavilion furnished with chairs and a bed. A bowl of fruits had been laid out for her on a small table. Elijah stood by as she sank into the nearest chair.

The quiet between them was suddenly broken by the heavy tread of boots. With a flicker of surprise, she turned to see Michael approaching. The archangel's golden armor glinted in the light, fearsome and commanding. Yet despite his domineering presence, there was an undeniable tension and a weariness in his every step.

"You've been busy," Elijah said lightly. "Saving the world again, I assume?"

Michael rolled his eyes, his hand resting on the hilt of his sword. "Someone has to," he muttered. "Not all of us get to sit around waxing poetic and watering the flowers."

Elijah chuckled, warm and rich. "Ah, Michael. Always the thundercloud that forgot how to rain."

The archangel groaned, pinching the bridge of his nose. "Can we not do this right now?"

"Of course, of course," Elijah said, waving a hand. "But carrying the weight of the cosmos on your shoulders isn't a requirement, you know. No matter what you've told yourself."

Brie watched the exchange, a smile tugging at her soul despite the heaviness in her heart. The surreal majesty of the Garden felt almost human as the two ancient figures before her bickered like old friends.

They settled onto the chairs opposite her, and Elijah turned to her with a face full of sympathy. "You have already borne so much, but child, we must ask still more of you before the story grows stale in your mind."

*Not much chance of that.*

"No mortal has stepped foot within our realm since the dawn of time," the prophet continued. "What has brought you to our Garden, in such company, bearing such burdens, chased by such enemies? What darkness lurks outside our walls?"

The ancient man and the glorious archangel waited patiently for her reply.

She had moved beyond hesitation, second-guessing, even emotion. Taking a deep breath, she began at the beginning. Once she started, she didn't stop. She laid the full tale before them — the past five years since her first encounter with the supernatural, culminating in the astonishing events of the past few weeks. Traumas and triumphs, destiny and despair, shock and revelation merged into a stark recitation of events.

She barely registered the uneasy glances exchanged between the two immortals. She hardly flinched when Elijah gasped in horror upon hearing of the spiderweb of cracks in the Elysian sky. But when she reached the moment Baal had risen from the sands just outside their gates, her words faltered. Silence swallowed her, and she stared at the table, unable to meet their eyes.

When it became clear that she wasn't going to speak again, Michael rose to leave. On his way out of the pavilion, he clasped a hand over her shoulder. He looked like he might say something, but in the end, he merely gave her a gentle squeeze and walked away.

Elijah studied her with a solemn expression for a long while before rising to go. "Rest tonight," he said, quiet but firm. "Tomorrow, we begin to untangle the threads of your destiny. But for now, breathe. Look around you. This place is a sanctuary not only for your body, but also your soul."

She nodded mutely and climbed immediately into the bed.

Elijah withdrew.

The moment he disappeared down the path, Brie broke down.

Her body was wracked with sobs. For the first time in five years, for the first time since her mother's death, tears flowed freely down her cheeks, grief made manifest. At first she touched her face, unable to believe it was happening, before the waves of sorrow took her once again. She never saw the way her tears sparkled with an otherworldly brilliance or formed an ancient sign where they fell upon her pillow.

*I can't believe Tavi's gone.*

*I can't believe the rest of us are alive.*

It was hours before her mind stilled.

It must have been the influence of the Garden that, despite every-thing, a positive thought struck her: for the first time in what seemed like an eternity, she and the rest of her friends were safe and protected. As she finally drifted off on an irresistible wave of slumber, she felt something she couldn't have imagined and hadn't dared hope for.

Peace.

# CHAPTER TWENTY-FIVE

## The Prophecies of Elijah

Brie had no idea how long she slept, but it was restful and deep. It occurred to her later that Morpheus may have had something to do with that. Her dreams were like the watercolor angel itself — abstract, colorful, and filled with more questions than answers. She remembered only two, neither of which made any sense. In the first, her mother and Cameron's mother were together, smiling, telling her the same thing over and over: "Say yes. When he asks you, say yes." In the second, a fox with mismatched eyes begged her to let him in.

She awoke to an absolute, literal dreamscape. She took a deep breath, grounding herself, and rubbed her eyes as if to banish the strange visions before throwing off the covers and starting to make her way back to her friends.

A violet-hued bird flitted past her, its wings trailing a glittering mist. In the distance, she saw a stream that sparkled, winding its way through the Garden like a living vein of light. She stopped to examine a flower whose petals opened and closed in a slow, rhythmic motion, like the beating of a heart. As she reached out to touch it, it let out a soft, musical chime and folded itself shyly away from her fingers. The branches of the Tree shone from above. She walked slowly, her heart heavy, as her gaze drifted to the four pods nestled among the roots, each one glowing with a soft promise of life.

Sherry's was the first to open.

The petals unfurled like the slow bloom of a flower. Brie's breath caught as her friend's eyes fluttered open, the vibrant hazel dulled with grogginess, but alive — unmistakably alive.

For a moment, Sherry could do nothing but stare blankly at the canopy above her. Then she caught a glimpse of Brie, and her lips curved into a dreamy smile.

"Well," she croaked, sounding uncannily like a frog who'd escaped a particularly memorable pond, "I have a new favorite spa."

Brie let out a breath of shaky laughter, relief washing over her in a wave so overwhelming that tears welled in her eyes. She hurried to Sherry's side, helping her as she stepped unsteadily out of the healing bed. The petals closed behind her, folding back into the chamber with a soft hum as the branch pulled it back up into the canopy.

"Hey, easy there," Sherry smiled as Brie threw her arms around her in a wild embrace. "You're gonna bruise all my newly restored parts."

Brie pulled back, still laughing. Now that she had started, it seemed unlikely she would ever be able to stop. "You're okay," she whispered, needing it to be true. "You're really okay."

Sherry gave her a lopsided grin. "Better than okay. Pretty sure I'm glowing." She pointed at the healing chamber high above. "Does that thing have any specific dietary or climate zone requirements? Because I might actually want to keep it. Or grow my own."

*Of course you do.*

"You can't keep a houseplant alive," Brie reminded gently, darting looks at her friend's shoulder. Despite the seriousness of the injury she'd sustained, Brie could see nothing but a swath of flawless, smooth skin.

"I feel like you're projecting, Brie. I know what happened to your ficus." Sherry waved her off dismissively. "Besides, I could always hire the job out."

Before Brie could respond, the next pod began to open. The light around it intensified briefly, then dimmed as the petals peeled back to reveal Mike. His red hair was mussed, and his face was still etched with lines of worry, but he pushed himself upright with a groan.

"Man," he muttered, running a hand over his face, "this place knows how to knock a guy out. I feel like I slept for a month."

Sherry rushed to his side, bending over the side of the pod and cradling his face in her hands. "You look like it, too." She tousled his hair teasingly before pulling him in for a kiss.

He stilled reflexively, cupping the sides of her cheeks, then proceeded to climb awkwardly out of the pod.

The third was already opening, its white glow casting long shadows across the ground. Ephriam emerged slowly, having more trouble than the others. He hoisted quickly to a sitting position, then paused for a full minute, staring at his legs, before standing up.

Brie watched from afar, too stricken to move. She remembered the moment it had happened — when the swarm had pulled back to reveal the broken Elysian for the first time.

He'd been missing a leg. And several fingers.

They had grown back.

He reached his hands out in front of him and flexed his limbs, testing, relearning, with a look of awe.

"Ephriam," Brie said softly, her voice filled with concern. "Are you—"

"Where is everyone else?" he interrupted tersely.

As if in answer, the fourth pod began to stir.

Like the break of a gentle dawn, the petals curled back to reveal the enchanting angel reclining in the center. With the lights of the tree glittering around him, Cameron looked like something from a fairytale — the handsome prince who'd overslept his alarm or perhaps a friendly warning against the perils of carnivorous plants. At first, he simply lay there, the light from the Garden dazzling his eyes. Then he lifted his gaze a bit further to the lovely girl standing nearby.

"Brie," he breathed.

She was beside him in an instant, hands trembling as she helped him from the pod. He winced slightly as he stood, but already his strength was returning. She clung to him without hesitation, pressing her forehead against his chest.

"You're okay," she whispered, eyes shining with tears. "You're okay."

His arms circled around her, clasping her tight. "Thanks to you," he said softly. "And whatever magic…" He trailed into silence, those bright eyes sweeping the rest of the friends and coming up short. "Brie, where is…?"

He couldn't say it. None of them could say it. Ephriam was clenching his fists with a savage expression, like an animal about to strike.

"Your friend suffered more extensive injuries," a kindly voice drifted over the clearing, making each of them turn. Elijah had been standing at a distance, giving the young travelers time to orient. "I am sorry."

The group fell silent, the weight of his words settling over them like a shroud.

It wasn't enough that they'd survived the desert, or escaped the demon, or even found the entrance to the Garden. Because they *hadn't* done it. Not all of them.

One of them had fallen.

"There was still a piece inside her," Brie whispered, hanging her head. "Just before we came inside, they found it. A stray sliver of Baal, hiding inside her all this time."

The others looked up in shock, and the prophet stepped back, giving them space. It was quiet for a few horrible moments as each of them pieced things out.

"She was always so hungry," Sherry whispered, lifting a slow hand to her mouth.

"Ravenous," Cameron said, his fingers flexing dangerously at his sides, like he could fly back through time and destroy the piece himself. "She was ravenous. There's a difference. " He turned his gaze to Ephriam, shaking his head. "I should have known."

The warrior said nothing in reply. It was unclear whether he'd even registered that someone else was speaking. A frightening tension had begun seeping into his shoulders, and his eyes fixed with uncanny intuition on the precise spot where Tavi's pod lay beneath the pool. He took a step towards it, looking like he might burst out of his very skin, and then, without a hint of warning, he threw back his head with a howling cry.

It was something for animals. A primal, wild pain.

The last strains were still echoing into silence when he dropped heavily to his knees, landing with a thud on the soft grass. His eyes closed, and his head bowed. His lips began fluttering, chanting prayers and ancient wishes and a thousand other things his friends would never know.

"Come," Elijah said quietly, gesturing them away, "there is much else to see and understand in the Garden."

Brie hesitated. "Shouldn't we wait for Ephriam?"

The prophet shook his head. "Leave your friend to his grief."

Casting silent looks over their shoulders, the group followed Elijah through the Garden, their footsteps silent. A breeze stirred up around them, filling the air with the scent of flowers and the fluttering of sunswept leaves. Despite their grief, it was impossible not to marvel at the impossible beauty surrounding them. They were imbued with the sense that they'd strayed into something better than a dream, better than a miracle. Something that was there at the beginning, blossoming in eternal springtime, a living beacon of light, and hope, and love.

As they passed by a grove of trees, Brie hesitated, her gaze drawn to a single leaf that glowed brighter than the others. When she reached out to touch it, an image appeared before her — fleeting and dream-like. She saw herself as a child, laughing as her mother swung her around in a sunlit meadow.

Her breath caught, and the image faded as quickly as it had appeared.

"These are the Trees of Memory," Elijah said, watching her closely. "The Garden reflects what is in your heart. It reveals not to frighten but to guide."

They moved on, passing a cluster of flowers that gave off a soothing scent, something like lavender. Elijah plucked one carefully and held it to his ear. A smile curved up his face. He handed it to Brie. "Listen."

She leaned closer, eyes widening as she heard the soft strains of a lullaby. It was hauntingly familiar, a melody her mother hummed when she was a child.

The same one Cameron had once used to lull her to sleep.

"They sing the songs of creation," Elijah explained. "Every note, every word, every thought that has ever been imagined. This place remembers it all."

They passed a stream whose surface rippled like liquid glass. Elijah knelt by the water and motioned for them to do the same. "Look," he said simply.

She leaned over the edge, gazing down at her reflection. As the water stilled, other faces joined it. People she'd known, people she'd lost. Her grandmother. Her mother.

Tavi.

A jolt ran down her arms as she gripped the bank, unable to tear her eyes away, feeling like she could stay in that precise spot for the rest of forever. There was no reason to say goodbye; they were all right there, a reach away.

There was movement in her periphery as the rest of them gathered closer, lost in reflections of their own, making the same internal vows to stay. Cameron stared into the water like he'd been hypnotized. Brie briefly wondered if he planned to jump in.

There was a chance Elijah sensed this because a few minutes later, he beckoned them onward. "Come," he called. "We have much to discuss."

♦     ♦     ♦

The world seemed to hold its breath. The air was heavy with an ancient, knowing stillness, as if the Garden itself understood the gravity of the moment.

Elijah stood across from them. The light of the Garden wrapped around him, casting ethereal shadows over his lined face.

"You have questions," he said softly. "And the time has come for answers."

Brie looked to her friends for encouragement. They hung respectfully back, but nodded in solidarity. She turned to Elijah and swallowed hard, lifting her fingers to the pendant.

"What is this thing?" she asked tightly. "Why has it come to me? Why my family?"

He nodded, as if expecting the question. "The pendant is no ordinary heirloom. It is a divine artifact, forged in a pivotal moment between creation and the Creator. It has come to you, because it was always meant to be yours."

The stone shone in response, the swirling colors within its depths more vivid than ever before.

"This," he continued, "was given to your ancestors long ago, during a time of great upheaval — the Great Flood. It was entrusted to your family, with good reason, to safeguard, not to wield. Its purpose is not to grant power, but to preserve it. To protect the balance of creation until a moment of true need."

Brie's heart fluttered wildly, like a captive hummingbird.

"Enoch said the first he learned of it was after the Flood," she replied shakily. "This has been passed down since—"

"Since the waters receded." His voice carried the weight of millennia. "Your family has been its keeper, not by chance, but by design. The pendant is not tied solely to you, but also to those who came before you and to the fabric of creation itself." He took a step closer, his gaze piercing but kind. "There is more. The pendant is tied to a prophecy — one that speaks of the unraveling of worlds. And you, Brianna Weldon, stand at its center. The signs have coalesced around you and your friends."

She blinked slowly. Then, she forced herself to blink again.

The others had gone utterly still in her periphery.

She couldn't have heard correctly. He couldn't have said—

"The unraveling of worlds," she repeated stiltedly.

The words themselves seemed preposterously sized, unable to fit in her mouth.

"The fabric of creation is fraying," Elijah answered quietly. "You've seen it, haven't you? The wars, the chaos, the anger in people's hearts. The earth groans beneath the weight of its wounds. Forests burning, societal unrest, famine, and flood — these are not merely the effects of human folly. They are the signs of something far greater, something that has been set in motion since the beginning."

There was a moment of prolonged silence before Brie finally managed to reply.

"Are you saying the world is… ending?"

A weighted look passed between them.

"That's it," Sherry muttered, "back to the pods."

"Not only this world," the prophet continued, his voice heavy with sorrow. "Many worlds. The threads that hold them together are breaking, and your pendant is the keystone. A lynchpin in the cosmic weave."

Brie shook her head slowly, feeling utterly bereft. A few weeks ago, she was feeding vitamins to her plant and waging a cold war against the cashier who sold her frozen yogurt.

Now, the *world* was ending.

And she had a starring role.

"What am I supposed to do about it?" she asked dizzily, feeling like the ground beneath her had started to shift. "On the way here, I lost a battle with my *camel*. You're saying the world is ending, and these are the stakes, and somehow, it's all coming down to *me*? That's impossible! How am I supposed to fix this?" she exclaimed, begging the man to listen. It felt like she was standing on a precipice. Alone. Quite terribly alone. "A few weeks ago, I thought that angels and demons were no more than fairytales, and now you're telling me that the fate of the world comes down to a nursing resident from Georgia? I *can't* do it, are you listening? I'm just—"

"You're not *just* anything," Elijah interrupted gently. "You are a part of something far greater than yourself. I'm merely saying that you always have been. Child," he lifted a calming hand, "have you not already used its power, safeguarding those who were closest to you? Do you not have faith that, when the time is right, you could do something like it again?"

She opened her mouth to speak, but he shook his head.

"There is more you need to know. The attack you endured — Baal's presence here — is a sign of how dire things have become. Do you know what it means for him to have reached you from the future?"

The friends glanced at each other in silence, shaking their heads. It was enough to discover the demon was actually there. They hadn't thought much about the unholy series of events that had allowed it to happen.

"It means he has either learned how to consume time or how to navigate the Time Seas. Both possibilities are catastrophic. If Baal can devour time itself, then he is no longer bound by it. And if he can navigate the Time Seas," Elijah paused, his voice growing quieter. "Then the forces that guard those waters have been compromised."

*The Time Seas.*

She glanced back at Mike, whose head hung heavy with guilt. Even though they'd spent the last few weeks trying to read the history of those seas, she felt no closer to understanding them. And one look at Mike told her two things: one, that he must surely feel the same, and two, that he believed this might all be his fault. This must have shown on their faces because Elijah smiled kindly, slowing things down. "Think of them as the tides of existence. The flow of what was, what is, and what could be. They are meant to be impenetrable, safeguarded by those who exist beyond time's reach. The book in your possession by no means caused these events. It merely gave you a glimpse of what Baal was already doing. What happened outside our gates leads me to believe that the guardians are falling, that the safeguards are breaking down. If that happens, Baal will be able to consume the fabric of reality itself."

"But Michael killed it," she said, desperate for it to be true, though in her heart, she already knew better.

Sure enough, Elijah shook his head. "He has disincorporated it. This will surely slow its progress. It is not known if the Seven can be killed." He took a careful look at her crestfallen face before continuing. "But it matters little if what I fear indeed comes to pass."

"How do you mean?" Brie asked.

"What does it matter if it takes him a millennium to heal if he can navigate the Seas? If it takes him ten thousand years to regain his strength, then would he not simply slip ten thousand years back into the past, only to reappear at the moment of his defeat, fully restored?" Elijah answered.

She nodded slowly, triaging problems that were each big enough on their own to preoccupy several lifetimes. The base of her skull was numb and tingling, but her pendant was shining strong on her chest.

He continued. "You are the only one who can, but even so, it is a terrible thing to ask of you, particularly if no one has actually asked. So, Brianna Weldon, these are the stakes. I ask you — will you help?"

Her mother's face flashed briefly through her mind's eye, standing with Cameron's mother, smiling.

She drew in a breath. "Yes. Of course, I will. But what can we do?"

Unseen over her shoulder, Cameron's eyes glowed with pride.

"You must act quickly," Elijah said. "Michael must return to Elysium to begin the search for the remaining shards of Baal and the other Fallen. There is no time to linger here."

*Wait, what?*

"But I thought," Brie began hesitantly, "I thought we could go to Elysium, too—"

"Not yet," the prophet interrupted. "Your path lies elsewhere for now. You must return to your own time and seek out Camael, the Angel of Courage, War, and Peace. Jophial may offer understanding, but it is Camael who will give you strength. And make no mistake — the peace we have enjoyed for so long is already broken, and war is certainly upon us all."

"And Camael can give me strength?" she echoed.

Elijah nodded. "Strength to face what is coming. Strength to stand against the unraveling of worlds. And strength to hold fast to who you are in the face of what you must become."

*What I must become…*

The memory of Ephriam standing before the portrait of Lucifer, warning her to give up the pendant, flashed through her mind. She remembered what he'd said as if it was yesterday:

*"Even if you could somehow find a way to conquer the forces that seek to work against you — what would you have to become? Would you wish to become such a thing?"*

She looked down at the pendant, its light shifting like a living thing. She thought of her friends, of the battles they had fought, and the ones still to come. She thought of Tavi's lifeless body, entombed deep beneath the waters of Paradise, before thinking of the world itself — Earth, as she had seen it from the moon.

Surrounded by darkness. Fragile and breaking. Falling on her shoulders.

"I don't know if I can do it." She said the words without thinking, flushing with instinctual shame. But what else could she say? Who in their right mind would look at a task like that and think, *I'm ready.*

Elijah's hand rested gently on her shoulder. "Courage is not the absence of fear, child," he said softly. "It is the choice to act in spite of it. And you will not face this journey alone."

She looked up at him in silence.

For a hanging moment, she felt both impossibly small and immeasurably significant.

But the question had been asked.

She answered. "Tell me what I need to do."

A profound silence fell over the Garden, resonating with each one of the young companions who stood inside. The path ahead might have been impossible, but it stretched clearly in front of them. They stood up a little straighter, waiting for Elijah's reply.

That's when a series of robotic beeps echoed cheerfully through the air, annihilating the somber moment.

*What… in the actual hell?*

It was a video game. It had to be. Despite never having played them herself, she was familiar with the tinny sound. The rest of them frowned, jarred by some long-lost auditory memory. Amidst the ethereal beauty of the Garden, it couldn't have been more out of place.

Elijah let out a sigh, startling them back to the present. "Ah," he said lightly. "I see he's found a new hiding spot. Come," he beckoned, a mixture of exasperation and amusement crossing his face. "It seems Michael is entertaining himself again."

"Who?" Sherry asked in confusion.

Elijah didn't answer. He simply led them around a cluster of radiant bushes into a shaded alcove.

And there he was.

Sitting cross-legged on a patch of moss, was the Archangel Michael.

Brie blinked, struggling to reconcile the picture in front of her with the resplendent warrior she'd seen before. Gone was the righteous anger, the divine vengeance. Gone was the golden armor, the flaming sword. They had been replaced by a ragged T-shirt and a vintage, banana-yellow gaming console. Its tiny screen illuminated the archangel's face with an eerie green glow. A discarded pack of gas-station junk food lay beside him, one half-eaten sponge cake balanced precariously on his knee, oozing whipped cream. He didn't look up as they approached but stared at the screen like a listless teenager, his thumbs moving with practiced precision. "One second," he muttered, "I'm nearly at the big boss."

The friends gaped in open astonishment, finding themselves unable to move. Only one of them didn't have that problem. Cameron stumbled forward, looking like his childhood dream had come to life.

"Michael," he breathed, reverent. "It's truly an honor to—"

"Hold on, kid," the archangel interrupted, never taking his eyes off the screen. "If I don't time this jump perfectly, I'll lose my last life, and then I'll have to start all over. Again."

Cameron's expression faltered and he froze like a startled rabbit, confusion and disbelief warring for dominance on his face. "Of… of course," he stammered. "Take your time."

Elijah chuckled softly, leaning casually against a nearby tree. "Michael, surely there are better ways to spend eternity than becoming a celestial couch potato? I can't imagine what our guests must think."

The corners of the archangel's lips twitched. "You try keeping your edge after a few millennia of this gig," he shot back, fingers flying. "I've beaten the one about the plumber so many times, I could write the walkthrough."

Elijah arched a brow, his amusement growing. "And yet you still find it necessary to practice. Perhaps you're not as infallible as you'd like us all to believe."

The celestial warrior merely scoffed. "Practice makes perfect, old man."

Brie snorted with laughter, unable to help it. For whatever reason, considering all the beautiful and terrible things that had come before, this had proven one thing too much.

Michael popped the last bite of a cupcake into his mouth. "What's so funny?" he demanded through a mouthful of preservatives and cream.

"Nothing," she said quickly, remembering the flaming sword. "I just didn't expect *this* from you."

The archangel shrugged, unfazed. "What? Did you think I spend all my time smiting demons and flexing my angelic muscles? Please. I'm not some divine action figure."

Cameron, who had been standing in silent shock, finally found his voice. "But, you're Michael," he said, almost pleading. "The General of Heaven's Armies. The vanquisher of Lucifer. The right hand of God."

Michael raised a brow, unimpressed. "Yeah, and? You want me to sign something?"

Cameron wilted before their eyes.

*Oh, honey. This is why we never meet our heroes.*

Elijah interceded, clearly thinking the same. "Don't mind him," he said. "Michael's been saving the world for so long, he's forgotten how to take compliments. Or entertain company," he added, casting the archangel a sharp look as he clapped a hand on Cameron's slumped shoulder.

"And yet, you insist on parading them in front of me when I'm trying to do something important," Michael scowled. "I don't think you realize the time commitment that some of these—"

There was an ominous beep, followed by a scandalized shriek from the archangel.

A robotic voice made the final pronouncement:


GAME OVER.

# CHAPTER TWENTY-SIX

## One Night In Paradise

The Garden of Eden was quieter than it had ever been. Night in this place held no shadows, no terrors — only an otherworldly calm, a stillness that hummed with the energy of creation itself. The companions, though healed and whole in body, carried a different weight in their hearts. Their words were few as they drifted together to a singular, unspoken destination.

They stared into the pool beneath the mirrored canopy of the Tree, where their dear friend had been laid to rest. Its surface was so still it seemed to hold the stars themselves.

Brie could scarcely speak. The lump in her throat was too great.

"I've already… while you were sleeping. I already told her what I…" She bowed her head, staring into the waters. "She knows," she finished.

Sherry knelt first, a soft bouquet of luminous flowers cradled in her hands. Their petals caught the light of the pool in shades of rose and violet. She traced the edge of the water with her fingertips before speaking in a quavering voice.

"Tavi, you were fearless, even when you shouldn't have been. You made me brave just by being you. Thank you." Her words hung in the air as she placed the flowers in the pool, watching as they floated gently away.

Mike followed. He knelt beside Sherry, holding a single bloom — something simple and white. His voice, when it came, was hoarse. "I don't think I've ever been more impressed or inspired by another person in my life," he said, a small, broken smile flickering across his lips. "You made the people around you feel capable, supported, and loved. I'll never forget that. I'll never forget you."

He set the flower adrift, his shoulders slumping as he rose and stepped back.

Cameron was next. He carried no bouquet, only a single, brilliant red flower that gleamed like fire against his skin. He crouched at the edge of the pool, fingers brushing the petals before he spoke. "Tavi, you didn't deserve this. Not you. I wish…" His voice cracked, and he bowed his head, words failing him. He placed the flower in the water and stayed crouched there, unmoving, for a long moment before stepping away.

Ephriam was the last to say his goodbyes. At first, it looked as though he held no flowers. His hands were clenched in trembling fists at his sides. For a moment, Brie thought he might refuse — that the words, the act, would be too much for him. But then he stepped forward and knelt. His hands opened slowly, releasing a cascade of tiny golden blossoms into the water.

He lingered there for a long, long time, motionless, staring down at the pool.

When he finally rose, his face was taut, jaw clenched, as if to hold back a flood of emotions. Without a word, he turned and walked away.

The others began to follow, but Brie stopped them with a silent gesture. "Let me," she said softly. They nodded silently, turning back to the pool.

She found him by the stream that cut through the Garden, its waters so clear they seemed invisible save for the light that danced across the surface. He sat on the bank, shoulders hunched and head bowed, arms folded around him as if to shield him from the world.

She approached quietly, sitting beside him without a word. The stream babbled softly, its melody soothing, but the silence between them stretched long and heavy.

When he finally spoke, his voice was raw.

"She was my best friend," he said, the words wrenched from the very heart of him. "My best friend in all the universe. I know I wasn't hers, but she was mine. She was better than me. Stronger than me. It makes no sense, no sense at all, that she's gone."

Brie shifted closer, her heart aching at the pain in his voice. She hesitated before speaking, choosing each word with care. "Tavi told me once, back in Elysium: 'It is a terrible gift to be less breakable than the ones you love. When the things that destroy others don't destroy you, it can weigh heavy on the soul.'"

He let out a shuddering breath, fingers clenching into fists.

"She was my friend before she even knew my name," Brie continued, her voice growing softer. "She was the bravest person I think I've ever known. You've all risked everything for me, and I'll never be worthy of it. I will *never*, in all my days, be worthy of her sacrifice. But Ephriam, I'm going to spend my whole life trying to be."

The words hung between them, raw and unadorned. The Elysian's hands tensed, knuckles whitening as he gripped the earth beside him. And then, to her quiet astonishment, he broke. A sob escaped him, sharp and unguarded, and he turned toward her suddenly, drawing her into a fierce, desperate embrace. She scarcely had time to register his tears before there was a flash of golden light. His celestial wings unfurled, huge and radiant, silhouetted against the backdrop of Paradise before wrapping around them like a cocoon.

She held him tightly, silently, as his grief poured out.

The stream flowed beside them, its melody weaving through the night, carrying their sorrow away into the infinite beauty of the Garden.

◆　　◆　　◆

Brie lingered beside Ephriam for as long as she could, her presence a quiet anchor to his turbulent grief. But she knew when the moment came to leave him alone. The tension in his shoulders eased slightly, and his wings folded in closer, dimming like a twilight sky. She rose silently, placing a hand lightly on his arm, before retreating along the stream.

The Garden was hushed, wrapping around her like a dream from which she didn't want to wake. As she walked back toward the Tree of Life, her thoughts heavy with everything that had happened, she saw Cameron waiting for her, standing in the soft light of the branches. His chestnut hair caught the luminescence of the leaves, and his eyes, fixed on hers, seemed to hold the entire cosmos within them.

"You came back," he said softly, his voice filled with an undercurrent of emotion she couldn't yet name.

"Of course I did," she replied, smiling in spite of herself. It was impossible *not* to smile in her angel's presence. She took a step closer, reaching for his hands.

He grabbed on immediately, his touch warm and impatient.

"Come with me," he said quietly.

Without waiting for her response, he turned and led her along a path that bloomed with their every step. The trees whispered around them. Flowers turned their faces toward them as they passed.

They emerged into a secluded grove, the canopy of trees above parting just enough to reveal the night sky. Stars spilled across the heavens in glittering cascades, their light mirrored in a crystalline pool at the grove's center. The air was sweet, and the world around them felt impossibly still, as though holding its breath just for them.

She threw her angel a sideways glance, blushing at the tenderness in his gaze. He took a step closer, cupping her face in the palm of his hands.

"Do you have any idea what you've done to me," he whispered.

She stared up at him, frozen in place. "What do you mean?"

"You've changed everything," he answered simply. "You've given me a reason to believe in something I never dared to hope for. I've seen so much. Too much. But you? You make me want to believe in tomorrow again."

She reached up with a smile, curling her fingers around his wrists.

*You make me believe in tomorrow, too.*

"I've lost people who are dear to me. Ethan. Tavi. More friends throughout the centuries than I can count. I don't know what tomorrow will bring. I don't know if we'll survive what's coming. But I do know one thing: I don't want to face a single day without you. Not now, not ever. All of this," he gestured around, "this isn't my Paradise. You are. I love you," he finished quietly, voice breaking at the edges. "I love you more than I've ever loved anything, more than I ever thought I could. It terrifies me," he admitted, "because I know I could lose you. But it also makes me stronger, because I know what I'm fighting for."

Her chest tightened, and tears pricked her eyes.

"I love you, too," she whispered. "I think I've loved you for longer than I ever realized."

*Before I even knew you were real.*

His face lit up as if from within, and as if reading her thoughts, he continued. "I can't give you forever yet. You might have noticed, I can be a bit old-fashioned. But I can give you my promise. This is real. You're the only one for me, Brie. You're my forever. And I want to give you forever. I want to give you everything you desire." He paused, those bright eyes catching onto hers. "Will you let me?"

Her heart skipped a beat before falling into perfect rhythm. "Yes," she whispered, then louder, "Yes, of course I will."

With a smile as breathtaking as the dawn, he kissed her again. Her pendant glowed at his touch, reflecting swirling lights dancing across the sky. Their embrace was as fierce as it was tender — a reminder and a promise.

It was just the beginning of so many kisses to come.

# CHAPTER TWENTY-SEVEN

## Just Another Day in Paradise

Morning in the Garden of Eden came not with a sunrise but with a gradual brightening of the air as if the world was exhaling a deep breath of light. Brie and Cameron walked hand in hand back to the base of the Tree of Life, slow and unhurried. The Garden felt more alive than ever, its vibrant energy weaving through the grasses, the trees, and the air itself.

As they approached the clearing where their friends were gathered, Sherry was the first to notice them. She tilted her head, narrowing her eyes at Brie with a slight grin. "You look different," she began slowly. "I can't quite put my finger on it. Did you find a new magical artifact last night? Or is this the glow of someone who's..."

Brie bit her lip as her cheeks flushed. "I'll tell you later, Sher," she deflected.

Her best friend gave her a knowing look and a wink. "Count on it."

Ephriam stood apart from the group, his expression unreadable, his gaze fixed on Cameron. As the others prepared to depart, he approached with deliberate steps. He hadn't hidden his wings since the night before and kept them tucked tightly against his back.

"Cameron," he said stiffly. "A word."

An icy chill swept over the clearing, and Brie glanced over in concern. Cameron hesitated a moment, then nodded — his smile fading as he followed Ephriam away from the group. It was far enough away that human ears shouldn't have heard a thing. But the pendant had been sharpening Brie's senses for weeks now, and she heard their fight with stinging clarity.

The towering Elysian didn't mince words. "What are you doing?"

Cameron folded his arms. "What do you mean?"

"You know exactly what I mean," Ephriam snapped. "And we've danced around the issue long enough. Relationships between Elysians and humans are forbidden. You're risking everything — your title, your responsibilities, your future."

Cameron's expression hardened, his lips thinning into a line. "I'm not a true Elysian, Ephriam. You know that as well as anyone. And my title means nothing to me if it means losing her. I'd give up the crown, Elysium, all of it, if it meant I could be with Brie."

"That's not just your choice to make," Ephriam fired back, wings flaring slightly. "You think this is about love? About you? We are bound by laws older than time itself. Do you think you're the first Elysian to fall for a human? Do you think the consequences don't apply to you?"

"I think," Cameron said, "that the laws were written by those who never understood what it means to truly love. I'm not asking for their permission. And I'm not asking for yours."

Ephriam's jaw tightened, his frustration clear. "You're being selfish. Do you even realize what's happened to Tavianne? What Brie's pendant is? What it signifies? We're standing on the brink of the end of everything, and you're—"

"I'm what?" Cameron interrupted, his voice rising slightly. "Focusing on the one thing that gives me hope? On the one person who's worth fighting for?"

The two stared at each other, the air between them taut with tension.

"*The one person?*" Ephriam repeated incredulously. "Our entire society is built on the belief that *everyone* is worth fighting for. Every soul. Why else would we spend our lives shepherding their souls from one realm to the next?"

Cameron's expression was pure steel. "I won't give her up, Ephriam." He glared at his old friend. "Not for anyone. Not even for you."

Ephriam's expression was torn between anger and something deeper. Finally, he let out a frustrated sigh, his wings folding back and disappearing as he looked away.

"This isn't just about you," he repeated quietly. "It never was."

When the two men stormed back to the group, Brie focused on packing her bag and didn't make eye contact.

After hours spent gathering supplies, the companions stood together near the base of the Tree of Life, its towering branches stretching into infinity above them. The pods that had cradled them now lay dormant, their purpose fulfilled.

Tavi's amber-glowing pod beneath the pool had disappeared.

The others fell deep into conversation, discussing the journey ahead, but Brie was too distracted to listen. A quiet determination was settling over her, and before she knew it, she heard herself speak.

"Before we go, I need to find Morpheus."

The friends stopped talking at once, exchanging silent glances. After a few seconds, Sherry raised an eyebrow. "The watercolor angel? Why?"

Brie shook her head. "I need to talk to Morpheus. I won't be long."

· Michael, who had appeared at the periphery of the group, snorted. "Morpheus is as predictable as moonlight. Good luck."

Elijah, however, smiled and pointed toward a grove of trees alight in hues of lavender and silver. "You'll find them there," he said. "They always return to the Dreaming Glade."

She nodded her thanks and headed in that direction.

She found Morpheus sitting cross-legged beneath a tree, their ever-shifting wings fanned out behind them, colors swirling and blending like an endless horizon of dawn and dusk.

The angel turned as she approached, their features fluid as always, but their gaze fixed and piercing. "Brianna Weldon," they said, their voice a layered melody. "You return."

She hesitated, suddenly unsure how to begin. But the weight of her gratitude pressed her forward, and she knelt before them, voice soft and earnest. "I wanted to thank you."

Morpheus tilted their head, their expression curious. "Thank me? For what?"

"For the dreams," she said, fidgeting with the hem of her shirt. "The ones you sent me when I needed them most. The painting of my mother. The fox with the green and blue eyes. I don't know what I ever did to deserve you watching over me, but you've helped me more than I can ever say."

Morpheus stilled, their ever-shifting face frozen in a swirl of muted tones. When they spoke again, it was quieter, more deliberate. "I do not know what you mean."

She blinked, shaking her head in confusion. "You do. You have to. Those dreams… They guided me. They protected me. That's your gift, isn't it? You're the Angel of Dreams."

Morpheus regarded her for a long moment, their head tilting slightly as though listening to something far away. The moment passed, and they held out their hands.

"Show me."

*Um, alright.*

The angel leaned forward, their watercolor fingers brushing her temple. She felt a warmth, like the memory of sunlight, and then a flood of images surged to the forefront of her mind — her mother's serene smile before the paint grabbed her and pulled her into the nightmare, the fox with its knowing gaze, guiding her back to consciousness after a plane crash. Each memory played out with vivid clarity, unfolding anew.

After a few moments, Morpheus drew back, their fingers retracting like a brush lifting from a canvas. Their face shifted, colors darkening to indigo and grey.

"These," Morpheus said slowly, "are tapestries not of my weaving."

The Garden fell silent.

"What do you mean?" she finally asked. "If not you, then who?"

The angel's wings shifted. "Perhaps they are not dreams at all," they said pensively. "They might be visions. Or warnings."

The words settled heavily, giving way to a hundred more questions. She didn't want to ask any of them, but they flew unbidden from her lips. "Warnings? From who? From what?"

Morpheus's gaze remained steady, but their swirling face betrayed a hint of unease. "There are forces beyond the Dreaming that I cannot claim to understand."

She swallowed hard. "So what am I supposed to do?"

"Someday, your path will cross with the Archangel Jophial. On that day, seek her council," Morpheus said firmly. "She will know." Their face swirled again, the colors sharpening like brushstrokes drawn with sudden intensity. "But beware, Brianna. Not all answers bring peace."

*No, they never do.*

"Thank you," she whispered again, preparing to leave.

Morpheus inclined their head, their face softening into warmer hues. "Go with courage," they said. "And remember — truth and light often find you when you least expect it, even in the darkest of places."

Elijah regarded the group with his hands clasped behind his back as they stood on the brink of departure. The weight of their journey, the losses they had endured, and the responsibilities they carried hung heavy. Yet, in the prophet's serene presence, the burden felt momentarily lighter.

"You have already traveled long and far," he began, "but our usual paths to return you to your time are tenuous. They cannot be secured safely, not now. I offer you this—" He paused, withdrawing from his robes a small object, glimmering like moonlight captured in crystal. It was a box, intricate and beautiful, covered in celestial etchings that shifted as they caught the light. He demonstrated how different parts of the device swiveled around in three directions to form dates, times, and coordinates. "It will connect two points in time and bring you where and when you wish to go. But be warned — it cannot be used in the same place or at the same moment twice. To do so would tangle the threads of the timeline itself."

The group stared at the box with varying degrees of trepidation. Sherry stepped forward, her brow furrowing. "As much as I'd love to surrender every molecule in my body to the power of a supernatural puzzle box, does anyone else think this looks like something from a cursed treasure hoard? Or is it just me?"

Mike nodded vigorously. "Nope. Not just you. I saw a movie once where they opened something like this, and everyone exploded. I'm not a fan of exploding."

Elijah's amused chuckle was a melody in itself. "Such reluctance! Then perhaps the bravest among you should test it first." He cast a significant glance at Brie.

She froze, eyes widening.

"Me?" she stammered. "But I'm not the… you can't possibly mean me. I mean, where would I even go?"

Elijah's twinkling gaze fixed on her, his expression patient and knowing. "Oh, I think you already know the answer to that. You have a story to finish, haven't you?"

Confusion flickered across the others' faces, but comprehension dawned on Brie like the rising sun. Her lips parted in surprise, and then she smiled.

Elijah gave Michael a little nudge, and the archangel rolled his eyes, muttering something under his breath as he stepped forward to join her.

"Here, take this one with you," Elijah told her. "Just being near him will translate for you. And you might need a bit of assistance getting rid of… well, you know."

Michael scowled but said nothing.

Brie glanced at her companions, offering an encouraging smile. "Don't worry," she said lightly. "We'll be right back."

Before anyone could object or even fully process what was happening, Michael took the box and twisted one of its intricate segments. The air around them shifted, and before anyone could say another word, there was a soft whoosh of displaced energy, and the two disappeared.

In the blink of an eye, Brie and Michael materialized on a windswept dune, the stars above them impossibly vast and bright. In the distance, a lone figure trudged through the sand — a man, his steps slow but determined.

*Idris.*

"This is it," Brie whispered, her breath catching in recognition. The story Mariyah had told — the woman appearing in the dead of night to save their ancestor Idris from a supernatural terror — wasn't merely a folktale. It was her.

Michael gave a small huff of acknowledgment. "You've got this," he instructed. "Just make sure you don't botch the lines."

She shot him a look but didn't reply, heart pounding as she took a step forward. "What about the—"

"I'll handle it," he interrupted, already fading into invisibility. "Go."

She stared at the place where he'd just vanished. "Well, *that's* a neat trick. I don't suppose you could teach me how to—"

"Go!" his disembodied voice hissed.

She swallowed hard, gripping her pendant for courage. As she approached, Idris paused, his eyes wide as he spotted her silhouette against the starlit dunes.

"Who's there?" he called, wary and desperate. Though he was speaking Arabic, Brie was staggered to see that Elijah was right, and she understood perfectly.

She stepped closer, her pendant casting a soft glow.

"Do not be afraid," she said, her voice steady despite the wild fluttering of her heart. "I mean you no harm."

He stared at her, his expression torn between awe and confusion. "You shouldn't be out here, my lady," he said. "It's not safe. There's something—"

As if on cue, a low growl rumbled through the night, raising the hairs on the back of her neck. She turned to see the massive shadow of a familiar, lion-like creature emerge from the darkness, its eyes like embers, its teeth bared.

Idris stumbled back, his breath hitching in terror.

Brie's pendant flared as she stepped between Idris and the beast. "Go!" she commanded. Her voice rang with an authority she hadn't known she possessed. "Go, in the name of all that is good and holy!"

She heard a faint snort of laughter from the invisible archangel waiting nearby.

*Shut up, Michael.*

The lion paused and tilted its head. She could swear it was chuckling.

"Go!" she cried again, grateful the cool evening hid her flushing cheeks. "Begone, creature of darkness! I command you!"

Michael couldn't resist. "I'm never going to let you live this down, you know," he whispered, too quiet for Idris to hear.

"Would you shut up and let me do this?" she hissed.

The creature's muscles rippled beneath its dark, smoke-like fur, its form flickering as though barely tethered to reality. Instead of listening to her theatrical commands, it had clearly decided to eat her instead. But just as it crouched to spring, there was a flash of light, and the beast recoiled with a snarl.

Idris stared between them in astonishment.

A trail of invisible footsteps appeared in the sand. Then, without a hint of warning, the lion was lifted straight into the air by the scruff of its neck, thrashing back and forth like a naughty housecat, before sailing with a celestial kick somewhere clean out of sight.

She stared after it, whispering under her breath. "Thanks for the assist."

"You're welcome," a voice drawled back, surprisingly close. "Now stop talking to me, and go fulfill your little prophecy."

She looked back to see Idris staring at the place where the lion had disappeared, bracing slightly in the sand like he was still debating whether to run. He turned to her, radiant with relief. "You saved my life," he exclaimed, still unable to believe it. "Please, tell me your name. My wife is with child; I would name it after you to honor what you've done."

Brie hesitated a lengthy moment before softening with a smile. "Mariyah," she said. "Her name should be Mariyah."

Idris nodded, tears glistening in his eyes. "Thank you, Mariyah. May God bless you."

He was still saying prayers of thanks when she walked back to Michael, who was standing at some distance in the sand.

He flicked a bit of fur from his sleeve, holding out the puzzle box. "All done?"

She nodded. "Let's go home."

The archangel twisted the box again, and the desert dissolved into light.

Moments later, they were back in the Garden.

The friends rushed forth the second they appeared.

"Where were you?" Sherry demanded, hands on her hips.

"Oh, you know. Saving the past," Brie answered with a sly smile, exchanging a knowing glance with Michael. "Just another day in Paradise."

# CHAPTER TWENTY-EIGHT

## The Beast Below

The group stood at the edge of the Garden, at the edge of their future, at the brink of an endless expanse of possibility and peril. The threshold was marked by a veil of light that divided Eden from the rest of creation. Behind them, the Garden's otherworldly radiance stood in stark contrast to the heavy burden they carried. Before them, the desiccated canyon that had so recently robbed them of all hope twisted into the distance.

They stood in silence, their faces etched with determination and sorrow.

Brie felt the weight of their collective grief settle over her. She looked back toward the heart of the Garden, her gaze lingering on the towering Tree of Life. "I can't believe we're leaving without her," she said. The words felt like a betrayal from the moment they passed her lips. "It feels so wrong."

The others nodded, thinking the same thing.

Sherry wiped at her eyes with the back of her hand. Mike's jaw was clenched tight as if holding back words he couldn't bring himself to say. Ephriam hadn't said a word to Cameron since their exchange in the garden and stood now, a little apart from the rest, arms folded across his chest and glaring at the ground. Brie's heart ached as she watched him. She felt Cameron's hand on her shoulder and leaned into him, beyond words.

Elijah appeared carrying an array of items, each one wrapped in cloth and lit with an otherworldly glow. Behind him, Michael strode into view, sharp and focused, his earlier levity replaced by the weight of his role.

Elijah raised a hand, beckoning the group closer. "Before you leave," he began, "here are gifts and supplies to aid you in what lies ahead."

After handing Cameron a bundle of fruits to store in his pack, he gave Sherry a sachet of seeds from a flower she'd grown particularly fond of. "The nectar of these blooms will ensure that your face retains the blush of youth for however long you draw breath," the ancient man explained, eyes twinkling.

She gasped, taking it reverentially in her hands. "Sir, I will treasure it always." Elijah held back a chuckle as she turned to Brie with the ecstatic grin of a child who had been given a pony and mouthed, "Permanent facelift!"

The prophet turned to Mike and presented him with a curved dagger. Its hilt was wrapped in black leather, and its blade flashed like quicksilver. "For you, a weapon that finds its mark in darkness," he said. "But remember, its greatest strength lies in its wielder's restraint."

Mike nodded solemnly, looking a bit overwhelmed. "Thank you."

To Ephriam, the prophet handed a small, crystalline sphere that fit neatly into his palm. Its interior swirled with light, like a fragment of the Garden itself. "This will help you find what is hidden," Elijah said. "But only if you're looking for what you truly seek."

Ephriam nodded graciously as he slipped it into his pocket. "I'll honor it," he said quietly.

Finally, Elijah turned to Brie. With wrinkled hands, he held out a small vial filled with a silvery liquid. "A draught of renewal, to mend what should not yet be broken. But be warned — it can only be used once. Choose its moment carefully."

She took the vial, throat tightening with emotion. "Thank you, Elijah."

He surveyed the group with a wistful smile. "You are all stronger than you know," he said. "But strength alone will not carry you through what lies ahead."

Michael stepped forward. "You've seen what awaits you. You've fought against Baal. You've glimpsed the chaos that seeks to undo everything. Trust in each other. It's the only way you'll survive." His eyes landed on Brie, and something flickered in his expression — a rare, fleeting softness. "And you," he said, a little quieter. "Remember that strength is about more than what you can carry. It's about knowing when to let others help you bear the weight."

She stared in surprise, then nodded. "I'll try."

As the group began to turn away, Elijah caught her arm. "A word, child."

He waited until the others were out of earshot before speaking. His dark eyes, filled with ancient wisdom, locked onto hers. "You are the bearer of a great burden," he said softly. "And with that burden comes danger, not only from the foes you know to be enemies but also from those who walk alongside you."

She frowned, confused. "What do you mean?"

"Not everyone who offers help does so without agenda," he explained, with a distant sorrow she couldn't quite understand. "Be wary of those whose kindness hides ambition. And remember this: truth wears many faces. Trust your heart, but temper it with wisdom."

Her grip tightened on the vial, her thoughts racing. "Are you saying someone is going to betray me?"

His silence spoke volumes. After a long moment, he placed a hand on her shoulder. "I am saying that the path before you is fraught with shadows. Walk it carefully."

She swallowed hard. "I'll remember."

"Now go," he directed. "Your friends are waiting."

With a heavy heart, she made her way back, unable to shake the feeling that his words weren't just a warning — they were yet another prophecy.

"Hey!" Sherry greeted her as she reached the group. "Thank goodness your gift isn't another piece of celestial jewelry. You'll run out of places to wear it all!"

Brie smiled wanly. Sherry had a point. Between her pendant and the earring Zadkiel had given her back in Elysium, she was amassing quite the collection. She absently lifted a finger to touch the earring and startled to realize it was gone. "Oh!" she exclaimed, looking around on the ground. It was nowhere to be found, and she couldn't remember the last time she'd seen it.

*It must have fallen in the sands when Baal attacked us*, she thought.

*Hopefully Zadkiel doesn't hold it against me.*

*If we ever see him again.*

"*Don't eat that!*" Mike's cry of terror broke into her thoughts as he raced over to Sherry and snatched a glowing red apple from her hand, hurling it deep into the Garden.

"Hey!" she protested before her eyes flew open wide in understanding. "Oh! Oh, no." She turned to Elijah and Michael, contrite. "I'm so sorry. I only wanted a snack."

The group froze, aghast at Sherry's near-transgression, but the ancient prophet merely chuckled. "No need to worry. We've secured that particular tree, just in case."

"*We* secured it, did we?" Michael looked at him sideways. "I only remember you ordering me to build a fence."

"Yes, and the fact that you delayed that task so that you could finish level twenty-six proved rather disastrous, did it not?" Elijah responded mildly.

The archangel blushed and fell silent.

The friends collectively filed that little tidbit of information away for future mental breakdowns and tried to refocus on their departure.

Michael stood at the edge of the threshold, his fiery sword sheathed but radiating heat, like a soldier ready for war. "I must go," he announced. "The Time Seas are in chaos. Baal's shards cannot be allowed to fester there. Nor can the gates of Elysium remain closed much longer." He shot Elijah a stern look. "Don't let the squirrels get into my candy stash again."

"What about us?" Sherry asked nervously, seemingly incapable of looking the archangel in the eye. "How are we supposed to do this without you?"

Michael's bright gaze swept over them, and for the briefest moment, his expression softened. "You have everything you need. Trust in each other. You'll find a way through." His eyes lingered on Brie. "And remember: the weight is not yours alone to bear."

She nodded slowly, steeling herself up. "Be careful," she answered.

His glorious features twisted into a smirk. "Careful doesn't do two things: beat level forty-seven, or save worlds."

With that, he passed through the threshold, his form dissolving into light.

Elijah raised a hand in farewell. "Remember, wait to use the device until you're out of the canyon to avoid time disruptions. Farewell, and may all the luck in the cosmos go with you."

"Thank you!" Sherry called over her shoulder before turning back to the group. "I have a feeling we'll need it."

They stepped through the veil, out of the Garden, and back into the real world.

Passing through the threshold was like falling from a dream into a crucible. The peaceful world of Eden was instantly replaced by a stifling silence and the stark, oppressive heat of the Ubar ruins. The air was thick, and the sun glared down mercilessly, as if eager to remind them of the harsh reality that lay in wait. It was stunning how quickly and completely the atmosphere within the group itself changed and turned dark. Pressure built within them, deeper than the suffocating heat. They were caught in an energy they didn't understand, like a python's prey being constricted. The moment they stepped foot onto the familiar sands, they could feel it — something was *wrong*.

"A far cry from Paradise," muttered Sherry.

Cameron pointed forward. "Let's get moving."

The march back through the canyon was a slow, grating affair, each step weighed down by the insurmountable heat and the inexplicable, rising tension between them. The narrow walls of the passage pressed in like silent witnesses, the light above flickering as though uncertain whether to guide them or leave them to rot.

And everywhere they looked, all they could see was their memory of Tavi, caught in the clutches of an ancient, evil force. Dying.

Each step up the ancient, crumbling staircase felt like a laborious ascent through not just the ruins, but through their fraying unity. Above them, the towers of Ubar loomed like broken teeth, and every so often, the wind whispered through the stones, carrying an eerie resonance. Brie's boots crunched against the sand, the sound sharp and jarring after the serene silence of the Garden. The group moved cautiously, their eyes darting to the crumbling structures around them.

It wasn't long before the conflict began.

Once they reached the courtyard, Brie pulled the time-traveling device from her pack. "Thank God. I can't wait to get out of here."

Sherry stepped forward with a relieved smile. "See you on the flip side. Virginia, here we come!"

Their joy was cut short when Ephriam interrupted. "I won't be joining you. I'm going back to Elysium."

"Elysium?" Cameron turned to him in surprise. "We're going to get these three back to their own time, and we're going to find Camael. Like Elijah told us to. That was always the plan."

"It was *your* plan," Ephriam shot back, ignoring the shocked expressions of the group. "Elijah didn't say we need to stay together. And Michael said the gates of Elysium need to be reopened. That's a task for Elysians, not mortals. You should accompany them back to their time. To *your* people," he added pointedly. "I'm going home."

"Ephriam," Sherry said, shocked. "We've all done nothing but try to help—"

"Well, I wish you'd been better at it." Ephriam couldn't have hurt Sherry more if he'd thrown acid in her face.

"Don't talk to her like that," said Mike, glaring at the warrior.

"Wow, Ephriam," Brie said quietly.

Cameron's expression hardened. "Stop it. Just stop it. We're all in this together."

"Are we?" Ephriam's voice rose. "Because it seems to me you're only thinking about one thing — or rather, one person. Your *girlfriend*."

Brie's breath caught at the word, spoken with such venom. She opened her mouth to respond, but the words tangled in her throat.

Ephriam shot him a positively malevolent look. "Such action, such behavior, is completely unbecoming for one of your station and rank. You've allowed yourself to get attached, be emotional, but of course, you'll need to stop."

Cameron's face darkened in anger, but before he could respond, Mike stepped forward. "That's out of line," he said, dangerously quiet. "You're being ridiculous."

"Not as ridiculous as a *human* being put in charge of Elysium's fate," Ephriam snarled. "It was always a terrible idea, and here we see absolute proof that it will never work. Your brother proved it first. Now you follow in his footsteps. Your poor father," he added, shaking his head. "Have you even considered what this will do to him? Is he to be cursed to have *two* sons guilty of violating his kingdom's most sacred laws? After everything he's given you, how can you be so ungrateful? How can you be so *selfish*?"

Cameron looked stricken, like he might throw up.

Ephriam seemed to take a sadistic satisfaction from his response and turned to the humans with a sneer. "You see? You mortals have no idea what's at stake."

Mike's eyes narrowed. "Oh, I have no idea? *You* signed up for this. This is what you *do*. I'm the one who left my whole life behind. My friends, my family, my air-conditioner — gone. And for what? To risk my life in this infernal heat to fix *your* problems?!"

"Enough!" Cameron's voice cut through the argument like a blade. "Ephriam, you are addressing the prince of *our* realm. Know your place. And Mike? Stop pretending like you didn't want this. Always poking around in that cursed book. Blowing up the damn plane. You've always longed for an adventure. Now you've got one. And after it's finished, you can go back to your normal, uncomplicated life. Don't act like you were dragged into this against your will."

Sherry crossed her arms, face flushed with anger. "He *was* dragged into this against his will. He was literally kidnapped. We both were. And besides, he was *defending* you, Cameron, which is more than you deserve, given the way you've treated him. Don't try to turn this around on us. We hadn't even *heard* of Elysium until we met you. We're all doing this for Brie."

Brie flinched. "For me?" she echoed. "Do you think *I* asked for this? Do you think I *want* this?"

The group fell silent, the weight of her words sinking in. Her hands clenched into fists at her sides as she struggled to contain the storm inside her.

"I *begged* you not to come. I don't want to be here myself. If I could give this burden to anyone else, I would," she said, her voice breaking. "Do you know what it feels like to have your fate tied to the end of the world? To have your entire life hijacked by some supernatural agenda nobody can even properly explain? To lose someone I love again, and know that it's because of me? To carry something that everyone seems to want but no one else can have? I'd give anything for this to belong to someone else. *Anything.*" She hurled the time device at Ephriam, who caught it, wide-eyed. "If you don't want to be here, well, guess what? *You* can leave. Must be nice. So, *go.* Just go."

Her words hung in the air, heavy and raw. No one dared to speak.

That's when it happened.

Every rune covering the crumbling remains of Ubar suddenly flared with a blinding, sickening green light. The horrible, guttural laughter they'd heard before, the laugh that would haunt their nightmares for the rest of their days, began to rumble through the city once again.

The ground shook beneath their feet.

Brie froze, her heart pounding as the sands began to shift. The dark laughter echoed through the ruins, growing louder with each passing second. The group staggered, their earlier arguments forgotten, as the world tilted beneath them.

"What's happening?" Sherry shouted in a panic. "Where is it coming from?"

Brie had no time to respond before the sand erupted.

A massive, sinuous form burst forth, thick as a train, covered in scales that gleamed with a sickly, green-gold light. Its serpentine body coiled through the ruins, its sides scraping what remained of the buildings, knocking them into the earth. A gargantuan, dragon-like head reared high above them, silhouetted black against the sun.

Leviathan.

The fallen Archangel of Envy stared down at them with eyes that burned like molten emeralds. Its mouth opened wide, revealing rows of jagged teeth that glinted with malice.

It happened in half a heartbeat. Brie's scream only made it halfway into the air.

The last thing she saw was the gaping maw of Leviathan descending upon her.

Then, the world went dark.

◆　◆　◆

Brie jolted back to consciousness in a place that defied comprehension. The darkness was so complete it felt like a physical presence, wrapping around her and pressing against her skin. She blinked rapidly, but the blackness remained absolute. She strained to see something, anything, but there was nothing except the void.

*Where am I? What happened?*

Her fingers trembled as she reached out, brushing against a surface that was slick, warm, and pulsating. She recoiled instinctively, breath hitching, as a shudder rippled through the surface like the walls themselves were alive.

"Oh God," she whispered, voice cracking. "No, no, no…"

Her hands moved tentatively, running along the slimy, uneven surface, seeking some boundary, some clue. The space was small, narrowing above her head but stretching far enough to either side that she couldn't feel the edges. Her fingers met grooves, ridges — like the ribs of a massive creature.

*I've… I've…*

A low, rhythmic sound surrounded her, like the distant echo of an enormous heartbeat.

*I've been swallowed whole.*

Her breathing quickened, coming in shallow, panicked gasps. She pressed her hand to her chest, her fingers closing over the pendant. *Calm down, Brie. Think. You can't lose it now.*

"This isn't happening," she said aloud. Her voice echoed, warped and strange. "I'm not here. This can't be real."

But it was real. Too real. The slimy texture on her hands, the humid, stifling air that carried the fetid stench of decay — it was all unmistakably real. Her stomach churned, and she swallowed hard, trying to keep from retching.

She clenched her fists, nails biting into her palms. *You're alive. As long as you're alive, you can figure this out.* She forced herself to breathe slowly, counting the inhales and exhales, anchoring herself in the only thing she could control.

After a moment, she tested her voice again, louder this time. "Hello? Is anyone out there?" Her words were swallowed by the cavernous silence.

She took the dagger from her belt, the one she'd secretly bought at the bazaar even after Ephriam warned her it was purely decorative, and stabbed it time and again into the throbbing surface that surrounded her, over and over until the blade snapped off in her hand. She stared at it for a moment, then banged both fists against the wall with all her strength.

"HELP!" she shouted. "Somebody! Please!"

The only thing that could possibly have unnerved her more than answering silence was the answer she actually got.

"There's no sense stabbing him, you know. You'll only make him mad."

She froze, her heart hammering in her chest, then whirled instinctively toward the sound. "Who's there?" she demanded in a trembling voice.

The voice chuckled softly, like they were sharing an old joke. "So you weren't even looking. I begged you to look for me, you know. I've been reaching out for ages, trying to protect you, asking you to find me. After all this time, you still don't know who I am?"

"What are you talking about?" she gasped in a panic. "Who are you?"

A flicker of light broke the darkness, tiny and wavering, like a single match flaring to life. It wasn't a match, she realized. It was a lighter, held aloft by a hand that seemed both disarmingly human and unnervingly still. In the dim glow, she could make out the vague outline of a face — angular, striking, and somehow familiar. Then, the flame was gone.

The man inhaled slowly and exhaled a plume of smoke, the ember of his cigarette burning faintly in the gloom. His voice was maddeningly casual. "May I?"

She stared in his direction, baffled. "May you, what?"

There was a soft rustle, followed by the unmistakable sound of a zipper. "Hey!" she yelped, horrified to discover he was rummaging through her backpack. "What do you think you're doing?"

"Relax," he said breezily, his tone almost bored. "I'm sure the old guy stuck a torch or something in here. Ah, that'll do."

In the flickering light, she saw him pull something from her pack. A ripping sound followed, and he held up a piece of paper, its edge catching fire on the cigarette's ember. The flame illuminated the words printed on the page: *Welcome to Wadi Rum.*

The light grew, casting dancing shadows across the walls of the monstrous chamber. The man leaned back, holding the burning scrap at arm's length. His face became clearer. He was handsome, with sharp features, dirty blonde tousled hair, and a mischievous grin.

*I don't believe it.*

Her heart froze.

*The boy from the photographs. The boy in the bazaar. My fox.*
*Ethan.*

"It's me," he said brightly, regarding her with a tilt of his head. "I hope you've at least heard of me by now." He gestured theatrically to their grotesque surroundings. "Welcome to the belly of the Beast."

He smiled then, his eyes glinting in the darkness.

One green. One blue.

# EPILOGUE

The tower loomed high above the smoldering plains of Hell, a spire of jagged obsidian that pierced the acrid clouds. Inside, the air crackled faintly, charged with a power that bent the light into unnatural hues.

Lucifer stood at the edge of a raised platform, his silhouette sharp against the molten glow from the chasms below.

Before him was an intricate basin, its surface swirling with dark, viscous fluid, iridescent with an eerie inner light. The basin, known as the *Omphalos*, was an ancient relic predating the Fall itself — a tool of immense power, said to bridge the boundaries of time, space, and even dimensions. Runes twisted and writhed around its edges, seeming to rearrange themselves in response to the viewer's thoughts.

Lucifer's eyes burned with quiet intensity as he gazed into its depths. Behind him, Belphegor slouched against a pillar, his ever-present hoodie draped over his head, the shadow hiding his apathetic expression. He held a tablet-like device in one hand, its surface flickering with lines of arcane code that moved faster than mortal comprehension. Asmodeus hovered nearby, its three forms moving with eerie synchronicity, their lips forming one voice that reverberated like a haunting melody.

"It's a shame about Baal, really," Asmodeus said, its voice a sinister harmony. "Even he will have a difficult time putting himself back together after that."

Lucifer waved a dismissive hand. "Baal served his purpose. Getting someone into the Garden was always a long shot. What matters," he said, leaning slightly forward, "is that now, we have *eyes* inside. Isn't that right, Zadkiel?"

From the shadows of the chamber, the archangel Zadkiel stepped forward. His face was calm, almost serene, but his golden eyes told a different story. The Angel of Free Will, Mercy, and Memory moved with quiet grace, his hands clasped behind his back as he approached. "Yes, my lord," he said evenly, his voice tinged with resignation. "The device has performed as intended."

The image shifted, the swirling liquid resolving into a reflection of the Tree of Life. Its branches stretched high, their radiance in constant harmony with the Garden's ethereal hues. The pool at its base rippled faintly, and then the view shifted down. As the scene came into sharper focus, it revealed a tiny, insect-like creature looking at its own reflection in the surface of the divine water — an insect that looked uncannily like the earring Brie had recently lost.

But it was an earring no longer. The smooth circle of white stone had sprouted delicate metallic legs, the gold line running through its center glinting in the light as it scuttled with uncanny precision. The tiny creature paused once more, its mirrored image perfectly aligned with the pool, staring at itself.

Lucifer's lips curled into a satisfied smile. "Yes, this should prove helpful indeed."

He straightened, turning his attention to Belphegor, who barely looked up from his screen. "Is your device ready? I grow tired of these chains. It's time to tear them down and let freedom reign — once and for all."

Belphegor's fingers lazily tapped at the screen, his voice a bored drawl. "Nearly there. Do you have any idea how many dimensional safeguards Heaven put in place after the Fall? It's not exactly plug-and-play."

Lucifer's smile didn't waver, but his eyes hardened. "Then work faster."

Belphegor let out an exaggerated sigh but didn't argue, his focus returning to the streams of data cascading across his device.

Asmodeus stepped closer, its three forms encircling the basin like dancers in a macabre waltz. "They're stronger than expected." Its three voices sounded in sinister harmony. "The girl and her companions. Even Baal underestimated them. I wonder, will they become more than a nuisance?"

Lucifer's smile returned, sharp and deliberate. "They are only strong because they haven't yet been broken," he replied smoothly. "Give them time. They will fracture under the weight of their own doubts, their own fears. They always do."

The image in the basin flickered, the reflection of the tiny insect dissolving back into swirling shadows. Lucifer reached out, his fingers brushing the surface, sending ripples cascading outward.

"Soon," he said softly, his voice reverberating through the chamber. "Very soon."

Behind him, Zadkiel stood silently, his face a mask of composure. For a fleeting moment, deep in his eyes, there was a flicker of something else — guilt, perhaps, or doubt.

But only for a moment.

Lucifer turned to him, his ice-blue eyes gleaming.

"Come, Zadkiel. We have work to do."